Broken Ones

Mallory Bautsch

Copyright © 2023 by Mallory Bautsch

All rights reserved.

No part of this publication may be reproduced, distributed, or transmitted in any form or by any means, including photocopying, recording, or other electronic or mechanical methods, without the prior written permission of the publisher, except as permitted by U.S. copyright law.

The story, all names, characters, and incidents portrayed in this production are fictitious. No identification with actual persons (living or deceased), places, buildings, and products is intended or should be inferred.

Cover by @oliviaprodesign

Ebook ISBN: 9798387672842

Paperback ISBN: 9798218956837

*To my twin, my soul sister, my mirror:
Maranda.*

Broken Ones

Mallory Bautsch

Prologue

Darkness consumed her every thought.

Evalyn Impur was dead.

Or she would be soon, when the lashing winds froze her paralyzed body and her frosted skin melded into the forest's snow-veiled floor.

The rushing waters of the river still filled Evalyn's ears. She'd been on its bank when the searing pain had begun, dripping from her nape to her toes. Her muscles weakened, the world swaying with the wind, and the girl thrusted her hands toward the ground in an effort to stay upright, but with fading vision, her fingers slipped on the snowy dirt. She slumped onto frozen, damp earth, body immovable.

Evalyn willed her eyes open, her sight landing on the couple standing feet from her body. "*Fifteen years* we cared for you, girl," the male sneered from above. "We gave up *everything* to keep you. You should be thankful we didn't leave you on our doorstep, cradled in your white wrap with a measly trinket, barely weeks old."

The girl's lips trembled, although her cheeks remained dry. "I know you never wanted me."

Although Evalyn wouldn't have thought her parents capable of *this*—drugging their daughter and leaving her stranded for creatures of the night to feast upon. She should've recognized the dark and swirling Winter storm making landfall while they'd lured her deep into the woods with promises of new beginnings. It was the perfect cover for their tracks and act. The river splashed along its bank, freezing water marking her eyelids and nose, the cold blueing her lips.

"We yearned for a child of our *own*, not the scum of another. We won't waste more years of the good life we almost had," her mother scoffed, gripping the cloak over her day-gown. "We should've let our sight drift over you and find in the morning that a poor babe's fate had been left to chance in the night."

Even though they'd never wanted Evalyn... the girl tried to budge her bones, tried to speak—to ask them to stay; ask them how she needed to change; ask them *anything* so they wouldn't leave her. She didn't want to be alone again. Not like she had been, in that warped upstairs bedroom for fifteen years.

But she couldn't move. Breathing became an effort.

The couple regarded the girl with relieved smiles as they shuffled away in the pearl-white snow, gone in a blink. Evalyn couldn't tell whether her immobility was from the drug... or the fear that had consumed her mind. Because she *was* alone.

Her eyes fluttered as she surrendered to unconsciousness.

The soft crunch of leaves echoed in Evalyn's head. It took a valiant effort to open her eyes. The girl glimpsed the old woman with fire-red hair, frowning upon her, before blackness returned.

The swinging of Evalyn's body partially eased her.

Warmth spread across her skin as she met a plush surface, and feeling drizzled through her veins. The girl's breaths came soft and light, as if her body needed to remember how to inhale. Exhale.

After a minute of wiggling her fingers and toes, she dared a look at her surroundings.

In her first glance across the room, Evalyn made out a timeworn fireplace with glowing embers at the base, faded gray curtains, and the shabby emerald sofa she resided on. She shot up after a second look, noticing the rescuer in a chair across from her.

Or... would this be her killer?

Her blazing red hair revealed that it was the same person she'd glimpsed before. The elder woman wore a dragging layered skirt with a black cardigan tucked under the waist. A dozen rings littered her hands; innumerable hoops pierced her ears.

Evalyn had heard stories about the stalker in the Mediocris Woods: a mute lady, who watched travelers and adventurers from the treeline. She'd never been able to check those rumors—the girl's boundaries had been well confined around her cottage, nowhere near the deep forest—but if this was the maddened crone...

Evalyn sunk into the sofa, wary of the woman's every move.

She inspected the girl with a hint of a smile before standing. Thick-heeled boots clunked against the wooden floor as she neared Evalyn. "My name is Kinz. You're safe here." Her voice croaked, yet it was... gentle. Soothing.

Still, Evalyn whispered, "I don't believe you." She wrapped her arms around herself. How could she trust anyone? She'd never felt safe with her parents; never knew home. Perhaps this incident was a sign she was never meant to be with that family.

Or anyone at all.

Kinz strolled to the window, moving the curtains to reveal a lustrous moon. "You can trust me, Evalyn."

Chapter One
Four Years Later

Evalyn used to hate the sun.

It once meant waking up to a silent and cold house, where the only greeting was the empty kiss of solitude.

But the burning, golden rays peeking over the horizon now prompted a daily caress of company. Kinz Alatar had made it habit to walk the forest each dawn.

"The columbines bloomed overnight," she observed as they ambled along the flower-lined trails. "Your special touch persists, dear."

Evalyn rolled her eyes. "My diligent watering skills, you mean." She decided months ago that she should improve if she wanted to see her flower beds blossom. Evalyn knelt to the trailside, pine needles tickling her bare feet, and brushed the blue petals of a columbine with gentle fingers. "Even without rain in a fortnight, not a single flower under my care has died." The girl smiled proudly.

Kinz halted her response as a ginger-coated fox crept towards Evalyn. Its thick, bushy tail swung behind as it cautiously neared the girl until it was a foot away from her outstretched hand.

"He's intrigued by your presence," Kinz whispered.

It wasn't the only creature that had lately dared to meet her. A drove of hares, a lively owl, and many kinds of wild game had approached the girl on her wanderings around their cabin. Evalyn stilled, not daring to breathe for worry of scaring the fox off, but it lifted a twitching charcoal nose, sniffed once, and darted into the morning shadows.

Evalyn breathed a laugh and rose, lifting the skirts of her day-gown as they retreated home.

The cabin was petite, with bedrooms for both of them and a living room that opened to the kitchen. Evalyn hung her cloak on an entryway hook and followed Kinz to the mouthwatering scent of stewing porridge.

"I'll get the drinks," Evalyn said, opening the cupboard to a neat line of wooden mugs. The girl reached for two—but a pair of shimmering eyes stared back from the depths of the shelves. Evalyn paused, blinking once as half a dozen golden-winged creatures fluttered forth, each an inch and a half tall. Humanoid yet bare and green skinned, they smiled with faint whistles. The girl had seen them before—the tiny things had begun, weeks ago, lurking in the kitchen when she cooked and appearing in her flower beds when she tended to them.

Evalyn hadn't been frightened. Appalled, at first, yet she'd never been scared by the mysterious beings. When they disappeared from her sight in a blink, Evalyn went on pouring herself and Kinz cups of water. She was half inclined to mention the creatures to the woman, but Kinz lugged over the pot of porridge from the fireplace and all of her curiosities vanished.

Evalyn slung herself into a stool at the kitchen table, wove her blonde hair into a plait, and devoured two bowls and a handful of berries in what felt like one breath.

"There may be a guest visiting us soon," Kinz declared.

The girl froze mid-chew. "Who? When?" They seldom entertained guests, but various travelers and companions of Kinz' had visited their cabin in past years.

"Oh, you mustn't speak with your mouth full. How many times do I need to remind you?"

She swallowed. "Who's visiting? Why and when?"

"You'll meet them eventually. My elders taught me that the best skill to—"

"To acquire in the heart is patience," Evalyn finished. "Sure. But you must tell me *something*!" She didn't trust new guests—didn't trust anyone, frankly, except Kinz. Evalyn had learned her lesson about succumbing to false security.

So Kinz had agreed that there would be no secrets or lies between them, and no strangers unless Evalyn approved. The girl lifted her cup. "What if they've been secretly tasked to deliver packs of toxic tea under the guise of selling a world-renowned recipe from an ancient brewer who doesn't exist?"

The woman smiled. "His visit has not been initiated for as elaborate of a scheme. And the time of travel has not yet been confirmed, so I cannot say when, either."

Evalyn bit into a berry. "So it's a *guy*." Kinz shook her chin, sighing, the confirmation Evalyn needed. "Oh, please tell me it isn't Mister Prent again. He stares at me for far too long, and after three visits, you'd think he'd show a hint of acquainted recognition, but his perpetuating interest in my existence is just *disturbing*."

Kinz sipped at her water. "No, Mister Prent's visits are temporarily suspended. And before you get any ideas, it's not the delightful young man who sings praise over your floral arrangements every time he delivers his danishes and pastries."

"You mean Sandin." A nod from Kinz in return. "Well, I don't have any *ideas*. I don't desire him." The woman smiled, inciting the corners of Evalyn's lips to lift. "*Come on*, Kinz—I barely know him, how could I? But that doesn't mean I have to avert his presence... *What?* He brings those little candied tarts too!"

Kinz chuckled. "Enjoy the unexpected, dear. You trust my invitation hasn't extended to a criminal or fraud, yes?"

"Yes," Evalyn grumbled. There was nothing else she could do to uncover the identity of their next guest. Kinz gave a satisfied nod in return, but Evalyn plopped her chin onto the palm of her hand. "I hate surprises."

It was midnight when Evalyn silently slipped out from the embrace of her sheets and scanned her room, candles still burning. She'd fallen asleep glazing over the sketches of a floral study, waiting to see if Kinz' private guest would show. The girl returned the book to its shelf before glancing to her window, where a bright crescent moon glowed in the sky.

The view was wide enough to encompass the paths from which travelers would come, but shadowed enough by the roof's edge that Evalyn could wait and watch without being seen. She unlatched and opened the wood-framed panes, sitting on the ledge with a breath of the still night air.

Then she spotted them.

Not a visitor... but wolves. Giant and beautifully made, resting on the pine-needle strewn ground, their coats blurring with the dark forest floor. Five edged the cabin; based on their spacing, she guessed more surrounded the entire place—watching her every move. Every breath.

And although her curiosity might get her killed... she wanted to see one up close. Like the fox and wild game she'd met... she felt bonded to the creatures, felt connected by some strange link in the shifting winds and step-trodden dirt.

In the moonlight, the girl made out one's silvery-blonde coat, a long stripe of black down his spine. She lowered off the windowsill, toes meeting soil, and his eyes locked onto her, as if aware of her racing heart. Step by step, she neared the wolf, neither him nor his companions shifting a hair. On his stomach, his snout reached her waist. The wolf was larger than the others, too, yet she'd been lured to him. Lured to his dominance, like a vast and strange power.

But this was where she met her end, because he seemed to dare her to come closer.

Without thinking, she reached for his snout and met fur softer than anything she'd ever touched.

He didn't budge. Just watched her, accepting the intimacy.

When voices sounded from the front of the cabin and she stepped away, he closed his eyes as if regretful of her departure.

But she could hear Kinz, and shot for her window with only a second-long glance at the majestic creatures. Passing through her room, she skulked along the dark hallway into the sitting area, where the remains of a fire sizzled and cast a faint light upon the furniture. Her eyes scanned every corner of the room. Where had the voices gone?

"Evalyn is in her room." Kinz' hushed croak and the scrape of the opened entrance sounded, followed by the indistinct mutter of a deep, husky voice. "No," Kinz responded, "she still doesn't know a thing, but that's not my decision to make, is it?"

Evalyn hurtled behind the sofa.

What didn't she know, exactly?

"She's a few months from coming of-age," the new voice remarked. "You should start seeing the Signs, and she will too—questions in tow. I understand orders, but you have to tell her *something*. Soon."

A moment of silence. Evalyn peered over the edge of her spot. Two pairs of staring eyes greeted her. One belonged to Kinz, the hunch-backed woman holding open the door to their cabin. The other belonged to a young man clothed in a sage green uniform with ribbons and patches at the breast pocket; his dark, bronze hair shone under the starlight from the window. One of his eyes was blue, the other a brown-spotted green; both squinted as Evalyn observed him. Despite his muscular build and height, the stranger couldn't be but several years older than her. Her breath hitched when she noticed his ears were delicately pointed at the tips.

He matched an attentive stare towards Evalyn. She regained her composure, crossing her arms. "Who are you and why are you talking about me?"

No matter who he was—or how attractive he was—she didn't trust strangers. Of course, Kinz had emphasized this guest's acceptable reputation quite thoroughly, but Evalyn would take her time to deem his suitability.

Kinz cleared her throat. "Evalyn, this is Walfien Pax, a very dear friend of mine."

A friend. Evalyn felt an unrecognizable urge to believe Kinz, who had never introduced a visitor as a... friend. But unlike Mister Prent or other guests, even Sandin... something about Walfien was familiar. Comforting. It was a peculiar instinct.

The corners of his mouth flicked up, a movement so small she thought to have imagined it. "We were just—"

"Saying our goodbyes," Kinz interrupted, watching him. "Yes, yes, we prattled far longer outside than I suspected, and I don't want you traveling any later into the night than now, dear. You'll have to visit another time, Walfien, when Evalyn and I can prepare a nice meal."

Walfien smiled tightly. Evalyn had learned to read Kinz' expressions—and those of the unusual visitors—well, and quickly, but Walfien Pax was different.

He only showed what he wanted, which annoyed Evalyn more than the fact that she couldn't interpret him in the first place.

"Yes. Another time, then, Kinz. Evalyn. I'll see you again." There was a spark in his eyes, one the girl hadn't noticed a moment ago, but she didn't have time to understand before he swept from the room.

"Who is he? How do you know him so well that you can call him a friend? And what are the chances that he arrives this late and is sent away upon my arrival? You didn't want me to hear your conversation," Evalyn spewed, back in bed. Kinz leaned on its edge.

"You've always been a clever one. But we must talk, my girl."

"Because Walfien told you to."

Evalyn was closer with Kinz than anyone—it didn't matter that she'd only ever gotten the chance to befriend anyone *after* her adoptive parents had tried to do away with her. She wouldn't have wanted anyone else to find her that night. But although Evalyn loved and trusted Kinz with every part of her soul, there remained oddities that the woman had yet to explain.

"If there are things you have to tell me, then answer this: what happened that night? How did you know who I was?" She'd never asked before—always wondered, but never dared to question. Kinz liked to talk when she believed them both ready to learn.

But after so long, didn't Evalyn deserve the truth?

Kinz observed the wall beside her bed. "Walfien and I befriended each other many years ago. He was with me that night—we were visiting when we discovered you. He brought you here after watching those people leave you."

Evalyn waited—silence followed. Fine. One answered question was better than none.

"Can you feel it?" Kinz added, fingers sweeping the air.

"I feel your vagueness putting me to sleep, if that's what you're asking."

The woman wholly ignored Evalyn's snark. "The atmosphere is altering, and times are changing. *You* are changing." Kinz reached for Evalyn's hand.

"There's much you don't know—but you will, soon. So prepare yourself, my girl. You mustn't have fear or hesitation. Remember that."

No fear, no hesitation. The woman had never been blunt in her words, but this... what news, what *things* was the girl supposed to ready herself for?

She set aside her uncertainty. Kinz' advice had always proved valuable.

"Why did Walfien say I was months from coming of-age? What does that mean? What Signs was he talking about?"

"I don't have the answers you seek, dear girl. What I *can* say is that Walfien will help you. You see, I'm not like him... but *you* are. And that makes all the difference."

After Kinz left, Evalyn observed the ceiling until her eyes burned for rest.

She was like Walfien.

But what—or who—did that make *her*? Walfien acted... normal. Had looked it.

Except for those daintily pointed ears. So unusual and striking and...

Her hands roamed her own ears. Rounded, she knew—yet she released a small sigh and closed her eyes. Whoever he was, however he related to her, was a mystery.

But she'd always hoped there was more to life. More to her. So if Walfien was a mystery... was it wrong for her to want to be one as well?

Chapter Two

The snow had nearly frosted her eyelashes together. She blinked quickly, heart pounding slowly; she needed to breathe, but the inhales of air only brought the stinging cold inside, debilitating her lungs.

Water. She needed water. Now.

Her mouth was dry, lips cracked but sticking together, and the desire for replenishment took over all instincts. She crawled to the river's edge. Scooping stiff hands into the icy depths, she drank and drank until her tongue turned numb—but the girl slipped down the steep bank and before she could catch herself, the current sucked her under, and she was rolling and thrashing within the slush surface of the river until she couldn't breathe—

Evalyn flew forward, gasping and smoothing her hair before gripping the warm sheets around her as her racing heart calmed. She'd gotten used to having frequent nightmares, especially about what had happened that day—before Kinz' rescue. Their realness continued to evoke the same panic and terror. It took her many minutes to breathe evenly once more.

She rubbed her eyes and fell into motion. Evalyn paced to the kitchen, rummaging for a goblet in the cupboard as the scent of lavender and chamomile tea flooded her nostrils. Kinz knew the girl's fitful sleeping too well. The herb-infused concoction had proved to cure the ugliest of illnesses and soothe Evalyn after her most petrifying terrors. She downed a serving and began pouring herself another when voices sounded from the cabin entrance.

"We thought things were calming, but—"

"Not anymore," Kinz interjected. "Look what happened to the clan, just months ago. Two dozen members, gone in moments. That's no sign of peace." Evalyn drifted to the edge of the kitchen as her guardian appeared in the doorframe, head bowed and shaking.

On her heels strode Walfien Pax, gaze wide and hair disheveled. He wore the same uniform from when they'd met two weeks prior, the shorter sleeves an indication of Spring's arrival. "Agreed; we can't risk doubting them. But if they know, then we must go immediately," Walfien exclaimed. He sank onto the side of a chair, so overwrought compared to before.

"Another meeting without me?" Evalyn drawled, still half-asleep.

The two turned to the girl as if they hadn't sensed her presence. Walfien's lips thinned into a line and he faced Kinz, voice lower. "It's what's best, Kinz. We can reach the border in little over a day if we hurry."

Evalyn set her goblet beside the teapot. "What's going on?"

Walfien ran fingers through his hair. "After so many years..."

"It's a good thing we planned for it then," Kinz said, hobbling to the wallspace by the door, retrieving a hung satchel and nearing Evalyn. She held out the bag, eyes pleading. "Pack what you can stand to carry for a while." She sighed. "A long while. And take some fruit, dear."

"What? Why? What's going on?"

Walfien met Evalyn's stare. "You should do as she says."

The girl reluctantly took the bag and followed Kinz' instructions, but kept her ears open to the conversation that continued on the other side of the wall, muffled yet intelligible.

"How?" Kinz demanded.

"It's beyond us. We don't know their method of border crossing, so it's difficult to estimate when they would arrive—if we would even catch them before it's too late. Anyhow, we know that they know, and that's enough to elicit relocation. I won't take risks with this."

Evalyn returned to the room and Walfien rose. The glint in Kinz' eyes said something was wrong.

"It's because of how close she is. Lineage is more easily detected at this stage," Walfien finalized. "And there's no one else down here like her."

At the edge of the sofa, Evalyn lifted the satchel. "I have everything. What are you talking about?"

Kinz smiled solemnly. "Dear, you... you aren't safe here any longer. You must go with Walfien. He'll take you where you're promised to see another wisp of sunlight on your flowers."

"Why aren't you coming?" Evalyn questioned.

"My girl, what have I been reminding you?"

"That's not an answer—"

"What is it?"

"No fear," Evalyn retorted. "No hesitation." She swallowed those emotions. "When will we return?"

The woman's lips twitched. "Stay with Walfien. Listen to anything he tells you. I'll see you again, eventually. I promise."

Evalyn's eyes grew. "I can't just go! Not after everything we've been through, Kinz, you—you helped me out of that dark place, how can I—"

"You'll go with Walfien. That is all I ask of you, my girl." The woman met Walfien's eyes as he approached the exit of the cabin. "There is no one I trust greater than him to keep you safe."

Evalyn's response was half a breath. "All right." She would go if Kinz was willing to ask. So Evalyn squeezed the woman in an embrace, wiping away the tear that streamed down her cheek.

"Go. Hurry," Kinz said, pulling away, features melancholic but lined with a gleaming relief that proved to Evalyn that Walfien truly was her best option for safety—whatever it was she needed to be safe from.

As they ventured into the forest in the waking breaths of the morning, away from the cabin and Kinz... Evalyn memorized the shapes and shadows of her first home.

Somehow... she knew she wouldn't be back.

Evalyn didn't expect to travel all day, but as the sun crept overhead, Walfien didn't slow his pace. She, on the contrary, was exhausted. And even more confused when they didn't stop at the river, but crossed it along a path of stepping stones at a section calmer than the girl had ever seen. It was the farthest north she'd ever traveled—when her parents had left her at its bank over four years ago. Kinz called it the Aternalis Creek; apparently it had once been a miniscule stream, but she'd only ever seen it as a rapid, half frozen river with the intent to suck her under its depths in her nightmares.

By the time all light disappeared, her back was drenched with sweat and legs were steps away from giving out. She'd eaten every scrap of food packed, with Walfien rejecting any she offered—like he'd done to her questions. Where were they going? Why? What was so wrong that she had to abandon everything?

Passing through a dense cluster of pine trees, Evalyn couldn't control her body from slumping along one. She closed her eyes with a huff, stopping Walfien in his tracks. "Can we take a little break?" she exclaimed, throat dry.

He marched over and scooped her into his arms.

Evalyn wondered if he remembered doing the same thing that Winter night.

"We can't afford a break yet," he muttered. She didn't have the energy to ask when they would. Evalyn didn't remember falling asleep in his arms, but when she awoke, they resided in a small clearing.

They sat against pines, facing each other with a foot of space between their shoes. She blinked against sunlight; she'd slept until midday. Peering around, something about the woods struck the girl. She could hear true sounds of a forest—birds chirping, wind rustling the limbs, crisp needles crunching under the step of wandering creatures. It had been far quieter at the cabin. But here, even the forest floor seemed more vibrant, the trees thicker, taller... welcoming. She felt protected, somehow, in this embrace of nature. Walfien leaned his head against the tree behind him.

Evalyn cleared her throat. "Are we... here?"

"You could say that," he responded.

Evalyn crossed her arms. "Where *is* here?"

"Past the border."

"The border?"

"That's what I said." Walfien's eyes crinkled as he stood. He glanced about the pines, eyes darting across their surroundings. "We need to keep going." He didn't wait for her to follow.

"I—I thought we'd made it," she exclaimed, scrambling after him.

"There's a long way to go, Evalyn. We've made it to temporary safety."

Shortly after dusk, they stopped in a similar patch of trees. They were deep into the forest, the pines set closer. Walfien, after a few hurried moments of checking their surroundings, sat before Evalyn.

"I have some questions, and I'd appreciate it if you'd answer them."

Walfien tilted his head. "I'll answer *one.*"

She furrowed her brows. "Who are we running from?"

"Soldiers. People who want nothing more than to satisfy their leader in whatever way necessary."

Dread fell upon her, but she shut it out. *No fear, no hesitation.* "What... what happens if they find us?"

"They won't. But if they did, they'd have me to deal with."

Whether it was the mere confidence in his tone or the countless precautionary actions he underwent at every one of their turns, she'd seen enough proof that he possessed fine skills at whatever *this* was—the protecting and guiding her to safety. She trusted that even if the soldiers met them, they wouldn't make it back to wherever they had come from unhurt, if at all.

"What do they want?"

"That's question number three." Evalyn bit her lip sheepishly, but he answered, "They want you. And they want to take you to a horrible place. The soldiers aren't close enough to put you in immediate danger, but that's why we're traveling alone and on foot. If they get any nearer, they can't track us easily."

After the couple Evalyn once thought of as parents left her in the frozen extent of the Mediocris Woods, she succumbed to loneliness—had feared anyone she trusted would leave. It had taken her a long time to have faith in Kinz. But Evalyn never forgot that feeling; never once failed to recall what had been done to her, despite the care and patience Kinz had shown. After fearing abandonment for so long, she couldn't understand why people wanted to *take* her.

"Walfien, why do they want me?"

"There's a lot you don't know."

"Enlighten me."

He raised his chin. The shadows on his face lifted. "You're special to a lot of people."

"You aren't going to tell me how, are you?"

"I can't tell you anything. I don't have the right to. But you'll understand, soon."

Hours seemed to pass in the still night before Walfien spoke again. How he knew she was still awake, she didn't bother wondering. "We're called Fae—short for Faerie; Faeries." She raised a brow, but he said, "You can't deny you've noticed I'm different. I've seen your staring," he chortled. "Fae are greater beings than humans—greater than most creatures. We were superior because of our bodily manufacture, then our minds adapted to prevail over all others, leaving us powerful and dominant. Our Gods gifted the race with elemental magic for protection against elimination."

Evalyn tried not to balk—she was humbled in the face of other life. It was miraculous. Yet... "How can I know you're telling the truth? You could be making all that up to keep me quiet."

Walfien tilted his head. "We've been blessed and cursed with the inability to lie, as fate has it. We call it Viitor—the force that makes us withhold all but truth. Fae *have* learned to speak around it—indirectly lie—but we're born with honesty in our blood." A pause. "Still, I wouldn't lie to you."

Evalyn was too busy processing his first words to acknowledge the unprecedented kindness.

"Fae came to this continent; established separate Kingdoms; set their rulers. Three make up the majority of Liatue."

"Are you taking me to a Kingdom under the orders of your monarch?"

"Partially." His voice lowered. "I also want to. I'm not risking someone else ignoring how high the stakes of your protected travel are. Besides, Kinz wouldn't have let you leave with an unfamiliar official. We earned each other's trust long ago, and it's all I can do to upkeep it."

Walfien was growing on Evalyn. Slowly, but... she understood Kinz' faith. "So we're going to your residential Kingdom. To whoever you belong to."

"We're already within it—Faylinn." His lips twitched. "But I don't *belong* to anyone. I serve the Queen, yet I could leave at any moment. She knows I won't, though."

"So the border we passed…"

"An entrance to Faylinn, of sorts. The borders encase each Kingdom. Our eastern edge meets with the western side of the Kingdom of Ausor, and the third Kingdom resides in the far north. They're invisible, magic-bound borders, identifying adjacent areas of land as property of the respective Kingdom. The security embedded in the casting of the boundaries protects common travelers and alerts patrols about suspicious activity."

Evalyn nodded, thoughts spinning elsewhere. She was in Faylinn. A Fae Kingdom. It explained why the land here was *alive* compared to the dullness of the human territory she was accustomed to. She'd always thought there was more to Liatue, north of the land that humans inhabited, but Evalyn had only ever heard rumors of emptiness and horror. None she'd believed, though, because no one—no human—had actually explored the continent. They'd never dared venture beyond their bounds, excused by deadly storms, families left behind, and supply shortages. Perhaps they'd been cowards, frightened by what they didn't know.

Walfien raised his gaze. Evalyn didn't think they needed to be as scared.

"Kinz said we're alike," she said.

The Fae crossed his arms. "You feel things… and see things. Things you thought were unnatural. Impossible. Am I wrong?"

He wasn't. The creatures in the cupboard, her intimacy with the wolf… they certainly weren't normal occurrences. "And?" the girl mumbled.

Silence.

She was—she was human. Maybe he meant to convey they were both utterly crazy, because Walfien couldn't mean… Evalyn wasn't a *Faerie*. She'd know.

Wouldn't she?

Chapter Three

A drop of water found Evalyn's nose. Another splashed onto her forehead. Within moments, a light drizzle of rain greeted them.

Traveling for nine days hadn't been nice—a far too gracious way of conveying that she now detested sleeping on pine cones and needles with her entire heart—but the constant envelopment of nature had brought her to a state of tranquility that she welcomed each morning she awoke. And after prolonged marching under the steady rays of the sun, she also welcomed the rain that pounded harder.

A row of fine huts appeared in the distance, and Walfien motioned to head for the awaiting shelter. They arrived onto a deserted central path, the inhabitants of the village safe in warm, dry places.

Walfien led them to one of the larger cottages. "This is the village of Pheelo. We'll rest here tonight and arrive by midday tomorrow."

"You know, you never told me where we're going."

The sign above the door referred to the building as an inn—yet the sheer size of the place told Evalyn that if they weren't the only customers for the evening, they'd be sleeping outside again. But upon entry, the chamber was stuffed to the walls with dozens of tables and chairs, each occupied by lively, cloaked inhabitants. She spied a single hallway centered on the wall to their left. Inn *and* tavern. A wave of laughter and chatter hit Evalyn as the door closed behind them, and she attempted to glimpse the faces under the hoods, but the dim lighting served no aid and the girl met shadowed silhouettes.

"We're going to The Palace," Walfien responded.

"Palace? *A castle*?"

"I trust you know what that is."

She huffed, "Of course I do."

The thin man at the innkeepers desk lifted a bald head, his grin increasing the wrinkles around his face. But his ears—rounded. Another human? "Welcome! Welcome, Walf'en! Can't say I'm surprised to see ya, despite the rain."

"You know I've been in worse conditions, Soj." Walfien's lips lifted and he placed their payment on the tabletop. "One room, two beds—the one with the nice bathing chamber."

Soj looked at the emerald coin, translucent and the size of a thumbnail, then at Walfien. "I can't accept—"

"You'll take dues from anyone else who walks in here, so you'll take it from me as well." Walfien slid another over. "This one's for your unwavering hospitality."

"You and your selflessness," Soj grumbled. He slipped the coins in a drawer before gesturing down the hallway. "Last door on the right. I'll be 'ere if you need anythin'." He squinted at Evalyn. "Though with this one 'ere Walf'en, I don't see why you'd be anythin' less than satisfied! Glad to see you're takin' a well-deserved break from those duties. She's sure soft on the eyes."

Evalyn stilled at the assumption, cheeks flushing as she glanced at her companion, who chuckled and shook his chin. "You also know I'm not that sort of customer, Soj. We're passing through as we make for The Palace."

"Agh," Soj replied, waving a hand. "Y'know where to find me."

Walfien turned on his heel, Evalyn following diligently. "Is Soj human?"

The Faerie's lips lifted. "Partially. Soj is a wolf." She squinted in thought. "You heard me right," Walfien added. "All wolves in Liatue are supernatural beings; half human with magic in their blood that allows them to transfigure between their wolf and human forms at will."

Evalyn wondered who she'd met at the cabin. What wolf had allowed the intimacy, with the others looking on as if frightened themselves of her fearless stupidity.

They reached their room. "What are these duties and conditions you need a break from?" she asked. The quarters were compact, but spacious enough to edge to the bathing chamber or armoire. A cluster of candles claimed the wardrobe's top. The rumbling thunder became a soft beat lulling Evalyn to sleep.

"I don't need a break. I'm accustomed to the pace of my tasks." He opened the armoire. "There's clothes, if you want to change."

She nearly lunged at the thought of a clean outfit, but made herself nod her thanks and casually redress in the bathing chamber. Pulling her hair into a knot atop her head, she returned to the quarters. "Well, what do you do?"

Walfien leaned against the window. He ran a hand through deep-brown hair, still slick from the rain. "I'm Hand of the Queen."

"Hand of the—I've been accompanied by the *Hand of the Queen* this entire expedition, and you didn't think to say—"

"It wasn't important. You'd have found out eventually."

"Selfless *and* humble. You're a golden child to Soj."

Walfien simpered. "Soj has known me my whole life. He only ever says such things when he thinks I need to impress someone."

"And he thought I was that someone? Little does he know that your mere existence as a Fae amazes me."

Walfien squinted his eyes as if in peculiar thought, but parted from the window and blew out the candles. They settled in their beds. The warmth of the blankets seeped through her skin. "What exactly do you do as Hand?"

"I advise the Queen and deal with issues on her behalf. When she can't attend, I lead meetings for her small council. Anything she asks of me, I oblige to."

"And the tough part?"

Walfien's lengthy pause warned her she didn't want to know. His voice was soft. "I often deal with larger cases brought about by higher nobles—some of which lead to the execution of the offender. As one of the most favored trackers, I frequently have to pursue convicts; return them to the dungeons to wait out their trial and sentence. Often, they aren't willing—some fight back, and some would rather me end it there than spend months in The Palace dungeons." He cleared his throat. "That's when I have to choose: adhere to my duty, or put myself in their place, their social position, their mind. Do they deserve such a mercy? When the situation calls for it, I make it as painless as I can. They know if they go back... there are punishments worse than death. Things *I've* had to do for information." A pause. "But if sacrificing a part of myself—becoming that kind of monster—means a better world for everyone else, I'd do it a thousand times again."

Evalyn understood, although she'd never taken a life; had never purposefully inflicted pain onto someone. If she had to do things—even cruel, frightful things—for the good of others, she would. Especially for adolescents. She wouldn't wish unto anyone a childhood like hers. "You're no kind of monster, Walfien."

She didn't think he believed her.

Evalyn strode slowly, still half-asleep as they made the last stretch to The Palace. It was hours before they spoke, but the silence was usual and expected. They reached the edge of the forest, meeting an open land of softly rolling grasses around their path. In the distance, barely a speck in her vision, was a lone mound rising above the surrounding land.

Evalyn deemed the sun pitiful of their journey as it hid behind light waves of clouds stretching to the horizon. A gentle breeze swiped at her loose blonde locks, and she closed her eyes, breathing in the scent of trodden soil and ray-warmed grass.

They ventured ever closer to The Palace.

To the truth.

A nature-made staircase of rocks and indented soil grew more visible in the center of the vast hill—leading to the walls of a castle, seated neatly atop the leveled hilltop. A curving, wildflower-lined roadway extended north from the castle.

"It leads to Koathe," Walfien explained. "The capital of Faylinn."

They finally reached the base of the hill, feet-high stone walls guarding either side of the rocky steps. Moving up and up and up, Evalyn took in The Palace.

The first gateway was an entrance through the outer walls of the compound, as Walfien had informed her the night before, which surrounded grassy yards enveloping The Palace. The girl ran a hand along the glimmering, wind-and-rain-carved stone, slowing as a feeling of ancient familiarity streamed through her bones. Her breath hitched in her throat. An overwhelming sense of belonging trickled through her, and for a reason she couldn't describe... she knew she was supposed to be there.

Two stout towers sided a metal gate, which rose with a signal from Walfien to a silhouette above. They stepped through, onto the hilltop holding The Palace, and made way for another gated entrance—this one into the castle itself, made of swinging wooden doors rising four times over her. The inner walls of the castle were thick and gleaming, with four guard towers lining the front.

The groaning of thick chains claimed Evalyn's focus, then the wooden doors swung inward. Walfien caught her glance, continuing forward. The entrance opened to a broad courtyard; numerous sentinels marched passed pillars lining the walls, and a group of female Fae meandered across the lawn in dresses of pale blue, lavender, and cream. Under an overhang on the left stood countless horses nickering in their stables; to their right rang the clanging of metal and the whittling of stone and wood. Sets of servants dashed under the arched canopy outlining the quad.

Three towers—the center one grazing the clouds—stood within the middle of the keep in front of them, their peaks needle-pointed tips. Windows lined the keep walls, more than Evalyn could count, collecting sunlight overhead. Banners hung between the windows: sage green fabric with a golden symbol—two crescents on either side of an encircled, seven pointed star—stitched in the middle.

Evalyn kept pace with Walfien along the gravel path through the middle of the courtyard and central archway entering the keep. The foyer was astonishing, with floors of flush, waxed stone and shallow green walls covered in intricate floral designs. A grand staircase sat in the heart of the spacious chamber, a lavish gold carpet running down it. Long tables lined the walls on either side of the stairs, bright vases and bouquets and colored decor nestled atop each one. Potted ferns and half-grown trees artfully surrounded the entrance to the courtyard behind them.

She'd never seen such an exquisite place.

Further sentries were stationed along the walls, and Fae males clothed in elegant attire marched about the hall. More graceful girls and suited servants swept through the doors on either side of the foyer.

A triad of maids, clad in cream uniforms and hair bunched into low knots, bustled for Evalyn and Walfien. The Faeries curtsied with smiles to Walfien, and in unison greeted, "Lord Hand." Petite hands gripped Evalyn's arms and attempted to pull her away.

She dug her feet into the ground. "Where are you taking me?"

The shortest of the three responded, "To your quarters, miss, to settle down. Come along." The girls continued to guide Evalyn to the staircase, but she spun towards Walfien in question.

An alluring, relieved smile lined his lips. "Welcome home, Evalyn."

Chapter Four

The maids pulled Evalyn through a long hallway. Taking a swift left at the end, she couldn't glimpse what the window-covered wall to their right overlooked. The girl was lost by the time they made it to her quarters. Everything looked the same; long, green corridors coated with dusty portraits of past rulers and warm pine doors scattered amidst branching hallways.

The Faeries ushered Evalyn inside.

"Here we are!" The short servant's round face brightened with a smile, but her nose scrunched. "We must clean you, miss. You'll need a bath and proper clothes." Her eyes glanced at Evalyn's attire—the since-dried gown from Kinz' cabin. The maids dispersed as Evalyn observed the chamber.

She breathed in potent vanilla, eyes wandering. A welcoming, fluffy bed stood before her, with two tables made from aged tree trunks on either side. Edging the tables were sheer curtains covering paneled doors that both opened to a balcony. In the corner to her right stood a vanity, tall and intricately crafted from a great wooden limb, with mirror pieces wedged between the branches.

One of the maids, a thin and lanky girl—a contrast to the matured figures of the other two women—strode into a closet on the left. It seemed capable of holding multiple times the amount of clothes Evalyn owned at Kinz', holding rows of dresses and elegant cloaks; jeweled and colored heels lined the floor. The green-eyed girl pulled out a silk nightgown and lifted it, color staining her honey-toned cheeks.

"Oh, that's beautiful," Evalyn confirmed. The girl simpered, peering at the shortest maid, whom Evalyn marked as a leader of the three. Plump hands grasped hers, and the four swarmed a second door beside the closet. "What are your names?" Evalyn asked.

The pink-haired maid spluttered, "Gods, I forgot! What a disgrace to my family name, neglecting *introductions* of all things!" She shook her head. "I'm Beverly. This is Ida—" she motioned to the thin girl clasping Evalyn's nightgown—"and Vixie." The third maid's curly, chestnut hair was uncontained in its knot. Vixie dipped a dimpled chin, a slight smile on her deeply tanned face.

They entered the expansive bathing chamber. Thick roots peeked out from the floors as if growing from the stone, and moss and curling vines draped the ceiling. An oval tub sat on the left of the chamber, and a smaller privy room opened from a door on their right. A variation of sweet-scented herbs surrounded the bowl upon the washing counter.

Vixie's fingers trailed across the tub. Water pooled at the bottom, filling to the highest edge, and gray-blue streaks of magic-dust floated in the wake of her touch. At her side, Ida splayed small hands over the water, heated bubbles rising to the surface. A steamed mist formed at the lip of the tub.

The first glimpse of Faerie power—water and heat and transfiguration—was miraculous to witness after the little Walfien had explained about their magic.

Her soothing bath awaited. She didn't care to tell the Faeries to turn around—they'd surely seen everything—yet they understood the routine and found other things to occupy themselves as Evalyn lowered into the tub. Thick, soapy bubbles floated around her, and she leaned her head along the edge, eyes closing.

"Is it too hot?" A light voice asked. Evalyn's lids opened to view wide, hazel eyes. Vixie bit her lip.

"It's perfect." The response earned a blushing, pleased smile.

The handmaids scrubbed her body and washed her hair, polished and painted her nails, and cleansed her face. Ida hauled her dirty attire into a basket near the door. By the time Evalyn stepped out of the cooled water, she was smooth, clean, and relaxed. Ida tied the nightgown strings at her back as Vixie combed her damp hair. Returning to the bedroom, Evalyn discovered Beverly with a sizable platter of food.

"Just in time for supper! I'm sure you're starving, it's nearly nightfall." Beverly, trays in hand, backed into a set of swinging doors across the room. Evalyn followed, the scent of roasted vegetables and spices wafting her way. A circled dining table sat closest to the chamber door. Behind it resided a smaller table, a game set and handful of shimmering balls atop it.

Beverly set down the array of food before curtsying. "Will that be all, miss?"

"Evalyn."

"Excuse me, miss?"

Evalyn took the center chair at the table, reaching for bowls of soup and the pitcher of water. She chuckled, "My name is Evalyn. You don't have to call me *miss*."

The Faeries stilled. The air thickened, tense—she wondered what they were thinking. But they replied in unison, "Yes, Evalyn."

She swiveled in her chair to face them, hair whipping around her shoulders. "Will you sit with me?"

"If it would please you," Beverly answered.

"It certainly would!" Evalyn gestured to the empty seats and the servants sat, hands clasped in their laps. She dug into the food, stomach grumbling. When was the last time she'd enjoyed such a delicious meal? Evalyn pointed with a fork to the additional plates—mouth half full. "Please, divulge yourselves."

"We mustn't," Beverly exclaimed.

Evalyn rolled her eyes, swallowing her bite. "As hungry as I am, I won't be able to eat all of this on my own. And I would hate for such a perfect meal to go to waste. Go ahead, help yourselves!"

Steadily, the women obeyed. In moments, the trays were spotless. Evalyn downed a goblet of water before pouring one for each of the Faeries, then leaned forward. "What's it like in the castle? Do you enjoy working here? Living here?"

Vixie spoke first. "It's wonderful, truthfully. I've made many dear friends, and it's delightful to see the active results of our labor assisting nobles. You'd be astounded how many Lords and Ladies triple their routine times without our help. Now, some of the Queen's Court are rather impolite and ignorant—" She slammed a hand to her mouth, groaning. The other Faeries' cheeks bloomed pink. "Forgive me for such words! Oh, if the Court found out I was muttering insults—"

"I won't tell," Evalyn reassured. "Who of her Court is unfavorable?" None of them answered. Evalyn knitted her brows. "You can trust me."

Beverly let on, "Pavan of House Ziffoy. He's dangerous. And cruel. He uses Ladies in disgusting ways, treats the other Lords as if they're beneath him, and servants like us... we're tools at his beck and call. I don't know how the Queen stands his disrespect."

Surprisingly, Ida piped in, her voice a squeak. "He's one of the most powerful Lords in Faylinn. He was one of the favorites under the Queen Mother, although she's long since passed. Queen Tania kept him close so as not to disrupt her mother's Court, for she was young at her Crowning. She has her reasons for him remaining in her Court."

The young Fae was educated. Or an adept listener.

"Are there any others?"

"Not in particular, miss—Evalyn," Beverly responded. "Most members of the Court are rather kind. Although, as Vixie said, some forget we're all the same, trying to manage fulfilling lives how we can."

"You're unlike anyone else we've served," Vixie exclaimed. She messed with her nail-beds, fingers entwining and picking at others. "You—you treat us not only warmly, for our positions, but as friends."

"You are my friends." Evalyn smiled. "I've been needing a few. I suspect being new and unknown around here won't grant me many chances for relationships." Once again, the Faeries looked at each other in their silently communicating way.

Evalyn pretended to ignore it, standing with arms stretched wide as she yawned. The maids immediately followed, reaching for their finished supper. Evalyn watched them work, their moves systematic and practiced from spending a great deal of time doing such actions in each other's company. She followed them into the bedroom, Vixie and Beverly with hands full of dishes. By the time she reached the bed, Ida had readied the comforter and pillows.

Before the trio slipped from view, Evalyn chimed, "Thank you." They spun towards her, and despite their full arms, curtsied.

As the door shut, a smile made way onto Evalyn's lips. Everything was strange and unfamiliar, but these women... they were good. Kind. The girl slowly exhaled—no fear, no hesitation. Suddenly, the demands were easy to follow. She'd uncover the truth soon, and had a feeling it wasn't all too bad.

Warm morning air flooded the room as Evalyn unlatched her balcony doors.

A range of mountains stretched across the horizon, a deep, clear rill running before them. The Aternalis Creek. A myriad of flowers colored the ground below, a mix of pastels against healthy, green grass within the castle's outer walls. Evalyn's quarters were at the corner of the castle, a guard tower feet to her left. Over the edge of her balcony, she peered along the rest of the castle—similar balconies lined the upper levels.

Evalyn was content to think about nothing except the awakening sky on the horizon as the sun rose at her back over The Palace, but a voice sounded at the door. "Evalyn?" It was a smiling Beverly, her pink hair braided into a high knot. "Breakfast is ready."

The girl willingly followed, stomach growling despite the amount of food she'd shoveled into her body the night before. In the dining chamber, Ida and Vixie set out an array of glorious cuisines.

Evalyn sat. "Have any of you eaten this morning?"

"Castle servants wait until breakfast hours are finished in the dining hall to accept their fill of what remains," Beverly stated.

"Well, I want you to eat with me from now on." Evalyn looked at the seats they'd occupied the night before and smiled. "Please, sit."

The group ate every lick of food.

"Let's get you ready!" Beverly said after, pulling the girl back into her bedroom to the vanity.

"For what?"

"Oh, to meet Queen Tania, of course!" Vixie answered brightly. "Her Majesty requested you to visit."

Ida scurried off to find a gown. Vixie appeared behind Evalyn and began combing and braiding and twirling; Evalyn's hair was pulled half up in an elegant style of pinned plaits. Beverly applied a thin layer of black pigment onto Evalyn's lashes and a rosy stain onto her cheeks before Ida stalked from the closet holding a lilac gown paired with short, silver heels. The back was open, yet delicate ribbons laced across her skin and tied above her hips. Evalyn couldn't help giving a twirl, the skirt fluid around her legs. A set of rings found her fingers, and jewels slid into her self-pierced ears.

The handmaidens stepped back, beaming. Turning to the branch mirror, a matching expression rose on Evalyn's face. She couldn't remember the last time she'd called herself pretty—the girl had never fawned over her looks. But she felt stunning.

Beverly seemed to agree. "You look astounding! Now come along, come along, the Queen is waiting in her chambers!" Beverly placed a hand on Evalyn's shoulder as they proceeded through the door. They passed the interior balcony overlooking the foyer and grand staircase, leading her to the opposite side of the castle. A turn later, they arrived outside the Queen's Chambers.

Vixie smiled. "This is where we leave you."

"Don't worry, at least it isn't the Great Hall before the Court," Beverly simpered. "A request to her chambers calls for informality. Take a breath!"

Evalyn obeyed. No fear. No hesitation. Trust the fate before her; this was what she'd been waiting for. To find out who she was and what she was doing here.

Light flooded the hallway as Evalyn stepped into a spacious chamber. The golden walls exerted their own light; the one across the doorway was covered in windows, revealing a sliver of green and a barrier of stone—the center rear of the castle was absent, a square of gardens in its place, stretching to the Palace's outer defensive wall. A canopy bed was centered on the right wall; five beautiful Fae females lounged on its edges and atop the thick, multi-colored rug on the floor, each clothed in translucent gowns of canary-yellow, cream, and velvet green. A voice exclaimed, "Pray, Ladies. They're expecting so much. The Gods know I can't fail this Kingdom—" It paused as the doors closed.

A hidden, sixth woman stood; the original five began chatting amongst themselves, voices harmonic and smooth. Without a doubt, Evalyn knew the risen Faerie was the Queen.

She was effortlessly flawless, with wavy, blonde hair that draped over her shoulders, framing a carved face. But her gentle appearance was overpowered by a darkened depth in the azure eyes that beheld Evalyn. She stopped herself from stepping back when the woman strode forward. A nude gown shaped her body, bringing out a blue tint in the woman's skin.

The other Faeries now looked at Evalyn, laughter dying and words falling to whispers—not from envy of the Queen's attention, but with... curiosity. Their eyes glinted and lips lifted. The Queen waved a hand, a casual gesture, and the women instantly rose, sashaying past the girl and out of the room.

The closing of the chamber door left them alone. Evalyn exhaled. "You wanted to see me, Your Majesty?"

"You can call me Tania." Evalyn stumbled forward, unsure of whether she should bow or kneel when the Queen added, "You need not submit to me." The girl obliged with wide eyes. "I'm necessarily skilled at interpreting expressions. You don't hide yours so well." The woman's face lacked visible emotion despite the humor lacing her voice. She gazed absentmindedly at the doorway. "It's been a long time since I last saw you, Evalyn." Her voice was pleasant, yet intimidating. Powerful.

"I... I think you're mistaken," Evalyn breathed. She'd never seen the Queen in her entire life. She would've remembered.

"Walfien has helped you understand some about Faylinn and Fae, has he not?" Tania returned.

"He has. Is that it? I'm here to learn more?"

"Somewhat. There is a greater purpose to your arrival."

Evalyn stood taller. "Walfien did say I'd receive answers."

The Queen's lips curled. "But of course he did. Please, sit." She gestured to the bed. Evalyn reclined on its edge with the Queen. Tania's eyes wandered around the room, her minute smile fading. She was so still, Evalyn didn't think the woman was breathing—then, abruptly, the Queen faced her. "Truth is not always so facile to comprehend. I've had to come to terms with many in my lifetime, and the effect of some... are strong and everlasting."

Evalyn studied Tania's eyes. There *was* something familiar about them. "If it reveals why I'm here, then I can take it. Whatever this truth is. I've been through things too." She swallowed. "You'll find I'm not so easily deterred," the girl insisted. She repeated Kinz' advice in her mind.

No fear, no hesitation.

After a slow inhale, Tania stood. "Two years after my coronation, I met a human. The Fae were never concerned in the lives of humans, and naturally, I was expected to marry a rich and important suitor from the Court. But this man wasn't like others. He was freeing and peaceful and generous, and relaxed me from the stress of ruling. Even if he didn't know I undertook such duties. Within weeks, then months, I learned to appreciate humans and their world. I grew to love *him*." She sighed. "Yet I had to keep the relationship secret. If the Lords of my Court discovered I wanted to marry a human—over the alternative Faerie options—they could withdraw support from my Crowning. Needless to say, no one found out. Private contact every few weeks kept us in love—and feeling as if we were again children with our sneaking. Luckily, my absences from certain meetings and appointments were overlooked, for I was still young at the time.

"A year later, I found that keeping who I was from him was draining and distancing us. So I told him everything. I felt obligated to; I loved him. I thought being a Queen—being Fae—would surely end things between us, and I prepared myself for that outcome. But by a Gods-given miracle, he accepted me, keeping my identity safe, and our feelings fell into place: we were mates. You see, every Faerie has a mate—a soul-companion, a partner—destined for them; brought together by fate. Finding and accepting your mate initiates the unbreakable, eternal bond that connects you on a level deeper than any magic. It's indescribable, discovering who you're meant to be with. I knew it was him." Evalyn was starting to lose grip on everything she once believed in. Being in a room with a Faerie Queen was proof that nothing was as it seemed in the world.

"We had a covert, human marriage ceremony... and soon after, I found I was with a child—a girl. The issue was not only that I'd begin to show, but that even if I managed to conceal my pregnancy, I could die from miniscule complications. I had to reveal the truth to my Kingdom. Surprisingly, they supported me further. Some shamed my secrecy, but the joy of the citizens was a far greater response. It was another miracle—after my mother and father's passing, I finally thought I could be happy, and my Kingdom as well." A pause. "But such events do not exist. My husband fell sick before my daughter was born. No Fae remedies worked, and he insisted he wouldn't die at the hands of an experimental human nurse. He was ready to go in peace with me at his side. He passed within the week." Her voice lowered to a tone Evalyn didn't understand. Melancholic and hurt in a way the girl suspected few others in the world had experienced.

"I became depressed. Distant. But as Queen, I couldn't show those emotions. We created a memorial for him at his grave, near his personal cottage. By that time, a neighboring Kingdom, Braena, had been founded—and its King, Oberon Romen, enthroned. He insisted on being married; allied. With a King over Ausor, and the southeastern continent of Alias too distant to coalesce with Braena, I was the only choice. He conveyed that having Braena as a partner would change Liatue for the better—as if such a declaration could sway me in the slightest. But after denying the marriage—and along with it, a potential alliance—the King threatened to overpower me, demolish the villages, attack my home." Her tone flared. "Having been born into Royalty, I was considerably more experienced than him, so the claim didn't frighten me, but upon the counsel of my advisors, the risk outweighed the hope he wouldn't act. So we married, and our Kingdoms became united.

"Halfway through my pregnancy, I began sensing bursts of feeling. It was power and strength. Utter *energy*. I merely thought it stress from the fresh alliance, but the sensation fatigued me so greatly that I rendered immobile for days at a time. Then, as if sent by the Gods, a matron showed at The Palace, requesting my presence. Matron Lessia Ruste of the Boltrum Tribe, she claimed. I summoned her, a new Queen intrigued by the desires of a witch from the Western Continent. The words she spoke to me were gripping, to put it lightly. The matron believed the babe I carried would grow to liberate Faekind. More than that as well, but... she made it clear the child was to be powerful. Influential. All I could dream for her, I suppose, is what the woman proclaimed for my babe. She explained that my weariness was from the child siphoning my energy to build its own. And I'd have taken it as blather, as nonsense from a mad buffoon, yet... the way the woman sat before me, not a hair out of place nor a syllable hesitant in her speech... I believed her. And although I've never heard a whisper of her since that moment, I've held to that foretelling."

Tania inhaled. "I gave birth to my daughter. Faylinn knew she wasn't the King's child, but Oberon attempted to act as a father figure for the infant Princess. I hid her among the castle for as long as I dared. He had made it clear that to disobey his wants was to personally inflict danger upon Faylinn—and I became afraid he'd take my daughter and raise her in the wrong ways he existed with. Every waking hour he asked after her, questioning where I'd taken her, what I'd done with my daughter. Oberon wanted her, for whatever sick motive, and began doing everything possible to retrieve her from the safety of Faylinn. Lackeys snuck onto our lands to kidnap her and he declared threats if she wasn't delivered. The King even sent an assassin. Not for either of us... but for my Kingdom. If I didn't comply with giving her up, my people would be greeted by punishment. I knew he'd do whatever it took to reach the Princess, but I couldn't risk her well-being. She was so much of the little I had left and I couldn't hand her over for a sacrifice." A pause. "So I sent her away; sent her to the human territory where she couldn't be tracked by any magic, into a family I hoped would treat her as their own." The Queen's lips wobbled, but she took a breath.

"I adored her. Faylinn did. And the pain of being without her, knowing she was in the world but outside of my embrace... I felt guilty for pushing her away, even though her absence from the King and Braena was best. Oberon couldn't discover where she'd gone—not that her disappearance ceased his scouring. Rumors spread, searches were formed—the Lost Princess, my Kingdom called her. Everyone questioned what I'd done. For months, I received inquiries and demands for her return, because she was my only heir to the throne. Eventually, I revealed that she was safe, and declared she'd return, one day, stronger and honored and unmatched—a fraction of Matron Lessia's prophecy. In turn, the questions died off, but the longing I had for her grew stronger."

There was something odd about the story that Evalyn couldn't put a finger on. She gulped. "What does this have to do with me?"

Tania's gaze wandered to Evalyn, and her mouth curved into a small smile. "My girl, *you* are the Lost Princess."

Chapter Five

Everything clicked into place.

Evalyn's feelings since arriving to Faylinn—whilst being in The Palace—those of belonging and rightness... this was why. And Walfien's words from the previous day...

She truly was home.

And she was Fae. Not only that, but a Faerie Princess.

"Why—why don't I look like you?" Evalyn inquired, fingers instinctively skimming her eartips.

"It's a glamour—a type of magic that hid your true heritage. I had aid from a witch when you were an infant. Neither you nor your human family would know your identity, and you wouldn't come searching until you came of-age. The magic breaks when you turn twenty."

Evalyn nodded but stood, unable to control the need to move, to pace—

Breathe.

No fear. No hesitation.

This was the truth she'd asked for; the one she'd been destined to uncover. Another piece of the puzzle locked into place.

"Kinz knew," Evalyn stated. Tania nodded. "And the visitors at the cabin... they weren't human, then?"

"Glamoured, as well. A temporary shield to keep the secret until you were older. Faeries from the Guard, our military force, ensuring your safety."

So Kinz' contact with Walfien had been more than friendship—it'd meant contact to the castle and Tania. Which meant the Queen—her *mother*—must have known what she'd gone through four years ago.

"Why was I kept away for so long?" Evalyn's voice balanced on the edge of composure and irritation. "They tried to kill me. But you knew that human couple drugged and left me that Winter, didn't you? Why keep me stowed away?" The girl couldn't say she would've wanted to live in fear of this King—but the thought that she'd endured that incident, let alone suffer fifteen years prior feeling so alone and hopeless, when things could've been better... it enraged her.

"It was the only way to keep you safe. Give you to a family unaware of who you were—of who you *are*—and be raised in a home where you could grow up without fear of Oberon."

"You wanted me *safe*? Without Walfien and Kinz, I would have *died!*"

"But you didn't. And such a horrendous act was never intended. The couple was inspected—"

"*Inspected?*"

"—before we placed you in their care. With a distant home and decent income, there was nothing indifferent about them."

"And you've resided in this castle, watching my life unfold?"

Tania lifted her head. "Once you were taken into refuge by Kinz... she checked in with me once a month. I couldn't miss seeing you grow up any longer. Oberon would've won, then. I couldn't let him triumph in that aspect."

"That sounds more selfish than caring."

The Queen swiftly rose. "You will *not* speak to me in such a way." She stepped toward her daughter with a pointed finger—shaking, amidst quick breaths. "I did everything I could to protect you. What those people did was a *mercy* compared to the actions Oberon takes to ensure power."

Evalyn believed the Queen. But some part of her wouldn't back down, wouldn't control her temper as she should and listen to everything Tania had to say. "I *suffered* at the hands of those people. I never knew love or kindness or what it felt like to *enjoy* waking up every morning for most of my life. You may have missed me, but at least you felt that longing. I had *no one* to miss while you sat in a fancy castle feeling sorry for yourself."

Tania looked like she'd been slapped. And although Evalyn immediately regretted verbalizing her thoughts, she realized she meant them. Were things supposed to continue smoothly? How could she accept these circumstances without retort?

Tania turned to the windows, her gaze cold and still.

Evalyn marched out. A tear slipped down her cheek, but the girl wiped her face. Curse her show of emotion. She somehow found her quarters, where already waiting within were the maids, standing before her bed as if they'd sensed Evalyn's arrival.

Her words were slow. "I presume you know who I am."

"Yes," Vixie quietly responded.

"We... we were forbidden to reveal anything," Beverly exclaimed. "We understand if you're cross with us."

Despite the shock thundering through her heart, Evalyn breathed, "We're friends, remember? I couldn't be cross with you." She tried to smile as the maid blushed, but another tear slipped down her chin and she stopped bothering to contain any others. The trio pounced to her side, instinctually ushering Evalyn into the bathing chamber and readying a bath.

Evalyn slipped into the tub and the three left her.

She'd always wondered who her real parents were; where she'd come from. This reality hadn't existed in her wildest fantasies: her mother, Queen, and she, the Lost Princess of Faylinn. She'd never taken on her adoptive parents' name; had remained Evalyn Impur for nineteen years. That distinction from those people—it'd always been special. Now, her maiden name identified her as the Royal heir.

The girl shuddered. She'd contemplate all that her future implied later.

Once the water was too cold to stand and her head too tired of realizing and wondering, she shrugged on a linen robe, hair dripping at her back. Finding her room empty, she strode to her vanity and began brushing out the knotted locks of her golden-blonde hair when Vixie and Beverly entered unannounced with plates of food; Evalyn's mouth watered at the smell. Ida filed in after.

With a look at Evalyn's state—stuck on a stubborn knot—Vixie handed her platter to Ida and swooped in to help. "Bring the food. This might take a while," Evalyn said, beckoning for the girls, who placed the soups atop the vanity. By the time Vixie detangled her hair, she'd eaten a whole loaf and half the array of roasted vegetables. For the first time, the trio finished the meal without Evalyn's asking. They ate in silence, a gift to Evalyn who had returned to dwelling over everything she'd just learned about herself.

A sudden knock sent the maids into a flurry of wiping their faces and smoothing their uniforms. Vixie pulled open the door, falling into a deep curtsy. "Lord Hand!"

Evalyn turned as Walfien strode into the room, uniformed as always.

"How many times must I ask you to call me Walfien?" His friendliness sent the maid into a scarlet mess. "I was hoping for a moment with Evalyn—if it's no trouble." He smiled. A simper found Vixie's lips as the other girls swept up the dishes, leaving in a giggling fit. Walfien strode to the edge of Evalyn's bed, eyes wandering around the room.

"It seems neither of us care for the formality of titles," the girl stated, returning to her vanity mirror. The Hand's questioning eyes reflected back at her.

Walfien tilted his head. "Your mother needed to tell you. You're clever; I know you were aware something greater was in play, but I couldn't share anything until Tania had her turn."

Evalyn turned on her stool to face him. "I understand."

Walfien stepped closer. "Then why are you upset?"

"I'm fine. Like I said—"

"You're not fine."

He saw through her so easily. Evalyn's chin dipped. "I don't know what I'm supposed to do. Everyone wants a reaction, but I don't know how to respond. I'm still comprehending."

"That's why I'm here," Walfien said. "To help you through the shock and confusion and everything else, if you'll allow me."

"You're just saying that."

"I'm not." A partial smile rose to Walfien's lips. "In three days, we'll start daily lessons after breakfast. I'll see you then."

With the click of her door, he was gone. The girl sighed, splaying over the bed on her stomach. A twist of the door handle and a chorus of giggles turned Evalyn on her back. Beverly, Ida, and Vixie skipped for the bed.

"What a gentleman," Vixie swooned, beaming. "If the Ladies of the Court saw you with Lord Pax, they'd curse you from jealousy. So many fancy him."

Evalyn's eyes grew. "We're friends, Vixie."

"Still, you have to admit he's *gorgeous*," Beverly exclaimed. A pillow chunked in her direction was the girl's response.

After the events of the day before, Evalyn had spent the afternoon lounging with the trio in her quarters. Somehow, the girl had woken up feeling renewed and clear-minded—and ready to shoulder the weight of who she was. Even if it took time to get used to her new identity—the *Lost Princess*—she was prepared.

For so long, she'd been fueled by a determination to be bigger than the girl who'd almost died those years ago. This was her chance.

Evalyn didn't anticipate her acceptance included allowing a constant eye on her whereabouts. When she begged her maids for a wander around the castle—because she was bored of staring over her balcony and playing cards until her lessons with Walfien began—they firmly insisted she stay in her quarters unless called upon. Only castle staff and members of the Queen's small council knew of Evalyn's presence in the castle, and it was safest that way.

"But if I'm the Princess, doesn't that mean I can do whatever I wish?" The maids shared hesitant glances. "I only want to know my way around The Palace. It wouldn't do well for me to become lost in an emergency."

"Oh, alright then," Beverly groaned. "We'll give you a tour, but you're to stay in our sight at all times."

Ida added, "Lord Pax would kill us if we let you get into trouble."

"Lord Pax is too kind to do that," Vixie said.

"It was a figure of speech," Ida returned.

The Faeries guided Evalyn through the castle. There were more than two levels—the higher ones within the three towers of the keep. The outer towers contained the Royal Library and Steeple—a place to praise the Gods outside of the Citadel in the city of Koathe. The centermost, highest tower—the Great Tower—was used for guardwork and servant travels. Only because of the maids' excessive stories—told whilst distinguishing the types of rooms and wings of the castle: north and south, separated by the foyer, grand staircase, and Great Tower—did Evalyn come to grasp the layout of The Palace with ease.

By midday, they had covered the entirety of the castle grounds except a section of the castle containing the infirmary, kitchens, and servant and staff sleeping quarters. Exhausted from walking, Evalyn reclined on a bench in the gardens within the three rear castle walls. Where a fourth one would've been was an opening to the flowering grounds that wrapped around the entirety of The Palace. Sunlight danced on her skin as she listened to the pleasant chirping of birds dancing between the trees.

"How about we peek into the kitchens?" Vixie hummed.

Beverly squealed, jumping on her toes, "Yes! I know where they hide the dessert reserves for special ceremonies and celebrations. Missy won't mind if we sneak a sweet loaf—she makes the best batch in all of Faylinn! You must try it, Evalyn!"

With that, they went on their way.

"Beverly knows The Palace better than most," Vixie explained.

Beverly rolled her eyes. "It's family tradition to serve the Queen and her Court. My mother was a handmaiden, as was my great-mother, when she was young enough to walk on her own. It's an honor for us to use our time and talents for the Royals and nobles."

"What magic do you have?" Evalyn asked. She'd seen Vixie's water configuration and Ida's heat production, but Beverly hadn't shown any signs of magic.

"Well, sometimes, magic can weaken as it's passed down a bloodline. Depending on the elemental branch prominent in one's family, magic can disperse into small amounts among more children," Beverly returned. "My family has dominant wind powers, albeit from a faulty branch of the air element. And with half a dozen children among even more folk, there's a lot of watered-down ability." She lifted a hand, palm up, and blew towards Evalyn, where a soothing trickle of wind slipped through her hair. "Faeries can store their magic—build it up by withholding it, then use a greater amount than they typically could summon when needed." The maid shrugged her shoulders. "I find the process boring, and I've come to terms with the usability of my magic, so the infirmity doesn't bother me. I don't need much magic as a handmaiden, anyway."

"You're stronger than me, in that case," Ida said, stroking the ends of her plaits. "Magic is one of my *only* skills. But your confidence reminds me that it's not the only thing that makes up who I am, Bev."

"You're a star, Ida," Beverly noted. "Don't let anyone forget so. When you arrived three years ago, hired at seventeen years old to save up for a remedy for your sick father, I couldn't believe it! I was *born* into servantry and couldn't have taken the work so early. At the same age I was wreaking havoc in lessons and barely making it home in time to have a meal before Pa forced us to bed."

Vixie giggled. "In my lessons, I was too busy plaiting my hair to pay attention. My mother always fussed over my results. It didn't take her long to realize my interests would serve me well if I served others." Her smile became lopsided. "I don't speak to my mother often; it feels like I was sent away a lifetime ago. Only when she sends me a letter every few seasons do I remember what I was forced to leave behind."

"You have us now. We're your family," Beverly said, gripping Vixie's hand. "Have been and always will be."

The maid smiled as they turned a final corner and entered the kitchens, where sizzling and beating sounded in an explosion of noise and waves of sweet-scented heat crashed into them. The room was crammed with tables; shelves filled to the brim marked every wall; even the ceiling was plastered with hanging pots and pans and serving utensils. Chefs and pastry makers crowded all leftover space, incessantly moving in the creation of exquisite dishes.

A baker of identical stature to Beverly ran up to them, smiling broadly. "Missy!" Beverly shouted, gripping the bun-haired and aproned Faerie in a hug.

"Don't tell me you're back for more sweet loaf, cousin!" the woman squealed, crossing her arms although a simper formed on her lips. "I just made a fresh batch for Queen Tania to try—spiced chocolate, my newest creation."

Beverly's eyes turned round. "Oh, Missy, just one loaf? For Evalyn here," she begged, tugging Evalyn forth who gave a small wave and nodded her chin eagerly.

Missy stared Evalyn down, but sighed and wiped her hands on her apron. "Fine. You can't say I don't treat you well, Bev." The maid beamed with giddiness as Missy strode to a table across the chamber, returning with two cloth-wrapped sweet loaves. Her voice lowered, and she inclined toward the four of them. "An extra for the Lost Princess, who's return the Gods have blessed us with."

Beverly accepted the loaves as the maids hummed their agreement. With a parting thanks, they exited to return to Evalyn's quarters.

"What happened while you were away?" Vixie inquired. "You've gone unseen by Faylinn for nineteen years yet it feels like you have no problems adjusting to this strange and new life."

Evalyn blew a long exhale. "That's because most of my life is easy to let go of. My parents—my human parents—despised and ignored me. I wasn't allowed to go anywhere or meet anyone or do anything outside of the strict list of chores and self-taught lessons they pinned on the door inside our locked cottage. For fifteen years... I had nothing. And then they tried to kill me." The maids gasped; Beverly halted in place, covering her mouth with both hands. Evalyn nodded in affirmation before swiftly moving along in the story—to happier times with Kinz. Even after reaching Evalyn's room, they laughed for hours about the stories from her and Kinz' time together: like Evalyn's first attempt at crafting clothes from scratch and Kinz' weeks-long effort to persuade the girl to wear something other than her successfully sewn, single pair of pants; or sixteen year old Evalyn venturing through the forest for a whole afternoon to gather ingredients for supper, only to return to the meal already made by her guardian, and Evalyn subsequently throwing her findings in the fire in a fit of aggravation.

When the Princess reached her trip with Walfien, Vixie slapped her hands to her cheeks. "Tell me you saw Lord Pax with his tunic off!"

"Why am I not surprised that that's your only comment?"

"Come *on*," Vixie laughed, "just tell us!"

Evalyn raised her eyebrows, silent.

"You *did*! You saw him, you saw him! Gods, he must be dazzling—"

"I only caught a *glimpse*, Vixie—and only did so once. We were at the tiniest stream and had been traveling for four days. Both of us reeked."

The Faerie giggled. "You're still lucky. Servants rarely cross soldiers during their training, but we clean their barracks afterwards—a horrendous mess of a place to sleep, I must relay."

"Well," Evalyn chuckled, "as the Princess, I'm sure I can sneak you into a training session at some point to ogle their sweaty chests." Beverly and Ida seemed positively disgusted at the thought, but Vixie's smirk told Evalyn that promise would be kept if it was the last thing she did.

Two weeks passed without notice, aside from the festivities of the Spring Equinox. Although Evalyn didn't join—to keep her presence in the Fae world private from King Oberon for a while longer—she witnessed the singing and dancing and glimpses of magic as the Spring celebrations began from her balcony. In the gardens below, females wore pastel gowns, frolicking with flowered crowns and bare feet while the males bore tunics of cream and pale browns, creating musical beats with pounding and whooping and deep hums. Evalyn settled with twirling in her bed chambers while her trio attempted to teach her the basic dances and songs of the celebrations undergone at the outset of each season. All four entailed specific practices and attires, but the gestures were the same: revel in the reborn phases of the year.

After breakfast the Princess began attending lessons with the Hand in his office—a stunning room with bookshelves enveloping the expansive chamber. Evalyn lounged on the sofa before Walfien's desk after laboring over books about past rulers, volumes of the creation of the Fae, and tales of their enemy and saviors. She let her head hang backwards, over the edge of the sofa. "Haven't I gone through enough basics, Walfien?"

"The history of Faylinn is important to understand many traditions, celebrations, and the foundation of our faith."

"At least the knowledge has some use. But I've studied so much that I can recite the beginning of Faerie existence in my sleep," she sighed. At his silence, Evalyn straightened to see Walfien's elbows propped on the desk and chin over his folded hands. She lifted her brows and began.

"The Faerie race was spawned at a sacred place called Coilum by the God, Omforteu, and his Goddess-wife, Deeam. Primascul Nemor was the first living Fae, blessed with the gifts of every element and a pair of radiant-gold wings to allow him to watch over Liatue—a trait never passed down. Frimpen mated with Primascul and began the first generation of Fae, which the Gods sparingly granted elemental powers in order to keep Primascul and Frimpen on top, to maintain their natural, born-for status as protectors, defenders, and leaders of Faeries. History never identified a cause to the Nemors' unified death, but speculation has it that they helped one another, in order to proceed into the afterlife together after a rich life of duty.

"Centuries after, King Dricormie and Queen Beolah founded Faylinn and became its first monarchs. They were idolized and praised for their parting gift to the rest of Faeries: saving them from destruction and death at the hands of their sworn enemy, Deilok. He'd been a well-known Faerie, mighty and adored before he was corrupted by greed. He wanted to be the emperor of all lands—to rule all Faekind. Even Dricormie and Beolah came to fear him—he was older, wiser, and a force to be reckoned with, with unmatched strength and legendary magic. Months went by as he stormed through villages and burned them to the ground, tortured mates and children, climbed fortress walls and assassinated Lords who had wronged him. But the time turned to years. The entire continent feared his breath, and prayed their own wouldn't be their last."

She gave a great breath. "But venturing through forgotten lands and unknown continents, under guidance from the Gods, Dricormie and Beolah reached the home of Deilok. They shot him down until he was weaker than the sickest human, and used every fragment of magic they could summon to conquer him. His body was never found—obliterated by their power. When they returned to Faylinn, their account was retold as consequence settled over their bodies. They'd used their powers without limits, and it had struck back. Albeit a glorious defeat, the Gods demanded balance. But Dricormie and Beolah were the sacrifice for a chance of peace. A pair of healers heard Dricormie and Beolah's account hours before they passed—a tale Liatue would never forget. But not all Fae kept to such beliefs; many think of the tale as fraud. The Rogues are careless for the past and for the bedtime story of Faylinn's saviors meant for ushering children to sleep. They wander the Kingdomlands, forcing their own truths onto any they encounter, with a dangerous following to be cautious of."

Evalyn slumped into the sofa in close. Walfien smiled. "Straight from the books. You could teach lessons yourself," he claimed, standing.

She rolled her eyes. "What's next?" She strode for the edge of his desk, placing her hands on the map covering the top. "Can we review some geography? I want to look into Alias and the Western Continent; how they differ from Liatue and the Kingdoms here."

He ambled to a shelf. "We'll do that next lesson. But not much is known about the Western Continent, and Alias has a relatively small Faerie population, so we'll pair it with calligraphy and code writing exercises."

Evalyn shrugged her shoulders, giving a smug beam. Walfien returned a title to the top shelf, and her eye caught his inked bicep, visible under a short-sleeved tunic.

"What's that?" she asked. "Isn't it Faylinn's emblem?"

Following her pointed finger, he lifted his sleeve. "Yes. It's an ancient, sacred symbol; when they turn twenty, every Faerie gets their Kingdom's mark inked on their body. It acts as the first show of loyalty as an of-age citizen. Our signarum."

"What else happens when I come of-age?"

Walfien's mismatched eyes twinkled. "Omforteu and Deeam granted Primascul and Frimpen powers that they were instantly gifted with. The rest of us don't receive them until we come of-age—on what we call our Bonum Vitae. You're then allowed to receive your signarum, and the Fae heritage in your blood makes its appearance—in looks and abilities. Your magic is revealed, if you don't know what type you possess already. Those whose parents have distinct, single powers often have an idea of what abilities they'll have. Once Fae reach within a year of their Bonum Vitae, they begin to notice the Signs."

"You mentioned them to Kinz the night we met." It seemed so long ago.

"I needed her to be aware. The most noticeable Sign is nature's response: healing fields and thriving forests surrounding the Fae, or the alternate extreme of hazardous weather. Then there's emotional adjustment: temporary bouts of optimism or pessimism resulting from the release of your forming magic. Some Fae get bad Signs, some get good. It depends on your body and magic.

The pixies can also sense a Faerie's age and like to show off faint trickles of their power in support; they're friendly things, green and winged and spindly—some of the Gods' other creations."

She nodded in recognition. The truth of her fate had sat in her lap for months.

"Physical appearance also alters on your Bonum Vitae; hair color, skin shading, irises." He made it sound as casual as shifting seasons. "You undergo the changes overnight. The process is harmless."

She watched him. Then suddenly asked, "Why are you doing this? I mean," she corrected, "why didn't my mother give me someone more... qualified to teach? Don't you prefer your work over this?"

"I do enjoy my role. But you're more important to... the Kingdom. And your mother." His mismatched eyes met the ground, and he cleared his throat, meeting Evalyn's gaze. "These lessons won't be forever, just until Tania deems your knowledge sufficient. The more accustomed and familiar you are to this life, the easier it'll be and the less time others will have to pick up the mess if you slip up. Which happens to all of us, but..." Walfien sighed. "In Court, everyone knows everyone—and if you don't, you're no one. And nobodies are spat upon as often as breath is inhaled. They don't get attention, don't receive respect, and aren't believed to be any kind of special. Being a Royal is almost worse. A mess-up to one Lord is the entire castle's gossip." A smile. "That's why I'm doing this. To help you. And because I offered in place of the librarian. You wouldn't enjoy her company as much."

Evalyn chuckled. "Thank you, Walfien. I *do* enjoy your company."

"And I, yours. But you should get going—it's nearing midday."

Evalyn nodded; she needed to return to her room where her friends would sweep her up in a madness of dressing and grooming. Today, she'd be reintroduced to Faylinn.

The Lost Princess found at last.

"Just... one thing," she said as she stood. "Why am I being so publicly announced if we want to shield my whereabouts from the King?"

Walfien returned to his desk. "The Queen wants to present you in such a way that demonstrates what the Kingdom knows of you so far: that you're strong and powerful and a ray of hope in face of the terror that Oberon Romen has put us through. And with Faylinn's awareness, you'll be protected from every angle. We just have to pray it's enough of a start against the King. We can't guess how he'll react to your return. He's been quiet." Walfien tapped a stack of parchment. "I'll see you at the capital."

The Princess was dressed in a pale blue gown that accentuated her curled hair and eyes, then she, her trio, and a majority of the Queen's Court were ushered through The Palace's gates. They descended the steps in the castle's hill, and on the path at the base of the mount, into carriages departing for the capital.

The journey was swift and quiet. Her hands were sweating and the girl's lip had tinted red from her gnawing, and talking with her handmaidens was the last thing on her mind—but she found a strange relief as Koathe loomed closer. The gates into the capital closed as the last of the Court carriages halted.

Stepping onto the road, she instinctively found Walfien up the path. His own stare landed on the Princess, and he gave a calm smile. She inhaled deep, mirroring his expression.

The Main Road stretched farther than she could see. A set of thick walls encircled Koathe, with the guarded, swirling metal-and-magic enforced gates on the north and south end of the city the only entrances. Cream-stone buildings siding the paved path towered high, with gold flourishes detailing the exteriors of lavish suites.

The only citizens in sight were a few Fae, strolling along and gawking at the arrival of superiors.

Vixie chuckled, "Everyone in the city has gathered at the Citadel to await your appearance! They were alerted this morning of the long-anticipated arrival of their Princess."

Evalyn followed Ida's westward-pointed finger, noticing the colossal fortress dominating the city, and gulped. "I suppose we shouldn't keep them waiting, then?"

They traveled so swiftly that Evalyn barely glimpsed the shaded alleyway ground before they were gathered near the entrance of the Citadel. A light, crystaled tiara was placed atop her head before everyone disappeared save

Evalyn, Tania, Walfien, and a unit of sentinels. The Princess was ushered beside her mother, where, Queen and Heir, they stepped into glaring afternoon sunlight at the top of the hundreds of steps leading to the dome-roofed Citadel.

Below them, swarmed along the broad stone path that met with the Main Road in the distance, stood tens of thousands of Fae. Evalyn was glad they were so far from the crowd as her heart pounded and a bead of sweat trickled down her forehead. Every citizen eyed the Princess.

And as one, erupted into a deafening cheer of joy.

A laugh erupted from her, and she couldn't help but beam and lift a hand to wave. They'd truly awaited her return for so long.

The Queen lifted her palms to the crowd, and at once, the Faeries quieted, so silent Evalyn could hear the wind blowing tunes over their heads. Queen Tania smiled and lowered her hands.

Evalyn felt a light touch on her elbow; Walfien stepped beside her. Her nerves dissipated with his steadying presence. The crowd murmured, strangely—it was a touching gesture from one friend to another, and reassurance that he was here from the beginning, and would be for the rest. As he promised. Yet it appeared to be an act of greater meaning, for even the Queen's eyes widened as she glimpsed the scene which had stolen the capital's attention. Tania's shock was hidden within a moment, replaced by a bright smile as she commenced with the first words and updates; unheard by Evalyn's ears, whose heart continued pounding, but for a different reason now.

"Citizens, friends, Faeries of Faylinn—many of you have come far from the comfort of your homes to be here today." The Queen's voice magically echoed to the farthest standing Fae, specks in the road. "You've heard of the future I believe for my daughter: that she will lead Faylinn in prosperity and joy, and be unmatched by any past or future rule. I confirm that she is mighty and strong-willed and benevolent."

Evalyn knew her mother's expression of delight wasn't a facade for the sake of the Kingdom, although the Princess hadn't made it easy to form their relationship. She'd make amends when they returned to The Palace. Have a fresh beginning.

"Today, we welcome Evalyn Impur, the Lost Princess of Faylinn!"

Beverly, Ida, and Vixie were already waiting at the carriage when Evalyn arrived, half a dozen guards surrounding her. The city had flooded its streets after the introduction, countless Fae hoping to glimpse their Princess up close. It took three times as long to return to the coach through the now-packed alleyways they'd come through.

"You were a glimmering angel up there! The capital fell in love with you even before Queen Tania's speech," Beverly chirped.

Ida grinned. "It's true. You were beautiful."

The Princess smiled. "Thank you for coming, even if you weren't up beside me as I would've wished." She was still jittery inside from the response of the citizens, the overwhelming cries of rejoice echoing in her mind.

Vixie leaned forward. "You had plenty of support, it seemed! Lord Pax stood so near you, the entire city was surely fuming with envy." They giggled.

"I told you, Vixie, we're friends!"

Beverly sighed, "And we heard you. But what a surprise that was, his first display of affection in front of the *capital*! After he hasn't shown such open devotion to anyone since Ahstra?" There was a moment of unresponsive quiet, then Beverly gasped, hand flying to her mouth as she paled with the other servants. "Gods, did I just say that out loud?"

"Who's Ahstra?" Evalyn questioned. The Faeries glanced between one another. "Who is she?" The maids stared at the floor; Beverly ceaselessly shook her chin. The Princess couldn't decide whether she actually wanted to know, but furthered, "Please tell me."

Ida responded, "They were lovers during the end of their childhood. Mates, most thought, until..." She glanced at the other women, who eventually nodded for her to continue. "Until she left. After some years together, she disappeared without a trace."

Evalyn watched their faces; observed their fidgeting. "And?"

Vixie exclaimed, "We shouldn't say, Princess. The Queen demanded her name never again be spoken—especially around Lord Pax. Oh, he'd be furious if he found out we'd told you—"

"Then we won't tell him," the Princess interjected.

The girls scrunched their features, but Ida said, "She went to Braena. She hoped to serve the King as..."

"As another common wench looking for the chance to warm a Royal bed," Beverly scowled.

Evalyn's throat closed. "How was this discovered?"

"King Oberon sent her to back The Palace," Ida whispered. "To the inner gate, where all could see." The others held their breath. "She was stripped naked... and had evidently been beaten. Magically strangled and tortured. Servants were called to take her body far away and bury it. One read the note tacked to her body—before Lord Pax burned it in front of everyone. It said what she'd done, and ended with... well, the King said he would make Lord Pax's real mate suffer for the inconvenience that Ahstra had caused him, no matter her status or blood."

The Princess' glee from the day disappeared.

No one spoke for the rest of the journey.

Chapter Six

The Princess had barely succumbed to sleep when she jolted awake.

She didn't know what had woken her—the room was still and quiet, and the sun had barely begun rising. She'd fallen into a deep sleep after her return from the capital.

Then she caught the voices in the hallway.

"... keep guard on both ends. Our exit route may already be clear, but stay *quiet*," growled a harsh voice.

Evalyn slid out of bed. An itch in her chest told her something wasn't right.

"Good luck," someone replied.

"We don't need *luck*," another rebounded.

The footsteps were louder. Closer. Her door handle rattled not seconds after she'd shoved her vanity stool under it. Evalyn darted to her closet, shutting the doors as softly as she could manage. Her palms sweated; her stomach twisted.

Silence.

Then an explosion echoed through her quarters.

Debris pounded against the closet door as Evalyn hid beside an armoire and took slow, soundless breaths. So much for their being inconspicuous.

"We're in!" one cackled. Cracks and crunches sounded—the wall they'd busted through.

"Can you smell her?"

The other Fae grunted in response.

Evalyn's throat dried. Were these Braenish soldiers? Had they known Evalyn had sent an ill Ida to her chambers the night before and ordered Beverly and Vixie to tend to her until she was better? How had they entered The Palace in the first place and crossed two floors pooling with the most elite sentries?

Light flooded the closet as the doors were ripped open. Evalyn squeezed her body as if it'd make her invisible, but a guffaw rebounded and a calloused hand gripped her arm, effortlessly pulling the girl from her place. Her nightgown tore, ripping a slit halfway around her waist. Despite the gown's length, she felt too bare. Exposed, with these crooks ogling her.

"What do we have here?" the Fae snarked.

His shove to a corner of the room slammed Evalyn's head against the wall. The Princess groaned at the sting and dizziness; attempted to catch her breath as she noticed his stringy, gray-brown hair draped over glaring, red eyes.

The second Faerie glanced at the hole in the wall. "Get on with it, Ailfbane."

"What do you want?" Evalyn blurted. They both showed her yellow, crooked teeth.

"You, of course," the one called Ailfbane answered. Then he lunged. Evalyn dodged to the side, body colliding with the destroyed wall before she slumped to the ground. Her head hadn't stopped spinning.

Four more soldiers barged into her room—but they weren't here to help.

"We have specific orders. Don't kill, just capture," one barked.

Ailfbane's mouth twisted. "What's a little fun gonna do? She'll heal in no time."

The group closed in. Evalyn's head throbbed. She couldn't back down—couldn't surrender like a coward. She was the Princess. The girl stood, clenching her fists.

No fear.

Stars danced in her vision.

No hesitation.

She lifted her hands, despite the fact that she knew nothing about defending herself, and when Ailfbane darted forth she swung wildly, fist colliding with what felt like his head, but maybe it was his shoulder—then sudden, spotted blackness enveloped her vision as pain seared across her cheek and she collapsed to the floor. But the Princess wouldn't give up so easily. She groaned against her dizziness and faced the Faeries again—

Walfien burst through the wall, a swarm of sentinels at his flank. They *were* here to save her. "Capture any Fae you can—take them as prisoners," the Hand exclaimed in one breath. "Whatever happens, we protect her." The attackers gave the Faylinn guards half a glance before returning to Evalyn.

"Let's get this over with," Ailfbane ordered.

The sentinels struck as the soldiers pounced. Red sparks flashed through the room; pounding fists and clanging weapons sounded. Every soldier was quickly taken down, but someone grabbed Evalyn by the throat, swinging her to his chest, momentarily winding her.

"Take us and the girl dies!"

All commotion stopped.

She gulped for air. Ailfbane held a dagger to her neck, burning at the weapon's touch.

Walfien stepped forward. "Don't." He glanced at her neck. "You wouldn't."

"Ah, but I *would,* if I wanted to. If my orders allowed me to. They *do* allow me an *unconscious* Princess," Ailfbane smirked. "I find females more fun to play with when unaccompanied by resistance, anyway." Evalyn winced at the pressure on her throat. His rotting stench filled her nose, and warm fluid ran down her neck. Pain shot through her throat and she cried out—but stilled when Ailfbane shrugged her closer.

Evalyn searched Walfien's eyes for answers, but curse his skilled secrecy, he let on *nothing*. The Hand had slipped into a mask lack of emotion as his duty called for—unyielding, unfazed, unrelenting. The Hand tightened the grip on his sword. "Let her go."

The Princess squeezed her eyes. No fear, she told herself. No fear.

"Now why should I do that?"

"Queen Tania may grant you a death merciful compared to those of your companions."

When she opened her eyes, Ailfbane began laughing at Walfien. "Oh, I couldn't accept. You see, I'm dead already."

It happened in slow motion.

Walfien pulled his arm back, throwing the sword faster than a blink. For a moment, Evalyn thought it marked her—her throat ached and blood dripped onto her nightgown—but her captor's body sagged. Ailfbane was right.

He'd been dead the moment Walfien had arrived.

Evalyn dropped to the ground. Crawled away from Ailfbane and clutched her stinging neck, taking thin breaths. But she couldn't remove her stare from the soldier, from his impaled chest and the dark blood seeping into his uniform.

A strip of cloth appeared in Walfien's hands and he pressed it to her neck, stopping the flow of blood that leaked down her front. "You can't stay out of trouble, can you?" he muttered. He twirled and flicked two fingers in the air, where a rush of white sparks streamed across the quarters and through the destroyed wall, disappearing from sight.

Evalyn tried to mutter a *no*, but used what felt like most of her strength to lean on Walfien's chest as he lifted her. As Walfien followed the other Faeries out of the chamber and into the Great Tower, she focused on his calm breathing rather than her own shallow inhales. "Mags is a florvi witch—one of the most gifted magical healers in all of Faylinn," Walfien stated as they descended the spiral stairs. "She's going to meet us in the infirmary. She's going to help you."

At ground level, they exited the stairwell, leaving the rest of the guards to descend to the dungeons. Walfien moved fast, clutching her tightly, but still revealed no emotion or sign of his thoughts. It frightened Evalyn more than if he *had* spoken fear about her state.

Outside the infirmary, Walfien paused at the sound of footsteps behind them. "Mags."

The woman was frail and gray-haired, but gentle-eyed as she said, "I received your sparks, dear; came as urgently as these legs could carry me." They turned into the infirmary together, where Evalyn glimpsed cots lining the chamber, curtains pulled around every other one.

A scrawny Faerie in a green and white uniform hurried over to them. "My, my! What is this?" she squeaked. Walfien gently laid Evalyn on a cot, whispering to Mags and the healer.

The Princess couldn't hold on any longer.

Snow filled her ears, mouth, lungs—she was stuck in a whirlwind of pounding ice and pearly-white downpour, skin searing from the cold. The girl dragged herself along, chest aching against the hard ground. Her vision was fading too fast to find shelter. Still, she kept moving—but when she pulled herself into shadow, blanketed from the suffocating snowfall, a growl at her front was the only warning before unknown teeth snapped inches from her face—

Evalyn woke to candlelight at her side. She sucked in toasty air that warmed her insides. Her head pounded; she needed tea. Luckily, Kinz always prepared extra servings; she was going to need more than one.

The girl shot up to shuffling feet and rustling curtains. Her neck stung and throbbed; she fingered a bandage around her throat.

She wasn't with Kinz. She wasn't in the human lands. Everything crashed back.

"Slow movements will most benefit your state," an elder woman declared at Evalyn's side, watching the Princess with a warm smile.

Evalyn grimaced but returned, "Lady Mags!"

The woman let out a bout of laughter, face wrinkling. Cerulean jewels dangled from her ears and laid around her neck. Layered, cream skirts bundled at her hips, with a bulky white tunic tucked into the waistline. "I'm not a Lady by any standards, dear Princess." Mags settled at her side; soft hands inspected Evalyn's neck.

"How long have I been here for?"

"Three days," Mags hummed, observing the wound. Evalyn could feel the scarred tissue like a faint touch.

"Walfien told me you're a florvi witch," Evalyn said.

Mags nodded. "I am."

"I thought Liatue was a Faerie continent. Mostly Faerie, anyway."

"Oh, it is," she chuckled, meeting Evalyn's stare. "There are a number of wolf packs across Liatue, and various creatures intermingled with us all, but this continent is certainly one in Fae hands. All witches are born on the Western Continent; I migrated here when I was young."

"So if you're a florvi... does that mean there are other kinds? Other witches?"

"Certainly. There is another central order, beside florvis; they sit at the opposing end of the spectrum. We rein in energy from plant life and living entities, whereas the magic of malythis witches is sourced from the dead and the evil in other beings."

Evalyn tilted her chin. "If you take energy from around you, does that mean you don't possess... pure magic?"

Mags laughed. "You're thinking about Fae magic. Faeries can use the elements; manipulate and control them, sometimes create them. Magic runs through their blood. Faeries need no source nor direction, and their power persists eternally." She picked up a bowl from the side table and patted a fragrant teal paste on the sensitive scar along Evalyn's neck. "Witches, on the other hand," the woman continued, "require an external source to fuel our magic; a dire condition. If a witch—florvi or malythis—runs out of the energy powering our magic... it means the dissipation of our souls. Based on their kind, witches tend to follow lifestyles depicted by their order to maintain sources for their magic." She tenderly secured a bandage along the injury, and smiled. "Florvis thrive as healers and herbalists."

Evalyn's fingers grazed the bandaged wound as memories of its origin flashed in her mind. "Thank you for healing me."

Mags pressed a palm to the girl's cheek. "There will always be someone who cares for you here, dear."

Evalyn smiled. "What happened to the soldiers?"

"Locked away like they should be. There's a council meeting tomorrow for an update about their questioning, but from what I've heard, there's no news about their motives or entrance into the castle—as if they appeared out of thin air."

Evalyn gulped. Hopefully, tomorrow, there was better news. "Am I cleared?"

"I'd think so. But I'll have you know that I'm always available for gossip over tea." Mags winked, waving a hand in parting.

Evalyn strode past countless sentries, stationed along every main doorway and patrolling outlying corridors. They inclined their heads to the Princess, content and unwavering at their posts. At least thrice as many guards as there had been three days ago were on duty, leaving no castle exits or entrances unminded—surely due to the crooks that had tried to abduct Evalyn from her own bedroom. Which was exactly the place she didn't want to return to, so she ambled aimlessly around The Palace, recounting the exits and hallways and rooms to grasp a firmer layout.

The girl paused at a window viewing the Timoke Mountain range and Aternalis Creek. Colors and scents flowed through her senses, luring the Princess to their touch. Her eyes burned at the thought that three days ago... she could've died so easily. Would never have seen the land or spoken to her mother again.

The girl took a steadying breath. She'd been gifted the fate of being the Lost Princess, and she'd use her power as Royal Heir to make a difference in Liatue before she *was*... dead. Content with this reassurance, Evalyn mindlessly rounded a corner—and slammed into solid, muscled mass. She stumbled as the stranger leaped aside, greeting the ground with her. Evalyn breathlessly assured a guard back to his spot as she rose; her neck ached again.

"I—I'm sorry," she apologized.

He jumped up with ease, replying in a husky voice, "As you should be." Evalyn's brows scrunched, but he added, wide-eyed, "Sarcasm isn't my forte. The fall was my fault." He jerked his thumbs at himself. "Swift walker." The male was extremely handsome; golden eyes suited his tan skin with dark, sandy-blonde hair. But his ears weren't pointed. Not a Faerie.

Evalyn straightened the gown that had been brought to the infirmary for her, and he proceeded to look her up and down. "Have you seen a girl before?"

"Have I?" He tapped his temple. "Quite a few, but none as forthcoming. Or as stunning." A smirk lit up his face; a natural reaction. "I don't think we've met. I'm Kalan Lupien."

"Evalyn Impur."

He bowed. "I'm pleased to make your acquaintance, Princess."

"Likewise."

"Unsurprising. All women who—literally—run into me say the same."

She couldn't deny, his humor was charming. She smiled. "Well, what has such an endearing suitor wandering castle halls on this fine day?"

His eyes twinkled. "I'm likely about to be late for an appointment with Milid Praesi. Hence my fast pace causing our stumble. Have you met the Commander of the Guard?" At her shaking head, he added, "Strict woman.

Dark humor. I was intimidated by her at my first council meeting, but you get used to it."

He was an important figure if he was in the Queen's small council. Evalyn stepped aside, albeit regrettably. "I suspect you should attend to the Commander, then."

A nod as he backed down the hallway. "We'll cross paths soon again, Princess. Don't fret!"

She chuckled. "With such promise, I could never!" When he rounded the corner, Evalyn slapped a hand to her forehead. *With such promise, I could never?* Her friendliness had come out of nowhere, and now she was allured by this Kalan Lupien, as if she'd forgotten what principles powered her the past three years: beware strangers, trust few, share nothing with anyone. Kinz was an exception, and her maids and Walfien were different; they *were* her friends, and she confided in them all.

But Kalan seemed different too. He was wild, but not like her—a wolf? The smell of nature, of forests and creeks and wind, traced her nostrils. Scents of the Mediocris Woods. And authority obviously rested on his shoulders; he'd be *someone*, if the male wasn't already.

She wanted to know more.

The Princess pushed open her bedroom door, where a faint creak echoed in response to improper repair. The rubble from the attack was swept away, but she remained... unsettled. She knew she'd have to return, eventually, which was why she'd ventured straight for the quarters after her mind had slowed its racing about Kalan Lupien.

But there in that corner, she'd been a hostage with a dagger to her throat.

Chills crawled down her spine. She'd become accustomed to that feeling with her adoptive parents—unchangeable weakness. Understanding what could've happened, had the soldiers' mission been successful... the helplessness was horrid and familiar.

Her head jerked at the creak of the door, snapping Evalyn out of the lonely spiral she'd nearly succumbed to; a difficult feat to overcome. She had yielded to sorrow countless times at Kinz' cabin when her nightmares felt too real or played out too long. But Beverly, Vixie, and Ida stepped through the threshold, and it was easy to return their smiles.

"I *told* Bev you'd be here!" Vixie proclaimed as they scurried towards Evalyn. "You must've been cleared from the infirmary just before we arrived—I knew you'd return here eventually!"

"It feels different," Evalyn returned. She stared at the space.

"Well," Beverly said, "you won't have to think about it any longer. Your things have been moved to the Princess' suite in the north wing."

They directed her to her new quarters; a larger, more spacious version of the room she'd been in, with a varied furniture arrangement and additional, elegant decorations that reminded Evalyn this space wasn't where she had been attacked. It was safe here.

She perched on the edge of the four poster bed while the handmaidens threw the balcony doors wide and opened the curtained windows.

"Who's Kalan Lupien?" Evalyn inquired.

Immediately, Vixie gasped. "Did you meet him?"

Beverly claimed between a laugh, "If you think Vixie adores Lord Pax, don't get her started about Kalan Lupien. She'll never stop gushing."

"Oh, I don't fancy him, Bev!" Vixie pouted her lip, hands on her hips. "He's just *gorgeous*. And has wonderful hair that I wish I could run my fingers through."

"He's the Alpha of the Moon Clan. Their pack has been our only wolf ally for centuries," Ida explained, settling onto a round cushion atop the rug at the end of the bed. Vixie and Beverly followed suit.

"I *knew* he was a wolf," Evalyn chimed, reclining on her side. "It suits him."

"Captivated, aren't you?" Beverly giggled. "The Ladies always are when he visits The Palace. Which he frequently has since becoming Alpha last Autumn. Almost half of his clan were viciously assaulted and killed by Braena, including then-Alpha Paiton, Kalan's father, so the power and authority fell to Kalan. The Moon Clan lives in the Mediocris Woods, so only their patrols often travel here, but he has to attend small council meetings and undertake alliance obligations, so he's gained admirers."

"It seems he's gained another," Vixie said smugly, widening hazel eyes in the Princess' direction.

Evalyn cleared her throat. "No, I just..." Even Ida tilted her chin in response to the excuse Evalyn was attempting to formulate. "Yes, he's charming and delightful to be around, but I know nothing personal about him. We only talked for a moment! I'm not captivated—*Beverly, I'm serious!*"

The woman doubled over, cackling furiously. Ida chortled, "Your attempt to deny your attraction is only proving that you like him. There's nothing wrong with that."

"Ida did the same when we discovered her relationship," Beverly choked out between chuckles. Ida instantly blushed, eyes averting from the other women.

"What? Ida! Why haven't you told me this?" Evalyn exclaimed excitedly.

Vixie raised her brows. "Because she hasn't told anyone. We're only aware because we accidently found out—"

"Oh, he wrote her the sweetest poem," Beverly interjected, to which Ida hid her face behind pink hands.

"—but she won't tell us who he is. And of course, their letters are signed in code to conceal their identities," Vixie finished. Everyone looked at Ida, who remained self-hidden, but was now accompanied by the brightest smile Evalyn had ever seen her have.

The Princess beamed. "No matter who he is, he's most fortunate, Ida. I hope he knows how special you are."

She peeked out from behind her long locks with a sigh. "He's special too. But we're keeping it private because we're taking things slow. That way, we can focus on each other and not what others think, and know our love is true."

Beverly placed a hand over her heart. "Oh, the preciousness of young devotion." She cracked a knuckle. "If he ever hurts you, I will pull the air from his lungs." Ida's eyes widened, but she chuckled as she nodded.

"You'll see Kalan tomorrow," Vixie moved on, "at your first council meeting. Talk to him; get to know him."

Evalyn was used to avoiding new relationships; she had always been wary of quick-founded feelings. It was better for everyone that way—there was no one to hurt or be hurt by. But... she was changing. The girl Kinz rescued was growing. Adapting to this new lifestyle and welcoming everything that came with it.

Vixie smiled. "Kalan may have a horde of Ladies questing for his love, but he's yet to give it to anyone. Maybe it'll be you."

Chapter Seven

All eyes shifted to the Princess as she entered the meeting hall. Everyone sat around an oval table except Queen Tania, who stood at the far end, arms crossed and eyes masks of stone until they found Evalyn—and softened almost imperceptibly.

Walfien rose from his seat, creating a succession as the remaining seven members stood. Evalyn found her place at the end opposite Tania, silent in wait for some signal about what to do next. She observed those around her; the small council was limited. Ida had informed her the night before that not many were asked to join, and no one left. Willingly, at least—it was an honor and privilege to be acknowledged in appointment.

Walfien Pax occupied the seat to the right of Tania; as not only Hand of the Queen but one of the most trusted and skilled trackers, and part-time sentinel in the Guard, Walfien was as close to a Royal station as one not born into it could be. Beside Walfien was Kalan, alert and composed and dressed in a uniform with Faylinn's emblem at the collar. At the Queen's left was the Commander of Faylinn's Guard, Milid Praesi, and at Milid's side sat Mags. The four Lords of the highest noble houses—making up the Conclave—sat across each other just before Evalyn: colorfully-clothed and smiling Miehl of House Blaze from art-filled Dusston, brawny but approachable Gerlen of House Relfou in the mountainous Lubbum, simply-outfitted, gentle-eyed Sorae of House Knapport in the city-port and farming plains of Flordem, and glowering Pavan of House Ziffoy, ruler over Mearley, the city of schooling and advancement.

At last, the Queen waved a hand and everyone sat; a gust of magical wind closed the hall doors. Minute chatter broke out among every neighbor; Evalyn observed her mother, who watched the Princess with equal intent and a slight smile.

"Council," Tania declared. All attention directed her way, but she continued looking at Evalyn. "Today we welcome Princess Evalyn to her first meeting. We pray the Gods provide knowledge and understanding, and encourage her fondness of this Kingdom and its people."

"As they will," reverberated across the chamber. Kalan placed a hand over his chest, fingers placed in a symbol as he momentarily closed his eyes; Mags drew in the air with her fingers and gave a swift mutter. Evalyn was honored by their prayers as much as Tania's to the Fae Gods.

"Thank you, Lords of the Conclave, for leaving the comfort of your cities to come to The Palace for more direct communication as requested. Obviously, there is a higher risk in sending our usual briefing letters." Tania said. "Let's begin with the most pressing matters. Do we have progress with the aggressors?"

Commander Praesi cleared her throat. "Unfortunately not, Majesty. How they arrived at Princess Evalyn's quarters remains unknown, although the Guard is following every lead provided."

Kalan said, "My patrol units found nothing in the Mediocris Woods. They likely traveled from the northeast and diverted all villages."

Evalyn tilted her chin. "So they *were* soldiers from Braena?"

Walfien returned, "Sent by King Oberon himself. His season-long repose lured Faylinn into a sense of false safety—a temporary one, but one which almost cost us everything." His jaw hardened. "And one that won't exist again."

The Princess hadn't thought about Walfien's rescue yet; for the second time, he'd saved her life. She didn't know how she'd ever repay him.

Mags said, "The most vital question remains: how did they reach Evalyn's room?"

Millo shook her head. "There is suspicion that they snuck into The Palace as nobles—or, rather, guests of a noble whose name we know and esteem."

Evalyn cast a glance at the Conclave. Lords Blaze and Relfou both appeared utterly appalled at the tactic and Lord Knapport's wide eyes danced around in confused comprehension; Lord Ziffoy's furrowed brows conveyed astonished annoyance. "There's no telling who, but gatekeepers are recounting the past week's logs. We'll know soon whether their effort had internal aid."

Mags lifted a frail hand. "Majesty, I sustain that this alliance—although incarceration better befits Faylinn's state—goes to the dirt. We are birds caught in Oberon Romen's trap, only surviving from the feeding of his hand."

"The marriage between Braena and Faylinn means nothing, then?" Evalyn inquired.

Tania sighed. "For a period, after our political unification, there were advantages. The alliance brought trade opportunities, surges in travel, and the northern culture refreshed the centuries-long customs and manifestations of southern Liatue. The newness of Braena was welcomed."

"But the King attempted to directly infiltrate The Palace, and you were sent away," Walfien said. "That's when the violence started. For nineteen years, Faylinn withstood Braena's threats, invasions, and assaults because we knew it would be worth it, once you returned and brought our home peace and power."

The Queen nodded. "Now that you are home... the next step is to formally annul my marriage to Oberon, and thus, our alliance." She tapped the table. "However, that matter will be additionally discussed in due time."

"As for the soldiers," Commander Praesi proclaimed, back on topic of the prior conversation, "the Guard has received all information that the men will willingly share. It's an unfavorable position, but we have to accept not gathering their means of travel directly from them. We must focus on tightening security for future threats."

The Queen interlocked her hands. "I retain that Evalyn's announcement was not a mistake; Faylinn needed the hope she symbolizes. But, agreeably, proactive measures are necessary. Lords of the Conclave, do you favor increased patrols and supplementary forces in your cities?"

Lord Relfou leaned back, his round belly grazing the lip of the table. His beard, although adequately groomed, shielded his mouth as he spoke. "I don't need noble men; I'll draft from my company. Though don't blame us if currency production dwindles, my emerald miners are the best I've got for defensive monitoring."

The other Lords responded as positively, except Lord Ziffoy. The Faerie cleared his throat obnoxiously, taking a painstakingly long minute to ready himself before he began, "Pardon my saying, Majesty—"

"If you're opening with a plea for forgiveness, Lord Ziffoy, I suggest keeping your comment to yourself," Walfien bit out.

The Lord merely sighed, ignoring the Hand's warning. Tania didn't reprimand his visible disrespect, however, Evalyn knew from her maids that the Fae—tall yet muscular with silvering russet hair, alluring to the elder Ladies of Court—wouldn't care if the Queen rebuked him. "Majesty, you understand that us Lords of the Conclave deal with our own trade and production, citizenry conflict, and slighter yet no less trivial matters within our cities?"

The other Lords rolled their eyes and crossed their arms. Lord Blaze, who's region sat opposite Mearley on the other side of the United Lake, sighed at his neighbor's embellishment.

Queen Tania smiled. "I do, Pavan."

"Then, surely, you understand the difficulty of maintaining excellent guarding? Simply put, I'd like the reassurance that negligible faults on Mearley's part won't be excessively scrutinized." He lifted his brows. "I also supervise the management of the border into the human lands—exhausting work, truly."

"I am aware of all proceedings in the Conclave cities," she replied flatly.

Mags' face was scrunched; she cleared her throat. "Pardon *my* saying, Majesty—" the woman turned to Lord Ziffoy—"but for the life of me—and I have had a long and filled one, I'll have you know—I cannot seem to comprehend what impression you have of this council that you believe it is acceptable to be so shamefully impolite."

Milid uttered, "I've seen men exhausted, Lord Ziffoy—with dirt and blood streaked on their scarred chests, unable to slow themselves enough to breathe." She chuckled deeply. "Gods, I'd like to see you with a sword in your grip and your feet in the mud."

Evalyn met Kalan's eyes; a smirk lined his lips. "I bet that fancy velvet-lined tunic is too valuable to take the heat," he said.

Pavan's face was turning scarlet.

"That's enough," Queen Tania commanded. But Evalyn wondered if it was, since she'd let the others go so long uninterrupted. "Internal hostility will not foster the genuine peace and comfort that needs to extend to the people of Faylinn. Nonetheless, if you *must* share appraisal, please take it outside of this room where the sentries can deal with it." She massaged her temples and turned to the windows at the side of the room. When it was clear that no more would be said, everyone graciously departed from their seats.

Evalyn monitored her mother, hopeful that they could finally resolve what had been said during their first conversation—but Kalan Lupien arrived at her side and her thoughts dispersed. He greeted her as they neared the entrance of the room; the Princess spared a last glance around the chamber, finding Lords Relfou and Knapport the only other lingering members, standing by the table in deep discussion.

She faced Kalan as they paused at the doors. Evalyn couldn't put blind trust into him—if he was going to turn around and leave her, she would be aware. But Vixie's words echoed in her mind, and she knew there was no harm in trying to be open. To see if he was as good as her instincts screamed he was. Gods aid her, this was her chance.

"I told you we'd cross paths again," he said.

Evalyn smiled. "You'll be happy to know that I didn't fret."

"No?"

"I do well on my own," she explained.

Kalan chuckled. "And that's where you were before your return, I take it? On your own?"

"For a while. I found a friend, eventually." She brushed at her gown, unbothered by his continued, curious stare, but went on, "I suppose you have a plethora of friends?"

He puffed out his chest. "I think that answer is obvious."

She rolled her eyes. "Anyone in the small council?"

"Walfien and I are as close as differing species often get. We met in the forest as toddlers—of course, a sparring session was inevitable. When I won, he helped me up. I knew my heartiness needed his calm resolve." Kalan shook his chin, grinning. "From that point, we were blood brothers. Without the ceremonial blood oath. Which makes us normal brothers. But figuratively."

Mid-laugh, a thundering collision sounded from the corridor, shaking the meeting hall doors, followed by deep, echoing shouts. Evalyn, Kalan, and the remaining Lords were out of the hall in a moment—where Lord Ziffoy snarled a retort at a glaring Walfien, panting in the center of the hallway.

"—and I will make them reconsider your role in this Kingdom," Pavan finished.

"Lucky for me, only our Queen has that power." Walfien pointed at the Lord. "Spread more of that slander and you'll be the one questioning his livelihood. *I* have the power to make *that* happen."

Evalyn didn't understand why they were arguing—like her mother, Walfien had seemed uninterested in the verbal onslaught on Pavan. Yet here they were, in a worse state than what had occurred inside the meeting hall. Apparently, one of them had taken the Queen's advice to heart.

Lords Relfou and Knapport stood with crossed arms, watching the scene unfold from afar.

Pavan stalked closer to the Hand, a smirk twisting his lips. "I'd think you were adverse to threats, Lord Pax. From what I know, a quite unfortunate one is why you're still mateless. Or did the King take his promise back?"

Kalan barrelled between the Faeries—Walfien had made to swing and Lord Ziffoy had been prepared, with hands raised in defense. "Stop!" Kalan boomed, pushing them apart with an arm at each chest.

Walfien huffed against Kalan's grip. "If you dare bring it up—"

"You'll what?" Pavan retorted across Kalan. He guffawed. "Resort to personal, physical blows? I knew you were ill-bred; I can't say I'm surprised you're a brute, too."

Without thinking, Evalyn gripped Walfien's arm and tugged him away as Kalan kept Lord Ziffoy at bay. Luckily, Walfien's office sat beside the meeting hall; before the Hand could respond, Evalyn shoved them into the office, and bolted the door behind her.

Walfien wordlessly crossed the room and paced behind his desk.

She raised her eyebrows. "Do I need to ask who started it?"

He glanced at her, his breathing slowing. "His leash has been loose for too long. He went after you because your mother shut him down during the meeting. I won't ignore his treachery anymore." He paused; leaned over the desk. "I apologize if I upset you."

"Lord Ziffoy had no right saying what he did," she replied. "I'm glad you took the initiative to put him in his place." He likely wanted to avoid Ahstra at all costs, but she couldn't think of a way to let him know that she understood what it was like to be part of something which you never wanted to talk about again.

Walfien met her stare. "I'm used to his taunts." He cleared his throat. "I've just been on edge since the attack. How are you feeling, by the way?"

How could he be concerned for her wellbeing when Lord Ziffoy had, only moments ago, bullied his role and reputation? "Don't worry about me," she returned.

"It's obligatory for the Hand to worry about the Princess."

"Well, I'm alive, thanks to you. And the best healer in all of Faylinn patched me up nicely."

His lips twitched into a simper as he strolled to the desk's front and reclined on its edge. At a knock, Evalyn bolted to Walfien's side, gripping his arm at the movement—as if her body responded before her mind could. She released her hold; his eyes widened.

With permission to enter, a curly, lapis-haired guard did so, holding himself tall. "Lord Hand—and Princess Evalyn." A beam lit up his deep tan face, hued a cool blue, and he bowed low. "It's true. Many within the Guard have raved about you; they weren't mistaken. I can't procure the words to perfectly articulate your beauty." Pink bloomed in Evalyn's cheeks, but Walfien chuckled deeply. The boy rolled his eyes. "Oh, I'm sure you, Walfien, know how to eloquently define her. Is that how you occupy your time whilst the Princess masters the art of shunning your pestilent presence?"

Evalyn exploded into laughter. Walfien crossed his arms and said, "This is Micka Roshium. Nearly the youngest in the field, at twenty—"

"And seven months!"

"At twenty and seven months," Walfien added. "He's the recently assigned Second in Command of the Guard. With the ability to manipulate his features, he's our most favored undercover scout. His was the best recruitment I've ever been part of."

"Your words honor me," Micka voiced, flattening a hand to his chest. "But don't be so humble—even without magic, few are as skilled as you."

The Hand shook his head, smiling. "What brings you here, Micka?"

"Oh! Commander Praesi requested you in the dungeons." With that, the young sentry turned to leave, but at the door frame proclaimed, "It was an utter *delight* meeting you, Princess Evalyn."

She hadn't stopped smiling. "Thank you, Micka." He retreated down the hallway.

Walfien sighed. "I better see the Commander. It's likely a tracking assignment. After a lecture about quarreling etiquette."

The girl nodded, gown fluttering as she plucked an herbal pamphlet from a shelf. Walfien neared the door, hand brushing the frame, but she exclaimed, "When I'm Queen, Lord Ziffoy won't be able to breathe a syllable against you. I won't allow it." After the Lord's insults in the corridor... something told Evalyn to ensure the Hand knew he was cherished and appreciated.

Walfien didn't respond beyond the dip of his chin, but the girl spotted a grin as he left.

The Princess turned past a wall covered in wooden-framed paintings. She'd spent the afternoon in the gardens, settled on a nook of grass hidden between hibiscus shrubs that had granted her enough quiet to skim the herbal booklet. Once the shadows were more shiver-inducing than cool, she'd turned to wandering the castle.

Evalyn slowed her walk as she came to a dead end. She hadn't crossed it before. A dainty, pine green door stood at the end, corridor walls bare. Thick vines grew along the doorframe; deep red and violet leaves sprouted in every direction. Evalyn edged towards the strange entry, finding the handle: a round, glowing, brass knob. Mysterious marks were etched in the door panels, the Faylinn sigil in the center.

The hairs on her arms rose. A voice, light and deep, of man and woman, echoed in her mind. *Come, move closer. Enter.*

To where, though? What was on the other side?

Come, move closer.

Enter.

The voice had shifted from a soft lure to a hoarse beg—and she was suddenly entranced, drawn to discover the secrets hidden behind. She felt the door was for *her*, that she was meant to open it. The Princess reached for the handle—

"Evalyn?"

She faintly heard the voice, but her fingers were inches away—

"Evalyn." It was louder.

Life was sound as she was pulled from the trance. The girl's hand dropped to her side as she turned, blinking in sudden light from the bracketed candles at the end of the hallway. Kalan Lupien's hands were on her shoulders, shaking gently. "Are you there?"

She gazed on confusedly, until—

"Yes. Yes." She exhaled a breath and met his eyes.

He stepped away, simpering. "What're you doing?"

"I—I don't know."

He looked past her. "Entrance to The Door was forbidden centuries ago."

"Why was it forbidden?" she asked slowly, although she had a feeling she knew at least one reason.

"No one knows. Nobody uncovered what it holds, but it hasn't provoked exploration."

"Why *not* explore, if only to prove its safety or danger?"

He shrugged.

She gestured to the markings. "What are those?"

"I've never seen them. Probably an old language; maybe a code."

Evalyn scrunched her face. "We should figure out what it means." She turned to Kalan. "Wouldn't you like to know what it's for?"

"I'm not sure, Princess. It *is* forbidden—"

"Only entering it is forbidden, as you said."

He smirked. "Are you sure you're not just trying to spend time with me?"

"That's for me to know," she replied, lifting her chin. "So? Will you join my investigation?"

Kalan laughed. "Lucky for you, I was only required for the small council meeting today. And I might know where to start." He grabbed Evalyn's hand, guiding her down the hallway; his touch sent a tingle up her arm she couldn't shake.

"I wouldn't have thought the Alpha of the Moon Clan had time for spontaneous Faerie outings." He lifted his brows and she added, "Were you *going* to tell me that you're the leader of Faylinn's greatest ally?"

"My withholding of that information was an attempt at humility," Kalan smirked.

"I don't think humility is your style. Feel better, now that I know?"

"Certainly. Now I get to flaunt my power to someone outside of my pack."

Evalyn grinned. "It is a magnificent accomplishment."

His expression slowly faded. "It doesn't make much of an impact when you've grown up as the son of a legend who abandoned you before birth." Evalyn's eyes rounded, and he grinned suddenly. "*That* is the part of my past you didn't find out?"

Her face reddened. "We didn't get that far down the explanation road." She cleared her throat. "I heard your father was Paiton. He wasn't the legend that left you, I presume?"

He gave an exaggerated sigh. "No. Paiton was my father in every aspect that matters. Recks Delta, on the other hand, is my true father, and the only remaining descendant from the most powerful wolf in history. It was his great elder who defeated the infamous Inimocc, a wolf who hunted, captured, and killed his own kind for decades. The Spirits—the first fallen wolves, who rule in the afterlife and watch over the rest of wolfkind—rewarded my father's bloodline with further power for his great elder's triumph. It became the mission of the Delta name to protect the wolf clans of Liatue. Thus, since his birth, Recks was a heroic symbol, long-praised... until he went into hiding over twenty years ago."

"You really meant... a legend."

Kalan chuckled, slowing their pace as they ascended the Great Tower's spiral staircase. "That's enough about me, though; what about you, Lost Princess? What's your story? Besides disappearing without a trace from Fae land for your whole life."

"My story isn't a nice one."

He smiled down at her. "Try me."

Evalyn's mouth itched into a simper. "Okay." She sighed. "When I was fifteen, my human parents left me in the storm-ridden woods to die. I didn't like them... but I wouldn't have thought them so cruel. I was quiet and well-behaved." The Princess tugged at a thread in her gown. "They didn't put me in schooling with the other children; I was taught at the cottage. Still, they were distant and uncaring. I had no one to look up to. I just didn't want to be alone, so when we traveled to the forest... I was overjoyed. For the first time, I liked their company and thought it'd be the day they accepted me." She frowned. "It wasn't."

Kalan returned, "I'm sorry you had to endure that." He tilted his chin. "You know that you *are* wanted here, though, don't you? Wanted and worthy of it."

"I do."

They entered the Royal Library through a set of towering, wooden doors. Straight ahead stood the librarian, a tall and placid Faerie whose eyes were a mirror of her flowing, sage green gown. The dark hair in a knot at her nape was streaked with silver.

"How may I be of service to you today?" She questioned in a slow drone, a stack of books tucked skillfully under an arm.

"We're hoping you can translate something for us," Kalan replied. The librarian stared blankly onward. Kalan glanced at Evalyn. "Uh... do you understand the markings on The Door?"

"The Door?" she repeated, sounding wholly uninterested in the curiosity of two youthlings in the only forbidden destination in all of The Palace. Evalyn and Kalan nodded eagerly, earning a shallow hum in response. With a lazy wave of her hand, they followed as the Faerie guided them along. A staircase wrapped around the edge of the tower, marking a path through the rounded, shelf-lined walls. Candlelit tabletops illuminated the floor, which they strode through to the other side of the library's bottom-most level. The librarian tugged a large book from a shelf, its wrinkled gray cover marred by dust.

"The Door has remained stagnant since its creation and therefore is of low priority to the monarchy," she said. "The markings upon it are written in Vynus, the original tongue of Faeries. But it is a dead and forgotten language, studied by few and fluently known by less. I cannot help you directly." She opened the book. "Should you find yourself further engrossed by the dormancy of The Door's unknown internal holdings—" she flipped through the thick pages, blotted with ancient ink and warped by time, until she paused and flattened her fingers along a particularly scribble-filled page— "then studying from this section should grant you a basis of knowledge about Vynus from which you can research thereafter."

She dropped the book into Evalyn's open arms, whose muscles strained against the strange weight of the title as she smiled. "Thank you!"

The librarian met Evalyn's eyes, bowed, and glided away. Exiting as swiftly as they could, the pair ambled past sets of guards as they departed the Great Tower.

"Can I escort you to your quarters?" Kalan requested lightly.

Flipping the book into one arm, she looped her free arm through his. "Thank you for your help, Kalan. I apologize if this was a waste of your leisure time."

"I'm sure I enjoyed this far more than you," he grinned. "Although, my presence *has* been said to be exceedingly entertaining."

She returned, "Truthfully, every moment with you is one on my toes, wondering what'll happen next."

"Like if the librarian will correct me for breathing the wrong way."

"I thought I was the only one! Were you nearly put to sleep by her answers, too? I hadn't expected a full-fledged lecture."

They erupted into laughter; Kalan replied, "I've met her only twice before, with Walfien, and let me tell you, she was worse. I'd rather she cared for noise level than wisdom; she once called me an imprudent beast for not knowing the founding of Dusston. Verbatim. From her scrolls. I'm a wolf, for the Spirit's sake!"

"Let's hope this book saves us another visit for a while," the Princess said.

They turned down the corridor to her quarters, and she breathed a chuckle at their shared distaste. The guards at the corner dipped their chins; Evalyn smiled brightly in return.

"Unfortunately, this must be the end of our evening together," Kalan said. "The full moon tonight marks Velit Tempus."

"Velit Tempus?"

"It's a traditional wolf ceremony held every lunar cycle, where we follow routine rituals and sacred worship practices to honor the Spirits. Basically, a monthly wolf celebration. And I'm obligated to commence the festivities. You should come to the forest and experience it one day."

"It would be an honor." Evalyn grinned.

Kalan sank into a bow. "My eventful company is yours, Princess, whenever you find yourself lacking entertainment."

Her cheeks reddened. "I'm sure I'll be spending a lot of time with my nose in this book. If that doesn't bore me—even with my curiosity about The Door—then I'm not sure what will. So... keep an ear open for my call."

"If it means time with you, I'll have to attend your reading sessions." Kalan backed down the hallway. "Until then?"

She nodded, unable to dim her beam.

He slowly turned and retreated past the stationed guards. Evalyn stepped into her bedroom, tossing aside the book and closing her eyes as she leaned against the chamber door. Her maids were gone—likely on other tasks before her nightly preparation. She was glad they couldn't see her flustered; their questions would go on forever and she barely knew how to breathe, let alone speak.

She jumped forward at a knock on the door, heart pounding. They *were* early, Gods help her. The girl forced herself to breathe and smoothed her gown before opening the door.

A servant nearly crushed the letter as he shoved it into her hands, words rapid and fearful. "I was instructed to deliver this to you immediately and to tell you to open it alone, where the contents can't be seen. I was also told to inform you that should anyone else uncover what's in the letter, I am to be punished accordingly." Then he darted down the corridor and out of sight.

Evalyn flipped it over. A lump formed in her throat.

"Is there a problem, Princess Evalyn?" called a sentry patrolling the end of the corridor.

She smiled, clutching the letter against her chest. "Not at all. Goodnight!" With a replying nod of his head, the Princess sealed herself in her quarters, the breath in her lungs gone not from the charm of the Alpha, but because of the emblem identified in the letter's black wax seal.

An infinity symbol formed of twisted rope.

Braena's sigil.

Abrupt tapping at the door sent a jolt down her spine. Again, Evalyn cracked open the door—only to grab Walfien Pax's hand and wrench him into the chamber. Before he could utter a greeting, she slipped the parchment open and read aloud:

> *I searched for you, Lost Princess, across land and sea, yet you managed to find home without finding me. Still I know you to a certain extreme; you hid with the humans as part of your mother's scheme, and curious you have become of this land much more green. So ask all of your questions. Uncover the strange door's theme. If I shan't obtain you, then its answer you must deem. But linger on 'til you're of-age... and I will surely see you soon, darling.*

Evalyn slumped onto her bed, eyes dancing between Walfien and the parchment. "It's a letter from the King."

"When did you get it?"

"A servant delivered it just before you arrived."

His mismatched eyes widened. "A *castle servant* handed that to you?"

"Are you going to tell me this is fake and part of a nasty stunt to scare me?"

"On the contrary... it's completely real. And only Tania is allowed to have direct contact with Oberon. So how he knew where you were, and had it delivered at a time when you were alone..."

She shook her head, unbelieving. "The servant said I couldn't tell anyone what this letter contains, otherwise he'd be punished. You can't tell, Walfien."

Walfien closed his eyes with a long exhale. "I won't. But I'm going to do some digging; figure out who the messenger was and how this managed to evade interception by mail inspectors."

Meanwhile, she would concern herself over researching The Door. Blatant curiosity was no longer the only thing spurring her on.

Uncover the strange door's theme. If I shan't obtain you, then its answer you must deem.

She wrapped arms around herself. Evalyn had been hurt by the King and his men, and it wouldn't be long before Oberon Romen tried to do it again. Especially when he wanted more than her company. He'd surely attack again to get the knowledge he desired.

And despite all of Walfien's preparation and protection, Evalyn would be helpless.

But she didn't have to remain so. She could learn to protect herself. Protect others.

The girl swallowed the lump in her throat. "Can you teach me how to fight?"

Walfien lifted his head; their stares interlocked. His expression shifted in thought for minutes, but at last, his lips upturned. "I'll train you. But we have to keep it quiet. Tania would oppose you handling weapons and fighting like the sentries around The Palace, and the Conclave would have similar disapproval. Not to mention that to most of the castle, training is a tradition among recruited guards, not Princesses."

She nodded. "I don't want anyone getting hurt if the King's threats are serious."

"I admire your selflessness, Evalyn, but *your* safety is my top priority. That's why I arrived in the first place; to check on you after I returned from tracking."

"How did that go?"

Walfien neared the doorway, rubbing the back of his neck. "He didn't fight back. Actually, he asked if I was there to detain him and willingly let me do so. I haven't had someone do that in a very long time." A smile. "Are you going to be okay tonight?"

"Yes," Evalyn returned. Even though she remained frightened by how the King had contacted her from his castle across the continent. Even though she was fully aware that Oberon could—and would—hurt her and her people if he didn't get what he wanted.

Only when Walfien slipped the letter out from between her fingertips did she realize she was shaking. In several swift movements, he lit the edge on a candle; his blue and brown-spotted green eyes sparkled across the flame.

Chapter Eight

Walfien scheduled their training for the hour before dawn, when only stationed guards and few servants were awake. It was the only time of day where her movements within The Palace weren't closely watched—except by Walfien, who monitored her daily schedule for security and lessons.

The practice quarters were on the ground level, just outside the sentinel's barracks. A large mat covered the majority of the floor, and a weapon-strewn wall and unit of dummies marked with colors at the heart, neck, and forehead edged the room. A small refreshment table sat in an empty corner by a single bench.

After stretching, a warm up, and beginner's practice, her limbs were pudding.

"The first thing to take notice of," the Hand said during her combat lesson, "is how your opponent moves." He faked a punch to her cheek. She flinched, stepping back as he continued. "To beat your enemy, you must become your enemy. Follow their actions—" Evalyn blocked her face as Walfien did—"and know what they're going to do before they think of it themself." He swung again, but she ducked into a crouch, earning a brief smirk in return.

She'd never pushed through so much physical exertion at once. But even when her breaths were lung-cutting gasps, she demanded to learn how to use a weapon, and after too quick of a moment to rest, Evalyn found her pick.

"Those are almost entirely useless," Walfien stated as she lifted a steel dagger. "They also mean a dangerously close fighting range, so most prefer to stick with swords and magic. They're seldom used, especially in battle," he emphasized.

"It's a good thing I won't be running onto a battleground anytime soon. This will do fine," she retorted, observing the intricate woodwork on the handle of the dagger instead of meeting his gaze.

"If you insist. But next time, we're practicing with shortswords."

Evalyn groaned her agreement. "Did anything come from the castle gate logs the night I was attacked?"

Walfien's lips thinned. "No unusual entries were noticed. I was going to tell you later, but seeing as we're on the topic…"

"Tell me everything you know!"

"Rear-wall watchers from the night of the attack are being questioned—apparently, several were incapacitated around the time of the soldiers' assault, but the sentries didn't report until the attack was brought to light. We assume their states provided the free window the Braenish soldiers needed to get in."

Evalyn's mouth plopped open. "How did Milid respond?"

"She was furious, but didn't dismiss them. It seems their incapacitation may have resulted from minimal doses of a poison slipped in their dinner."

"Doesn't this point to a traitor among us?"

"Perhaps—but we have no suspects. No high-placed and honored members of Court have shown a smidge of affection towards Oberon or his goals. I hate to say it… but I think the King's men were simply powerful and smart enough to get through. Let's pray evidence arises about their invasion plan. For now, we have to hope our increased security is enough to protect the castle and watch for suspicious activity."

Evalyn stared blankly, trapped in thoughts about how someone inside the castle may have helped the Braenish Fae find her—and nearly kill her.

Walfien cleared his throat, pulling her back to their training. It was why she wielded the dagger, no matter how *useless* it was. Evalyn focused on his basic instruction: how to hold it; how to stab; the vulnerable areas on the body to aim for… and where to conceal smaller weapons under clothing. She'd like to keep one close.

At her dominant side, Walfien positioned her stance, adjusting the girl's grip and describing the maneuvers for long-distance throwing. "Remember not to flick your wrist. Let it slide out of your grip here," he explained, extending her arm for her, his fingers gentle on her skin.

Evalyn turned her chin—meeting his face a hairsbreadth from her own, looking down and patiently waiting for her attempt. "Can you show me?"

Without moving his gaze from her, Walfien took the dagger, threw it at the target, and didn't so much as blink when it marked the forehead of the practice dummy.

She laughed through her nose. "How'd you get so confident?"

He crossed his arms. "I joined the Guard when I was young. Your mother greatly encouraged my training, and in turn, I pushed myself to be the strongest. The smartest. Even through the names and gibes from those born into the Guard, when they cornered me in the corridors and beat me into unconsciousness out of envy, even after the door to my chambers was sealed during dinner and I was forced to sleep in the stables for a week... I kept going. I'd give anything to protect Tania—and anything for her Kingdom. For as long as I can remember, my life has been dedicated to defending and representing. Being top of the soldier's rank for most of it built a little self-esteem."

Evalyn swallowed. She never would've thought Walfien was despised by anyone—except, of course, Pavan Ziffoy—but especially Guard members. She'd only ever seen love and respect and adoration for him by others. Yet his past sounded so cruel. And he stayed through the torment?

"I had many reasons to keep fighting," he said. "I know you're wondering why I didn't leave."

Evalyn turned, facing Walfien fully. "Perseverant, humble, skilled... what more about you don't I know?"

A small chuckle, but he looked at the floor. "Very few people know even that much. I keep my personal life to myself."

"Why do you share it with me?"

"I trust you," Walfien stated.

Evalyn smiled to herself. But Walfien leaned away, and she realized his proximity had captivated her attention from the task at hand. The Princess concentrated again on the red circle of the upper body: the heart.

She released a breath as she swung the blade. It sliced through the air before the thud of steel meeting fabric met Evalyn's ears.

The dagger pierced the target's heart. The red mark was wholly covered by the weapon, cutting into the dummy up to the handle, obscuring the colored material.

Walfien's lips curved. "Beginner's luck," he insisted, nearing the target and pulling the dagger out. "Aim for the neck."

Evalyn nodded. A breath, then a swift maneuver of her arm and wrist. The blade narrowly missed the blue-marked throat. She tried again and again, changing distance and angled positions at every target.

The weapon scarcely missed.

"You're a fast learner," Walfien proclaimed, tidying the room to hide their trace as Evalyn gulped water at the refreshment table.

"You're a decent instructor," she hummed sarcastically.

"A fine compliment if I've ever heard one." The Hand smiled faintly and turned to the sole window that viewed the gardens.

Morning sun licked the tips of the trees; Evalyn needed to return to her quarters before the castle awoke. She slipped a dagger in her boot before retreating from the practice area, careful of the eyes of the guards. Walfien assured her they'd keep silent, but she kept her chin low and wariness high. Evalyn didn't want twisted words finding her mother before she could explain herself. Eventually.

As soon as she closed her bedroom door, she shoved the dagger under her bed, concealed but capable of being grabbed if the need arose. She prayed it didn't.

Evalyn twisted around under her bedsheets, longing to find a comfortable position, but it was a hopeless wish. Her nameday was in less than twenty four hours, and after her substantial gain of energy several days prior, an adjustment before all Bonum Vitaes, her mind had become a restless storm of thoughts and emotions.

She was convinced she'd received bad Signs.

Evalyn stretched across the bed, yet she could neither abate her fidgeting nor stop pondering various ideas and issues that could arise with her nameday in the morning. Even after hours of watching moonlight drift across her quarters, sleep hadn't arrived.

All Evalyn wanted to do was weep into calm nothingness.

Every Faerie she spoke to reiterated that what she felt was an effect of Bonum Vitae: the wakeful nights, restive behavior, and sour attitude were results of her body bracing for the change.

Evalyn despised every second of it.

And she wasn't a fan of finalizing the preparations for her celebratory ball, which had occurred across a fortnight for the evening party to take place in mere days. Queen-sent maids had assisted Evalyn through decorating and food choosings and guest seating arrangements, and the girl's lessons with Walfien had temporarily turned into practices with a dance instructor, where she learned the key waltz of any Royal Celebration—the Libcerus.

She was ecstatic for the event, but there were too few ways of releasing her emotions until it arrived. The only thing besides tending to the gardens or training was studying Vynus; Evalyn had often taken to the Royal Library tower in hopes of deciphering the markings on The Door. Delightfully surprising, Kalan had joined her research one dark, stormy evening, although their time together had been more laborious than uplifting and she hadn't seen him since that exhausting night. And despite the hours of laboring over scrolls and titles, the Princess was no closer to understanding Vynus.

Evalyn groaned and threw her sheets across the bed. She pulled her knees to her chest, breathing long and slow—but on recently-adopted cue, Beverly appeared to quell her impatience and nerves by burning herbs whose soothing, scented smoke drifted through the room along the handmaiden's breezes, before she fetched a sickly-sweet drink that Evalyn had come to know granted deep and dreamless sleep.

Upon morning's rouse, Evalyn tightened her eyes. A deep breath revealed she was still in her castle quarters. Sometimes she feared the past four years were a dream, and she'd awake to her room in the human lands. No Kinz or maids, no Walfien or mother or magic. But she inhaled again: vanilla and fresh linen.

The scent of what had become home.

Evalyn opened her eyes to a brightening chamber. It was sunrise, as she'd hoped.

And life was... utterly breathtaking.

The white of her bed was a burning pearl, the ceiling a landscape of intricate woodwork. She clambered from her bed and gingerly stepped to her vanity mirror.

The twenty-years-long glamour was no more.

The Princess' ears formed soft points at the tip. Her eyes were as piercing as Spring's sky. Glowing blonde hair framed her recently sunkissed face. Evalyn traced the scar at her throat, a faint and pale line.

The chirping lured her to the balcony doors. Her motions were quick, every action instinctual. She'd stepped onto the stone balcony in half a second, nostrils detecting the thick scent of leather and steel lingering in her hair after the previous day's training, and the fresh florals from the gardens below. Shimmering rays danced on the distant mountains. She leaned on the railing as the sun rose and rose and rose.

The lightness in her heart was surreal. She'd never lived until this moment; she felt renewed.

Reborn. Perhaps in a way, she was.

This was the start of the life she had dreamt for herself with her human parents when she'd possessed nothing and loved no one. This was the start of the life she'd begun living with Kinz, where she pursued her passions and had found the world a warmer place than she'd grown up in.

The Princess was astonished by the castle's beauty. The green walls had never been less bare, gold patterns sparkling in the light of the morning. She mindlessly glided into the training quarters; although absent from the past week's training sessions due to tracking jobs and Hand duties, Walfien had promised to help her adjust. Luckily, they didn't have to keep their wanderings a secret today. Everyone knew it was the Lost Princess' Bonum Vitae. She had utmost freedom.

But it seemed Walfien took no excuses to go easy on the Princess. As soon as she was warmed up, he insisted on dueling.

Evalyn attempted a hit, but Walfien struck before she could sense it. The punch stung her side, but the girl regained her stance, lunging in the offensive. He ducked from her swipes, unmoving from center-mat. "You have magnified strength from the transformation," Walfien explained. His smile grew with every swing she gave. "You could beat me if you focused on applying yourself correctly."

Evalyn growled and punched, missing. For the entire half hour they'd been going at it, the Hand reminded her that she could claim victory. But she hadn't won yet, and she was becoming awfully annoyed at his consistent remarks about her capability.

"You're mindlessly using all your strength just to get a single hit in," he added.

Evalyn simply dove headfirst for his abdomen.

They crashed onto the mat.

He huffed, "A temper will get the best of you, Evalyn. You must hone your skills and adopt a style of fighting that suits your—"

"Strengths. I get it." Evalyn groaned, rising from his chest and making for the weapon-clad wall. Plucking a shortsword, she pointed it at him. "Let's try this, then."

In a split-second, a matching shortsword swung in his hand. He said, "Feel your body and muscles. Demand control over your exertion, and don't waste your energy within minutes."

Evalyn was half-inclined to ignore him and showcase her power, but... the Princess did as he said; control and focus. She dodged as Walfien struck, swiftly rolling across the mat and rising to face him.

Watch your opponent.

Become your enemy.

Walfien flipped his sword, meeting her own with a strong block. They both pulled away before striking simultaneously, metal ringing. Back and forth they went, blocking and striking. Somehow, she caught him by surprise in a dodge; the force of his swing sent him tumbling head-first to the ground.

The Hand sucked in a breath before rising, but Evalyn anticipated his movement. She pounced, slamming into his chest quicker than he could sense. Both of their swords clanged on the ground. The Princess felt his loss of breath, heard his heart speed up in realization of what she'd accomplished. Evalyn rolled as soon as they hit the ground, coming to a kneel. On his side, Walfien gaped, looking partially surprised but even more proud.

He shifted, but Evalyn flew towards him, slipping the dagger from her boot and under his chin before he could blink.

"I win," the Princess murmured. He simply smiled. Then gripped her wrist, turning it towards her chest as he flipped her to the floor and poised the dagger half an inch above her heart.

"You hesitated," he breathed. "*I win.*"

Their eyes locked, both breathing heavily, but Evalyn simply tutted and shoved him away. As soon as they were standing, she exclaimed, "Can we finally practice magic?"

A momentary pause, but Walfien nodded his chin.

"What can you do?" she asked; she hadn't seen his abilities aside from basic communicational alerts. Without answering, he lifted his palms and knitted his brows. The air in the room thickened; the hair on Evalyn's arms rose in response to the atmosphere's heightened density. She spun to see objects across the room rising, suspended in midair. Their shortswords slowly rebounded through the air at her touch. When Walfien dropped his hands, Evalyn jumped as the items clattered to the floor around them.

"It's a form of air manipulation," Walfien explained. "I can move anything—control anything, essentially. I've been building up my store of power for some years, so I can take on large masses, but I don't often need to use it for anything bigger than other Fae. It's a reliable combat aid." He chortled, "Kalan would say it's a fantastic party trick; the amount of times I've served an entire unit patrol with ale, flasks and goblets finding your hand..." He smiled. "My other ability is the Sight. It's a peculiar thing, but convenient. I can glimpse the future."

"What do you see?"

He paused in thought. "Well, the visions are more... instinctual. A deep wave of emotion that conveys safety or danger. Sometimes it's a puzzle, other times it's easy to understand."

"What about my mother?"

"As a master of the land element, her power is greater than the rest of the Kingdom's combined. Plantlife, stone, dirt, minerals; they each fall under her command. It's something no Fae has been able to do as effectively as herself for centuries. She also has powerful wind manipulation. Then there's empathy—a rare ability, since many who possessed it, over time, were forced to push it down until it was stifled from their bloodline. It allows her to read one's emotions and use them to influence that person. Mind control, of sorts." He met her look. "Don't worry; I could count on a single hand how many times she's used it. Now, we could assume her magic was passed down, but only *you* are able to discover what you possess, Evalyn. Close your eyes. Focus your mind where there seems to be... excess energy. Eyes, fingers, palms, lips."

She followed Walfien's orders, outstretching her hands and closing her eyes, becoming more still than she'd ever been.

There was nothing. She waited another minute before opening her eyes. "I don't feel it."

Walfien watched her intently. "Try again. Feel that energy. Try to understand what element it's calling out to be formed into."

She did. "It's a blank slate," the girl puffed. He gave her a look, but silence filled the room. "Is there something wrong with me?"

"No. Not at all," he answered. He tilted his head, hair flipping across his forehead. "But there are stories. Several Fae who prove it, too, despite the rarity—"

"Prove what? What stories?"

The Hand sighed. "My powers were a second part of me—they were there from the beginning." Something he'd certainly remember vividly. He had undergone his Bonum Vitae just two years prior. "But there've been Fae who were born without powers—without magic. Chormas. Perhaps they didn't look deep enough or in the right places, but..."

Evalyn didn't need him to finish. "Are you saying... I may not have abilities? I could be powerless?"

"We don't know that. It could take time before you recognize the magic."

She sucked in a breath. "There's something wrong with me—"

"Evalyn—" Walfien reached out a hand, but the girl ran fingers through her hair. "Go to Tania," he suggested. "She might know something. More than I do, at least."

The Princess nodded, biting her lip as she tucked her dagger in her boot. "Don't worry," he said. "It'll come to you."

Evalyn was gone in a moment.

The Princess didn't know when she started running, but was at her mother's chambers in seconds. She needed answers.

A chorus of delicate voices told her that the Queen and her Ladies were inside. She was lucky to find Tania outside a conference with advisors, or not hearing cases about civil altercations and noble disputes in the throne room. Evalyn entered, relaxing further at her mother's hunched figure on the side of the room. Five females turned to the Princess, standing with curtsies.

"Your Highness," a honey-skinned, brunette-haired one declared. "May verve and experience greet you."

"As they will," the others around her added. It was the Faerie adage for namedays; a well wish for a fulfilling life ahead. Evalyn smiled in responsive thanks.

"What brings you here?" the first one questioned.

Evalyn gestured to the Queen. "I'd like to speak to Tania." With a unified nod, the Faeries swept from the chamber; Tania hadn't lifted her chin from the desk. The Princess walked over, peering past the Queen's shoulder and onto the contents littered across her desk: corked vials of blue liquid, bottles of dried herbs, and gray marked parchments were scattered around a glass containing a dark, bubbling substance. And the writing on the papers—was it Vynus?

"Perhaps I should request Walfien to provide a seminar on privacy," Tania stated. Evalyn widened her eyes and stepped back. The Queen faced her.

Evalyn responded, "Do you know what those markings are? Do you know what they mean?"

Tania's face revealed nothing. After a moment, she simpered. "This mess is a result of concocting a basic herbal remedy. Nothing for you to concern yourself with. You told Lady Serene you wanted to speak with me?"

The Princess bit her tongue. There were more troubling matters at hand than the secrets of a Queen. "Yes. I do."

"Distress is written all over your face—something you'll learn to control, in time." The Queen gestured to the stool at the deskside. Evalyn slowly reclined onto it.

"There are two things I want to tell you," the Princess said. Tania didn't respond. Evalyn continued, "I came here because I thought I may not possess magic, since I couldn't feel anything within me, and Walfien told me about chormas and I became nervous that maybe I was one, but I figured you may know why nothing was happening or perhaps it'd taken *you* a while for the magic to appear—" Evalyn took a swift breath—"but I arrived here and realized we hadn't spoken since you told me the truth about who I was and I snapped at you because I was shocked, and I've wanted to apologize everyday since but so much happened and you're continuously busy with your duties and I just—" Evalyn sucked in a breath, face scrunched. "I just wanted to say I'm sorry."

The Queen's lips twitched. Her gaze wandered around the room. "There are a great many things you learn as Queen. One of the harshest things I've had to understand is that not everyone moves at pace with you." Tania looked at the girl. "You taught me that best. I was quick with my anger when we spoke... but I'm hearing that we both made choices we regret, and that speaks for a fresh start in our relationship, wouldn't you agree?"

"I'd like that."

The Queen clasped Evalyn's hands. "As for your magic..." The Princess held her breath. "I've met three chormas. One of them is a churlish, old man, who's spent a lifetime complaining to the Gods about what he calls a curse. Something tells me he has never felt anything beyond rage and loneliness. The other two, however, are the liveliest Faeries I'll ever meet. They're mates with four children in Dusston. They're the talk of the city for their behavior; for the way they inspire the weakest of magic-users to live on. They've proven that if *they* can be satisfied in lives without magic, the rest have no excuse. Perhaps you can meet them, one day."

Evalyn lifted her chin. It was a charming story, but the prospect of magic—of being able to fulfill a greater purpose—was what had propelled Evalyn so far. She couldn't help others—couldn't lead a Kingdom—with the strength of a human.

It was that weakness which had nearly killed her four years ago.

"Don't mope." Tania leaned forward. "Power lies ahead of you. Whether or not it's magic... only the Gods know. Persevere with what you *do* have: wisdom and determination and sympathy. You haven't given up yet. Don't start." A smile. "Happy nameday, Evalyn."

"Thank you." Evalyn sucked in a deep breath. There was nothing she could do, it seemed. Following her mother's advice was the next best option.

The Queen turned to her desk. "If you'll allow me to finish my work..."

Evalyn gave one last glance at the tabletop before excusing herself from the chambers. The potions and objects on the Queen's desk were strange... but something else tugged at her thoughts.

The markings on the parchments weren't just written in Vynus.

They were the exact ones on The Door.

Chapter Nine

Evalyn stood in awe before her mirror.

The sleeves of a pale blue ballgown fell off her shoulders; the bodice, covered in floral lace, distinguished her curves. The skirt flowed out in layers of a thin, smooth material, with stitched flowers at the hems, fading up the material to her waist. Golden heels matched her jewelry. Evalyn's locks were fashioned into waves that framed her face, and miniscule cream flowers wove through the elegantly small plaits Ida expertly formed.

She paced around the room, attempting to prepare for the long night of dancing and smiling and socializing with countless strangers, but her stomach twisted into a knot as she turned to the maids. "I didn't think I'd be nervous." Although she'd faced the entirety of Koathe at her introduction, countless influential nobles were attending her ball tonight solely to meet the Princess. The way the Queen listed their names hadn't calmed her.

Beverly clutched the hands that Evalyn wrung together. "If it's any consolation, your mother was tense at her first Royal Ball. The stories are bedtime tales to us servants. She was half your age, far less composed, and threw a tantrum when a Lord denied her a dance."

Evalyn chuckled. "I can't imagine her—"

"Having a fit?"

"Being rejected!"

The maids giggled, but a knock on the door quieted the Fae. A guard escorted Evalyn to the doors of the Great Hall; the sentries lining the corridor watched as Evalyn observed the tall, wooden entry. She glanced at the Faerie stationed by the door frame. He gave a reassuring nod as the handles turned. The chamber sparkled blindingly; a pleasant smile took shape on her lips as she admired it. *Great Hall* was an understatement.

It was expansive and luxurious, converted from the throne room into a celebratory ballroom like it often was. Arched pillars lined the walls, paned windows on the left and rear of the room allowing evening light to shine through the alcoves. The curves were lined with gold, and a monumental glass chandelier hung in the center of the room, illuminating the magic-painted ceiling of glowing portraits and abstract, sparkling landscapes.

All eyes, grouped on the other side of the dancing floor, turned to Evalyn as she crossed the hall. The Queen was at her side within a moment.

"Never stop smiling. Greet everyone with kindness and pleasure, even if your cheeks turn numb." Tania smirked as she locked arms with her daughter and faced the welcoming crowd. "Let the celebrations commence!" Her voice rebounded across the room.

Cheers erupted and music floated to Evalyn's ears as the crowd broke apart.

The Queen cleared her throat once; twice. Evalyn shifted her gaze when Tania broke into a soft coughing fit, grip tightening on the Princess' arm.

"Are you alright?"

The woman sucked in a breath. "Fine."

The paleness of her cheeks said otherwise. As did the well-hidden bags under her eyes. Yet it was too late to pry as Faeries strode forth, greeting and complementing the pair.

Tania introduced her to more nobles than she could count. Truthfully, each was more boring than the last, some richer and snobbier than others—even having the audacity to converse about Evalyn's limited knowledge of being Royalty. But her smile never wavered, however much she wanted to scowl at them. It helped that the Faeries had to bow before making their leave. She pondered why she'd been nervous.

Evalyn was on the verge of passing out when she slid onto a velvet chair. They hadn't even danced the Libcerus. Sadly, her trio's common handmaid positions meant they couldn't attend a Royal ball, so when her mother wandered off to meet other guests, Evalyn was left alone with no friends in sight.

The Princess stared across the room at mingling Fae when a triad of people ambled over. She straightened and smiled, ready to greet them, but her heart fluttered at the familiar face. Kalan Lupien.

He beamed, guiding an older woman and young girl forward. "Evalyn, I'd like you to meet Diana, my mother—" the older woman curtsied, a polite smile on her tan face— "and my sister, Felicity." The girl followed her mother's lead.

"It's a pleasure," Evalyn grinned. His mother and sister were as beautiful as Kalan, with matching deep-honey hair and golden eyes.

"Kalan told me lots about you, Princess Evalyn," Felicity exploded with a grin. Kalan pinched the girl's arm, but she added, "Kye told me you'd do that. He owes Bre and I three emeralds."

Evalyn laughed, "Kalan never mentioned how delightful his family was."

Felicity smirked. "I think it's safe to say *I* acquired the looks of the bloodline." Diana chuckled as the girl continued, "And I'd love to chat, but this is a fun song, and we *must* dance." She proceeded to pull Diana onto the floor as a cheerful, upbeat tune began. Evalyn watched them dance, feet gliding in tune with the music. They twirled and spun, happy as Fae children.

"They're wonderful," Evalyn thought aloud.

Kalan faced her. "Thank you." He gave a slight bow. "And you look stunning, Princess."

Evalyn blushed. "I'll have to disagree that Felicity took *all* of the beauty from your bloodline. It's a shame such compliments go straight to your head."

He smiled broadly. "Alas, I keep your compliments tucked close at heart. How are you liking the party?" They both shifted to watch the citizens dance.

"Everything's perfect." Their chatter was simple, but Kalan was addictingly pleasant and Evalyn was unhappy to see him excuse himself when the Queen met her side with a group of alluring Faeries.

"I thought it time you formally meet my Keepers. They're members of my Court who attend to personal tasks and my daily needs. You'll have ones of your choosing when you're Queen. This is Lady Serene Lyhn." Her mother gestured to the nearest one; she was the one Evalyn had spoken to in Tania's chamber on her Bonum Vitae. Serene gave a polite smile, her face chiseled and warm, before curtsying, revealing two high slits in her deep magenta gown. Paired with the Faerie's slim yet full body, the Princess had a feeling they weren't only there for fashion.

"Lady Nickie Dyse." The next Fae stepped forward on the other side of Tania. She was paler, with stunning gray-green eyes. Her dark hair, in a thick braid pulled over a shoulder, fell to her hips atop a shining, silver gown. Nickie beamed widely and curtsied.

"It's a pleasure to meet you, Princess Evalyn."

Evalyn beamed in response as her mother gestured to the third Faerie. "Lady Hali Maytora." Hali was the least revealing in more ways than one. Although her curtsy was deep, the woman's smile was subtle. She had small, brown eyes and blonde locks slicked into a knot atop her head, and her pale pink dress had a high neckline and long skirt that showed little of her tan legs.

"And Ladies Jeni and Juna Mim." The last two were twins, identical in seemingly all ways except the shade of their blue gowns. Even their wide, pearly smiles were mirror images.

"I'm delighted to meet all of you," Evalyn said. "I hope you've enjoyed the festivities so far?"

They nodded. Displeasure radiated from Tania's voice when she looked over Serene's shoulder. "It seems Lord Ziffoy has finally made an appearance." Muttering amongst themselves, the Keepers found elsewhere to be as the Lord reached the Queen's side, a boy in tow.

The Lord wore a suit of charcoal gray with gold-hems. His silver-streaked, russet hair was smoothed back. He grinned and ushered forth the boy, exclaiming, "My Queen, my Princess!" although he didn't seem inclined to bow nor give any ode of respect other than the swift acknowledgement. "This is my son, Jaino!"

Jaino, in contrast to his father, bowed low, reaching to kiss both Evalyn and her mother's hands. He looked nothing like Pavan, with cropped black hair and gentle features—from his mother, no doubt. Lord Ziffoy didn't hide the twitch of his lips. "Jaino has recently turned fifteen. I found it right he made your acquaintance as early as possible, since he'll be on your list of suitors. The longer you know each other, the better chance he has of becoming our next King. Isn't that right, son?"

Jaino winced, but nodded hesitantly with a sharp look from his father. He glanced at the Princess, who gave him a kind smile despite the fact that her chest tightened at the thought of males from around Faylinn coming as potential admirers. It was unavoidable, but she'd been consumed by the idea of Kalan and her being something to one another. However, now that she thought about it, there was no way the Alpha was interested enough in her to desire suitorship.

Her face bloomed pink.

Tania clicked her tongue. "You're aware of the relations between King Oberon and I. The time is short before I formally exterminate our marriage. Meaning I won't be dealing with matters of suitors—in both my life, and my daughter's. It's her choice as to who and when she chooses our King, if one at all. I do hope you catch my meaning, Pavan." A pause. "I wouldn't want your grooming and expectations to go to waste. Surely you have better ways to exhaust your time?"

The Lord stuttered, "Princess Evalyn is—is expected to marry someone of wealth and lands. You shouldn't consider anyone of lower station. You will need a *strong* leader. Jaino will inherit my holdings when my title is passed onto him—"

"As will every eldest son in the Conclave," the Queen countered. "Or did you forget there are three other Lords precisely as powerful?"

"I have not." His mouth thinned. "But I'll remind you that I own valuable land, control a large portion of impressionable citizens, and dictate much trade in this Kingdom. Those of the *Ziffoy* name are honorable and worthy of their station. I'm inclined to believe you're pushing aside my offer—one of the best you'll receive, I must say—for personal reasons."

"If you wish to further discuss these matters, Lord Ziffoy, I suggest scheduling a private appointment," Evalyn retorted. "You'll find I enjoy parties, and don't intend on wasting a good one in bad company." The Princess gestured to the dance floor. The Lord grumbled something about getting a drink and dragged Jaino away.

"Well said," Tania piped.

"He was on both of our nerves. How do you stand him?"

"He has significant influence within Faylinn. It's necessary to maintain cordial relations, if only for the reputation of the monarchy."

"Would it be wrong of me to want something awfully tragic to happen so Jaino can take over?" Evalyn snickered. "But speaking of suitors... I'm not wholly opposed to finding someone. Not Jaino, of course, but... someone."

Tania faced the girl. "I do not intend to restrict possible advances on your part towards a partner." She gripped one of Evalyn's hands. "But if my marriages are any indication of the pain that can arise with such a decision, I must remind you to be wary. Find yourself, and know what kind of leader you desire to be, before allowing another in. Sometimes, a Queen must think of herself before her Kingdom or any others."

Evalyn gulped. "I will."

"You need only yourself to rule. You have power and grace and strength. Be careful not to forget that such things are all you need to do good for this Kingdom." Tania patted her arm. "Nevertheless, we cannot fully dismiss potential suitors tonight," her mother added as the music slowed to a gentle beat. "You still must partake in the Libcerus."

Evalyn forced a pleasant beam.

As tradition declared, the Princess was required to dance with citizens in thanks for their coming. She was allowed to choose a partner for the initial dance, but had to join with any male that offered their hand after. The girl spied a familiar twist of lapis hair and rose onto her toes, echoing his name. Sure enough, the Fae strode out from the crowd and onto the edge of the dance floor, meeting Evalyn's eyes. She waved him over, and when he reached her side, held out a hand.

"Has the Princess requested my acquaintance, dare I ask?" Micka hummed.

"Yes. I..." she lowered her voice. "I thought it'd be less embarrassing if I stumbled with a familiar face rather than a stranger during my first Libcerus. You were the first friend I saw."

They chatted as they danced, Evalyn stuttering through their conversation while focusing on the movement of her feet and hips. She maintained her coordination and didn't trip a single time—but gave credit to Micka.

"My father used to tell me that a man who can dance on the battlefield but not at a party was no man at all," Micka said. They neared a corner before making the coordinated turn to the center of the floor. Evalyn chuckled. "He also used to say dancing was the fastest way to a woman's heart. That's when I started paying attention in his lessons," he continued. His grin never faltered. "I don't come from a lot of wealth, so I had to take advantage of other methods."

"Is that why you're a sentinel? I hear the benefits are uncommonly sizable."

"That is one of the reasons, admittedly. I thought it'd be the honorable thing to do for my family, but then I fell in love with what I do. And fell in love with a spirit sent from the Gods themselves. She's the reason I haven't ventured home in five seasons." He cleared his throat. "However, I do see my parents and brothers when they manage to visit. I doubt I'll retire from the Guard until I'm forced to."

It was nice to have such a casual conversation. Refreshing. Like Evalyn was discovering more about Faylinn with every word.

But a time later—thirty minutes or five hours, Evalyn could no longer tell—her feet stung and arms hung limp as she was pulled into another round of dancing with an unknown partner. Her mouth ached but she kept her lips turned up in the hopes of still appearing content. She hadn't grasped how many Fae had come, nor how long each would want to dance, but quickly realized that those who talked were greatly preferable to those that silently stared during their turn.

Yet the Princess withheld her thoughts and chatted without grimacing at every step. Her eyes wandered the room, and she found herself watching Lord Ziffoy. His young son remained close, looking at anything except his father. Evalyn blocked out the Fae's voice who danced with her, unable to look away as Ladies Nickie and Hali glided to the Lord. Their words were inaudible over the music, but it wasn't hard to discern their unified laughing as the Keepers encircled Pavan, closer than acquaintances in a Court would typically be. What was their intent? Seduction? She didn't know what they expected from their efforts, seeing as the Lord looked inclined to tear Jaino apart if the boy so much as thought about moving an inch.

The Princess almost left the embrace of her partner to rescue the Faerie, if only to offer Jaino an excuse to leave the conversation between the Ladies and Lord surely not meant for his ears, but she spun out of the male's arms and into another.

Kalan's smile entranced her immediately, every concern vanishing. She'd hoped for a dance with him since the beginning of the celebration.

"Tired already?" he chortled, guiding her through other Fae couples with ease. Of course he was one of the best dancers yet, with his wolfish grace.

"Can you tell?" she winced.

"Not at all." Her breath hitched as he twirled her, then they swung together, closer than before. Whether it was the rush from the feelings she was starting to acknowledge or the rebellion to proper spacing and dance etiquette... Evalyn preferred their proximity. It was exciting compared to the awkwardness of the older Lords that held her tight.

Evalyn's exhaustion disappeared as Kalan spun her again; the music and their closeness encaptured her thoughts as they weaved through other Faeries. She didn't notice the beaming bystanders or onlooking Queen; with him, the girl just felt... free.

But the music inevitably slowed, as well as her feet with Kalan's, signaling the end of his turn. She clung to him, unprepared to move on to another male.

"Surely my all-powerful designation can sneak me a few more dances," he purred.

"If it was up to me, you could have the rest," she replied. He huffed a laugh. Evalyn had rarely flirted before; she'd never said more to Sandin than quaint hellos and thanked him for his compliments. She certainly had never felt like... *this*. And the Fae could've sworn Kalan leaned in, but he glanced to the side of the ballroom and Evalyn followed his gaze to see Walfien alone at the edge of the floor.

The Princess crossed her arms when she reached the Hand of the Queen. "How come you haven't asked to dance with me?"

His eyes roamed over her dress and settled on her face. "I was waiting for you."

She squinted. "Why?"

"To ask *me*."

"Oh, if *only* tradition allowed me to dance with whomever I wished," the Princess lilted, rolling her eyes. "But as it seems no Lords are currently striving for my partnership..." She gripped his hand, pulling them onto the floor as a soothing melody echoed through the hall. They swayed leisurely.

"I haven't seen you all evening," she exclaimed.

He lifted his brows. "Maybe you weren't looking hard enough." The girl pinched him, scoffing. Walfien smiled. "I left for a tracking assignment before dawn then checked on the Braenish soldiers when I got back." His eyes lingered on Evalyn's.

Her lips twitched into a simper. "Why are you staring at me like that?"

"You look beautiful."

"Mhm?"

"Better than all others. Not that the same can be said for me," he chuckled. "I prefer my sentinel uniform over the flamboyant celebration garb." Evalyn observed his green suit, the color contrasting his deep bronze hair, his mismatched eyes glimmering under the lights. He was gorgeous.

She would never tell him so.

It took her a moment to realize the music had stopped and only she and Walfien remained on the floor. A shiver crawled down her spine as she pulled away towards Tania, who stood with two glasses full of golden liquid. A toast.

"Welcome, friends and guests of Faylinn who have joined us—and stayed until this hour." Her eyes crinkled. "We thank you for your kind words and presence tonight in honor of Evalyn. Over the past half season, she's grown into a strong-willed and lovable friend, daughter, and leader. May verve and experience greet you." The Queen raised her glass. Every Fae in the room followed suit.

"As they will!"

Clinks echoed. She took a sip of the sparkling liquid. Bubbles rested in her stomach, and she began laughing for no reason at all.

The drink.

She should sit.

No, have fun. Dance all night. The Princess obeyed. She didn't care how she looked; didn't care if everyone was watching. The girl spun, hiccuping, her dress flowing around her. She swirled the contents of her drink, bringing the cup to her mouth—

A shatter sounded from her side. The effects of her beverage dissipated as Evalyn took in Walfien, hand still raised where his cup had been. The glass lay broken on the floor, shimmering liquid streaming in every direction.

Walfien's body was unmoving, eyes clenched shut. Was he breathing?

Evalyn stepped closer. His eyes burst open, and he sucked in a breath, falling to his hands and knees over the cracked glass. She and the Queen met his side instantly. Guests watched in hush as Tania ushered him to stand.

"What did you See?" the Queen muttered. The Sight. It was a vision.

He whipped towards Tania. "They're coming," he gasped. "They're here." Spotting Evalyn, his face paled. What had he Seen?

Common, logical sense abandoned her as he sprang towards the Princess, wrapping his arms around her body before racing them both to the side of the room, faster than a blink. He pushed her against the wall, his back to the open chamber, as the oak doors of the Great Hall blasted open in a deafening blast.

Chapter Ten

Everyone rushed from the doors, terror twisting their alluring features as screams echoed.

Faeries streamed in. If the Kingdom's sigil on their maroon uniforms weren't clue enough about whose doing this was, the wicked grins were.

Braena was attacking.

Still pinned to the wall by Walfien, in the corner of an alcove, Evalyn watched in horror as the Fae stalked towards her guests, who quickly gathered into a group, no one daring to exit the hall. There was no escape.

The bolder citizens edged the crowd, their magic streaming through the room. Licks of fire and second-long gusts of wind impacted the soldiers, striking and marking—but not enough to make a dent. There were so many of them.

Too many.

Evalyn pushed against Walfien's chest. These people—*her* people, were going to die in seconds.

"Stop," Walfien demanded. "They want *you*."

Evalyn stilled at his tone.

The soldiers retaliated, their own powers blasting. Darkness and shadows encircled the crowd of citizens, forming an impenetrable wall around the shouts and cries. A barrier of magic to keep the guests contained. Where was

Kalan and his family? The Keepers Evalyn had met mere hours ago? Were Lord Ziffoy and Jaino in the crowd?

Where was her mother?

Evalyn's heart dropped as silence filled the hall. The Queen was dragged out of the crowd, struggling against five Braenish males; she sent one to the ground before her arms were secured behind her in a strangling grip. They made for the front of the hall, where Tania was shoved to her knees.

The wall of swirling blackness around the guests fell for an instant, long enough for the soldiers to grab random Fae, slamming them into the floor. The Faeries were ushered forward in a line and to their knees, each head pulled back by a soldier holding a shining knife to their throat. Obey, or die a slow, painful death.

A flood of soldiers rushed in, packing half the hall, shoulder to shoulder with swords and magic ready. Maybe... maybe they didn't want Evalyn. But why come to attack innocent citizens? Was this the cruelty of Braena? Meaningless havoc and bloodshed?

No, she'd heard the King was calculated. Motivated. This chaos had a greater purpose.

Many strangers Evalyn had danced with were among the pulled Fae—even women and children. They'd been merciless in their choosing. Evalyn clutched Walfien's suit. "We have to do something. Walfien, I've been training; I'm stronger than I used to be and I can help fight, help rescue those caught inside—"

"You are strong, but you're inexperienced, Evalyn. Besides, you have no magic to defend against theirs. There's likely a hundred soldiers." Walfien tilted his head, face calm and unreadable.

"Please. They're going to kill them," she breathed, blinking away tears. Crying would do no good.

"They aren't. Not yet."

Slowly—so unbearingly slow—soldiers trickled out from their crowd with strange, needle-tipped devices. A lanky soldier with stringy, black hair strode for the Queen. He clicked his tongue, hands clasped at his back. "Is it true our people are being held in your cells?"

She stared.

The Faerie—the leader—snarled. "Is it true Ailfbane was killed by one of the Guard?"

Evalyn shook her head. Faylinn's own Court hadn't even been told of the attack. How did *he* know?

The Queen of Faylinn returned, "His body is rotting like yours will soon be."

The male slunk to Tania, bending at the waist, his face mere inches from the Queen's. "Do not, for one *second*, think Braena can't—*won't*—take down Faylinn if you move a toe out of your fearing, submissive line." Evalyn could practically feel his hot, musty breath on her face, but Tania didn't so much as flinch.

"Oberon won't get away with this."

The soldier threw his head back in a laugh. "Oh, you poor, poor Queen, to believe you could triumph in War against our almighty King." The others mimicked his amusement. With a wave of his hand, the soldiers raised their devices.

"Why are you doing this?" The Queen's voice echoed across the chamber.

The Fae narrowed his gaze. "You already know that, don't you?" Tania's glare was of rock and stone. "Perhaps I should rephrase: what better opportunity for a test, Majesty?"

The needles plunged into the throats of the Fae guests. It took everything in Evalyn not to cry out as black liquid dribbled down their necks. The stench spread through the chamber like wildfire during a drought. Evalyn swallowed her gag; Walfien's posture was no less tense. With the crowd detained by the barrier, no one could reach the Faeries as they fell to their sides, heads colliding with the floor. Unconscious, but not dead—the faint rise and fall of their chests depicted lingering life.

The Queen jostled her body, managing to stand and strike one of the Braenish Faeries holding her arms. He impacted the floor with a heavy thud as her remaining captors scrambled to regrip. "You made your point—invade, frighten, wound Faylinn. But this is more than a *test*, lackey. *What does Oberon want?*" Tania sneered.

He chuckled, "My King had a minor side mission for us. We've accomplished it." He gestured to the motionless Faeries. "As for the main purpose of this excursion—well, that you *certainly* do know. Third time's the charm, isn't it? You see, you managed to get her through your borders to conceal her scent, and Ailfbane wasn't so smart in his scouring, but this time... we won't make another mistake."

First and foremost, this was a public display of strength. A means of showing that Braena could do whatever they wanted. The fact that they'd again crept into Faylinn so easily and unnoticed proved their power.

Evalyn had been holding onto the hope that the King would find her significantly less appealing now that she was returned to the public eye of Faylinn—enough so to give up capturing the Princess—but this confirmed her Kingdom's terrible fear: Oberon was still fighting for what he wanted.

"We can take our time with amusement... or end it early. Your daughter, or the lives of more citizens." The soldier smiled. "I suppose the choice is yours."

When several Fae made for Tania, the leader raised his hand, ceasing their advances. Either he didn't want his men to die within the walls of The Palace, or perhaps he was dumb enough to overlook the rage radiating from the Faerie Queen—the latter, Evalyn supposed, as he casually swung his hand to the crowd and more Faeries were pulled from small openings in the magical barrier.

The leader shifted, opening his mouth—but no words came out. His eyes widened as he clutched his throat, squirming and gasping. It was useless—he was choking on air.

No, not choking.

Suffocating.

But Evalyn's mother glanced about the room, as confused as any other. Until Walfien stepped away, fingers directed at the soldier. He was in the middle of the hall before anyone noticed him move, extracting the air from the Faerie's lungs, who thrashed on the floor in a spasm, trying anything to breathe. Walfien neared him, and the other soldiers backed away as if scared of the same end.

They should be.

Walfien looked over the Faerie's twisting body, silent as he began bluing. But then he coughed, turning onto all fours as air filled his lungs. His body shuddered and he glared at Walfien, who muttered something Evalyn couldn't make out. Walfien was emotionless in the face of the terror the soldiers had brought. He didn't blink or breathe or move. He wasn't a friend. This was the Hand of the Queen in the midst of his true duty to serve and protect the Crown.

The soldier smiled and replied in the same, inaudible tone.

A crack rebounded off the walls. The Faerie slumped to the ground.

Walfien faced Tania. The halted soldiers came alive once more, faces gnarled in deadly stares. One stepped forward, ignoring the dead body of his companion. "We came for the girl. We *will* take her. I suggest you move aside, or face the wrath of the King," he hissed, drawing axes from his sides.

No one glanced in Evalyn's direction; no one gave the Faeries any inclination of her location. She inched forward, but some selfish instinct kept her in place.

Would the soldiers wreak havoc through The Palace, the Kingdom, as King Oberon had done for so long, to find her?

She'd discovered unwavering trust and love from Faylinn. They would do it, places switched. Others would save her in a heartbeat. The right choice was obvious. And not only was it her obligation to help her people, but this was her chance—a chance given from the Gods to protect Faylinn. Maybe this was why she'd survived four years ago; to stop the King from his wicked measures and better the continent in sacrificing herself.

"Wait," she declared, making for the open chamber. All eyes found her. Her throat tightened, but she pushed the words out. "I'm here. I'm right here. Take me and spare the rest. Take me and leave."

A mass of soldiers lunged in Evalyn's direction. She stumbled back as they cackled.

"Let's have our fun," one smiled, arms spread wide. "I say we take down Her Majesty first. She's looking a little worn. Maybe it's time she turned the Crown over to someone a little more... suited for the role." A cluster of soldiers shifted to the Queen.

Tania smirked. "Even an aging Faerie such as I can take on a gaggle of fresh drafts." She twisted her fingers, wind swirling around the room, and the remaining soldiers shifted focus to the Queen, wholly ignorant of the Princess they had come to capture.

This wasn't how it was supposed to work. They were *supposed* to get Evalyn and forget everyone else; abandon all missions besides kidnap and return to Braena.

The girl started forward but a presence appeared at her side, strong arms gripping her own. Wide-eyed, she viewed Micka, expression unyielding. Evalyn didn't give herself time to wonder how he wasn't within the crowd. She tried to pull away, to reach Tania as the soldiers closed in around her, but Walfien appeared as well, and they both clutched her arms.

Tania was making a greater sacrifice—some bargain to protect Evalyn. The Princess jerked and yanked, but Micka and Walfien's hands tightened. A retort sputtered from her lips as she stared them down, disbelieving.

They weren't going to hold her there, make her watch—not after she finally connected with her mother. Her and Tania were going to make it work; this new mother-daughter bond.

But it was all she could do to behold in horror as the soldiers blocked Tania from view, lunging for the Queen with whooping howls. Evalyn could hardly feel anything—didn't want to feel anything—as the citizens screamed and hollered, banging against the impenetrable barrier, begging for the Braenish Fae to stop.

But the soldiers flew back, into the walls of the ballroom. The barrier of darkness fell.

Tania panted, unmoved from her spot. Her knees wobbled, and Evalyn tried to go to her, but Micka and Walfien pulled the Princess' struggling and growling figure away. She'd already caused more trouble than necessary. The soldiers rose as the Queen's voice rang across the chamber. "I have my own message for Oberon. Perhaps he'll learn to follow through with his threats."

The immobile Faylinn citizens were pulled into the crowd of guests before a clear, lustrous wave of magic flowed around them. It came from within, blocking the Braenish soldiers who advanced towards them. A shield.

"Ours goes up," Walfien hastily demanded. Micka's hands spread in front of him, and the two Fae wrapped around Evalyn. A field of translucent gold expanded over the three a heartbeat before it happened.

The windows shattered as rocks and debris flew into the chamber, rushing around the shields towards the Braenish Faeries. The chandelier swung wildly as the candles and light fixtures winked out. The room transformed into roaring, black night.

Evalyn searched for her mother against the awakening streaks of moonlight. Gravel and cobblestone rained on the soldiers; they scrambled for safety under the pounding of the rocks, jumping over their own as they attempted to retreat. Tania flipped her hands to the floor, and the commotion stopped as the last of the stones plummeted to the floor.

But Tania wasn't done. And Evalyn was certain of one thing: the night wouldn't end in Braena's favor.

The Queen lifted her hands, and vines along the walls Evalyn hadn't noticed before began growing and lengthening, reaching to the ceiling. The plants rose high before smashing to the ground, bashing the Braenish Faeries from every angle. Evalyn shivered under the shield as vines crawled over the floor after the leftover soldiers. They latched around their bodies, whilst the Fae thrashed and howled, but escape was nonexistent. The climbing plants flew through the shattered windows, halting their muffled screams with darkness.

It was silent when the shields dropped. Evalyn rushed for Tania, who fell to the floor, the woman's gown a heap around her. Evalyn crumpled at her side.

"Are you alright?" she asked, gripping her mother's hands.

Tania's eyes darted over Evalyn's face. "Mags," she whispered. "Mags." She sagged on Evalyn and passed out.

Chapter Eleven

The Princess reclined by her mother's side. Tania hadn't woken since she'd fallen unconscious the previous night.

Micka had carried the Queen to the infirmary, leaving Evalyn to view the Great Hall and its destruction. She restrained from hurling at the reek of the dead Faeries. Bodies scattered the room, and with tear-stained faces and quivering hands, the citizens fled for their homes. The families of the attacked Fae stayed by their sides to the infirmary. Evalyn had followed the sounds of fearful sobs—no one knew what the Faeries had been injected with or what would happen to them.

It was a matter of time before results emerged.

Evalyn hadn't moved from the wooden stool beside her mother all night. She peered at the sleeping Queen, who seemed so peaceful, so strong and powerful in her rest.

Evalyn knew something was wrong. Tania had yet to say, but the Princess had suspicions. The Queen's schedule, isolated for hours at a time; the coughing and pallor; her falling weak so quickly after the attack... it added up to a truth bigger than Tania made it seem. Worse than Evalyn wanted to hope.

The Princess observed bustling nurses. There were few of the magical healers in the castle, but their small number was made up with great skill. The women's delicacy matched the simply detailed unit: the cots were stout and colorless but luxurious all the same, with thick, white pillars separating each of them. Soft-green curtains were stationed at every bed.

The girl lifted her gaze at the echo of laughter across the chamber. She leaned around the pillar to spy a woman grasping a child on the floor.

"I thought I'd lost you! Oh, you mustn't wander off like that!" She kissed the young, giggling Fae's face and scooped the girl into her arms. "It's not safe. Not anymore."

It was true. How many had been hurt because of Evalyn? How many would continue to be hurt defending her?

"Sorry, Mama. I want'a see Princess," the girl simpered.

Evalyn curled into her seat and stopped listening.

"Evalyn. Evalyn." A breath. "No, no—"

The girl whipped towards her mother's words. "I'm here. Right here," she whispered. The Queen shook on the cot—a nightmare. Evalyn stroked Tania's silken, blonde hair. She'd said the same words two days ago in the Great Hall, willing to sacrifice herself for her people, for Faylinn. For her mother. Now, the girl didn't know what she'd have done if she was taken to Braena. If she would've made it before dying of dread.

Tania continued muttering. "N-no, no, Evalyn—"

"It's okay—I'm here, I'm here," Evalyn repeated, clutching the woman's hand. The Queen's words had become part of this waiting routine, as had the squirming, shouting, and crying. Her vulnerability was unsettling. Still, the Queen had never fully woken.

So when Tania sat forward, gasping with broad eyes, the Princess slipped off of her chair. Tania faced her daughter, gripping the hand Evalyn outstretched from the ground.

"I—I just—it was a dream," Tania rambled. The Princess remained a silent presence. She wondered what could make her mother so frightened. Were they similar to the nightmares Evalyn could so vividly describe—of being left alone in the woods, frozen and helpless and scared that no one would ever find her?

The nightmares that Evalyn could explain as if she were seeing them in front of her own eyes?

"Elyse, she's awake!" Evalyn called out.

The head nurse, Elyse, met the Queen's cot with a jar of dark liquid. The Fae wore a pale green robe, the Kingdom's signarum patched over the heart. "I see Her Majesty has awoken." Her voice was light and calming. The nurse poured a spoonful of thick, brown substance, which Tania consumed, trying to hide her coughing with an arm. Elyse chuckled, deep dimples appearing on her cheeks. Her entire figure had a pretty, pink hue to it, matching a rosy knot atop her head.

"Quite disgusting, isn't it?" the nurse laughed.

Evalyn turned. "Elyse?"

"Hm?"

The pair watched Tania fall into dreamless sleep, a gift from the dose. Once her breathing slowed into an effortless rhythm, the Princess spoke. "What's wrong with her?"

Elyse studied the Queen. "We call it burnout. All Fae have a limit to the magic they can use at once. When a Faerie reaches the depths of their power, and uses much of it, there's consequence. You see, everything comes with a price. In rare cases, burnout is just that—a sudden burning through the entire body, their powers searching for a source that doesn't exist, until it kills their host or suffocates their powers altogether. For most, burnout begins as an itch, warning you to stop early on. All you can do from there is rest. Restoring magic is a tedious process."

Evalyn fidgeted. Tania nearing burnout didn't explain her other symptoms. She'd have to pay Mags a visit soon; she needed more answers than one from the woman.

But first, the girl had to track down the Hand of the Queen.

The Princess trudged down the corridors, peering at every sentinel she passed. She didn't know if Walfien was on a shift or not; he took them whenever he felt like it.

Evalyn hadn't seen or heard from him since the night of the attack. He hadn't checked on Tania or the Princess or anyone else for that matter, nor given any recognition to his own well-being. The girl didn't realize her annoyance until she turned down a short hallway absent of extra sentinels and found Walfien closing a door. He stopped in his tracks when he noticed her. The Princess stared.

Despite an hour wandering the castle and its grounds, she was at a loss for words. The girl crossed her arms with a huff, but was greeted with stifling quiet. She could faintly hear his breathing, gentle and unchanging.

"Where have you been?" she blustered, stepping forward. "After the attack, you were gone. Gone. You didn't assist the cleanup in the Hall or help the attacked or check on your Queen. You just disappeared." He looked as if she'd walked up and slapped him, opening his mouth soundlessly. "Go ahead, state your excuse. You left when I needed you, Walfien. I'm trying to be worthy of this Kingdom, and you're running away."

Walfien didn't explode—he was a persistent, prolonged wave of calm. The polar opposite to how he should react. But as his hands gradually clenched into fists at his side, she wished he would instead shout. "I never talk about it. Don't allow myself to remember it, most of the time." His voice was low, tinged with something she couldn't place. Grief or... sorrow? Was it *shame*? Evalyn's stare faltered. "There once was a time when my parents were alive. And any of us ever being in a position like I am now would've been a miracle sent from Omforteu himself. I was young, barely a toddler, but I remember struggling to scrounge up enough money for food each fortnight; even clothes were scarce, and we lived in a hovel gifted from my elders. But one day, my father brought my mother and I here, to The Palace. It was a place of *miracles* for us who'd never left our home village. It was the first time I'd seen a dress like the one my mother was gifted. It was lavender. The ball was small, but we didn't care.

"We danced with nobles, with people we'd never heard of and families we didn't know existed. We danced day and night, and my parents drank and danced again. I'd never seen them so happy. I thought it was a dream." A pause. "It was the last memory I had with them before they died. When we decided to return home, the Faeries attacked. I learned they were no-name assailants with petty grudges against the Queen's Court. That was all that motivated their actions." Walfien's eyes locked onto Evalyn. "Every single Faerie at that ball was slaughtered in front of my eyes. I didn't know what was happening then, but... I can never unsee it. Perhaps it's my Sight that keeps the memory clear. I survived because your mother had left the ballroom by the Gods' mercy; I somehow made it to the door, and she saw me and snatched me into her arms, using what she had of her growing powers to save the two of us. It was already too late to rescue any others. We buried them after."

"I—I'm sorry," the Princess stuttered, otherwise speechless.

He steadily neared her. "So here's the excuse for my absence, Evalyn." It wasn't anger in his words, but dismay. Walfien had relived a nightmare. "You don't yet know the every in and out of this Court. Not like I do after a thus-far lifetime of experience. You don't yet know the *terrible* things that people have done and gone through to live in The Palace and serve you and Tania with expectations of nothing in return. So when you, the prophesied-about Lost Princess who it is my *primary* duty to shield and defend, were willing to sacrifice everything in an instant, I was horrified that you'd have the same fate as my parents." His lips thinned. "It wasn't painless to take that Fae's life the other night despite the loathing I have for Braena. He knew that I was taking revenge; taunted me about it before I ended him. For my parents and everyone at that ball, I would do it again and again to anyone who threatens this Kingdom. It is *all* I have left—to protect. To attempt to avenge those taken lives." Walfien whispered, "But the mass of bodies lying there, motionless and frail and forever gone... the scene set me on an edge I hadn't experienced in years. And I had to get away."

"I'm sorry," Evalyn said again, eyes on the floor. How had she gotten things so twisted, assuming he'd done it without reason?

Walfien gently grabbed her chin, pulling it up until she met piercing, mismatched eyes. "Don't *ever* be sorry for having it in you to want to keep the people you love safe." Walfien's heart pounded as fast as her own, but he stepped back, hands falling to his sides.

After a minute, Evalyn cleared her throat, words light. "When my mother rescued you... is that how you became Hand? Did she raise you?"

He loosed a breath. "Your mother... she'd lost so much already. Her human mate had passed, and with the new alliance with Braena and the King's subsequent threats to find you, she'd sent you away. After losing so many friends, so many citizens... Gods, I don't know how she pushed through it. But I suppose I became a lifeline to her. When I could handle my own, I was going to leave—return home after so many years. But she offered me a position as her Hand when I turned sixteen, against the pleading of the Conclave not to let a child in." A flicker in his eyes. "I accepted and didn't look back."

The Princess stepped closer.

"Evalyn?" sounded from the opposite end of the corridor.

Her heart skipped a beat as she spun. "Kalan!" She beamed. Her head calmed in relief as she scanned him: no scars or bruises or broken limbs. He'd sent a letter from camp saying as much, but she hadn't stopped worrying until there was proof.

"You're alright, Walfien?" Kalan questioned gingerly.

The Hand's smile didn't meet his eyes. "Always am."

The Alpha glanced at the Princess. "Well then," he said, nearing her side. "Could I offer you a temporary getaway? I heard you were crouched in that infirmary for two days."

"That'd be wonderful," she returned, taking his outstretched hand. Facing Walfien, the echo of memories from his past played in her mind. "Are you okay?"

"I'll be fine."

Evalyn dipped her head and turned with Kalan, but it was only when they reached the foyer that she realized what Walfien had meant. Eventually, he'd heal from that horrid night; from the scarring that had summoned with the ball and her own actions.

But right now... he wasn't fine. She didn't think anyone was.

Nevertheless, she couldn't help a faint grin as they ventured through the courtyard. Just being beside Kalan brought it out. The sun was far from setting—they had the rest of the day to themselves. "Where are we going?"

The Alpha smirked and continued leading. Gods, a *surprise*?

He never released her hand, even as a huddle of enchanting Fae girls stepped into their path, flipping their hair and giggling amongst themselves. Their dresses restricted airflow; the products on their faces were like clumped pastry. "Hello, *Alpha*!" The girls smiled at them—at him.

"If you'll excuse us, Ladies, my partner and I have business to attend to," Kalan retorted. He glanced at Evalyn, a playful glint in his eyes. The Faerie's expressions turned to scowls at their interlocked hands.

"You can do business with *me*," one pouted.

Kalan smiled. "Truly, Princess Evalyn and I must be on our way."

The girls' eyes widened and they fell into deep curtsies, gasping, "Your Highness!" Evalyn was more dumbstruck at their sudden respect than anything, but Kalan couldn't contain his amusement as he pulled them onward with a chuckle.

"Is this an attempt to woo me?" Evalyn questioned. "The Courtly suitors are falling behind on those grounds." Kalan parted his lips, but shut his mouth. The Princess simpered, taking it as confirmation. "I wonder if your efforts will surpass my standards." Not that they were high to begin with; she was wearing the same day-gown she'd changed into two days ago after the ball, her hair a tangled plait.

"They will."

Evalyn gaped, "You *are* trying to win my favor!" but the Alpha gave a look that half-heartedly suggested he was doing nothing of the sort.

They came to a halt outside the north wing of the castle, where the view overlooked the land reaching to the Timoke Mountains and Aternalis Creek. A multicolored, makeshift rug lay on the grass, littered with goblets and dishes, the aroma of a fresh meal filling her nostrils. Kalan ran a hand through his hair. "I didn't know what to bring, but—"

"This is more than perfect," Evalyn interjected, eying the setup so thoughtfully laid out for her.

He gestured to the awaiting foodstuff. "Shall we, then?"

The sun dipped towards the horizon.

"Tell me something about yourself," Kalan voiced. "Anything."

Evalyn gazed out to the landscape at their front. "When I was still with Kinz, a short time before I came to Faylinn, I saw a wolf outside our cabin." The Princess tugged at a thread in her gown. "Stupidly, I touched one, right on their snout." Kalan sat up, beaming far too excitedly for such a bland story, and she paused. Shook her head slowly, aghast. "It was *you?*" Evalyn squealed, hands flying to her mouth.

Kalan laughed. "I wanted to see how long it took to uncover it yourself."

"Why were you there?"

"We set watches at night around Kinz' homestead, and lightly patrolled the area during daylight. It was one of my first shifts with the patrol since I'd become Alpha. I didn't know it was you; Tania kept secret who you were, although clarified that your highly critical protection was from Oberon Romen. We put it together, eventually." He chuckled, "Everyone thought you were crazy and I, stupid, for letting it happen; Paiton would never have let anyone get so close nor intimate except my mother, and even then only in private company. My unit laughed for days about your bravery—with your glamour we thought you to be mostly human, and no human had ever mustered up the guts to so much as *look* a creature in the eye that was more than half their size. So... you can imagine their shock."

She grinned smugly; Kalan cleared his throat. "The monitoring kept my mind off of our fallen members. And it made me feel... full. After a long while of feeling empty. Knowing that although I couldn't save them, I could save you, if need be."

Her beam died. "I heard about the assault on your clan. How did you recover?"

"At first, I was enraged. All I could feel was fury and confusion for weeks. You see, they invaded on the night of Velit Tempus. For a time, I lost all trust in our Spirits. We dedicated our breath and energy to prayer and worship each month, yet I felt they'd failed us. Or rather, *we* had failed *them*. And the tragedy was our punishment.

"But eventually... the pack returned to its festivities. We reminded one another of the goodness of the Spirits and why we celebrate. Eventually, I came to terms with it. It's wretched, and the King will lay at our mercy soon enough, but what the Spirits decree is their will. I've regained my trust and hope."

Evalyn said, "You're a good leader, Kalan."

He smiled.

She sipped from her goblet; rays of gold and pink licked the grass. "Speaking of the horrid works of Braena... the Moon Clan was safe concerning my ball, I take it? I didn't see your mother or sister."

"They rounded up the few clan members that'd gone and returned to camp earlier. I was moments behind them, but Lord Relfou had interests about establishing a new clan patrol. Suffice to say, I ended up within the crowd."

"I apologize that you had to experience that. Truly, Kalan. After so much calamity, I'm sorry."

"It's not your fault," he returned. "As far as I know, they didn't have wolfsbane, and I doubt they cared to pack silver blades. They were focused on Fae enemies."

"Wolfsbane and silver?"

"Both are lethal to wolves. The former is a primitive flowering plant. A large enough dose can kill a wolf instantaneously. The touch of it causes common sickness, as well as burning welts, numbness—among other horrors. Silver is just as perilous; it completely halts our hyper-healing, leaving us to bleed out." Her eyes widened, but he shrugged. "As I said, Oberon will suffer consequences. That's all that matters." He brushed through his golden hair with a grin so contagious it wiped all thoughts of the King and his brutality from the Princess' mind. The Alpha's eyes darted to her side, and Evalyn turned to see a cluster of pixies stealthily crawling towards her.

Or, what would've been stealthy, had they not stood and begun skipping forth upon her stare.

One tugged at the waist of her gown; a whistling pair tucked loose strands of blonde hair into her plait. A dozen danced around her, snickering and spinning, while an outsider snapped its fingers repeatedly, summoning rose-colored magic sparks with every click.

As soon as Kalan let out a hum, the creatures plunged behind Evalyn with buzzing hisses.

The Princess cocked her head, looking around her. "Why are you scared, friends?"

The Alpha gave a long sigh. "Pixies are despised across Liatue for their chaotic culture of ransacking and foolery. Many farmers and city-dwelling shop owners have adopted the practice of trapping and killing them. That's why they're frightened; they are by most Fae, and still have yet to warm up to the clan, even though their central domain is the Mediocris Woods. Although it's one of the few remaining places not forbidden from pixie exploration, I suspect my father didn't provide the warmest welcome."

Evalyn shifted towards the pixies, and a couple bounced onto her lap. They all eyed Kalan ferociously, yet had stopped their cruel shrills.

"They mean no harm, but the majority have migrated to the Sacred Tree, their birth home in the heart of Faylinn's northern plains. Yet it's strange... I've seen more since your arrival to the Kingdom than in my entire life."

She whipped her head to Kalan. "Why is that?"

He tilted his chin. "Walfien once told me that the pixies know everything. Every conflict, every matter, every being. They hear and remember all. Maybe... they respect you. Adore you, even: the Lost Princess who filled dreams and prayers for two decades."

Evalyn wished she'd known with Kinz, when she had glimpsed them every few weeks in their cabin. They'd been her first sight of this world, of the future she'd been unaware of. The girl smiled at the creatures, who levitated higher and began spinning and sending colorful sparks in every direction until they flew away, down the hillside towards the creek.

"I have another surprise for you, Princess." She raised her brows. The title felt like an intimate joke between them; a nickname instead of a role that defined the course of her life. He stood. "Will you trust me?"

She rose, curious. "Yes."

He smirked, slipped off his boots, and shifted. The Princess couldn't decide whether she was in awe or shock as fur grew over his body, as bones rearranged and his clothes ripped apart until a human no longer stood there, but a wolf.

Kalan slowly strode around the girl. Circling her, his vast frame temporarily blotting out the setting sun as he passed her side. Evalyn faced him and reached out a hand, grazing the deep-blonde fur that shimmered in the setting sunlight. Her hand stilled at the black stripe down his spine: she was awestruck.

He was captivating.

Kalan turned, snout inches from her face. Meeting his golden eyes, she felt it. The power and domination that supported his position in the Moon Clan. He expelled a freedom and excitement she'd never known, but suddenly and fervently craved.

Evalyn stroked his head, to which he sat and closed his eyes. Who would have thought she'd fall for a wolf?

But she was as much a wild creature. And glad for it.

Kalan tilted his head. "I don't speak wolf," Evalyn mused as Kalan backed away, repeating his movements. "Fetch?" she tried. He gazed to the sky, and the girl wondered if he was praying for sense to be knocked into her.

After a moment, Kalan positioned his paws beside one other. A defensive stance; ready to run. He looked to the Princess, then snapped his head east, to the Mediocris Woods. Evalyn exclaimed, "You… want to race to the forest?" Kalan inclined his head with as smug of a look as he could have.

The Princess laughed.

And with a preparatory stare, set off in a sprint.

Everything around her was a blur. Adrenaline pumped through Evalyn's veins; her heart pounded with every breath. Her dress sucked at her skin against the wind, a petite hindrance to her speed, but a wild grin grew on her face. She matched Kalan's speed as they darted through the closing outer gate and down The Palace's hill. They reached the Mediocris Woods faster than she'd have thought possible—with Walfien, it took them half a day to cross the rolling plains.

But back then, as far as she'd known, Evalyn had been human.

They were under pine trees by the time the colored rays were replaced with glowing moonlight. Kalan was a flesh-and-bone embodiment of peace.

This was his sanctuary.

At the edge of a clearing, they slowed to a stop. She spied small cabins and sizable tents circling the area; multiple fires rose to her height in the center of the camp. People gathered around the largest fires, on stumps of cut wood or the forest floor. The Princess leaned against a tree, hardly fatigued as she observed the people. There were young and old folk, the latter with round, wooden cups in hand while they laughed and chatted.

The Moon Clan.

The Alpha watched them too. She stilled, feeling as if she'd caught him in a private state. He breathed deeply; his heartbeat relaxed and steady. When she smiled, he faced her. Evalyn glanced at the camp, attempting to pretend as if she hadn't been watching him—but it was a struggle to keep her eyes away.

Without warning, Kalan stalked over to a tree and shifted to his human form. Evalyn yelped, barely turning around in time to miss his unclothed frame. She waited for a clear signal, but a breath tickled her ear—

"You can look." His quiet voice was full of amusement. Still, Evalyn slowly faced him, eyes high. With an exhale, she glimpsed a dark tunic. He smirked and withdrew; despite the warming season, a chill traced her spine.

"When did you first shift?" she questioned.

"Most of us can start shifting on the cusp of pubescence; it's our first coming-of-age milestone. I was nine and a half."

Her eyes bulged out of their sockets. "So much pain, so young!"

Kalan chuckled. "It's certainly a strange experience, initially, but it doesn't hurt. The magic in our blood does most of the work, you just have to surrender to the transition. Once you taste the freedom of your wolf, transforming is peaceful and relieving."

They watched camp.

"And how is leading?" Evalyn asked.

"They trust me. Things were... different with my father. How he ran things; how he ran *them*. But I think they're beginning to see I'm not Paiton. Authoritative and strict in my own way, as I should be, but changing how we interact together and function as one. It was something that needed to be done long before my name came into the picture."

"It seems like you're doing a great job."

"Sometimes I think I am. I'm mainly... trying." He huffed through his nose. "What's it like being the Lost Princess? Foretold to be wise and mighty?"

"I'm mainly... trying." A grin. "I want to do something for the children of this Kingdom. Somehow provide schooling and housing and care to those who don't have it. To ones who grew up like I did."

"That's a powerful dream. I'd like to back it. Be part of its fulfillment, if you'd allow me."

The Princess beamed. He really wanted to accomplish it? Together, with her?

Kalan extended a palm. "I'm sure they know we're here by now. Would you like to meet the clan?"

Evalyn squeezed his hand and stepped out of the treeline—where, not a second later, someone boomed, "What a treasure Kalan has snuck from the castle!"

All at once the pack jumped from their seats with shouts of welcome. The Princess was swamped by pack members, embraced so tightly the girl struggled to catch her breath. She nudged Kalan, simpering. The clan settled to their places; Kalan guided them to an open spot.

"Dear girl, you're more beautiful than my four children combined!" A woman declared excitedly from across the fire. Her auburn bun frizzed; wide, dark eyes were paired with a grin.

"Kimi is our usual entertainment," Kalan explained.

Evalyn chuckled, "Thank you, Kimi. It's a pleasure to meet you all."

Kimi lifted her cup, sloshing liquid onto the needle-strewn floor. "Oh Princess, you mustn't be so *formal* with us! Come, dance with me!" She skipped around the fire, pulling Evalyn to her feet. Everyone began cheering and turned to a frail, balding man, as if his next actions were obvious.

Evalyn gasped. "Soj?"

The man grinned. "Just couldn't forget me, hm?" He winked. Those around the fire clapped to a beat, and Soj began singing, his voice full of beauty and wisdom.

The crowd joined in the dancing; the Princess found herself breathlessly chanting along to the tune as she flounced. Her hair loosened into waves around her as she spun. The Alpha stood beyond the crowd, mouthing the words to the song and tapping his foot with the beat. His happiness was as clear as their dancing.

When it ended, a triad of members appeared before Evalyn; one of the two uniformed males looped an arm through hers, pulling the girl in Kalan's direction, who rolled his eyes. "Couldn't restrain keeping your grubby hands off the Royalty, could you?"

The male grinned in response to his Alpha. Half of his shaggy, brown hair was tied in a knot at the back of his head, and the expression scrunched the freckles splattered across his cheeks. "I knew she'd come as soon as I heard our reception song. I sprinted over from the returning patrol unit."

The female twisted her long, brunette plait between the fingers of one hand and handed a goblet to Evalyn with the other. "You're mighty flushed after that dancing; it's water." She released Evalyn from the wolf's clutches before pinching his arm.

The other male was a stark contrast to the first, with cropped black hair and striking green eyes that lit up the rest of his face. He shook his head. "Kye, you have a girlfriend. Who also happens to be your *mate*. Do you realize how immoral and inappropriate it is to curry Evalyn's favor?"

Kye, the brown-haired male, returned, "Not at all. Bre doesn't even mind."

He turned to the female, whose full, rosy lips upturned in a smile. "Make one move and you'll find yourself another pack to join," she said sweetly, batting thick lashes.

Kye just laughed, pulling Bre in and kissing her forehead. "Thanks for ruining my chances, Jan," he said without looking away from Bre.

Kalan strode to Evalyn's side. "These are my closest friends: Kye Kallister, Janson Wren, and Bre Saber." He whispered, "I believe their presence indicates a desire to tour you around our camp. Kye and Jan have been *raving* about making an impression on you."

Evalyn chuckled; with the wave of a hand, she said, "Well, let the tour begin!"

Even Bre's face lit up. The males led proudly—Kalan included, after the begging of Kye and Jan—and first led her to the cabins on the outskirts of camp. They housed the oldest and most esteemed members of the clan, a different one chosen daily to serve meals for the pack and provide general rest or aid.

"Considering the amount of times I was forced to sit on these porches and count the stars as punishment," Kye cackled, "you'd think I'd be much less prone to fights. But I never left a ball at The Palace without one."

Jan snorted. "Because you were too immature to overlook the petty grudges of ancient, noble Faerie families."

"Actually, it was because their snobby sons always had something to say about the disgrace of wolf-Fae connections. Did you think I could leave without a nice pummeling of their pretty faces?"

Everyone laughed as they moved to the tents: the common housing for most wolf clans across Liatue. Some were massive enough to accommodate entire packs, although petite ones.

"Why did you join the patrol?" Evalyn asked Jan and Kye.

The latter said, "I'll join anything that grants me the opportunity for some good revenge."

"I joined to keep him tame," the former added.

"Yeah, right! I keep you on your toes and bring out your innate rebellion—"

"Don't let them start," Kalan piped. "Kye will maunder on about his duties to anyone who'll listen and somehow manage to force Jan to dissociate from his humility long enough to brag alongside him."

"Excuse me? Bre listens to my patrol recounts every time I return!"

"Because she's your mate, dimwit," Jan said.

Kye rolled his eyes but looped an arm around Bre's hip. She shrugged. "He had to have someone." Bre smiled at Evalyn. "Janson always sees the best in people. He knew he could help Kye do more than the brawling he claims to have been born for."

"Are you going to tell me I'm wrong?" Kye spluttered.

"No, but Janson's right that there's more than a fighter in you."

"Oh, don't let Jan sink his emotional claws into your heart." Kye turned, shaking a finger at Evalyn. "Next thing you know, he'll have you sitting down and releasing all your... emotions. Or whatever he talks about."

"Unlocking the unconscious motives of your being can only help you," Janson muttered as they moved along. "Beating someone up doesn't make you feel better. I've told you this *so many times!*"

They entered a section of the clearing empty of housing, replaced by trunks and boulders, and wolf statues and handmade obstacles, all of which formed a survival course. The elaborate array of material certified that it was the pack's favored training method; the worn and indolently replaced pieces conveyed active, heavy use.

"This course has waned off plenty of steam," Kalan described. He grinned, scratching the back of his head. "My father sent the four of us here almost everyday, ordering us to train until we were too taxed to breathe. But we got into enough trouble to deserve it."

Bre tsked, crossing her arms. "Let's not forget who spearheaded the adventures and forced our joining, thus getting us *all* into continuous trouble!" She eyed Kalan, who looked everywhere but at her and began whistling loudly.

Janson turned to Kye instead. "And which of us could never stand before Paiton without giving some idiotic feedback that put us into deeper messes."

Kalan burst into laughter. "Remember when you called him a *hypocritical disgrace*, Kye? He put *me* on bonfire cleanup for a week!"

"Yeah, well, I apologized, didn't I?"

"Because I *paid* you!" Janson declared.

The males began their back and forth, continuing their bickering over who was *most* at fault for their childhood punishments all the way back to the bonfires. Bre walked with Evalyn, arm in arm.

"So when did you and Kye get together?"

"Well, we grew up in neighboring cabins. Kye's parents passed away when he was twelve, so he lived with my family for a few years. He let down his walls for the first time to me, and we couldn't stay away from one another after. One day, it just became official."

"Yet somehow *they* were the only ones in the pack shocked by their discovery that they were mates," Kalan said, coming from behind to meet their pace. "It made sense for everyone else—and explained why Bre was one of the only people Kye listened to unconditionally."

Kye fake gagged as they seated themselves around the main fire and listened in on the clan's storytelling: some tales were legends of fallen warriors, others amusing recountings of friends' pasts.

Eventually, midnight had consumed the forest. Kimi's voice rang through the black woods: "... so I flicked my tail at him and strutted off. The poor bird didn't know *how* to respond! But let me tell you, those pixies enjoy every second of our weekly squabbles." The woman's gaze rose to the tree limbs. "Don't you, you wee tricksters?" Bright eyes and flickers of gold emerged in the darkness. A unified humming sounded.

"Alright, let's hear the rest," Kye said.

Kimi tutted, "There's no more to tell. That's what happened!"

The male rolled his eyes, swirling the liquid in his cup. "You either exaggerate or undershare, Kimi, no in-between. I'm sure the bird had the last word."

"*Spirits*, Kye, you don't say that out loud!" Janson cried, putting his face in his hands.

It was too late: the woman ran over and pinched Kye's ear until he released his cup into her hand with a howl. "Keep up that attitude," she said, downing the drink, "and I'll give you some last words to choke on." With a snicker, Kimi returned Kye his empty cup, at which he scoffed and tossed to the ground.

"You didn't have to drink all of it," he grumbled.

Standing behind Kye, Bre kissed his cheek before mouthing to the Princess, *He'd had enough ale for a week. Kimi did me a favor.*

Evalyn chuckled. A middle-aged man, Howler, barked into the night, "*Spirits Guide Us*, dear Soj! What better honor than to lift up a hymn for the Princess!" He lifted his drink.

The rest of the pack vigorously shouted their encouragement, and Soj's eyes crinkled in delight. "Alright, alright. One of our primitive hymns, eh?" The crowd hooted and hollered, cups shooting into the air. Soj lifted thin hands, crackling fire the only sound in the night.

It began slow and deep, the man's voice echoing far. The forest held its breath. Not an eye strayed from Soj.

All within their cabins settled around the flames as their song rose. Every soul in the pack, young or old, sang in the melody. Kalan slipped an arm around her. This clan had lost and sacrificed so much for her Kingdom, yet they'd found a way out of the darkness.

Silence settled. Evalyn whispered, "Thank you for letting me be part of that."

A woman seated across the fire proclaimed, "We decide who we love, not the substance in our veins. You're forever welcome here, Princess."

Kalan squeezed his arm around her, and Evalyn closed her eyes momentarily. Conversation rose; when the girl opened her eyes, she found the Alpha watching her. Evalyn hummed in question. He glanced behind, where a handful of young girls motioned for Evalyn.

"You have admirers," he said.

"Princess! Princess Evalyn, sit with us!"

She wandered toward the huddle at the edge of a smaller campfire and slid onto a stump as they watched her with... wonder. Or curiosity. Either way, their questions rose unannounced.

"Do maids wash your feet?"

"Do they brush your hair?"

"Oh, I bet they brush her hair! It's so silky!"

"She's a Princess, she's *naturally* pretty!"

Before Evalyn could respond, Felicity wandered over, beaming at the group. "Are we interviewing Princess Evalyn?" She placed a hand to shield her mouth, however useless it was as she whispered, "Kalan is the only one allowed to question the Princess, since he's the one that likes her." At that, the girls whipped to Evalyn and giggled.

The Princess placed Felicity's words aside, even as her heart beat faster. "Sometimes my maids wash my feet. They brush my hair if I ask. You're all kind and beautiful in your own ways." The girls melted at Evalyn's response. "And please, call me Evalyn."

"But you're *Royalty*!" one commented.

Another slapped the girl on the arm. "Lizzie, who cares! She told us to call her by her name, so we should."

The girl called Lizzie turned scarlet and began smoothing her black hair. "Apologies."

Evalyn laughed, "No need for it." She looked around the camp. "Do you come out here every night?"

One answered, "Not as often. We used to, but after..." The girl took a ragged breath. "Well, you know..." She abruptly broke into tears.

Felicity sat, placing a hand on the girl's back. "It's okay, Jesi. Evalyn understands."

The Princess opened and closed her mouth. What was she thinking, questioning these girls, making them relive a nightmare? The others crowded around Jesi. Felicity gestured away from the fire, and Evalyn followed her into a warmly lit cabin.

Felicity said, "No one in Jesi's family made it through the attack. She took one of the greatest losses in camp. But she's strong; she'll push through. She always has." The girl brought them to a tiny kitchen table and sat across from the Princess.

"And you?"

Felicity shrugged. "I'm managing. It was harder at first. It took me weeks to accept the fact that Father was gone. When I did, everything got easier. I've tried my best to move on for the other girls. I'm one of the oldest, so they look up to me. But I can't be there for them if I haven't dealt with myself." She paused. "I know you heard what I said about my brother."

"You meant for me to hear?"

"I'm fifteen, not five," the girl laughed. "I knew you heard every word. Kalan was worried you may not feel the same, but I can tell." Evalyn swallowed. She assumed Kalan felt *something*, but hadn't yet pondered it. "Oh, it's so *obvious*! I see the way he looks at you when he thinks no one's watching. And you admire him, if nothing else." Felicity's brows rose, and she glanced at the cabin door. "I trust you, Evalyn, but as his sister... I have to plead that you don't hurt him. He deserves a love that won't break him further."

Not a second later, a creak sounded, and Kalan stepped into the kitchen. "What do we have here?" Arms crossed, he leaned against the wall.

"Oh, just discussing the plentiful wonders of womanhood," Felicity said, giving Evalyn a small wink as she left the table, patted Kalan on the shoulder, and strode out of the cabin.

The trek home was dreadfully swift.

It'd become usual for any spare sentry to open a door or escort Evalyn back to her quarters. At first she'd insisted without their help, but they were so politely stubborn that when a chorus of "Hello, Princess Evalyn," sounded before the foyer doors had fully opened, it was a habit to smile and bid them good nights.

As they rounded the corner to her bedroom, Evalyn slowed her pace. Kalan immediately followed suit. At her door, he faced her, smiling. Evalyn wanted to ask about Felicity's words—to stop her feelings if they weren't truly reciprocated. After everything that had happened that evening... she needed clarification.

"In the cabin, Felicity and I weren't talking about—"

"It's true. What my sister said."

"But you... you're so caring, with a life full of opportunities and so many other amazing people in your life. And I'm just... new and ordinary. I can't dance or sing or use magic—" Evalyn took a breath. "Why me, out of this whole Kingdom—"

Hands settled on her cheeks, the words on her lips dying at Kalan's touch. "Evalyn." It was a moment like in the forest, where she'd caught him watching his pack, his family—but he watched her. And every emotion was visible in the eyes that wandered her face. "I can't control what I feel. It's *you* that I want. Out of this entire Kingdom—out of every creature in existence—you've made me feel *alive*. Some part of me—" She placed her hands over Kalan's. "Some part of me is untamed. Lost. But with you... I feel found. After the attack, after losing my father, I didn't believe I'd experience true happiness for a long time." Yet he had, tonight. "And as much of a stuck-up fool as I am, I've never let anyone see this side of me—so vulnerable and open. But I don't want to ignore the joy I get from being with you. From being *honest and real* with you and receiving nothing but acceptance in return."

Evalyn poked his chest, smiling. Her voice was a warm breath. "If you're a stuck-up fool, I must be pixie offspring." A weight lifted off her shoulders as Kalan chuckled.

Then kissed her.

She didn't care if the sentries were looking—there was only *them*. The Princess leaned in; Kalan's hands wrapped gently around her waist. Calmly. Unlike her heart, which was going to burst out of her chest. A thousand sparks rushed through her veins.

Was this what love was supposed to feel like? So freeing yet secure?

She prayed so.

When Kalan managed to drag himself back to the forest, Evalyn was sure part of her heart went with him.

Chapter Twelve

Evalyn leaned against a pillar by her mother's cot. "Is she going to be okay?"

Elyse observed the Queen, admiration visible in the healer's gaze. "Eventually... I think she'll be better. Better than she is at the moment. It's only been a few days, but normally one would be awake and talking." Elyse's lips lifted. "Let's hope a little more time will suffice Her Majesty's exhaustion."

"This is unusual?" Evalyn inquired. "What about our Fae strength? Don't we have invincibility against lesser forces?"

Elyse tutted. "Although we can overpower a human in moments, we do have weaknesses—few as they may be, they're ones you'd do well to remember." Evalyn's stomach plummeted to her feet, but Elyse said, "Iron is fatal to Faeries; its mere touch burns and itches. It has metallic properties which repel our magic: direct contact with the metal causes loss of function near the wound, wholly stifling power usage. It's the most common method of death to Fae—besides other obvious, horrific ways. We can withstand a great deal, but we aren't invincible, your Highness. Our fates lead to death, one way or another."

Evalyn's hands trembled. "When the Braenish soldiers attacked me... could—could I have died?"

Elyse shook her head. "You weren't twenty yet, so your heritage hadn't fully manifested. But even underage, many effects from the iron remained due to the emerging Fae lineage in your blood. That's why your burning and scarring occurred." Tania fitfully turned in her sleep. Elyse continued, "We must monitor our own wellbeing. The Nemors may have been immortal, intended to provide eternal protection to the rest of us, but their demise turned the story. It meant a greater need for self-care for the rest of the species. Despite Primascul and Frimpen's promised longevity, they're gone—like we all will someday be." With that, and an abrupt farewell, Elyse left the Princess.

Evalyn certainly couldn't leave Tania now.

Hours later, she remained in the chair by her mother, leaning drowsily against a pillar. Her eyelids fluttered, and thrice now she'd slipped out of her seat from a lack of will to stay upright, but her exhaustion vanished with a murmur from Tania.

Evalyn was at her side in a breath. "Mother?" The Queen slowly sat upright, eyes drooping despite her days of unbothered sleep. Tania's lips lifted. The Princess gripped her hand, speaking gently yet swiftly. "You were asleep for so long. Elyse said with what you did, it'd take longer to restore your energy, but I didn't think it'd take *that* many days—I've been here morning and night waiting for you, not that I'm bothered by your rest, but I was hoping everyday you'd wake and everything could be normal again." Tania smiled a second time, but the expression declared feigned hope. "What is it?" Evalyn questioned.

Tania's features never faded as she replied, voice low and raspy. "I've been bedridden and slow-healing because a disease unknown to our kind has tainted my body. It's weakened my powers and energy, and will keep doing so until nothing's left. There's no cure, nor any treatments to help my pain or fatigue." Her hand brushed Evalyn's arm. "This explains many things, does it not?"

Evalyn opened her mouth, but no words came out. Tears escaped her eyes in silence. The girl's mother was dying, and there was nothing she could do to prevent it.

"Mags has experienced the passing of a Queen," Tania furthered. "I knew she would handle the information in a quiet and collected manner. Even my Keepers know nothing. They questioned, but I ordered them not to worry over my symptoms."

"Nickie, Serene, and Hali came to see you. Nickie said a prayer over you," Evalyn recalled. Hali was characteristically silent yet seemed upset; the Princess had gripped her hand with a smile—and earned half of one in return.

"My closest. The four of us have been friends since we were young girls," the Queen hummed. Meaning her Keepers would have had more years with Tania than Evalyn.

The Princess hugged her mother before she realized she wanted to. Her arms wrapped around Tania's neck, not daring to let go. She *never* wanted to let go. Tears spilled down her cheeks, in choking sobs that made it a struggle to catch a breath. "I can't do this without you," she gasped. "I can't be Queen. You're too perfect."

Tania stroked Evalyn's hair. "There's time for you to learn. And when my reign is over, you'll be incomparable to anyone in the history of Faylinn. You don't need me or anyone else to tell you how to do what's right."

"How can you be so sure?"

The Queen simply smiled and held her daughter.

Evalyn cleared the fears of her inevitable future by pondering the more simple lives of the common-folk. She imagined young children, their only worry whether they can watch the stars dance among moonlight. She imagined Fae parents with their lovers, hoping to secure a second of alone time by themselves, and the lives of other girls, focused solely on what abilities they may receive on their Bonum Vitae or whether the village boys will look their way.

Evalyn didn't notice Mags sit across from her until the woman spoke. "Wondering how different life could've been?" She offered a cup of steaming tea to Evalyn, who gratefully accepted it. The woman always knew exactly what to say; seemed to know adolescence better than children themselves.

The Princess closed her eyes, sipping the tea. She inhaled the sweetness wafting through the air. "I don't wish to be someone else, but often it's easier to think of anything other than myself. I know it's selfish; my life is a blessed gift to so many."

Mags watched the fire across the toasty sitting area. Sparkling crystals and gems, chromatic liquids in bottles, and inked parchment clustered in every crevice around the room. The quarters were more than that—it was a small cottage home, with multiple rooms linked by a cramped hallway down the middle. "Feel what you feel. Embrace it deeply and thoroughly—then use it to push through the troubles. Life goes on, and there are actions to be taken through sorrow and guilt."

Evalyn swore the woman could read her mind; Mags always knew what the Princess needed to hear.

"I didn't tell you about Tania's sickness at her request," the woman said. Evalyn nodded mindlessly. "She suspected there was something I could do. Sadly, we both failed at uncovering any cause or cure to her sickness. I've been trying to make light remedies for some of her worst symptoms."

Evalyn finished her tea. Mags gathered the drinks, bringing them to her kitchen. There was a small hum and a rummaging of dishes with running water, then the woman returned.

Evalyn blew a sigh. "What would I do without you?"

Mags smiled. "Dear girl, you would live on."

The trees swayed in a breeze. The sun peeked over the land, shining warm rays of gold. The Kingdom of Faylinn awoke steadily. Fae lugged about, no longer needing their wraps for a morning chill.

Summer was near.

With it, work and chores. There was more than the return of cooler weather to prepare for in the later months.

"Wake up, Evalyn." Her body lightly shook and Tania's voice sounded.

Evalyn jolted up in the bed. She frantically searched the room until her eyes fell upon the Queen at her side. "What is it? What happened?"

"Everything is fine. I let you rest late; you needed it."

The Princess steadied her breath and rubbed her eyes. It'd been a month since the attack by Braena—and there hadn't been a single whisper from enemy forces. Evalyn hadn't rested properly in weeks. Sleep was no longer a necessity, but a distraction—preventing her from protecting those she loved. The girl wouldn't relax unless they received word from Braena—to know they may, perhaps, back down. Surrender.

It was a foolish wish; the alliance between the Kingdoms was gone.

They were at War.

Her mother had sent the declaration to the King—ending their marriage in the process. She belonged to herself, and their Kingdom was free of the King's political clutches. For now.

The small council was hoping to gain reinforcement for an inevitable great battle from Ausor—the third Kingdom on the continent and Faylinn's neighbor in southern Liatue. The citizenry was composed of gentle, compassionate people, and the Kingdom was well-established although not as old as Faylinn, so Tania was confident they would support the possible demolition of Braena and Oberon Romen. The issue was getting through to Ausor before it was too late.

As for internal struggles, there remained no leads about the Fae injected during the attack at Evalyn's ball. They'd spent the past month in a half-slumber, stuck between hours of moaning consciousness and silent sleep. No one could talk to them, to try to understand the changes happening within their bodies. Their necks had since healed, but without knowledge of the danger, there was no way to guess what the internal effects were until someone set out to uncover the problem and find a cure.

If one existed.

"How are you feeling?" Evalyn questioned, slipping out of bed. She'd stayed in her mother's chambers since Tania had been cleared from the infirmary a fortnight ago. Evalyn never knew the hour of night when she finally drifted into dreamless dark, her body exhausted from watching over her mother. She always woke before dawn in a panic.

Something in Evalyn felt guilty for sleeping in, but a greater part reminded her to be thankful that things were steadily going back to normal. A decent night's sleep was evidence.

"I'm regaining my strength. The weariness has faded."

Evalyn could sense her mother's distaste for her condition. Tania wouldn't allow herself, nor anyone in the Kingdom, to believe her as inadequate. She was in no way or form weak—just a bit out of practice.

Still, the Princess had insisted her mother stay bed-bound until she could stand without Evalyn's hand.

"Come along, Evalyn. It's time I confront our home."

Tania's Keepers trailed them as they descended the grand staircase. Guards bowed low at their sight; a warm breeze swept their hair in the courtyard, where servants, sentries, and nobles wandered under the favorable morning sun.

The ride to Koathe was relaxed; the capital's gates swished shut as they unloaded the carriages and started down the Main Road. "We're here to go to the Citadel," Tania declared, shaking a leather pouch that jingled from the coins inside. "I have business—delayed due to my recent circumstances—with the High Minister and Elder Council that must be conducted shortly."

The Queen made a sudden left onto a narrow, cobbled road. The height of the multi-leveled homes blocked the sunlight, and a gale of wind had Evalyn tugging her cloak tighter. Ash-colored roofs sloped sharply inward into ridges; each window was claimed by beds of light-emitting florets, and overgrown, flowering vines lined every wall. A huddle of Fae children played in the pathway. Tania slipped three emerald coins into Evalyn's hand.

Instinctively, the Princess crouched beside the children, gown puffing around her. "Hello."

The children halted and watched her. One showed crooked, growing teeth. "That's a mighty fine coat you've got there. Are you from the castle?"

"I am. What game are you playing?"

He scratched his chin and threw a rock into the pile between their feet. "Made it up. New one everyday. Winner gets the leftover pudding-treat tonight."

"Well, I have another treat for you and your friends." She flicked the shimmering currency in her hand. The huddle gasped sharply, and their fingers scrambled to grab the coins as she held out her hand. When all three coins found an owner, the group scattered instantaneously.

The Princess straightened. "Why did they run?"

A pleasant smile lined her mother's lips; Tania's Ladies giggled from behind. The children reappeared with folks at their hips, streaming out of their homes.

"*My Queen!*" a young mother squealed, running up to Tania. "You saved our lives those weeks ago." She grinned. "We owe everything to the Crown. It's because of you, Your Highness, that my mate and sons are safe. Thank you for your coin." She curtsied deeply.

Tania brushed the female's shoulder. "It's because we're strong, and because we are united as a *Kingdom*, that so many were able to live through such a treacherous time. It's because of us all."

The Faerie nodded with glossy eyes. She curtsied again, returning to a doorway. The mate and sons she'd spoken of smiled as the Royals moved deeper into the city.

Again and again, they were approached at countless thresholds with gratitude. Tania conversed brightly with everyone. Some Fae cried in her presence; more begged to provide services or offer personal gifts in return for the Queen's visitation. It was moving to see them touched by her presence.

They reached the Citadel with onlooking folk in their wake. The Queen's Keepers followed up the steps, their faint chatter succumbing to the hush that enveloped the opulent fortress.

"Her Majesty occasionally meets with the High Minister to discuss the state of the capital and to make personal payment for his service to Faylinn," Serene whispered in Evalyn's ear. "He receives half a dozen sapphire pieces each year." The Princess gaped at the amount with the Lady. Where castle servants and soldiers were paid in common bronze chips or emerald coins, and the wealthier nobles with gold coin, a single sapphire piece could excessively support a lowborn family for a lifetime.

Advancing through the entrance of towering, wooden doors, Serene gripped the Princess' arm. "We're to wait while Tania attends to the Council. Usually we favor mingling amongst ourselves, but I think you'd appreciate a wander."

Evalyn lifted her gaze. The chamber was vast, the ceiling a dome of stained glass. The midday sun cast colored stripes of light across the stone floor and cream and gold walls. Pillars lined the edges of the round-walled fortress. Two sets of stairs opened on the left and right, leading below the Citadel and underground, to holy spaces of rest and worship.

"I would," Evalyn responded.

Serene smiled sweetly. "As I surmised." The woman locked arms with the Princess. "Hali, join us." Hali shifted, wide-eyed, before stepping to Serene's side. The three made for a staircase, the Queen retreating down the opposite one. Sages ambled up and down the steps, their shrouding cloaks sweeping along the stone. Shadows bristled the hoods, and shimmering-pearl hair draped to their hips. "No one has seen the face of a Sage. They keep their wisdom in the darkness of their faces. Even in the brightest daylight, they remain unknown," Serene muttered, close to Evalyn's side. The girl returned a wary look. "No need to fear," the Lady smiled. "They've sworn to exist peacefully. They dedicate their lives to honor and serve the Gods. Ask them anything, and you'll be answered—although not without a price."

They reached the base of the stairs. The landing broke off to hallways on their sides and a door at their front. Serene pulled them forward, pushing through the entrance to a room that stretched as far as her eyes could see—filled with aisles upon aisles of books and scrolls and Fae art. Candle-lanterns hung from the end of the shelves, lighting the path until it converged into a blur of golden color. Sages plodded through the aisles. Evalyn could feel the spirits of the Gods in the chamber, a delicate pressure at her shoulders.

"What kind of price?" she questioned.

"Anything," Hali answered. The Princess spun. "A Sage can ask for anything they desire as payment." The lightness in her voice was... haunting. "It depends on your questions. How many and what you ask about. How desperate you are for answers."

"Hali's right. If you dare seek out knowledge meant only for Omforteu and Deeam, you must pay. Unsurprisingly, many are willing."

"And the High Minister? What does he do?" Evalyn asked. Hali was silent; her usual self once more.

"He's the public face of the Citadel and leader of the Elder Council. Chosen by the Gods, he has the highest word outside of The Palace. He administers ceremonies, rites, celebrations; his attendance represents blessing and peace. The High Minister is a holy being, revered and adored across Faylinn. He possesses more than the Sages—all knowledge, and even glimpses of the future—but can only reveal what the Gods allow. A blessing and a curse, some say." Serene turned down an aisle, abruptly chattering about a petite sculpture. There was an eerie glint in Hali's expression, as if apprehensive of Serene's description of the High Minister.

Evalyn faced her. "Is something wrong, Hali?"

The woman's eyes darted across the room. She licked her lips.

"Hali?"

The Keeper sucked in a breath. She stepped forward, clutching Evalyn's wrists. Her hands were freezing. "When the blistering starlight fades, the right comes to fruition as we remain."

"Who?"

"Only we will remain. Feel the touch of our crusade; be rendered extraneous as we remain. *Only we will remain.*" Her voice rose to a squeal, and Evalyn's skin burned—veins of ice snaked around her arms. As swift as she began, the girl stepped back, emotionless and still. The ice stripes on Evalyn's arms melted instantly. "*Only we will remain,*" Hali whispered.

The Princess returned to the main floor without another word and her eye on the Lady for the remainder of the day.

Starshine flooded the Royal Library tower's uppermost floor through a cone-roofed skylight. Princess Evalyn exhaled a breath as she flipped a book page, and the candle flame before her flickered, darkening the scribbles in the title. Kalan had done the same ten times already.

"Why do you think The Door was created in the first place?" he asked from a table over, scrolls and books littering the wooden surface.

"According to castle maps, the dimensions of a room behind the door could, at maximum, hold three people," Evalyn returned. "If they stood back to back. But I don't believe it's just an old closet—I think ancient magic is involved, and The Door houses... something else. Something special. I'm not sure what, just that we haven't thought of it yet." She closed the book under her fingers. "But the librarian was right. Vynus is a pain to learn."

"I think I've finally grasped how to decipher between words." Kalan leaned back in his chair, lifting a scroll. He described the markings which he surmised as intervals defining a space between words. "It's not much; maybe we can figure out how many words are written on The Door."

"That's a great deal more than anything I know."

Kalan neared her seat and leaned against the table. He gazed at the moon, visible through the ceiling-window. "After we figure this out, what excuse will we have to be together for so many hours?"

"We have a dream, remember? To help the children of this Kingdom. To give them love and knowledge and homes." Evalyn smiled. "When I have the opportunities and resources, we can be undisturbed whenever we want."

He peered down at the Princess. "Are you ready to have those opportunities and resources?"

She swallowed the lump that rose in her throat. "I'm hoping I will be when the time comes."

"I never thought I'd be Alpha this young. If I'm decent, then you're going to be an exceptional leader." He winced. "I thought that'd make you feel better, but I expect I rather sounded like an arrogant prick."

Chuckling and shaking her head, Evalyn returned a handful of books to their shelves. Kalan followed her across the floor, trailing fingers along the stacked books. The girl rose on her toes, unable to reach the home shelf, but the Alpha was there instantly, placing the book in its slot.

Then took the remaining titles from her hands and sorted them back. "I have to return to camp soon. The evening patrol is returning and they have to check in with me."

Evalyn nodded as they met their candlelit tables. "Were Kye and Janson with the rotation?"

"Always. They spend the majority of their waking hours on patrol. They're some of our best detail units, so they have priority placement."

"How does Bre manage with Kye being away so often?"

"As mates, they have a constant connection, made stronger in our wolf form. Apparently it's a mental and emotional linkage; they can use their most intense feelings to communicate if need be. They're never truly apart."

Evalyn smiled at the fact. She wasn't sure about mates... but she and Kalan understood one another in a way that made her sure she could tell him anything and he wouldn't turn away.

"Have you had any... romantic partners?" she questioned lightly. They began their descent down the staircase.

"Before you?" Kalan replied with a laugh. Evalyn smiled, but his expression faded as he answered, "Truthfully, a couple. My favorite was my month-long relationship as a pup. We spoke only three times because she was too scared to sit with the Alpha's son alone for longer than a minute. Have you?"

"If you count mindlessly flirting with the only male that stepped foot into Kinz' cabin a handful of times before I left for Faylinn, sure." She couldn't withhold her blush. "I know: my inexperience is appalling."

"Inexperience determines nothing."

Evalyn blushed more. He clasped her hand as they slipped through the doors and traveled down the Great Tower. At the castle's ground floor entrance, Evalyn turned to him. "Is your schedule full tomorrow morning?"

His eyes twinkled. "No."

She beamed. "It is now, because you'll be having breakfast in my quarters. I'll have my handmaids bring something especially tasty."

Kalan didn't respond—instead brushed her hair behind her ears before kissing her left cheek, then the right. Evalyn laughed as his lips brushed her chin and her forehead and the tip of her nose. She wrapped her arms around his neck and kissed him fully.

The Alpha chuckled against her lips, and the sensation tickled her own. He leaned in for more, and her back grazed the framed entrance as they seemed to meld into one. Evalyn's fingers tangled into his golden hair, gently pulling him closer for more, an urge that he submitted to.

The aroma of pine filled her nose, and his lips were seducingly soft. Lightning flooded Evalyn's veins as they pressed into the wall. He brushed blonde curls over her shoulder; she hummed a laugh as Kalan's lips marked her jawline and below her ear, sweeping along her neck.

But at last they slowed, cheeks flushed and heated, bodies reluctantly parting, fingers dragging along any last skin. When a chilled breeze swept past, Evalyn opened her eyes. Although Kalan was gone, the Princess didn't stop smiling.

She fell asleep in the castle gardens. It'd been for less than an hour, but when the sentry woke her, she'd been too embarrassed to stay at the bench between the rose bushes and a hawthorn tree. Evalyn had essentially skipped there after Kalan went home, not tired at all but wise enough to attempt to restore her energy by relaxing among the flowers. Now, her nap left her ready for bed.

She strode through the wooden double doors into the castle, pace slow and gown bouncing with each step. She was a foot away from the Great Tower's entrance when a figure shot from the opposing corridor and into the center of the hallway before her.

Evalyn halted, heartbeat steadying as she recognized Walfien's uniform patches, then his hair, before he faced her.

A slice marked the Hand's cheek; the blood dripping down his chin was dark and fresh. He rubbed the back of his head with one hand, the other sat around his sword hilt.

"Walfien, what happened?"

Crimson dropped from his chin to the floor. The Faerie winced, "Tracking."

"You need to see a nurse."

He shook his chin. "Too many questions. I can take care of myself."

Evalyn tilted her head. The male's eyes were too unfocused, his words too hurried and excusing. He'd only hurt himself more. "Can I help you?"

Silence returned, but when Walfien entered the Great Tower, she followed. He stepped leisurely, yet the Princess had a feeling he was more exhausted than calm. They met the second level, and he guided her through a set of corridors until they reached a doorway identical to her own quarters. This was the hallway where she'd accused him of abandoning everyone after her Bonum Vitae ball. Guilt plagued her at the memory.

He flicked his fingers. A rumble sounded from the other side of the door. When he opened it, a wooden stool continued floating to a long, wooden desk on their left. A gray bed took up most of the chamber, backed into the right corner. Curtain-blocked windows sat between it and an empty wall. The room was bare, a contrast to his decorated and lively office.

Walfien silently entered the door beside the desk. When Evalyn entered the bathroom, he hissed against the water that he splashed into his face, leaning over a basin atop a wooden counter.

Evalyn tutted, clutching his wrists when he stuck his hands in the bucket of water again. "Sit," she demanded. "Let me help you."

He slowly plopped onto the wooden countertop. Bracketed candles in the ceiling corners lifted the shadows from his face, lighting the deep cut along his cheekbone.

She fumbled through the cabinet, tugging out a cloth and a basket of corked, finger-length glass vials. Evalyn opened one filled with pale yellow powder and poured it into the water. She couldn't remember what it was called, just that Beverly had once dissolved it in a goblet of water, rubbed it on a scratch on the Princess' ankle, and the pain had instantly ceased.

She wiped the blood from Walfien's face, then dunked the cloth in the water, ringing it out before cleaning the wound. "Kinz taught me about healing and treatment. The first time I severely injured myself was when I slashed my palm after breaking a vase in the middle of the night. She gave me a lecture on everything she knew about how to fix a wound."

He seemed to smile, but grimaced at the action. "I didn't realize how deep it was," he groaned.

Evalyn sifted through the vials, lifting each and smelling them—the oil was lavender. She dabbed the end of the cloth into the bottle and patted along his cheek. "You said the nurses ask too many questions. Should I be surprised you don't tell anyone about your jobs?"

"No one needs to know. Commander Praesi assigns them, but doesn't care what I do, so long as they get done."

The words were resolved, but something in his voice sounded pleading.

"You can talk to me, Walfien."

"I don't mind doing it," he replied after a moment. "Everything I do is for Faylinn, and I would gladly die for this Kingdom or Tania or you."

Evalyn paused her cleaning. "It is okay to be exhausted, Walfien—"

"Not when acknowledging it hinders your daily obligations."

The Princess sighed obnoxiously; didn't respond for long enough that the Hand looked up at her, and didn't take her eyes from his once their gaze locked. Her voice was light as she asked, "What happened today?"

Relief. There was relief in his eyes.

He rubbed at his face, flinching at his wounds, and said after a grumble, "Trackings like the one tonight... they drain me. Pull me from reality and pressure me to forget how to be good. Because she deserved the punishment that she provoked with her crime. She was riled and fierce and fought back, and made it a whole lot harder to remember mercy is an option." Evalyn inspected the back of his head—just a swollen bruise. His gaze had shifted onto nothing.

"By the time I got her to the dungeons for interrogation, I was someone I didn't know. I can't recall the questioning because I was too busy trying to sort the Fae from the monster in myself. Trying to remember that I'm doing the right thing. That I'm nowhere near as cruel as her, even with the torture I enacted to get her here."

The Princess touched his temple. His eyes focused on her. Came back to life.

"I told you before, Walfien. You're no kind of monster."

He exhaled a breath. Maybe he believed her this time.

"Thank you," he said. His feet brushed the floor at her sides as she leaned off the countertop.

"You trust me for a reason." She smiled. "I have to live up to such a dire responsibility."

"You don't need to go out of your way to do that for others. Especially me."

"I do for those who matter to me. *Especially you*," she said. He didn't respond, just swayed in place. Evalyn tilted her chin and wrung out the dripping cloth. She was suddenly aware of the small inches separating them—but Walfien cleared his throat, and Evalyn stepped away, brushing her gown as the Hand slipped off the counter and returned to the bedroom.

She didn't know what that situation was. What feeling had just clawed its way from the bottom of her heart and cried to be let loose. She pushed it far down. Far, far, far down.

Because Walfien was so much to her, and it meant he couldn't be more. Because he was her trainer and defender, Tania's Hand and her teacher and a perfect friend—and a brother to Kalan. The Alpha had essentially made their relationship official, so she had to set aside whatever *this* was. It'd hinder both her and Walfien's duties.

"I should head back to my chambers," Evalyn said in the bedroom. Walfien was shirtless on the opposite side of his bed, slipping off his boots. The Princess took his absent response as a sign and made for his door.

"Evalyn."

She turned. Walfien was a step away from her, and she quickly restrained from observing his toned chest. The pace of his heart locked her eyes to his.

"Thank you, again." He rubbed the back of his neck.

The Princess released a breath and opened the door. "Like you said—through it all."

Chapter Thirteen

Two evenings later, Evalyn strolled through the nobles' quarters in an attempt to relocate Mags' cottage-suite; her first visit to the woman's stay had been led by the witch herself, with the Princess in too deep of a stupor to pay attention to direction.

When she heard back-and-forth whispers around a corner, she halted, instinctively straining an ear to listen before her presence was uncovered. Curiosity lured her to peer into the corridor before resuming her cover. Hali Maytora stood cross-armed at the open doorway of some noble's chambers—a male from the opposing voice—but the argument was too rapid, too hushed, and the girl could make nothing out before silence fell—

Hali stomped in front of Evalyn, fury brimming her dark, red-rimmed eyes. No words would form on Evalyn's lips—all her body did was stand there, stupefied and silent.

"Don't you have grander tasks to do than spy on a Keeper of the Queen?" Hali barked, hands squeezing into fists around her thin, cornsilk yellow gown.

The Princess narrowed her eyes. "Don't you have grander tasks than sneaking around with a nobleman?" Hali stuck her nose in the air, unfazed, and smoothed down the edges of her brown hair, slicked into a knot. "Or have your quarters been relocated from the Keepers' quadrant?"

"Don't pretend you know anything worthwhile about this Kingdom."

Evalyn's eyes widened. "You know, you haven't granted me the kindest welcome, Hali, so I'd appreciate it if you joined me for a moment of amiability." Evalyn sucked on the inside of her cheek. "Look, I have no ill thoughts about your wanderings; just slight curiosity to the workings of my mother's Court. I *am* new to all of this, as you seem to be well aware." The Princess folded her arms across her chest. "Were you meeting with a suitor? Is he favorable?"

Hali's glare hadn't wavered across any of Evalyn's gentleness. The Lady gave no signal of answering.

Evalyn snapped, "You weren't nearly as quiet with your partner back there—"

Hali shoved Evalyn into the corridor wall. Frost crusted across the Princess' shoulders as she hissed, "You saw *nothing*, Princess." Something different than anger lined the Keeper's eyes now: fear. Terror, at Evalyn's words. Because Hali believed the girl had heard.

"If you don't let me go, I'm reporting you to my mother." Evalyn pushed against Hali's hold.

Needles of ice scraped against Evalyn's skin, even through her gown sleeves, and she cried out against the burning. Hali tightened her grips on the girl's wrists, and white clouds of breath brushed Evalyn's ear. "*Only we will remain.*"

Then the Lady was gone.

Evalyn barged into Walfien's office after a single knock to find him at his desk, engrossed in writing a table-length letter. He glanced up as she closed the door. "Evalyn." The corners of his lips lifted, then dropped at her expression. He paused his writing. "What's wrong?"

She sucked in a deep breath. "I believe Hali Maytora is involved in something she isn't supposed to be. Something sinister or dangerous or just... wrong."

"Why is that?"

"I found her leaving noble quarters... she wasn't overjoyed to find me listening. She grabbed me again."

"Like at the Citadel? She used her magic again?"

Evalyn pulled at the fabric of her gown, revealing raw, red skin.

He stood instantly. "This is unbelievable—attacking you, *twice*? What's her motivation?"

"I'm going to tell my mother. I should be going straight to the rest of the small council, let them uncover her secret and deem sufficient consequence—"

"No." He shook his chin. "Evalyn, I know this is outrageous, but did you think about the fact that declaring even slight rumors could arouse unnecessary speculation against Lady Hali? If her actions are harmless and she's just atrociously private, a false accusation could irreversibly ruin her reputation and future."

Evalyn eyed him. "I'm certain she's up to no good. You should've seen the way she jumped at me, Walfien. She was *terrified* that she'd been caught. I'm going to find a legitimate reason and divulge my suspicion to Tania, if no one else—"

Her rant was interrupted by a knock on the door.

"Come in," Walfien casually declared as he sat, documents and ink scattered around his folded arms.

The Princess heaved a sigh as a girl entered, clutching a folded note. She curtsied deeply to Evalyn. "This was just delivered to The Palace. I was informed to bring it straight to you, Your Highness."

Evalyn reached the Faerie in a second, accepting the note and sending her off within a breath. When the door closed, she glanced at Walfien, who stared from across the room.

"Are you going to open it?"

"Of course." She flipped the note over, and any thoughts of Hali's ventures vanished as she found the sender's signature. A black symbol of infinity. "It's from Braena."

Walfien stood, nearing her side as she scanned the contents. "What does it say?"

She lifted her eyes. With shaking hands, she slowly, hesitantly, read it aloud.

> *Your Highness, please accept my sincerest apologies for your losses. I hope you can understand the necessity of my experimentation. This is War, after all.*

She gave a shuddering breath. "What does it mean?"

"I don't know."

"Why is it addressed to me again, not Tania?"

Walfien didn't respond but trembled, eyes closing as he inhaled sharply. She gripped his sleeve when he stumbled, but not a second later, his eyes opened, alert and clear. "Tell me what you Saw," she demanded.

Walfien's mouth tightened as he shook his head, hair falling over his forehead. "It was just... terrible. Something terrible is about to happen." He turned to the door, but Evalyn caught his arm, waving the note wildly between them.

"It was Oberon. Whatever it is—he caused it." A pause. "Our *people* were the experiments." It connected as she spoke the words.

His eyes turned round. "You don't think—"

The office door slammed open as two guards rushed in, faces ghostly pale. They didn't bother with bowing or formalities as one declared, "The Faeries... the—the injured citizens from the ball are dead. All of them."

Evalyn clenched Walfien's arm. They slumped onto the sofa as the guards explained how it'd occurred.

"One minute, they were asleep—with nothing and no one able to wake them. *Weeks*, we've been working to figure it out. But suddenly every single Faerie was out of their cot, attacking anyone and destroying anything they could find. But... they were changed. Their eyes were black, teeth razor sharp. Their blood was darker than night itself. They'd turned into otherworldly creatures." The sentry gulped. "We tried to restrain them, but it was no use. It took an entire unit to take them down. Micka and Loatan and some folks who'd been visiting were injured."

"What do we tell their families? Everyone else who knew about them?" The Princess inquired.

Walfien said, "We tell them they passed in their sleep. The injections were lethal, and they stopped holding on. All Guard soldiers can keep this secret. As for the couple, and anyone else who saw or heard anything..." Walfien glanced at Evalyn. "This calls for a rare use of Tania's empathy. Making them forget the tragedy is the only way to keep the truth in." The Hand looked to the guards. "Aid in the cleanup, then take the evening off. Say nothing of this."

As the males left, Evalyn lifted the letter. "What about this?"

"We have to keep the Kingdom calm—they can't know we're losing this War before it's started. Tell your mother, then like the last one... burn it."

Chapter Fourteen

Five days later, Evalyn still couldn't get the letter out of her head. The Fae's legs trembled as she sprinted east across the rolling plains; her recent lack of exercise had taken an aggravating toll on her physique, and left her mind empty to worry-filled pondering.

The sprints were something Evalyn had done since her first training with Walfien—she'd endured them daily until a few weeks ago. Until the ball and its injected citizens and the King got in the way. Exercising was one of the few things she could fully commit to: the sting of wind on her face and freedom in her lungs. It took her mind to a place of calm and life; one she hadn't visited in a long while.

Evalyn didn't stop for a break as she reached the Mediocris Woods. She'd had to formally document the training session—including getting Kalan's signature—to manage traveling outside of the Palace, all the while sneaking around her mother's security measures, which had tightened tenfold since the Queen had learned about Oberon's latest message. Evalyn darted through the scent of pine needles and soil as the sun broke over the horizon, heating already warm air. She finally slowed, throat burning and soreness blazing in her legs. When her body no longer clung to fatigue, her vision lifted to the tall pine a pace away. Jumping with all her might to grip a limb, she shimmied up the trunk, skin clinging to bark. But she felt herself slipping, and without a foothold, the air knocked from her lungs as she slammed into the ground. The

Princess sat there, struggling to breathe, when a wisp of laughter exploded from her lips.

"It *was* rather funny."

She sprung to her feet, heart racing—Kye, Janson, Bre, and Kalan watched her, each smirking, although panting and sweaty from their own group warm up.

"Need some tips from the creatures of the forest?" Kye jested. He punched the air. "We can show you how a real man—or woman," he added with a look from Bre, "brawls."

She narrowed her eyes, but failed to hide the growing smile on her face.

Janson exclaimed, "It was her first try. Cut her some slack!" He slapped Kye on the shoulder, to which Kye swung for Jan, ushering the pair into a swing and dodge match. After a moment, they were off into the woods, chasing each other with howls.

"Spirits help them," Bre muttered, rolling her eyes and jogging after.

Kalan shrugged from a nearby tree. "Perhaps you need a different challenge."

"Oh, really?" She tiptoed forward. "What did you have in mind?"

His eyes grazed up, down, up. "Perhaps something a little more... interactive?"

"You're on, Alpha. Just remember you asked for it."

They circled each other, waiting for the first move, but his first step forth was so slow, so casual, that she was unprepared when he actually darted toward her. A punch to her side resulted. It stung, but he was going easy—his full power could leave her in pieces.

She returned to position. Kalan swung; she blocked, then sent a kick to his chest that forced him to the ground. He growled as he rose, and Evalyn tackled him whilst his mind was penetrated with annoyance—but he'd suspected it. When they landed, he pinned the Princess' wrists against the soil.

Evalyn scrunched her nose. Yet Kalan bent forth; his kiss was unhurried but passionate. She kept her eyes closed even after he pulled away. "What was that for?"

"My way of saying that we're going to be okay. Despite the chaos and destruction consuming our Kingdom."

Their lips reunited before they'd fully risen; Evalyn backed into a tree, hair grazing the bark as the Alpha's hands roamed her hips. He kissed her slowly, across her jawline, along her collarbone, returning to her lips when she let out a faint breath, and their legs entangled, bodies pressed against the pine—

Kalan reluctantly leaned away, palms flattening on the sides of her head against the tree. Their foreheads rested upon one another's. He took several deep inhales while she steadied her own heartbeat. In a gentle breath, he voiced, "You should return before we get carried away. Before others get worried." Disappointment saturated their presence, but he was right. Evalyn couldn't be out of sight for too long anymore. People would notice her absence, and panic was easily resorted to. No one knew what tragedies might strike them; the small council could only guess what extremes the King would pursue in order to attain the Princess, or otherwise force her to succumb to his bidding.

But she brushed Kalan's lips once more. There was no pain or drama with him. His hand slipped to the back of her head, pulling her closer, closer—

They broke apart, laughing. They couldn't keep going.

She'd taken five steps away when a crack echoed through the forest.

Every instinct said to run; to escape the woods. But she wouldn't leave Kalan.

A snap. Those were breaking branches. Rustling leaves.

Their gazes rose.

A dozen soldiers perched in the tree canopy. In less than a breath, the Faeries dropped into the space between them, the symbol of Braena proudly evident on their uniforms. With a shout at Kalan, they lurched for the Moon Clan camp, but the soldiers swarmed around, gripping Evalyn's limbs until she was forced onto her knees, writhing and struggling. Evalyn willed a punch at the closest Fae, hitting her mark, but earned a strike to the face that sent her to the ground in a breathless, shocked heap. Her face was shoved into the pine-needle strewn floor.

They smashed a purple, flowering plant against Kalan's cheek. Fresh wolfsbane.

"Stop! *Let him go!*" Evalyn shouted, digging her fingers into moist soil. Kalan hollered as his skin hissed, blistering welts forming.

The soldiers backed away. Kalan slumped to the ground, unconscious yet alive—but completely overtaken by the poison.

A kick to the girl's stomach returned her glare to the soldiers. One knelt down with a wicked grin as she sucked in air. "Say goodbye to your lover, darling."

There was searing pain, then blackness.

Chapter Fifteen

Evalyn first became aware of the distant pain in her head.

Then realized she wasn't in The Palace.

The girl rolled over so forcefully she fell from the bed she'd been on. Evalyn caught herself before fully impacting the stone, but soreness pounded in her body. However she'd traveled, it hadn't been a relaxing ride.

The Princess surveyed the room as she rose. The walls were a murky, blood-red; the cracked stone floor was covered in grime and dirt. Candles about the room were no aid to her vision, and the single, curtained window behind the bed: pointless for lighting. Evalyn neared a splintered, wooden door, gripping the handle and shoving with all her strength. It was useless. She'd expected it to be locked, anyways.

When the Princess shifted to the chamber again, understanding struck her frozen.

Braena.

Evalyn was in Braena.

In the King's castle, if the size of the quarters were any indication. The muscles in her legs melted, and she crumpled to the bedside, dizzy and nauseous and weak.

It'd happened so fast in the forest, she hadn't realized until it was too late.

She'd been kidnapped.

Through a nick in the window curtains, she detected a setting sun. How long had she been gone? After how long would her mother attempt to retrieve her from their adversaries, if at all? Countless citizens had been killed and taken by Braena, their minds enslaved, bodies used, knowledge exploited—there wasn't a soul in Faylinn that would allow the Queen to save Evalyn on her own. She'd be a fool to dare think a unit of the Guard would be dispatched. Faylinn wasn't prepared for the combat a rescue mission would likely bring.

Ferocious, hot pain throbbed in her head.

The Princess would have to escape.

She'd figure out how to reach Faylinn after she got out—first, the girl had to escape the castle alive. The sickness in her stomach settled into determination as she scoured the room—but not for long. She stumbled back at the click of a lock. The door slammed open.

The Faerie strode in with her chin so high Evalyn thought she'd blindly collide with the bedpost. Strawberry blonde hair swayed as she halted before the bed, perching too-long nails over the wooden frame. The tautness of her corset sucked the breath from Evalyn's own lungs.

"Well?" the Faerie inquired. "Aren't you going to bow or cry or something? Don't just sit there like an imbecile."

Evalyn scowled. "Am I supposed to know you?"

The woman gasped, "I would hope so, from my various feats! There *are* so many to pick from." She pouted her lips, but laughed, "Pellima Nomote, darling! The King's mistress, although he doesn't like to reveal so in open company. He's a smidge shy." The Princess stared blankly. Pellima stepped around the bed and pulled them to recline on the edge. "Look, darling, I know you're confused and scared, but everything's going to be fine. You'll fit right in, as soon as you get out of this..." She eyed the room. "*Predicament.* I'll talk with Oberon; discuss this living matter. And darling, when you meet someone," she patted Evalyn's cheek, "you're supposed to be as pleasant of a recipient. It's only proper. I've been *nothing* short of welcoming, hmm?"

Evalyn glared, mind transfiguring an insult. "Since when does the King dig into fledglings?"

Pellima's eyes darkened. "How sweet. He *does* admire the innovative wisdom of my youth. But the King has told me *much* about you, Princess—let's hope you fit in." She patted Evalyn's cheek again.

The Princess pried Pellima's hand away. "If you haven't realized Oberon is using you and will rid of you once his needs are satisfied, then you're the one who'll need to fit in before you're thrown out."

Evalyn swore Pellima's arm twitched, her hand lifting to swing, but she stopped as a presence interrupted their battle.

Neither had previously noticed the door open or the Fae standing in its frame. She wore an ash-gray uniform, a black ribbon cinching her waist. She tilted her head, and a long, black braid fell behind her shoulder, revealing shining accessories on her ears as the corners of her lips tugged up. She cleared her throat.

Pellima rolled her eyes. "What is it, stray?"

"You're being summoned." The girl crossed her arms. "And you're clearly wanted elsewhere." Her smirk faded. "So get out."

Pellima smiled and strutted over. She gripped the girl's chin, nails deep enough to mark. "You may be allowed to stay in this castle for your duties, but if I hear another *peep*..." Pellima released her hand. The servant scowled. "Well, there'll be one more child waking up as an orphan in the morning." Pellima slammed the door behind her.

Mindfully, the girl stepped out of its impact and stared silently at the wall opposite her. Before Evalyn could say a word, she approached the Princess, voice calm as she ordered, "Sit."

Evalyn did.

"I'm Luca. I know you're Evalyn. I'm at your assistance, but I have my requirements, so you'll listen to me when things must be done or we'll both face the consequences. We have little time to prepare for dinner." Luca entered the closet, reappearing with a long, dark gown.

"Why did Pellima say that to you?"

Luca stared at Evalyn. "Two years ago, I gave birth to my girl." Her voice quieted. "Damira: my secret child, forbidden for my traitorous bloodline. Pellima found out and, since then, has threatened me with our lives if I disobey her. I assume the reasons are purely taunting—everyone knows my own parents were killed for rebelling against the King in the Great Uprising." Luca paused; straightened. "I don't know why I told you that."

"I have no one to tell your secrets to, Luca. I wouldn't, even with the chance. If your daughter has a good life, I would never dare fracture that." The Princess held her stare. They both needed a friend in this place.

At last, Luca gave a miniscule smile. "Change into the gown. Dinner is approaching and I have to check for alterations." Evalyn eyed the dress. To accept a fraction of their culture... Luca huffed, "Look, I don't know why you're here or what the King wants with you, but trust me, you must do what he asks. Whatever you mean to Oberon and this Kingdom—it won't matter if you don't adhere to rules and standards."

Evalyn obliged, albeit grudgingly. The maid adjusted her waist, then combed Evalyn's hair into a knot at the back of her head. No further details, no jewelry.

"Thank you," Evalyn stated. Luca half-smiled again, and ushered the Princess down a dark hallway; few candles flickered under the low ceiling. The walls matched those of the bedchamber, but the floor was a dark, worn wood that creaked as they stepped. There were no guards or passing servants; not a single being in sight besides the two of them. It was deafeningly mute.

Luca's voice was quiet. "The basic points: never disrespect a guest, although you're partially one; finish your meal; only speak when spoken to; be on your guard—you're the only person who will look out for yourself. And no matter what—" They met a wide hallway, where a double-door resided at the end, its pristine condition out of place with what Evalyn had viewed so far. "—you mustn't attempt to leave. There are punishments harsher than death."

She'd heard the same about Faylinn.

But something told the Princess that, here, even death was worse.

"Remember what I've told you." The maid scurried out of sight.

Before Evalyn reached the doors, they flew open, sending her into a frenzy of maintaining her composure. She hadn't prepared for the brightness of the room; everything else was so dark and bare. Yet the dining hall was different. In no way did she want to compare this place to her home, but... the lightness almost reminded her of The Palace's Great Hall. Almost.

The chamber was an off-white stone and pale-timber flooring, the table a marble slab with gold kitchenware and glasses placed neatly upon it. A magnificent chandelier hung from the ceiling, hundreds of glass beads strung between candles.

A voice snapped her eyes away. "Evalyn. Come, have a seat. You're late."

Evalyn's body was numb as she forced herself to shuffle to the open seat at the nearest end of the table.

Opposite Oberon Romen.

The King of Braena.

He wasn't as she'd imagined. He looked as normal as any other Fae, save the contrast to those at the table. Where their skin was moon white, his tan was scarlet-tinged. The color perfected his outfit—a thick, navy cloak, lined with jewels and his Kingdom's sigil, sat over a tight-fitting, maroon tunic. His crown was an obnoxiously large and gaudy object atop dark, chestnut hair; a simple show of wealth and dominance.

Stark, blue-gray eyes curiously squinted at her, a violation of sorts; as if he could peer into her soul.

He possibly could.

Evalyn perched in the chair, hands folding across her lap, appetite gone. Despite Luca's warning, there was no way she could take a bite of the food before her.

"Meet our guest: The Princess, Evalyn."

She raised her chin as he gestured, the many Faeries around the table glancing her way—as if they were to take a quick look or risk provoking her. A wise action. A gaze too long and she might've broken Luca's first warning.

"You'll adjust to her presence," the King declared. "She'll be joining us from now on." A moment of silence, then small conversation broke out. She glared onto her plate. How long did he plan on keeping her? How long had it been already? She was torn between defiance and compliance; every shred of her being twitched with thirst for revenge.

Right here and now, unexpected and defenseless, she could attack the King.

If the girl was stupid enough. He wasn't defenseless by any means; it was common knowledge that his magic rivaled Tania's. Not to mention that such insolence would surely mean consequence—slow and painful punishment, if his past actions were any indication.

Evalyn picked up her fork.

If she wanted to escape, she had to keep up her energy. She'd eat and suffer, but eat and live.

How Kalan had suffered. The Princess already craved his warm comfort, his smell, his voice. As much as she ached to return home, Evalyn hoped he knew that coming here for her... it was self-destruction. He couldn't risk himself. Not for her. She hoped the same for Walfien. Her stomach twisted and knotted. Evalyn had failed him—she'd ended up in the *one* situation he'd forever take blame for. However impossible it was to save her, Walfien would feel at fault. Evalyn knew him too well to not understand that. And her mother. There was no doubt Tania would let anyone take the Princess without retaliation. They were at War, and Oberon just crossed the farthest line.

The fork clinked on her plate—empty. Good. One less thing to worry about.

Returning to reality, she grasped with alarm what was occuring. The guests began to exit the room as bustling servants cleared the table.

"But surely I can stay?" Pellima whined, hand grasping the King's.

"There are many things to discuss in the privacy of my fellow Royal," the King returned, tone allowing no room for debate as he slipped his fingers away.

Pellima pouted her lips, but her deep brown features transformed into glee as she stood. The woman joyfully kissed Oberon's cheek before strutting from the chamber.

Evalyn had no fear nor hesitation about how she'd handle Oberon. She wouldn't give him the satisfaction of being scared. He didn't deserve such control over her feelings. Being afraid was giving up—and she had plenty of fight left.

Oh, she was just getting started.

The door shut into place, but her stare was unwavering. "Tell me why I'm here, Oberon."

He tilted his head, yet his crown stuck in place. "You seem to have forgotten, Evalyn—I am *King* Oberon, even to you. Be careful not to forget so."

"You're no *King* to me."

He studied the Princess. "I'm rather upset about the disruption of my experiment; I was hoping for grander results. How are their families coping?"

Evalyn sprang from her seat. "Don't act like you cared about those Faeries for a *second*. It was all part of your plan."

His face remained expressionless at her outburst, yet a strong force, like tethered rope, wrapped around each of her limbs. The fallen chair flew back into place with her planted in it. Her wrists affixed to the armrests, legs immovable.

"I most certainly *did* care. So much so that I couldn't even wait to personally be in The Palace when I admitted their early Rising. A pity to miss, but I heard they made quite the show."

Evalyn's eyes grew at the concept of his magic, at the strength he possessed to use it across the continent, but her thoughts were on her physical predicament. "Release me," she demanded. She had no control over any part of her body.

"Why should I do so? I've received only disrespect from my guest of honor."

Her nostrils flared. "Let me go, *Your Majesty*," she spat, emitting as much calmness as she could muster. Evidently enough—she regained feeling in her limbs.

The King's chuckle was a deep, raspy noise that reverberated through the hall. "At last, I have your attention." Evalyn showed no interest. He couldn't know she was listening to his every breath—her own depended upon what came out of the King's mouth. Anything was necessary to relay to Faylinn. "What a plentiful assortment of things we must discuss! But first, darling, tell me: how vile of a father would I be to begin without first welcoming you to Braena? My daughter, home at last."

Chapter Sixteen

Evalyn's hands began trembling. Sickened heat coursed through her body. She was related to this Fae? This *monster*?

"You don't believe me." He stood from his place, slowly inching nearer. "You know that my words must be true. *You are my daughter.* You are the Princess of Braena."

"How."

"Only by a matter of twisting words and means. When I was with your mother, I glamoured myself to appear fully human. She couldn't sense a shred of Faerie in me." His eyes glimmered. "I did love her. Tania. Before I grew tired of following her around and having nothing to say of it." The King was halfway down the table. He leered. "So I ventured and founded Braena. We are an infant Kingdom, yet my citizenry greatly amassed due to my provisions of power and wealth. Even after two decades, Fae from Faylinn and Ausor continue to migrate for Braena's intrigue. After I gained my original following... I pretended to die."

Evalyn didn't want to listen anymore.

"Believe it or not, Tania was once a gullible and foolish Queen. She truly thought I couldn't be helped, and obliged to every word that my perishing body could muster."

"What of the service? Your body was buried. Everyone saw it."

"Glamouring a sacrificed body was nothing grueling."

As if the life of one was nothing but a strategic part of the game.

Oberon reached her side. "I deluded them all. I could start fresh—start my new life. This time, I had Ultimate Power. I was King."

Evalyn had never imagined to be in this place, but *this*, being a *part* of him—this had to be a nightmare. She was asleep, and this disgusting story was all in her head. "Why are you telling me this?" Something inside her caved open, flickering and sparking as it spread through her veins. Anger and confusion took her breath away—her chest was too tight, the air too thick.

This was real.

He tilted his chin. "You appear to be falling ill. Leave me—new chambers await."

Without parting, she exited the dining hall. Evalyn didn't pay attention to where Luca took her, as long as it was farther from Oberon. As soon as Luca guided them inside, Evalyn couldn't contain her dinner.

The maid summoned a pot, and Evalyn was thankful her hair was secured. Luca didn't speak a word when she dragged herself into bed and didn't move again.

The memories of the night haunted Evalyn's dreams. She sprung awake in a cold sweat.

"King Oberon requires your presence," Luca announced at the door. Evalyn hadn't sensed the maid. She shoved down her nausea and exhaustion; she'd push through the day and find an escape: her only hope of returning to Faylinn.

Luca clothed her in a black uniform that hugged her hips, and she gathered her surroundings. The new chamber was similar to the last. There was a wide canopy bed; sheer black lace draped over the corner poles, reaching down to a deep red comforter. Multiple windows lined the wall behind her bed, opening the quarters, but the chambers were no better.

Evalyn concentrated on the turns and surroundings this time as Luca guided her. The quicker she learned the layout of the castle, the easier she could find a way out.

The girls greeted the King in the center of a corridor. Sneering, he was unbothered by the Princess' glare. "Daughter! After last night's outrageous fit, I've arranged training. Perhaps the working of your measly form will effectuate your understanding of the standards of Royal behavior." Evalyn's lip curled, but she restrained her retort. He rapped a knuckle on the door at his side. "Asodu will set you in shape swiftly." Luca bowed deeply, and the Royals entered the room.

There was no way Evalyn could train with this male.

Asodu was a buff, hulking Fae, his head shaved and black eyes shining with malicious excitement. Wan skin exploded from his uniform. Evalyn would be crushed from a tap of his finger. Her practice with Walfien barely gave her a sliver of a chance of making it out of the room alive.

The girl gulped. Instead of isolating Evalyn in her quarters, the King wanted her to become strong. A warrior-Princess. But although the King was forcing her... this would help her escape. Knowing Braenish combat strategies could help Faylinn survive this War if she made it back.

When she made it back.

Oberon was a shadow in the corner of the training quarters; his eyes pierced the back of her neck. Asodu cackled. "You're puny an' weak. We start wi' little."

She could barely interpret his words, but straightened. The girl understood taunting.

He swung for her face, and Evalyn reflexively ducked, immediately realizing she needed to reduce her strength. Evalyn didn't trust Asodu wouldn't restrain himself if he knew the true extent of her skill.

"Tha' was luck," Asodu tutted, stepping forward.

Good that he thought so. After she predicted his next move—and the steps to deflect it, along with an ensuing counterattack—it took everything to surrender her defense and let his fist meet her stomach. The impact was worse than she anticipated. The girl flew onto the mat, clutching her chest, gasping for breath. Her panic diminished as air filled her lungs. Again and again, Asodu struck, and Evalyn let herself be beaten down. Every few moves she allowed a dodge or a jab to his side, but by the time Oberon spoke, she was aching and bruised.

"What a feeble thing you are! I thought I'd have produced something better." Evalyn shoved herself to stand, heaving as he added, "I daresay your magic may mitigate this... disappointment."

The Princess' chest seized again, and she stilled. She'd nothing to show. It would add to her facade of weakness... but she hated the humiliating sting it gave her.

Oberon tilted his head, smirking. "My offspring is no chorma. No, no, no!" He neared Evalyn, gripping her chin with one hand, stroking hair behind her ear with the other. "I could sire a thousand children and the last would still control unstoppable power." His expression changed. "Fix yourself before I must. You wouldn't appreciate what I can do to procure your magic." She jerked her face away, unshed tears burning her eyes. She wouldn't cry. He couldn't break her with mockery and threats. "Your real training commences tomorrow at dawn. Clean up for breakfast; we have special guests this morning."

The Princess observed the cutlery on her finished plate. No one had yet joined her and the King during their soundless mealtime. She was blank of expectation, and by the Gods' grace, felt deep in her soul that it was no one from Faylinn. The King would've made a grander scene.

But Evalyn didn't expect her human parents to enter the hall, shuffling with frightened stares at the guards holding them.

Her head whipped to Oberon. She hadn't thought about her childhood beyond swiftly passing thoughts; hadn't desired to remember the fragility and self-hatred that had consumed her for fourteen years, nor question why her needs were neglected like some savage creature.

Faylinn had helped her finally push away the last memories, but they all flooded back.

"My childhood was *torture* because of those people—"

"These are two captives of Braena," Oberon interrupted. Evalyn froze. "Tania thought they were a wealthy couple, far from human neighbors; kind and caring and longing for a child. She believed them to be perfect: exactly what I wanted her to." The humans shivered at the closing entrance. "The plan was to drug you when you were old enough. They'd leave you there, never to be seen again, and my men would do the rest. You'd awake to find my Kingdom had rescued you after a young life of pain, and we'd raise you under my protection and care." A pause. "But that witch and bastard of a Hand ruined your chances of being free—of being in your true home. Tania poisoned your mind and positioned you against me."

"What do you want?" Evalyn hissed.

Oberon fastened his stare on the Princess. "I've injected common prisoners with blood concoctions. These Faeries have become ruthless masters of death—the Sanguin. My army of them will be indestructible against any force." The King grinned. "If Faylinn doesn't surrender, if Tania will not bow... I will spare no one when I invade to take it for my own."

"You long for domination? All of your destruction and manipulation... because you desire to control my Kingdom?" The concept sounded even more naive out loud.

"Oh, but how foolish would it be to reveal the grand scheme here and now?" Yet his lip twitched. She'd pinned him. There was more to his plans—but they meant nothing if she could protect Faylinn and hinder his first step. "Like *that*—" Oberon snapped his fingers and a flicker of magic swept through Evalyn's curls—"I could command my army to rise and attack. And you understand my power; I think you know that Faylinn would, very swiftly, fall." Another flicker of his magic traced her cheek. "You'd leave it with such a fate?"

Evalyn stood. "Your first letter claimed you want to open The Door—and now you desire to overpower Faylinn. But it's clear you can't do either without me. If you attack, I'll be sure not to make it out of the crossfire. Where would that leave *you*, Oberon?"

"Clever indeed. But your claims lay idle. Enact any suicidal efforts, and I'll show you exactly why we Fae flee from Death."

Evalyn sucked in a breath. The King tapped his fingers against the marble table. "You're an adored, important face in Faylinn, Evalyn. All surely know of your absence, and I have no doubt those in power are formulating a plan to release you from my restraints. However... they'd never accept my terms of compromise, so the resulting choice is up to you. Join me in building this army, rule at my side, and I'll provide you safety and care."

She swallowed.

"Or," Oberon rose, edging down the table, "you will condemn your parents to death. The first of many casualties on behalf of your decision."

He was a finger's width from her side. Evalyn didn't know if she was breathing. These people had given her a lifetime of nightmares; a childhood of suffering. But did she have it in her to choose their fate? To as good as kill them herself if she denied Oberon?

"Please, girl, don't do this!" the male exploded. The Princess didn't budge. Did he remember her name? "Our part in this is done! We never meant to harm you. This was forced upon us!"

The woman began weeping. "Please, please. We're sorry! We're sorry! Negotiate, do—do something—"

Evalyn blocked out their pleading. Her innocence had long since been seared away; Oberon couldn't damage her in that way. But her people's chance at freedom lingered. There was a possibility of victory, however slim. For them... she could sacrifice this good part of herself. And hope a tendril of it remained to combat the aftermath.

She hissed through clenched teeth, "Produce another heir. I won't be your lackey."

Instantly, Oberon cast out a hand toward the humans, his gaze transfixed on her. Two prolonged gasps, then the slump of bodies meeting the floor. Something swirled through her veins, sharp and warm and heavy that gave her the strangest sensation of power, yet frightened her so much that it disappeared.

Oberon placed his hands behind his back and inclined to Evalyn's cheek. "I suppose we're more alike than I thought."

Chapter Seventeen

Evalyn sat atop her bed, knees to her chest.

Who was she becoming?

Luca materialized at the door, silent and stealthy. Dark, unbound hair draped over a shoulder. "You don't have to tell me what happened—you don't need to tell me anything at all. But you deserve someone to be here for you."

Evalyn withheld her breakdown.

The past day had been misery, and for someone in this Kingdom to care for her... it was more than she could ask. "I miss home. I want to see my mother and friends and the peace of my Kingdom." The Princess reminded herself what she was living for. Prosperity for the Fae-folk, life and love for the children. She could give the citizens considerably more—but not from here. "Braena is nothing like Faylinn. The death, the pain, the authority you endure..." Evalyn gripped the maid's arms. "Luca, we can't stay here! Let's take back our freedom!"

Luca gave a sad smile. "I know why you want to go back... but the King would have my head if I thought about leaving. Even so, there's no way—no safe or easy way—to get my daughter and I out of here. There's too many risks and complications." She gave an abrupt sigh; met Evalyn's gaze with a fierce one. "I know I told you not to leave—but for me and Damira... perhaps I can help you go home."

Evalyn rose for dawn training each morning, where she began loosening the block on her strength—although Asodu remained appallingly strong.

"No whinin', eh? A step above m'last trainee." The brute paced before Evalyn, whose arms were clasped behind her back, anticipating his move. "Bu' he does no more whinin' after I finished him." He grinned. A swipe at her face sent the Princess colliding with the ground, but she caught herself, jumping into defense. Blood trickled down her cheek; it'd hurt worse tomorrow.

Asodu prowled for her, but his hulking mass gave Evalyn the advantage. She sped under his swinging arm and to his rear, throwing a kick to the male's hip.

His body barely dipped. Asodu growled, "Think you can defea' me?" He shadowed her figure. "You are weak. No muscle. I win 'cause I am with power." She eyed the Fae's flexed limbs. The Princess would *not* become a full-fledged beating machine like this... creature.

A sudden hit to her chest, and she hit the floor. The girl stared at the ceiling for the second she lost her breath, but with a gasp, returned to her feet.

On it went.

She was pushed and shoved down—every one of his attacks forced her to the ground.

Yet she rose. Again, and again, and again. Asodu wouldn't steal her determination. Although she loathed the Faerie, she respected his strength. She had to be smart; use him against Oberon. Walfien was right: to defeat your enemy was to become your enemy.

Yet every morning, Evalyn would stand, barely clinging to consciousness, ready for the next strike—and every time, Asodu sent her away. As if aware she could push no more.

Luca was always in her chamber, ready to bathe and clothe the girl, with fresh meals and loose talk. The Princess looked forward to their conversations, where she could sometimes—*sometimes*—forget she was captive against her will.

Slowly, their pasts slipped out. Luca was from Goamar, a petite fishing village east of the castle—which citizens labeled the *Shadow Compound*. Barely a teen, Luca's parents left Goamar for the Compound in hopes of a better life—one where they consumed more than shellfish and saltwater. Their wishes ended there; her parents hadn't thought they'd enact the start of the only rebellion in Braenish history—one that would conclude with their deaths, and Luca in indentured service to the King they'd fought against.

Although the Princess grew to care for the girl, there was a greater focus: her gradually forming escape plan. Whether it be exits, guard shifts, or schedules, Luca had excelling knowledge of them all; the only disadvantage was time. If they stayed together too long, suspicions could rise—and no one could find out.

Days swept by. Evalyn didn't notice the Summer Solstice; couldn't participate in the celebrations in Faylinn. Every look out the windows was into gray sky and bare mountain. Heat, life, and joy, all a dream. But enough relied on the Princess' concentration that she didn't ponder the time—thinking about it meant wasting it.

So it was train, eat, scheme, sleep. Despite Oberon's insults and Pellima's taunting during meals, teachings never arose. So she was left with little to guess Oberon's real truth, alongside his desire for her partnership to topple Faylinn.

With training her only duty, the Princess finally let her restraint go—nearly defeating Asodu in a combat match.

He beat her into unconsciousness afterwards. To him, winning and losing was a poor mindset. Unless your opponent succumbed into nothing, a duel was far from over. But she didn't say a word. Evalyn wouldn't give him reason to further inflict his power.

Two hours into their session, she shook the fuzziness from her vision. Warm blood streamed down the girl's temple, but she lifted her chin. *Hit me.*

Asodu stomped forth, yet the Princess wasn't scared.

Not anymore.

He swung a calloused fist at her head; she dodged as the punch landed where she'd been. Asodu's arm rose and she leapt onto her toes, the dimmest of smirks rising to her lips. Evalyn had concluded his offensive pattern early on; it was moronicly simple.

She lifted her chin. *Hit me.*

He tried. She dodged them all, furthering his fury.

But when he marched forward so swiftly that she hit the mat's edge and stumbled back, her concentration was pierced. He picked her up, throwing her to the wall some feet away where she crumpled to the floor.

Her grin broadened at the pain, and that strange sensation returned from the dining hall. It flowed through her veins, an imbalanced weight of ancient strength and power. She shook her head; shook it away, too concerned with her attacker to desire to ponder it.

Evalyn had gotten under his skin and outsmarted her father's trainer. She cackled and spat scarlet. Her lip was busted and a swollen lump had already formed on the back of her head. The Princess leaned into the coolness of the wall.

Asodu snapped, "Ge' up. I am no' done with her Royal Highness."

She closed her eyes, content with ignoring him if it meant he might beat her into dreamless nothing, but another voice had Evalyn involuntarily tensing. "I believe we *are* done, Asodu. You're dismissed."

Evalyn opened her eyes. Breathlessly, she muttered, "Your beast of a slave is strong, I'll admit, but he's not the wisest."

Oberon said, "I'd recommend advice, in that case... but I doubt he'd appreciate it. You know what he can do to those he detests, especially when I permit him free rein."

She glared. "Threats don't make alliances."

He smiled. "No. Actions do." They stared at one another. "You have an hour to clean up and meet me in the Consultation Chamber."

The King left her seething and limping to her quarters.

Luca dressed Evalyn in a long-sleeved gown and combed her hair into a slick plait. "The Consultation Chamber is where the King holds conferences with the High Houses every few days. They mostly discuss politics, potential warfare..." She paused as Evalyn flinched under her hand. The dark bruise on her cheek stung. "Or extravagant social conflicts," Luca finished with an apologetic smile.

"Why does Oberon want me at a meeting? I have nothing to contribute to this Kingdom."

Luca shook her head, then gestured away. "Go along before you're late. It's down the hallway towards the East Tower. Take the first right at the double conjunction, then a left."

The Princess arrived at the Consultation Chamber no sooner nor any later than the half-hour given. A wide, oval table was crowded with Lords and Ladies. As the door closed, their eyes shifted in her direction.

She was stationary and unfazed. The judgments of these strangers meant nothing.

Oberon stood at the far end, a smirking Pellima at his side with an arm looped through his. "Evalyn, darling. Come stand with me." His voice rebounded through the room, and he outstretched his hand to the side in wait. She met his stare, unmoving until a tap of magic had her legs lurching into motion. Evalyn huffed as she met his side, dismissing his hand and crossing her own over the table. To her surprise, Oberon made no move to reprimand her disrespect. "This is my daughter, Princess Evalyn," he announced.

If this was the first the nobles had heard of her, they withheld questioning the King.

"Princess Evalyn *Impur*," she adjusted. The inclusion of her maiden name identified her as Heir to Faylinn, and she'd make sure no one forgot so. Oberon was silent, even as two noble boys mocked her, cackling. The girl scoffed, "And you are?"

The taller one scowled, puffing out his chest, "I'm Jacobi of House Fansole." He looked at his red-faced friend. "This is Huwer, son of—"

"Son of Lord Pol Dril, Your Highness." An older male stepped beside the so-called Huwer. His father, presumably, who gazed upon the boy with great irritation. "Apologies for my son's... discourtesy." Pol Dril was larger than his son, with a thick beard in contrast to the boy's near-bare head. He wore clothing of brown-gold and navy; most of the nobles were grouped according to the colors of the High Houses.

Oberon cleared his throat, a noise that echoed across the chamber. "Let us begin."

The discussion was frustratingly commonplace, consisting of three hours of tedious exchange between differing House Lords and Ladies and the King. Evalyn hadn't expected conversation about War plans or secret motives, but remained surprised to hear about crime rates, inter-House trade, and accommodation and employment for migrants. Her only notable observation was of the King's constant interruptions, where he rambled about how his authority or riches could clearly solve the issue at hand.

She tried not to fall asleep.

The Princess popped her hip to the side, legs weary and stance more uncomfortable as time wore on. What was the point of her being there? To show that despite the evil of Braena, normalities existed within the Kingdom?

Her thoughts were interrupted by a hand on her shoulder; they were alone in the chamber, other than Pellima, who smiled over Oberon's shoulder. Evalyn shivered with revulsion. "I hope this portrayed the reality of my home. *Our* home." The King stared down his nose at her. "Next time, you'll participate more. To the High Houses, silence screams ignorance and stupidity. I can't have the Lords realizing their Princess lacks knowledge of vital aspects of ruling." His fingers squeezed her shoulder. "Return to your room."

Although Evalyn marched away from Oberon, she hadn't a drop of satisfaction—because beyond the bitter insult, these meetings would leave less time for Evalyn and Luca to engage.

She slammed the door on her way out.

No magic responded. Evalyn stalked to her quarters, thoughts of nothing and everything weaving through her mind; how she might deter her father, how she could return home, if her family was managing well—but Evalyn didn't sense the presence behind her until it wrapped stone-cold hands on her elbows and slammed her into the corridor wall.

Chapter Eighteen

Evalyn's eyes broadened, shock overwhelming her intuition to strike back. In a split-second, the Faerie was an inch from her face, cackling as his grip tightened on her slowly healing bruises. She swallowed her wince.

"What's the little Princess doing wandering around the Compound alone? If you're looking for trouble, I can give it to you," he spat through crooked, brown-flecked teeth. She attempted to lean away from his hot breath, but met solid wall.

Scanning him, her throat closed. The Faerie bore a sentinel uniform, a longsword sheathed across his back. Mangy, gray-brown hair was pulled back, tightening the skin on his forehead and accentuating leaden, red eyes. "Stunned to meet the mighty Rouhs?"

Her mouth opened and closed. Evalyn couldn't think clearly enough to remember how to fight.

He jerked his head into a horrendous laugh. "Didn't think I'd get to repay you for my brother's demise, but here I am," he grinned. "And I'm gonna have some fun with it."

Dread enveloped her.

She'd never forget Ailfbane's face.

"*Stop*," Evalyn demanded. She dared a kick to his legs, yet he was a step ahead. The Fae struck her shin, almost sending the girl sliding to the floor, but she growled at the pain and stayed upright. "I'll tell Oberon of this. What he'll do when he finds out what you—"

He laughed. It wasn't the arrogance, but the lack of fright in the sound that froze her. "Oh, poor Princess! The King is overtly aware of the vengeance sought among his followers—do you believe he'll protect his defiant child from rightful punishment?" She squirmed. He inched his body closer, digging a knee into her hip. "What a shame to know he sent me to do whatever I please."

Evil Come Flesh, she realized. That's who this was.

Despite the horror coiling in her gut, Evalyn snapped, "*Get off of me.*"

It did nothing to stop him. A hand snapped the ribbon tying her plait. Blonde locks flowed over her shoulders, momentarily obstructing her vision. "Such lovely, Royal hair," he uttered, sniffing along its length from her scalp to the ends. She shuddered. "I know a merchant who'd pay nicely for some of this."

His grin didn't falter as he yanked.

She shrieked at the agony and collided with the floor. A multitude of stars danced in her vision. Evalyn was sure the Fae had ripped out half of her hair, yet when he released his hold, and she staunched her whimper before facing him, Rouhs was empty handed.

The sting at the crown of her head was unabating as the Princess slid herself from the sentinel. She hit the opposite side of the hallway and dizzily stood, but it took Rouhs three steps to reach her. Her movements were so restricted from the tightness of her gown that Evalyn couldn't react when he swung for her stomach. She doubled over, unable to catch her breath before the Fae shoved her against the wall. The Princess barely felt the impact over the fright from her lack of air—but just as her head felt near to bursting, she inhaled a thick, sweat-filled breath. The Princess couldn't contain the tears of relief that slipped down her cheeks.

Rouhs sneered at her struggle, his legs set around Evalyn's to lock her in place. In her panic, he'd managed to bind her hands with his magic—a cord of flowing, silver sparks burned at her wrists, pinning them to the wall above her head.

Without magic of her own, she was helpless. "*Stop,*" she muttered again, nausea crashing down. Her lips wobbled.

The magic restraining her right arm ceased. But when the sentry pulled up her sleeve and set her arm against the stone, lifting a jagged blade, she began shaking. That was iron. When he placed it to her forearm, sending blazing fire across her skin, Evalyn started screaming. Ear-shattering, high-pitched shouts for help, for *anything*.

But she was alone. No one cared to rescue her.

Evalyn was back in her parent's cottage, locked in the cramped bedroom where she'd spent so many years suffering starvation, loneliness, and despair. Not a single time had anyone aided her.

Saved her.

Evalyn understood with a start that she'd been unworthy from the beginning. That so many times, there had been chances for a savior—but they'd never shown because she didn't deserve one.

And she was going to die.

But Rouhs stepped back, the tip of his blade slick with crimson, and the Princess dropped to the ground. She'd stopped yelling and quivering. Stopped reacting. Although the sentry stalked off, he wasn't done.

There were two letters. B and R.

It was nasty, cragged lettering on her forearm—unless she wore sleeved gowns, it was visible to all.

The Princess didn't tell Luca how it happened.

For the most part, she tried to shove the memory into the same, far-away pocket that contained her childhood, despite the fact that nightmares—of her under a thousand blades, locked in place and frozen by their touch; of Rouhs chasing her down, determined to finish what he started; of the King onlooking as sentries took their turn to mark her like Rouhs had—stole most of her sleep every night. The faintest rustle of bedsheets against the wounds woke her instantly.

Evalyn put her time into everything else that formed her life in Braena—the only way to stray her mind from the terrors. She endured the hours in the Consultation Chamber, pitching in her thoughts—although each was swept aside—if only to satisfy Oberon. She'd rather endure noble sneers than more of the King's *punishment*. Training grew rougher with Asodu's increased motivation not to be defeated by his trainee; the Princess had to push her hardest not to be simply demolished.

It took time to remember that Luca cared.

Atop Evalyn's bed one evening, after a match of jokes, the Princess exclaimed to a laughing Luca, "Thank you for your kindness and care. I don't deserve any of it."

The maid smiled, but her eyes proclaimed her surprise. "Evalyn, you're my first friend in this place. You deserve *all* of it. And more." The Princess dropped her head; Luca clasped Evalyn's hands. "Would you like to meet Damira?"

"You—you'd risk bringing her here? For me?"

"She's never met a soul beside myself in her two years of life. It's far past time—and I want the first to be you, Evalyn."

The maid was gone before she could retort.

Evalyn beamed. She hadn't realized how starved she'd been of youthful joy. There was something irrevocably magical about children; about their laughter and soft flesh and innocence, unblemished by the misdeeds of their elders.

Banging and shouts sounded outside Evalyn's door, then a horrendous scream.

The Princess lunged from her bed, whipping open her door without a second thought. Her father stood in the corridor, dutifully dressed and groomed, one hand swirling dramatically in a circle in the air. Luca levitated in the air, arms lightly outstretched, sobbing vehemently but unable to pry a limb out of the King's hold. Blood rolled down her temple and dripped off her chin.

With his other arm, Oberon held a crying toddler. Damira wasn't moving either, but her deep emerald eyes looked up at him under long and full lashes, tears spilling down pink cheeks. Her hair was exactly like her mother's—shorter, but the same jet black in a plait, with a dress that seemed to be made of scrap material from Luca's uniforms.

The King stared down on Damira, and he blew a soft breath that rustled her hair.

With a *suck*, Damira disappeared into thin air.

Luca howled. Evalyn restrained from covering her ears as the maid shrieked, "*What did you do? What did you do with my girl?*"

Evalyn started crying too, even before Oberon responded, "I sent her to my military General to be dealt with. I've warned of the ruin that extra baggage brings to your focus."

Luca screamed and cried, her skin turning red from fighting against his power.

"You have a task at hand to tend to my daughter." He clenched his jaw. "I've granted you more than enough mercy after the contention your parents caused, so it seems you need reminding that my orders are final and foremost."

The maid dropped to the floor, knees crumbling upon landing. She gave another breath-stopping scream and Evalyn made to meet her side—but the King grabbed her arm in a bruising clasp.

"Leave her be. She'll come to understand my intent."

Evalyn's mouth dropped, saltwater disfiguring her vision. "You've *destroyed* her life!"

Oberon tsked. "No, I *fixed* it. As I am yours." Ignoring the maid, he said, "Come along; it's time you meet some friends of mine." His arm wrapped across her back, magic aiding in pulling the Princess away from a now motionless Luca. They came towards a strange, eerie wing of the castle, where the air grew stale and cold and dried Evalyn's throat whilst they descended never-ending stairs. Her sobs subsided; chills crept down her spine.

They passed through a metal doorway with far too many locks along its edge.

She gulped. "What is this?"

Oberon ushered her toward a row of cells. "These... are my creations." A sole wisp of fire formed on his fingertips, and a collective shriek pierced Evalyn's ears. "Forgive their attitudes. They've been extensively undisturbed in their darkness."

The Princess shoved away the chills threatening to consume her body. She could only see shadows.

Again, that unfamiliar power surfaced, as if in response to the hidden creatures. It heated her bones, flowing between her limbs, but left a sharp ache in its wake. The Princess wiggled her fingers anxiously, as if it would drip from her fingertips and dissipate into thin air. With a quick inhale, the feeling vanished, along with the pain and pressure on her chest.

"The original concoction was made with my blood, of Fae power and magic, and the blood of a foul beast, which enacted the turning. I housed the injection in a host body, allowed it to simmer and rest, and there formed the first Sanguin. Its venom can turn any being into one of its kind. Once tinged by it, the host will succumb to wakeless sleep, constantly Changing, until my power enacts their Rising." A chorus of thrumming hisses rose, then deafening silence.

Evalyn bit out, "I suppose your death would then equate to theirs, too?"

Even the flames from Oberon's fingertips couldn't defrost the stare he returned her. She couldn't determine the truth of her speculation. He went on: "When a Faerie is turned, it begins slowly. Their blood alters, then the physicalities form; over time, the Changing strengthens until they're as I want: invincible, unstoppable, and consensual to my every command."

"That's why you sent the letter. You'd woken the citizens."

"Such a wise inference," the King hummed. His fingers drummed on her shoulder blade as he jerked his head to the cell. "Unless I use my power to staunch their own, they will kill until they are killed. But you'll find that no one can get close enough for a fight before they meet their end."

"Death is inevitable for all creatures. Including *you*."

A chuckle. "Even Death fears me, darling. The question is..." He faced her. "Do you?"

He shoved Evalyn into the cell bars, the girl's face smashing against rough, freezing metal.

The force holding her against it—Oberon's magic or his own hand, she couldn't tell—disappeared as the reek of the Sanguin flooded her nostrils. She jerked back when it lunged for the spot where her face had been.

She realized her mistake too late.

Another pulled Evalyn against the bars at her back. Thick, pale-white claws gripped her upper body, marking her shoulder in deep, fine slices. The Princess cried out, throwing herself as far away from either cell as she could manage, whilst searing pain mingled with the blood dripping down her front.

Looking back at the cell, she glimpsed the monster's face.

Evalyn found its eyes first—wide, depthless, and not a shred of white within them. The Sanguin was human in shape; his skin was gray and ancient, with armor of dangling chainmail over a thin jacket of fabric that defined the creature's skeletal frame. It had no hair, and his snarl showed a row of razor canines. The claws that'd marked her were inches-long and blade-sharp, clacking against stone as it slunk for Evalyn on all fours.

She gagged and slid towards the exit.

Her father's face was wholly empty at her fear.

Rouhs was right.

A flick of the King's hand had the Princess involuntarily snapping her eyes to the creature, her body immobile as it neared the cell's edge closest to her.

The Sanguin was her last memory before she collapsed.

Evalyn woke to scorching pain. Her head pounded and she moaned as she rolled over, but a hand shoved her down. The Princess' eyes fluttered open to her candle-lit bedchamber.

Luca leaned over, pale and sickly-green but holding a cold, wet cloth to the Princess' head. Healing amidst her grief and anger.

Evalyn broke into tears. "I'm sorry," she exclaimed, voice cracking. "I'm sorry."

The maid shook her head.

"He will pay," Evalyn forced out.

Luca straightened; swallowed. "A guard brought you back, bloody and unconscious. The King ordered you to be patched up and ready to return to work in a day's time."

Evalyn sucked in a breath, calming her sobs. She groaned as she forced herself to sit; the thought of training in her state was unfathomable. Her shoulder seared in pain and body burned, aching *everywhere*.

"I stitched your wound," Luca added. "You need to rest if he expects you back so soon." No questions about her location or what had happened. There was only one thing on the woman's mind: she was a mother no more.

Luca retrieved her belongings and slept in the bathing chamber.

Her sobs told Evalyn neither of them slept that night.

It took another two and a half weeks before the plan was concluded. The Princess rarely saw Luca outside of dressing; it didn't help their efforts that neither of them slept more than a few hours each night. She had a feeling their cries kept each other up even more than their nightmares.

But new ones haunted the Princess—in addition to those about Rouhs. And worse than her childhood fears of being left in the cold snow, alone in a pine forest. Those were bedtime tales in comparison.

Instead, she saw a Sanguin in her bed chamber, crawling and hissing until it was at her throat, claws impaling her cheeks; herself in pitch black, the sounds of the creatures filling her mind before jumping at her from every direction, tearing her apart; Luca and Damira feet before her, joyful and dancing until the monsters snatched them into darkness, their screams ending abruptly.

Evalyn woke drenched in sweat the night of her escape, gasping roughly as she threw the blankets and sheets from her body. She endured a shockingly cold bath until she trembled, then prepped a boiling one—but the Princess couldn't rid of the Sanguin's stench and its sour breath; the sickening touch of Rouhs on her skin; Luca's cries and Damira's laughter.

It'd been the same for a fortnight. She stalked back to bed feeling no less unnerved by her nightmares than before, curled among pillows until Luca arrived.

It was time to return home and end the wrath of this King.

Faylinn would win this War.

She would win this War.

Evalyn stripped from her night clothes and layered on the sentry uniform; Luca stepped into the bathing room, silently closing the door. They gripped each other tightly. "I *promise*, I will find you again," Evalyn whispered. "You'll come to Faylinn, and you'll have quarters next to mine and we can enjoy the rest of our lives away from this place. We'll rebuild what we've lost. I promise." Her eyes burned.

"Just make it home." Luca's quiet voice broke as tears slipped down her cheeks. Evalyn pulled her friend into a final, firm embrace, then steadily made way to her door frame.

Time was of the essence. The Princess had to go.

"I don't want to see you—" Luca pleaded, "—until the King is dead."

Evalyn nodded.

Luca headed down the hallway as planned. Evalyn turned left at the opposite end, towards the south-eastern exit; towards freedom. The maid was right: no guards were stationed until she neared the main gate. Every step closer made her heart pound quicker.

Two sentries paced along the ends of the central corridors that opened into a large, circular foyer. Counting the exact half-hour as instructed took a lifetime, but on cue, the guards headed to their next shift, leaving the third one slumped against the gated entry, eyes closed and breathing even.

The Princess paused her own breathing as she slipped past him and onto the cobbled pathway. There was one last sprint out of the sight of the castle's guard towers and into the mountains for protection, then she was gone. Safe. On her way home.

With a glance behind, to Luca somewhere in the castle, Evalyn began running. She'd have to be a shadow not to be spotted. After her pain and struggles, it hit harder than Asodu that she could leave everything behind in a matter of minutes. It'd been so easy.

The girl sucked in a breath and increased her pace—but a sentinel appeared in her path with a grim smile.

"King Oberon will *love* to hear of this," he chuckled. "To the dungeons, Your Highness." Before she could react, he slammed an elbow into her chest.

Chapter Nineteen

Evalyn didn't know how long she'd been there.

Hours, days... weeks.

Her perception of time was lost, along with any chances of seeing Faylinn again. She knew her fate: rotting in this dungeon before Oberon ever considered freeing her.

The chamber was different than in Faylinn—different from the cells housing the Sanguin. Evalyn's wrists and ankles were shackled, the latter chained to a cold, rocky floor and the former embedded in a large, stone pillar at her back in the center of the dungeon. No magic—no visible magic—imprisoned her. Four mounted candles burned high in the corners, barely allowing Evalyn to see well enough to take in the surroundings.

She was, unsurprisingly, alone. Considering Braena's proclivity for threats, perhaps the fear of Oberon was enough to maintain low citizen crime. But for those who had done wrong—they were likely Changed.

Was she next?

Chains and manacles drenched the walls, the ground spotted with dark, dried substances—she knew without the metallic stench it was blood—and a lingering hint of decayed flesh and bone pervaded the air.

Evalyn couldn't guess why the plan had gone awry; how she hadn't sensed the sentinel. But it was too late to ponder her escape. She'd failed, and was stuck in here with her thoughts to haunt her.

But they were better than her visitor.

The King of Braena stepped into the dungeon with a sniff of the air. Evalyn silently cursed him.

He took an eternal pause. Observed the chamber. Then, slowly, "My daughter? Attempting to desert her Kingdom? Her own family? I didn't believe it at first. I never trusted you, nor did I think you'd want to stay here under your own will... but I wouldn't have thought you so foolish." He twisted his fingers; Evalyn barely contained her flinch. In here... she was well aware of her powerlessness. "Oh, don't cower, darling. Those are the reflexes of subjects—not the Royal Princess."

She pulled herself to stand as high as she could, and spat at his feet.

He beamed, and the crown atop his head shifted. He punched her face so forcefully that her neck snapped to the side. If Asodu's hits taught Evalyn anything, it was that such a strike would leave a weeks-long mark. She shoved aside the throbbing burn and blurred vision.

"Have you not yet grasped your inferiority?" Oberon swung again, this time a punch to her stomach. But not with his hands—with magic, a phantom limb he could contort into any weapon he desired. "You say I'm *nothing*." A kick to her shins. "Yet I am the absolute rule of this Kingdom. Without me, Braena would resort to chaos, descending to poor folk and youth as their authority. They would, perhaps, attack Faylinn with squandered hope of gaining power, thus fabricating a battle ending in atrocious losses for both sides." A tightening in her chest—her lungs. "I don't think I'm the reason they live and thrive. I *know*."

A minute passed.

Her body panicked, face blueing and chest twitching as it longed for air.

The pressure released.

Evalyn inhaled quickly, sharply. "Try... again." She huffed a laugh; everything ached. "A few nicks doesn't mean I'm broken. I will continue pushing for Faylinn because they kept pushing for me, and I'll do it until there is nothing left *to* push. So try again."

The King stared. "Challenge accepted."

There was a flowering weed in a crack on the floor. Just a foot to her right, the yellow petals sprouted from the center like rays shooting from the core of the sun. The stem was a twisted, knobbly thing, with leaves too big for the plant to carry, and it casually drooped over, yet remained standing. Defying the law of nature as if saying, *I can survive. I will make it.*

Evalyn didn't know how, seeing as it was stuck in this dungeon with her, rotting and starving and without sunlight nor rain, but at least she had company. The girl dipped her chin to the weed, head throbbing at the motion, and leaned against the pillar behind her.

Laughter outside the door jolted Evalyn—she'd fallen asleep. By the time she willed her eyes open half an inch, Rouhs was a foot in front of her, scarlet irises drilling into her own.

"Didn't I warn you, Princess?" he drawled. Strands of hair clung to sweat droplets on his forehead. "I see you're too repelled by my presence to respond."

He wasn't wrong. But her jaw was too swollen to move, and she was too stiff, too weak, to bother trying. The Faerie leered at her silence. When he sprung for the girl and forced her to stand, the sound came out.

"*No.*"

Rouhs cackled. Humid breath brushed her face. "Didn't I claim to love my fun?" He traced a finger down her bruised cheek, leaving a stinging ache in its stead.

"*Don't touch me,*" she hissed, pulling on her shackles. Each word shot lightning through her jaw.

"A challenge indeed." Rouhs stroked a hand down her arm.

Evalyn's legs buckled. Her father had ordered this. She'd essentially asked him to.

Try again.

Challenge accepted.

Rouhs clicked his tongue. "Ailfbane didn't favor ones like you. Luckily, I prefer the resistance in my females. What a fitting turn of events for his fate to be in your hands... and yours in mine." The Princess tried to shove Rhous away as much as she could, squirming and squealing under his hold. But his magic wrapped around her chains, bridling any of her remaining self-control.

Again, she was vulnerable.

She knew her nightmares were about to become reality.

Rouhs shifted forward. "How'd you kill him?" The Princess shut her eyes—anything to control her fright. "Did my brother suffer? Or was it quick? He made his end grand, I'm certain. He always had a flair for dramatizing his missions." Sharpness traced the curve of her ear, a thin stream of warmth and wet following its path. In his bind, she was more powerless than the child in that forest.

He sniggered and groped her arms. She let out a harsh, pained scream, "*Get away—*"

"You're an exciting one, aren't you?" Rouhs declared, dragging nailed fingers down her side, slicing through tunic and skin.

She resisted the urge to sink to the floor, and instead blindly struck, slamming her forehead into his. He stumbled back as they regained their composure. Fresh, hot tears slid down the Princess' face and the male shook his head, scowling. Pink already marked his face, a sure match to the one she felt on her own.

He snarled, "My brother didn't have the choice—to live. Though I knew his ambitions would grant him a premature end, you can never really prepare for the day your last family member doesn't return." If he was anyone else, Evalyn might've pitied him. But not this male. She had no sympathy for his loss. "King Oberon won't let me kill you, but I pondered doing so. You took Ailfbane from me; how perfect that I could take you from the Kingdom you so dearly adore. But death would be too gentle a gift. Putting you on its edge—making you wish you were dead, only to withhold it… oh, it sounds much more wonderful than definite demise."

All of this for a stupid, wicked revenge story.

Evalyn dared a glance to the dungeon door as steps sounded.

"You still believe someone is coming for you, after all I've advised!" Rouhs guffawed. A hand gripped her chin, tugging Evalyn's face to his. She groaned as he squeezed her purple skin. "Go ahead. Yell. Shout with that burning fire inside. It won't make a difference."

He was right. The girl had already tried.

Yet when he lifted his fingers, his magic raising her forearm, Evalyn's cry was harsh enough to momentarily pause Rouhs. But he laughed and continued, and that irregular dagger appeared from nowhere whilst he tore the fabric from her limb. The since-scarred markings still ached at the slightest touch, and the Princess shook when he gripped her wrist. With a burning and shredded throat, all she could do was take wet, gasping breaths.

She shoved aside her exhaustion to make a last plea, to bargain or ask for any alternative means, but Rouhs scratched down her thigh, scarlet soaking the servant trousers, and pain took over any conscious thought.

Iron pierced her skin.

The Princess lost whatever shred of dignity she had left and began crying once more, uncontrollably and wildly. She'd never felt a pain like it—as if her body would simultaneously burst into flames and freeze from the inside out. He pressed against her, clutching her forearm tighter to moderate her movement.

Everywhere—she couldn't get rid of his stench, of his magic and hands and the blade's sting everywhere on her skin.

Minutes, weeks, decades passed as Evalyn was consumed in splintering ache. She was sure her skin was liquid, melting off her bones and flooding the dungeon; her insides had disintegrated and she was going to fade into the wind as nothing more than ashes. Gods, she wished she would—more than anything in existence, she just wanted the pain to stop, wanted to forget about her father's cruelty and this brewing War and plummet into the dirt as fuel for the next Faerie to finish what she couldn't. This torment was what she'd inherited as Liatue's wretched, prophesied hope—

But she didn't want to be a leader anymore. Evalyn screamed for him to *end it, end it, end it,* because she didn't want a single thing except for this suffering to stop, for her life to be over—

The dagger clattered into Rouhs' sheath.

Her arm fell to her side, numb, the damage drenched in crimson from her elbow to her fingertips, a never-slowing flow.

Rouhs smiled. "It seems I've found my new toy."

He strode away, advancing to the exit, and saltwater trailed down Evalyn's face.

The Fae turned back, his irises staining every thought in her head. "I don't think I'll be so neat next time." When he closed the door and her magic binds released, the Princess slumped to the floor, empty.

Chapter Twenty

Broken.

It's what he carved into her skin, scarlet and blistered, deep and uneven and disastrous.

The Faerie crouched against the stone pillar at her back. She was tattered and used and worthless—her father had outdone himself.

Hours later, Rouhs' damage was wholly unabated. Evalyn grimaced at the swollen bruises dotted along her body, at the cuts and scratches she hadn't felt in the moment. Her shouting and crying hadn't aided her weariness, yet Evalyn did everything to stop unconsciousness from taking over. The only time it did, her dreams were the entire incident played on repeat, every one of Rouhs' actions magnified. She awoke weeping in a shivering ball, crying out as she pulled her arm from underneath her side. Red pooled the floor; marred every inch of her pants. She tore off what clean fabric remained of her tunic and wrapped the wound tightly.

The tremors were nowhere near subsiding when Evalyn spotted a source of light behind the exit. Footsteps and grunting echoed outside the door, along with the slow, heavy sound of a dragging figure. Undoubtedly a body. She wondered what kind of culprit had earned housing in this hellhole with her.

But Evalyn stared, immobile and speechless, as sentries unlocked her door and Kalan Lupien was thrown towards her, his body slamming into cold stone.

"Caught him sneaking about the corridors. Nice try, wolf." The guards cackled, sealing the door shut behind them.

When her eyes burned from lack of blinking, another part of her cracked.

The world crashed onto her shoulders and she sprang forth, pulling on her cuffs to grasp his clothes, struggling to lift him close. The girl let out a shuddering sigh at the faint pump of a pulse.

His eyelids fluttered and he groaned.

"Thank the Gods," Evalyn breathed. She tore a strip of cloth from her tunic and wiped at the mess of his wolfsbane-induced blisters. Kalan hissed, flinching to sit before he shifted and took her in—then flung himself onto the Fae.

"I'm so sorry. I tried to get you out of here." His voice trembled in her ear. "*I tried.*"

She pulled away, restraining a grimace and attempting to ignore the flames across her entire body. "Why?" Her voice rasped. "Why would you risk so much?" Despite the utter solace of seeing him alive and speaking... "I had a plan, Kalan. This wasn't how it was supposed to work. You could've *died.*"

"The small council spent weeks formulating a plan, too. The platoon was taking an eternity to round up since so few volunteer soldiers wanted to journey to Braena, and the Conclave was adamant about each of their own proposals having the most secure route. Of course, all were completely different." He rubbed his face with a groan. "Tania had called on a mass council—a stupidly vast amount of voices, but the Conclave was *also* adamant about assistance and additional input. After two months without you, *two months* knowing you were in Oberon's grasp... I couldn't stay. I left alone nine days ago—I wasn't going to put the pack into a position to choose to help me or not, but I wasn't going to leave you here and wait for backup that might've taken weeks longer. It's not private knowledge—what this place does to people."

She leaned away as she recalled what it had done to her. The Princess cleared her throat, lifting her chin. "I've handled it." Thus began the construction of her facade. Unscathed and safe. Internally, at least, since her physical wounds were on clear display. She put a finger in his direction. "But *you* can't barge in thinking you're invincible, Kalan."

He gripped her hand. She bit her tongue to staunch the cry in her throat that rose at his touch, at the throbbing in her wrists. "I know I'm not. But you eased me from the verge of a dark place, Evalyn. After the attack on our clan, Paiton's falling... I had this aching, gaping wound inside that I thought would remain perpetually hollow. And after a lifetime of believing I'd never live up to the Delta legacy, I had a taste of hope when *you* believed in me. So I couldn't lose you. Not after I'd finally found myself." There was apology in his eyes... but something else, too.

She bit her lip, words unable to rise above a whisper. "You have a life to live, though, Kalan. There are so many people that want you safe, and need your leadership and care. You can't just throw everything away for me—"

"'I'm in love with you," he interjected, voice calm but breathing heavy. "That is why I traveled to Braena and attempted to rip you from its clutches, and I will be forever indebted to you for my failure. But I love you, Evalyn Impur, and there was nothing anyone could've done to stop me."

Rouhs prowled into the room, sneering; Pellima Nomote backed him, hips swaying as she gasped, "What a *heartfelt* confession!"

Evalyn froze; tightened her grip on Kalan and mustered every ounce of hatred she had into the glare she returned to the pair. *"Do not touch him,"* she snarled.

Rouhs laughed. "As if you have a say!" Evalyn cried out as he dragged the Alpha along the floor and to the wall across from her. With the Faerie's magic, cuffs slithered around Kalan's limbs, lifting and chaining his body upright to the stone. The Alpha sucked in a breath, coughing and gaping.

"How sweet it is, the healing of young love," Pellima purred. "Too bad you're unpracticed with the art of poison resistance. Maybe, if you had been, you would've withstood your capture and helped your sweet, *sweet* Princess out." It wasn't heat that radiated from Kalan, but intense, expanding rage. Pellima stalked before him, giggling. "Or not. Dare I say... you would never have been strong enough to overpower King Oberon's forces—"

Kalan spit in her face.

Evalyn sucked in a breath. The Alpha's head snapped back and he groaned in pain, but Pellima secured the fist with which she grabbed his hair and pulled his face close. "Do that again, and you'll see how fiesty I can get." The woman took a slow, joyful breath before dropping her fingers. The Alpha panted.

Rouhs switched places with Pellima, clicking his tongue, eyeing Evalyn with a beam grander than any she'd ever seen him conjure. The male leaned into the crook of Kalan's neck; gave a smile darker than a moonless night. "I have a feeling you'll last longer than your lady."

Kalan's tunic was ripped in half, revealing his chest.

Evalyn exclaimed, "Don't. You can have me, hurt *me*—"

Her words cut off as a hand flung in her direction. Evalyn lost her breath, choking on nothing. When her vision blurred, a gust of air ripped into her lungs, searing her throat. She folded over, coughing.

"I think he can withstand her pain, several times over!" Pellima shrieked from the side. "By the end of it, of course, he'll wish he never insulted me... but he'll hold on until then."

It happened before Evalyn could comprehend the movement. Rouhs' *cursed* dagger flashed, then Kalan grunted and his body tensed. Blood dripped to the ground in a thick stream from the base of a deep cut crossing his chest.

A sense of foreseen horror settled over the Princess. "Please, Rouhs, stop!" They'd ruined her, but she couldn't let them damage Kalan. Even after what Evalyn had endured hours before, she exclaimed, "Take me, hurt me instead! *Take me!*"

Because she was already broken.

Rouhs' eyes widened. He stepped towards the Princess, grinning. "You grow more foolish by the hour, it seems. Yet what an intriguing idea! We know what you mean to dear Kalan—"

"*No!*" Kalan's roar echoed, his chains clacking as he attempted to free himself from their hold. Rouhs was before the Alpha in a moment, a cry of pain rising from Kalan's lips. Another slash across the first—but Evalyn watched his skin inch closer. The wolfsbane was wearing off. He was healing.

Pellima noticed too. "We can't have that, can we, Rouhs?" She giggled and pulled a vial from the folds of her gown, snatching Rouhs' dagger and dipping it into the substance before slicing into the wound that'd started to heal. A bellow rose from Kalan, and Evalyn couldn't stop the tears dripping down her face. Would he heal before he lost too much blood? Or would the Faeries make him beg for death before it reached that point, like Rouhs had done to Evalyn?

The Princess' pain was nothing compared to Kalan's, but she couldn't take it anymore—

Oberon appeared in the doorway. "That's enough fun. For now." His gaze darted between his daughter and Kalan, both faces streaked with tears and their bodies bloody messes. "Clean yourselves up," he grimaced. Pellima and Rouhs strolled out of the chamber after him, snickering.

Kalan took shuddering breaths, his head leaned against the wall. Evalyn scrubbed away her tears. "If they dare come back in here..." She didn't finish her sentence, instead attempting to free herself from her chains. The cuffs on her wrists tore at her skin, but some part of the Faerie hoped her diminishing strength was somehow enough to break loose.

It wasn't.

"Stop," Kalan grumbled. "Evalyn, stop."

She didn't. How long she struggled, how hard she pulled, she couldn't care less. Whether it meant meeting Death or Faylinn, the Princess just wanted to be out, away from it all. Not only from her father and his army, but Pellima and Rouhs.

The Princess used everything left within her to yank at the binding metal.

"*Evalyn!*" Kalan shouted. The Princess whipped up to face him, but she could barely see—when had she started crying again? "Look at what you're doing to yourself. Please, stop. I can't take it."

Evalyn quivered at her burning wrists. Both of her forearms were covered in sticky, deep scarlet. Bruises already formed under the gashes at her wrists. At least she couldn't see the scored word in her skin anymore.

Broken, broken, broken.

"I'm—I'm sorry," Evalyn gasped. Kalan's face was near emotionless, save for a tremble in his lips. They'd gotten themselves into this situation and there was no way out. Not with their states.

"It's my fault." Kalan's voice was deep. Exhausted, like herself.

"No, it isn't. We wouldn't be here if I'd been more careful in the forest. If I had taken better precautions or—"

"*This is not on you!*" he exploded. "This is because of that *atrocious* King and his puppets. All Oberon wants is to hurt and separate us. Neither of us... neither of us can take the blame. It won't do any good down here." The deafening quiet of her response was cut by the drop of blood meeting stone. The flow had slowed, but Kalan's wounds were no better. The King had ensured they would never forget their weakness.

Evalyn achingly bent down until she was crouched into a chained ball, her rough breathing echoing through the chamber. Despite the trauma, the emotions surely pungent in her scent, her voice was merely a whisper as she stated, "I love you too, Kalan."

His head slowly lifted.

The Princess had never thought her first love would exist among such an absence of... light. She couldn't recall how to laugh or smile or anything more, but her words were the truth and she wanted them heard. If not for herself, then for him. If they didn't make it out of the dungeon, at least he knew.

But they *would* make it out. They... they had to.

Chapter Twenty One

The King left them for ten days.

The only way to track was from the meals thrice a day—leftovers they forced themselves to eat. Neither spoke a word. They both were in enough pain not to want to, and the Princess had nothing to say, anyway.

Her last words were a parting she'd gladly accept.

A week ago, she thought they could've made it out if they gathered their strength. Timed everything right. Now... her hope was dim. There was little chance of returning home. Kalan was healing, especially after the wolfsbane effects had worn off through his wounds, but any rough movement would send him crashing. There'd be no savior unless Omforteu and Deeam themselves came down in rescue.

And although she dreaded to think it, Evalyn hoped her mother was wise enough to leave them be. Faylinn didn't know about the Sanguin. If the Queen dared march soldiers to Braena, the wreckage would be incomprehensible. And Oberon still wanted Evalyn on his side—despite this dungeon and her treatment, he wanted *nothing* more than to keep Evalyn alive so she could join his conquest, because he couldn't get all he wanted without her. The King would forever emerge victorious in the fight for her.

She sighed into the darkness of the dungeon; the candles had burned out long ago. It'd been so long since she'd last seen the sun. Felt the wind in her hair. Breathed in the fresh scents of pine and fruitful gardens. She'd nearly forgotten what the Aternalis Creek sounded like. Her once-sunkissed skin had faded to a lifeless pale—from more than a lack of warm rays.

Evalyn's mind was the same, almost slipping into lifelessness.

If Kalan hadn't emerged from the shadows as if sent by the Gods, it just might've.

The Faerie dragged her eyes to the Alpha. His head leaned into the wall, wrists hanging against the constraints. She released the hold on her knees, stretching out her legs with a groan. The worst bruises and scratches continued to throb at any movement, and in effect of the iron that'd created them, the gashes in her forearm remained aching and unfading.

A grumble sounded from outside the door a second before it slammed open. "I've brought consolation," King Oberon crooned.

Evalyn made to retaliate, to curse him for what she and Kalan had endured already—but she recognized the body carried by a pair of sentinels behind the King. The frail, small figure, whose loose, blonde hair mirrored the Princess'.

Two months or two centuries together... Evalyn would never forget her mother.

The Princess pulled at her chains. "What did you do? *What did you do?*"

The guards dropped Tania's body with a thud, their exit hurried. Tania gently stirred, and Oberon grinned. "I suspect this sickness has consumed her." It was a lie—something of the sort. The Queen would be okay. "It's a shame she was in a wave of indisposition—a shame for her, I suppose. For me, it was an excellent opportunity to collect my next... hostage." He chuckled. "Ransom is a delightful game, isn't it, darling?"

Evalyn scowled. Her scarred wrists rubbed against the shackles, crimson flakes drifting to the ground.

Oberon raised a hand, and Evalyn rose into the air, every part of her body falling to the will of the King. "I'm going to ask you one last time, daughter." Kalan's face turned a ghostly white—she'd forgotten to explain her true heritage, of the monstrous blood running through her veins. "Your lover hasn't been informed?" Oberon tilted his chin. "She is my daughter, and subsequently, Princess of Braena."

"I am the Heir of *Faylinn's* Crown. *Nowhere else.*"

Tania pushed herself to sit, skin a sickly green whilst she glared at Oberon between light, strained breaths. "Evalyn is nothing to you. Her *father* died from that illness along with whatever innocent life you took." Oberon smiled. Tania huffed, "You're surprised? I've spent twenty years putting together the mysteries, and your pretense is not so well established." The Queen's voice thickened. "Put my daughter down."

Evalyn immediately fell to the floor, legs giving out.

But Tania shot towards the wall, pinned in place by Oberon's force. The woman coughed, a dark liquid spattering down her chin. The scent of blood plugged the Princess' nostrils.

"Now that I'm able to state my piece, allow me to continue," Oberon boomed. He faced Evalyn. "Join me, and we will become the most powerful duo to rule these lands. We will rise and dominate. Or," He gestured to Tania, dangling helplessly under his control, "face the consequences."

"It doesn't matter what she chooses," Kalan snarled. "If Evalyn joins you, there's no going back. She'll never escape your control. If she denies you... I doubt you'd grant any of us a clean death—or death at all."

"It seems we're on the same page, Alpha." King Oberon fanned his cloak, crossing them. "Now you understand: no one and nowhere is safe. I can, and will, take down whomever I please."

"You won't," Evalyn growled.

Oberon whirled. The Princess couldn't stop the memory from playing in her mind—the vision of the Sanguin so close to her, trapped in those dungeons, her father exactly the same. She barely contained the nausea that overcame her as the King interpreted her widened gaze, sending his magic grazing over the scars on her shoulder. "You're ready to choose, darling? I do hope you've made a wise decision."

Chills crawled down the Princess' back. But she knew what she had to do—and prayed the Gods forgave her.

Because now... destruction was inevitable.

"You know where I stand," she said. "You're on your own." Because although the King was all-powerful, there was a chance Faylinn could win this War. And Evalyn wouldn't surrender without attempting to take it.

Oberon's grin faded. He hurled his force over Tania, who rose before smashing to the ground in a crumpled heap. "Stop!" Evalyn screamed. "I'm begging you, please!" Stupid—she'd been so *stupid* to think Oberon would hurt only her for the defiance. With the King's lifted hands, Tania's body rose, and with clenched fingers, she fell, crashing to stone.

Over and over again.

It could end in an instant.

"*Fine!*" she screamed. "*I'll do it, I'll join you, just stop, please!*"

Tania froze, suspended between life and death. The King's smile conveyed he was enjoying every second of their pain. "Finally, you come to your senses."

Evalyn opened her mouth—but a crash sounded outside the dungeon. Shouts from guards rose with cries and muffled groans. The Princess' tear-flow halted as the door swung open, giving way to a towering figure that barely slipped through the door frame.

A wolf. Its gray and brown coat was slick with blood, and the stench of sweat and flesh filled the chamber. The animal was twice as big as Kalan's form, dominating the space of the room, showing long canines and squinted, golden eyes.

Oberon began laughing.

The horrendous sound echoed through the chamber. The King dropped his fingers and Tania plunged to the ground in front of Evalyn, who swept the Queen into her arms.

Oberon stepped towards the creature. "If I recall correctly... I get to kill you, Recks Delta."

Kalan froze, eyes widening—his father was alive. Still, the Princess tugged Tania close, wary; bloodlines did naught to warrant allegiance.

The King chuckled, "I have to say, this isn't the turn of events I was expecting!" When the wolf remained silent and still, Oberon cast out a hand. Recks' legs buckled, but he shook his snout—fighting off the King's magic. A rumbling arose in his throat, and the King smiled, dropping his arm, leaving the wolf panting. "Not as strong as you once were," Oberon declared, "but a respectful effort. It's hard to believe we were so close as to train together. Not friends by any measure, no, but we relied on one another's strategies and counsel. I always knew you despised me, but you strayed from meeting my bad side. Especially when you discovered your partner had birthed a son." Oberon eyed Kalan. "Recks abandoned you because he didn't think he was prepared to raise a child. I, never being one to reject a spectacular guest, allowed him to shelter with me until the rumors about his disappearance faded. Not yet King, no one suspected his sanctuary with me. He went away for a time, returning when my Kingdom was established.

"I welcomed you in, Recks, and you used me—took advantage of my willingness to provide you care and safeguard from your kind, who'd ventured off in search of their great legend. You trained behind my back, ignoring my efforts to reach a deal for additional refuge. You became a stranger in my own Kingdom." The King tilted his chin. "So I forbade him from entering Braena. Yet here he is, despite my threats—my promises of death if he were to return."

Evalyn squeezed Tania's shoulders as she lugged the Queen closer, who sucked in crackling breaths and wheezes. The Princess' head swam and a searing pain flared across her body, in her bones and through her veins. The stupid, strange power—not now, *why now,* when she needed her full bearings and focus? Evalyn bit her tongue to keep from crying out from the burning; a metallic tang filled her mouth; coated her teeth.

"This isn't how you imagined to meet your father, is it, Alpha?" Oberon piped to Kalan.

"Don't speak to me as if you know me, Oberon. You may have lived a life with my father, but I have the luxury of not trusting you. Of being on a side worth fighting for."

Evalyn balled her fists. Her hands throbbed and eyes watered—the girl hunched over, expecting another fierce pang, yet was met with a tingling warmth, coursing from her head to her feet. A wonderful strength covered the soreness in her bones.

The King blinked. "What a fine speech."

Evalyn knew what the sensation was. What she'd been feeling since her arrival here; what had attempted to surface for weeks without her realizing, and which she'd pushed away out of fear of weakness and hurt, when all along it could have provided the opposite. Perhaps, in other life, saved her from breaking.

Magic.

The King chortled, "I must say, this is an overwhelming surprise. The most powerful Fae family of Liatue and the only living descendants of the legendary Delta line, joined in one presence. What an unlikely reunion!"

The Princess stood easier than ever before, arms lifting her mother. Oberon turned, amused; Recks Delta twitched and inched towards the door as soon as he exited the King's focus. Evalyn took a final breath.

"No. This is War."

She didn't comprehend what she did—only felt the magic respond to her unspoken will.

A wave of fire blasted through the room, so mighty Evalyn feared her own destruction, but it sensed her fright, heeding her command for calm. A violent surge of wind gathered the flames. It took nothing to pry her shackles from the stone pillar; the metal around her limbs melted into liquid.

Evalyn hurled another blast of fire towards her father, and she blindly stumbled for Kalan—untouched, due to the unyielding individual shields the Princess had created around herself, him, and Tania. His eyes were broad as she removed the chains from his body with a tug, then he collapsed onto her.

Roaring wind whipped through the dungeon, obliterating the chamber, but the fire quelled, leaving embers and cracking flames, the room coated in dark ash whilst shards of chain-metal and stone soared through the room.

Oberon was an unmoving heap of darkness on the ground, his glittering crown feet away. No doubt knocked out—but not dead.

Neither the King nor his daughter were finished.

Evalyn willed her power to quicken, to magnify as they neared the door. It responded in seconds: a deafening gale whipped around and living fire scaled the walls. The heat grew, her forehead slickening and body drenching with sweat; affected but unhurt by her powers.

Recks was absent at the exit. Not dead, either—there wasn't a body in sight. He'd gotten out.

The three trudged out of the dungeon, and Evalyn's magic swarmed out of the chamber, following them down the corridors. They met a set of stairs, hurling themselves up through the castle. Evalyn was tiring; the weight was slowing them. She'd be exhausted soon, unable to hold herself. They had to find safety.

Miraculously, the main halls were deserted. Kalan gestured, and they entered a dark corridor abandoned by surveillance. Their escape was so easy. Too easy. Something in her gut said Oberon wanted it that way.

Evalyn didn't care. They'd return to Faylinn if it was the last thing she did.

They stumbled into chilly evening air, slivers of gold rays warming their skin. Sunlight. *Sunlight.* Evalyn restrained her joy. Keep moving. They had to keep moving. However much she resented it, the night's arriving darkness was their friend and cover. They plowed through the rocky outskirts of the Dumon Peaks, the range rising high. The mountains were eternally dark and frozen; the perfect shield for an army of Sanguin. The Shadow remained on their left as the Dumons curved to their right—forming an opening to the south, straight ahead.

The trio was clearing the Shadow Compound, but not far enough, not fast enough—

Evalyn stumbled over her feet, the weight of Kalan and Tania overpowering her speed. They slammed into hard, grass-spotted rock, skin stinging against the half-frozen dew coating the stone. Summer was nonexistent in the north.

Meaning the trek home would be tedious. In their states, the journey could be weeks longer.

With Tania's sickness and her and Kalan's wounds, they couldn't wait that long.

As they pulled forward, a shadow rose over them. Evalyn glanced up—then crawled away from Recks Delta. But Kalan, groaning at her side, waved his fingers. "Go with him. I'm right behind you." She scanned Recks before pulling her and Tania onto the wolf's back.

The beat of his steps matched the pace of her heart and lured her into empty sleep.

Chapter Twenty Two

They had to keep going. The sun had long since broken the horizon.

But with her cheek on Kalan's shoulder, Evalyn pretended to remain asleep. The Alpha seemed relaxed, leaning against the wall of the cave Recks had brought them to, head grazing cool rock. Although the Princess knew he hadn't closed his eyes once, she didn't want to disturb his conscious rest. So she kept silent and still, even though her body ached and mind wouldn't cease spinning.

They had to get home.

They weren't safe.

They would never be until Oberon was rid from existence.

Even with her eyes closed, Evalyn knew Kalan was staring at Recks. The Alpha had been silent since she'd awoken some minutes ago, so the suddenness of his voice, although soft, made her jolt.

"Is it true? What Oberon said?"

He was asking his father. Because after two decades of absence, Recks was back. Had helped them escape. So what was his motive?

The wet padding of the wolf's paws on stone indicated his pacing along the edge of the cave. When was the last time he'd been human? Whether his silence included a nod, she had a feeling Oberon had spoken utterly true, for Kalan tensed at her side. "You may have been accustomed to the benefits of the *legendary* Delta line, but my mother was pregnant when she became an omega. When she was cast out of her pack, into the wild, with nothing except her resolution to keep us alive." His words turned to a snarl. "Did you know your disappearance was the reason she was labeled a disgrace? Because her parents were mortified that she hadn't been good enough for the *Almighty* to stay?"

A huff of breath in answer. Evalyn cracked open one eye. Recks' silhouette sat at the cave entrance, facing away from them, head bowed and body still.

Kalan was equally motionless, but exhaled heavily through his nose. "I always said that when I met you," he whispered, "I would exact the humiliation and suffering you put her through. But you saved my life, as well as Evalyn and Tania's. I can't very well attack you in return."

His father turned, and Evalyn forced her face to relax, lips parting slightly to feign deep slumber. She knew they were looking at her and Tania, who leaned into Evalyn's opposite side; Kalan shifted his body to warm her in the frigid shadows as he added, "You don't deserve to know who she is. To me, or to my Kingdom. But you're going to help us get home safely." A pause. "And you'll explain yourself. I deserve that much, if nothing else."

After what felt like an hour of responding silence, Evalyn inhaled deeply and sat up. Kalan sprang into action as Tania stirred to consciousness too, aiding both Fae to stand.

"How do you feel?"

Tania smiled weakly; Evalyn sucked in a breath and said, "Alive." Because she remained as exhausted as before, if not more from their solid rockbed. But they were breathing and they were out of that dungeon.

"There's a village at the base of the Dumons, in the distance, between us and the Frost River. We can refuge there for the night. Possibly get a decent meal and finer sleep," Kalan mentioned. Recks paced out of the cave and onto the slippered rock that lined a path towards the mass of buildings clustered in the far south; Evalyn tightly gripped her mother's elbow as they began the trek.

Thick, gray clouds covered any trace of blue, blotting out what miniscule sunlight may have reached them. With the prospect of rain, they hobbled faster to the village.

"Keep your heads down," Evalyn voiced. "We don't know how far out Oberon may be looking for us."

It was near dusk when the group arrived, slinking against the canopied backs of the first cottages and shops they met, many of which were luckily already quiet and closed. With a sharp left they shifted into a short and cramped alley that forced them into a single line with the wolves at either end; the shadows kept them hidden from the eyes of the villagers. The end opened to a side-road, where a pair of washmaids giggled and sang gently around a tub of murky water.

Kalan looked over his shoulder at Evalyn, who observed their next steps. Overhead the door of a tall, mud-and-plaster building at the opposite end of the street hung a sign that identified it as an inn. A neighboring board called the town *Hembourne*.

The Princess pointed it out. "We'll have to put ourselves in the open, but if we hurry, I doubt they'll take notice of us. We'll get a room and keep to ourselves, then leave before dawn tomorrow."

Despite steering clear of the main road, there were a plethora of folk at the end of the gravel path, starting evening chores and cleaning from the day's work. Evalyn kept her eyes trained on her feet; her blood-and-dirt stained shoes seemed to make the loudest squelches as they approached the inn.

She could hear the other Faeries conversations as they passed, unbothered by a stray group of travelers passing through. She may have even called them safe—had a figure not halted a foot before her and Kalan, and the group of villagers instantly silenced and turned to watch as if they'd known what was going to happen all along.

Evalyn dragged her stare upward.

The dark-haired woman was tall, with a sharp, defined face, and observably older than the companions that slithered to her flank a moment later. Their outfits weren't noticeably Braenish; male or female, they all wore hooded tunics, trousers, and boots, with thin sashes of fabric knotted around their waists. Each one had double weapon belts, with a hatchet and dagger at either hip, as well as two shortswords sheathed across their backs, the handles poking over their left shoulders.

She realized she was gaping when the woman spoke. "Don't like what you see?"

Evalyn straightened, lifting her chin. "No, she likes me, I can tell," a male to the female's side said with a smirk, flipping the hood off his head. "It's you she's frightened by, Millo." He was muscular and just as tall, with shaggy, brown hair that curled at the tips.

"Whatever you say, Grae," a second female responded, pulling down her hood too. "Not everyone we meet falls in love with you on the spot." She was an exact copy of Millo, albeit shorter, with chin-length hair where the woman's was plaited down to her waist.

Grae rolled his eyes. "I see what I see, Kaye. You're jealous because you're unapproachable; no one wants to befriend the Overseer's kid."

The fourth Fae, another male, chuckled deeply. His forest-green eyes gleamed within the darkness of his tunic covering. "Kaye's not wrong, Grae." The deep calm of his voice soothed Evalyn's ears. "I could count on a finger the number of lovers you've enjoyed. You certainly aren't going to catch the eye of the Lost Princess."

Evalyn paled. Kalan sidled up to her, Tania taking the other side as Recks gave a low rumble—

Millo sighed with a short smile. "There goes our welcome, Willsom." But they didn't bow. Because they were loyal to another monarch? "I'm Overseer Ten, Princess. I'd like to talk."

"Concerning what matters?"

"The lore of my people: who we are and what we believe. What we want."

Evalyn's stare was unwavering. "What part do I have in such things?"

Millo chuckled, but there was no humor in her words. "You have every part."

"What if I deny you? We could leave right now." They wouldn't get far, but these strangers didn't need to know that.

"You could," Kaye said, picking at her nails. "But you're too intrigued to do so. Besides, it was your fate to come to Hembourne. Now we talk." She wasn't mistaken; Evalyn's wariness simmered with curiosity.

Tania's whisper was nearly imperceptible. "They aren't with him." Her mother's eyes were shut—using her empathy magic. "We can trust them—for now."

"It is our aim to gain your trust indefinitely," Grae retorted. Evalyn shifted to him tapping a finger against his ear. "And for your reassurance, Queen Tania... we *certainly* aren't in cahoots with the King."

"Who said anything about Oberon?" Kalan questioned from behind.

Millo answered, "We won't pretend we don't know what you're doing here either, Alpha. Recks Delta, however..." The wolf's ears twitched. "Your life's purpose for the past twenty-three years remains a mystery."

Tania tilted her head. "Who's banner holds your honor?"

"Our family has its own," Millo said, spreading her hands before her. "With secret habitation in every Kingdom, our ears stretch far and wide."

Grae smiled, jerking a thumb towards himself. "She mostly means mine."

"She doesn't," Kaye argued.

"She certainly *does*. How do you think Blare knows about your *shrine* for him—"

Kaye whipped around, hatchet swinging in hand as she faced Grae, who silenced instantly as Willsom whistled, "Too far."

"You—you were *across the village,* Grae! How am I supposed to keep *anything* from you?" Kaye stormed into the inn behind her companions.

"You're Rogues," Tania voiced. Evalyn's heart stopped.

Grae smirked as a low chuckle came from Willsom's hood, and Millo simply waved a hand, signaling them to follow Kaye inside. The inn was buzzing, packed with chatter and laughter around the circled tables. It was clear all were Braenish folk; the pasty-white of their faces, as well as the various fur-lined cloaks thrown over stools and strung along the walls indicated their time spent in the ever-cold, sun-lacking North. From some corner, the playing of a soft yet upbeat song on strings disrupted any lingering quiet.

As soon as the door closed behind Recks, a lanky, bearded male skipped forth, clapping his hands together. He wore a stained apron over a brown outfit, pockets filled with used rags and wooden utensils. His voice was as light as his sand-colored eyes. "How special it is to attend to you, Overseer! Can I offer drinks?"

Millo gave Evalyn's bunch a once-over. "Drinks... and as much of your finest soup as you can procure."

Only after they all—including Kaye—had sat around a huddle of tables that they pushed together, emptied their cups, and filled their stomachs to near-bursting did Evalyn say, "We know what the Rogues live for."

Millo returned, "Our lifestyle has been horribly misinterpreted."

"Along with our reputation. Among other things," added Grae. He was no longer smiling, but in his eyes... a hopeful glimmer. For what?

Millo's sight was unmoving from the Princess. "Little is actually known about the Rogues of Liatue, especially our beliefs."

Willsom tilted his head. "We all know the tale of Dricormie and Beloah. The fact of their existence is certainly true—they did live and die. But the rest of their story is unproven. Perhaps not all is false... but over time, their tale has become twisted; formed into a bedtime story for children. For older folk, to maintain the look of a front unified since the beginning."

"What they don't tell you..." Kaye interjected, leaning so forward in her seat that she knocked her drink to the floor, "are Deilok's last words. His parting."

The innkeeper clicked his tongue from across the room, but with a swing of his arm, the cup wobbled back onto the table.

Willsom continued. "They were once taken from the retelling to not scare the children, yet Deilok's proclamation continued to be pushed away as another version was accepted. In reality, he declared in a vision to Dricormie and Beolah's descendants that the death the Rulers witnessed had not been his final one. He said that one day he'd return and exact what was done to him, tenfold. Our ancestors kept to this version—the real tale—and passed it on as a means of safety. Of preparation. Because we know Deilok isn't gone."

"He never was," Millo said. "How he saved himself from death, how he survived this long, has never been guessed. But we believe it's true. Some of our elders are direct descendants from the first generation of Faylinn-born Faeries, and they have passed down the true telling of Dricormie and Beolah's mission. Deilok is out there, rising to power, and we've spent the generations since his fall preparing for his return. Perhaps, with enough of us, we'll be able to do damage before he secures his revenge."

The Princess found herself desperate for a reason not to understand their beliefs; the story they told of Deilok. Because something about it made sense. Some part of her mind screamed that she knew it all along. Evalyn couldn't shake the chills that snaked down her body. "Why tell us? What could I grant you in return for our acceptance?"

Grae said, "We don't want land or coin. We have home wherever we go, and we have each other. We're content with our ways of life."

"Then what do you desire?"

Millo returned, "Your support. And a promise that if—when—the time comes, you might help us defeat the true enemy for good."

Evalyn was unable to say no. If Deilok never came—if the tale proved false—then she had nothing to lose. But if Deilok did return... was it not in her best interest to ally with those who'd spent lifetimes preparing for him? "On one condition," Evalyn said, folding arms across her chest.

The Rogues lifted their brows.

"I'm sure you've heard that War has begun. I hope battle is not too soon," the Princess began, "but in return for my support and that promise... I ask that the Rogues join my side in defending Faylinn against King Oberon. I understand the fear of your own fight, but I need you to trust that if we don't defeat him... there'll be no one for Deilok to seek revenge upon."

"Done," Millo agreed. They both had too severe of threats—whether present or rising—to decline such a deal. The woman looked over Evalyn curiously. "We will be forever grateful for this pact, daughter of Oberon."

The silence of the inn hit Evalyn. Everyone inside was staring, listening intently to the conversation unfolding.

"Your ears are incomparably skilled," Evalyn jeered.

The Rogues smiled. Millo said, "Our ears have tracked villages just like Hembourne across this Kingdom. Ones that desire to support you rather than King Oberon. Many have been in communication with another about beginning a second Great Uprising." Millo crossed her arms. "I believe they would rather share their weapons, soldiers, and funds to Faylinn over wasting it on a civil conflict they know will end badly for them, despite their fervor to oppose the King."

A lanky, pearl-skinned woman stepped forth, emerald curls bobbing at her shoulders. "He has tormented Hembourne for many months; taking our loved ones without warning and not returning them, despite our pleas. If they're gone, we only desire proper burials."

Those around the female nodded, murmurs rising as they proclaimed the small wishes of happiness that Oberon had denied.

Millo cleared her throat. "I know this War means much to you, as our cause does to us. But if we survive... I'd consider living under your rule, if you'd have me. Us."

Kaye gasped, whirling for the woman. "*Mother!* We haven't pledged ourselves to a monarch in centuries! We live for our freedom—plan to fight for it. You know that *best*."

"And no Royal has ever listened to our truth quite like Evalyn." It was the first time Millo had used her name. "Times are changing. Perhaps we should, too."

After a moment, Kaye faced Evalyn with crossed arms. "Perhaps," she muttered.

Evalyn dipped her chin. "Should we win this War and defeat my father, the Rogues will have a place in Faylinn. If you should want that." There was something about her home—its life and joy—that she couldn't keep to herself. Offering it to those who deserved it—the used and misunderstood—made her feel like a portion of the future Queen she was supposed to be. Tania dipped her chin in agreement. "When the time comes... how will we find you?"

Millo's lips turned up at the corners. But instead of answering, she looked to the other side of the inn and declared, "Beds, baths, and a change of clothes for your guests, Jon!"

The innkeeper's face popped around an edge of the kitchen door, and he immediately shouted at two Fae to follow the demands.

"You'll have to cross the Frost River after you leave Hembourne," Millo declared. "We don't yet know what you were involved in last night, but the bridge and boat-crossings started being inspected and monitored by packs of the King's men. Overall security has exploded. The only way you're getting out of Braena is to swim. There's a spot just south of here, past the old spruce woodland, where you can cross."

Evalyn gulped. "Thank you. For everything."

Millo smiled. "I suspect your room is ready."

Indeed, it greeted Evalyn and her companions with warmth and light. Candles perched on every inch of furniture except the beds, and a faint steam escaped from the cracked entrance to the bathing chamber. Evalyn rushed her mother into the room and helped the Queen into a tub.

Tania hissed at the heat, but lowered herself fully into the water. Evalyn marched across the chamber, hands folded above her head as she pivoted towards the other side. The Rogues were here, in this town with her, and had just pledged themselves to Faylinn's cause—Evalyn dropped to her knees, unable to suck in as much air as her lungs needed. And across Braena—*across Braena*—there were more villages and citizens that despised their own ruler as much the other Kingdoms did. They wanted to aid *her* in this War. But... they had no idea what destruction they'd gotten themselves into, what army she'd set loose on Liatue by escaping—

"Get in, Evalyn. Get in and breathe," her mother murmured. "We can later ponder all that we've been told."

Evalyn gave a long, slow breath. Gave two more. Then did as her mother said.

Warm yellow and brown spotted the Princess' abdomen, limbs, face. Her once-shackled wrists remained swollen and purple, and thin, pink streaks rose to the surface of her skin from the water's heat. The triple-clawed mess of a scar on her shoulder was pronounced against her colorless complexion; the Faerie's forearm throbbed as she traced over the carved letters with a finger. And the soreness in her bones returned as she recalled what each wound was from. Her father, Rouhs... herself.

She had no one to blame for it all but herself.

The Princess selected a cloth and began scrubbing. Scrubbing away the pain and the trauma. Attempting to rid her body of the memories; of the terror that overwhelmed her with any mention of the Shadow Compound; of the disgust and hatred for herself. She'd allowed things to get so far and had let herself become so helpless. Become that fifteen year old girl once more, drowned in stupidity and fright and unable to defend herself.

Broken,

Broken,

Broken.

Evalyn didn't stop scrubbing, even when her flesh became a tender, raw mess. But when steam obscured her vision, she halted with heavy breaths and realized the water in her tub had disappeared.

A new response of her magic to the frantic emotions. Evalyn closed her eyes. Inhaled. By the time she released the breath, warm water reached her upper body once more.

She gradually faced Tania, whose head was tilted and eyes observing.

The Princess' gaze fell.

"Do not look away from me," Tania croaked. The girl returned her gaze. "I don't know what he did to you; what others may have done to you. Your time there..." She sighed. "It was my deepest fear. But we made it out—*you* made it out. That is enough to be asked of you."

Evalyn didn't break her stare.

"Are you okay?" her mother questioned.

"No."

Yet her eyes were tearless. She was tired of crying.

They remained there, silent, until the water grew cool. Recks laid asleep on the floor at a bed's end, which Tania settled into. Evalyn hadn't seen the wolf relax since they'd met. After his own washing, Kalan exited the bathing chamber shirtless, revealing thick, pink scars as he peered through the closed window curtains, then faced the Princess. "How are you feeling?"

Evalyn left Tania's side, meeting the second bed and pulling its blankets over her legs. "Warmer."

Kalan sat next to her, gaze tired but awake. "You know what I mean."

Evalyn exhaled thoroughly, unable to find the words—especially as his closeness brought forth a multitude of emotions: ease, trust, comfort... but also anxiety. Panic. She tried to shove it down. Kalan wasn't Rouhs. Finally, she said, "I never thought we'd get out of there."

"But we did."

"Not unscathed. In more ways than one."

She observed his chest; ragged scars stretched across his muscled figure. Evalyn gaped at the size and sheer look of them, worse than what she'd perceived in the dungeons. Evalyn met his eyes. When Kalan leaned down, she involuntarily flinched away, earning a frown.

"I'm sorry. I thought..."

"No," she breathed. "Don't be. I—I'm sorry." Evalyn looked around the room—anywhere but at him. She wanted to reveal the truth, wanted someone to understand... but she couldn't tell Kalan. What would he think of her? How would his feelings change once he found out how weak she was? The ways she'd been fragmented and defeated?

She folded her arm into her lap.

"I never noticed it in the dungeons," he whispered. "Only yesterday. In the cave."

"I never let you. I don't want the questions."

"Then I won't ask them," he assured her. "Only when you're comfortable."

Perhaps she was a coward. Perhaps she'd returned to her old self—a scared and lonely child—but Evalyn nodded. He dipped his chin and shifted across the bed; giving her space. For some reason, she felt guilty about it.

They left the candles burning into the night.

The group woke before the sun. After a swift yet large breakfast, the Princess shivered behind Recks, who led them down out of Hembourne, following Millo's instructed trail to the Frost River. Evalyn pulled her hooded cloak tighter, wrapping an arm around her mother in the hopes of providing some repression of the day's biting wind. The quad marched due south, only slowing their urgent pace after passing through the crumbling spruce woodland and meeting the frozen edge of the Frost River.

And as one, halted. The river was dark and rushing; a deep abyss that would suck under all who entered its grasp. Pearl froth surged along the bank, lapping at the lichen crusted in the jagged, rock shore.

The crossing was going to be rough. Even with the rising Summer sun, the river remained lethal, and if they didn't move fast enough, the current would take them under. If they didn't shut down from the temperature first.

They quickly waded into the depths before anyone acted on the appeal to turn back.

Evalyn had never been so cold in her life. Even with the cloudless, sunny sky, she couldn't tell where the northern waters met her skin—they'd flooded her veins, freezing Evalyn from the inside out.

She was halfway across when her strength began dwindling. The river was wider than she'd anticipated. Kalan sucked in a breath and her magic flared out—a now-instinctual reaction. So far, her control spanned across fire, wind, and water—wind from her mother, leaving the others from Oberon. As if she needed more connection to him. But Evalyn barely gave a thought, and the current slowed and warmth enveloped their submerged bodies.

Then disappeared.

Evalyn waited, expecting the relieving heat to return—but it didn't. If she couldn't warm the water, if the cold seeped into their bones... the Princess slowed. She couldn't swim, couldn't breathe against the tugging current. Evalyn squeezed her eyes, crying out, hoping for some flicker of power to respond.

Nothing.

Her magic—the inkling of power that meant she could make some change... she'd lost it, as if she'd never found it at all.

Something pounded into her side, the girl's head dipping halfway into the river depths. She faced Kalan, the wolf's head the only thing above the surface with wide eyes and flared nostrils. His teeth were clamped around the knotted and secure satchel containing medicinal aid, spare clothing, and food—although it was certainly watered-down mush now—from the Hembourne innkeeper's spare stock. But Kalan's fighting figure settled something in her—fear, determination, she couldn't decipher between the two—and Evalyn swam faster than before.

They had much farther on their journey. She could finish this task.

Evalyn coughed and sputtered as she crawled out of the Frost River. She rolled onto her back, pulling her toes from the black channel, blurred gaze meeting the Shadow Compound standing on the horizon. As elegant and towering as it was, she shuddered at the looming stare of the castle. Its carved rock walls sat in the valley of the stretching range of the Dumon Peaks; the black mountains touched the clouds, their snow-capped peaks brushing the sky.

It might've been beautiful, had the King not come and torn peaceful existence to shreds.

The Alpha nudged her hip: *keep going.*

Following their southern travel, the air became steaming with the sun overhead; they were lucky to find shelter from the dry winds when darkness fell. Nonetheless, as they finally exited Braena, Evalyn welcomed the warmer greeting of her first Fae Summer.

But four days into their travels, the first obstacle marked the trek: massive, noiseless hills loomed before them.

The Silent Slopes. They were about to enter strange territory.

According to the stories, the hills used to be full of life. Loud, echoing, jubilant life. But when the Crawlers arrived, infesting every peak and nook, any wildlife that existed escaped, and Fae were warned not to venture close. All that remained were thick, twisting trees dotting the grassy slopes, caves nesting the predators, and the unending holler of nothing.

No Faerie had ever seen a Crawler—none that lived to tell the story—but it was advised to steer clear of the hills at night, and never travel directly through the slopes, unless one wanted to become the hunted.

They were doing just that.

It wasn't an intended death wish, but according to Kalan, pathing through the Silent Slopes rather than detouring around was the quickest route. And although they'd successfully retreated from Braena, free of trackers and a trail, speed remained a necessity. As long as they took cover from dusk to dawn, they had a chance of making it through the hills without confronting any Crawlers.

Recks and Kalan led the Royal Fae through the first of countless valleys minutes before sunrise; as early as they would dare. It wasn't a struggle not to talk; their only sounds were strained breaths. No one had conversed greatly in the past few days, anyway. Evalyn barely participated in the meaningless discussions between Tania and Kalan, and exchanged only mumbled words to her mother before sleeping. Recks was yet to show his human form to communicate.

Nightfall devoured them quickly, forcing the group to rest. After intense scouring by Recks, their chosen area was declared clear of Crawlers. They sat snugly, legs and fur touching, the contact necessary in case any of them were swept away in the night.

Evalyn didn't think anyone closed their eyes for hours.

She woke while dark lingered. At her sides were Kalan and her mother, Recks curled beside Tania's other leg. They leaned against a steep dirt hill, trees shielding their front. Evalyn's neck was stiff and heavy as she straightened. She didn't know why she'd awoken—yet after a long minute, she felt it.

Her throat closed, all senses alert within a second. Chills dripped down her back.

Crawlers were out there. Close to them.

Against the instincts howling to sustain her state of quiet motionless, Evalyn stood.

It took a tense moment to ensure the group didn't stir at her movement, and then she was at the opposite edge of the tree clump, still within sight of their overnight stay. More awake than she'd been in days, the woman tiptoed ahead of the treeline, if only to catch a glimpse of the Crawlers from afar; she refused to believe these creatures were worse than the Sanguin.

Oberon's experiments flashed in Evalyn's mind. Her night scares had disappeared for the time being; she'd been able to sleep the little she dared try.

But a snap rang through the hill-valley.

Evalyn spun towards the treeline, finger to her lips as she faced Kalan paused mid-step, brows furrowed. He looked even more exhausted than she felt, his sleep-wrinkled gray tunic fluttering in the pre-dawn breeze. She slowed her breathing; Kalan highered his chin as a manifold of purring growls rolled across the hills.

Evalyn's stomach plummeted to her feet. Her magic had yet to resurface since the river crossing; she'd tried summoning it during their trek to no avail.

Powerless. She was powerless.

She choked down the burning in her throat. Soundlessly, Kalan beckoned to run.

They sprinted. She followed him, but not towards their camp—higher, through the trees and out of the valley, where Tania, on Recks' back, met their side. A patterned clicking echoed, their claws or nails or teeth or *something* against the dense bark of the warped trees. Not even the dawn light streaming over the treetops eased her dread, but they entered an open clearing, where piercing sunlight formed a border between them and the hidden, shadowed Crawlers.

Their yaps continued, and Evalyn counted her breaths whilst the quad huddled together, waiting for the attack of the infamous dethroners of the wild. A sweep of Tania's hands raised mounds of dirt around them, forming a meaningful—although helpless—perimeter of soil and stone. The Queen grumbled at her feeble attempt of aid. Nevertheless, the Crawlers came no closer, continuously unseen yet endlessly felt from the branches and shade, their strange dominance leaking through the Slopes like liquid pooling over the grassy hills.

Evalyn crouched down when her legs began cramping and placed a palm against the hilltop. The Faerie closed her eyes, ears straining to sense movement from the Crawlers beyond their noise and energy. On her left, their stepping limbs patted soft grass—she raised her hand and a stream of fire shot into the shadows. Their clicking and howling grew louder, but Evalyn wasn't rendered still by the Crawlers.

Her magic remained.

She was strong.

It seemed her emotions influenced her abilities—but too much rendered them uncontrollable. She'd have to learn the balance. Tania held fast to the Princess' free arm; Evalyn shook her head, remaining prudent to the necessary actions at hand.

After seventy-three exhales, silence consumed the quad—the Crawlers' noises dissipated so suddenly it felt as if they'd been a collective hallucination. But the group breathed normally once more. After another hour in the clearing they moved on, wary and careful, if not more unnerved than they had been, and kept every step within paths marked by the sun.

When darkness returned each night, they hid in deeper tree nooks and empty hilltops and didn't budge until far past sunrise.

It took four more days to reach the Central Lowlands—all that stood between them and Faylinn.

Home.

The thick, endless field of grass stood tall year round, three heads taller than Reck's standing height; another obstacle too large to detour around with their haste. Which meant they'd have to proceed southwest through the most dense areas.

They rested at the edge of the grass, a deep green casually striped with teal expanding past the horizon. Evalyn turned from the field, the sunset's pink rays tickling her cheek. Trees trickled down from the Silent Slopes and scattered around them. Tania reclined against one with upside-down curving branches that warped away from the ground at waist-level, her head leaned against the trunk with closed eyes and steady breathing.

Evalyn said, "We're about a week from Koathe. Kalan said we could make it in less if we pushed hard enough." The Royals' gazes met. "We can do it."

Tania nodded slowly, a wordless response. The Princess stowed away her fear—her mother's sickness was worsening by the day, but the Queen had insisted she'd be fine—until they returned home, at least.

She settled beside her mother and laid her head upon the woman's shoulder. Perhaps it was the Queen's last dreg of magic, but Evalyn was certain the ground was more comfortable that night than it'd been before.

It was habit to wake when the sun did.

The air was still and quiet as the group began the end of their journey.

Kalan led as usual, supernatural senses searching the path ahead for threats. With the grass height hindering their vision, they had to rely on his scent and intuition. Evalyn followed; Recks took his spot at the rear with Tania after resorting to carrying her completely, the Queen too weak to sustain even an hour trek. They'd emptied the resource sack from Hembourne while still in the Silent Slopes; Kalan and Recks were now prone to hunting rodents, and the Princess to delivering water from the palm of her hands.

Although without altitude changes or the consistent cold of northern Liatue, hiking through the Lowland grasses demanded strict stamina and willpower. The Princess' lingering wounds left her skin sensitive to the touch of the serrated-edged plants.

And just when Summer weather became a holy grail, they encountered a rain that poured for two days. Swallowed by an ocean of grass, they were left unsheltered from the needle-sharp drops. The Princess tried her magic—wind to block it and flames to stifle it—but instead intensified the humidity and sent harsher, swifter rain pounding upon them. A full day after the downpour, Evalyn remained damp.

Kalan woke her the next morning, uncut and unkempt hair flipping across his forehead as he rose in their patch of grass which Recks had flattened the evening prior to sleep upon. When they exited the Central Lowlands, the ground shifted to denser soil, grassy and clipped and sloping up and down—transitioning into the lovely, rolling plains of northern Faylinn. The scattered trees in the distance were vibrant and welcoming; all was covered in lingering morning dew.

The Princess suppressed a smile. Not yet. They weren't there just yet.

She wouldn't process how far they'd come—that they had returned in one piece—until she was standing in the keep entrance, marveling and delighting at all that was The Palace.

An hour later, they reached the border. She hadn't before been awake when crossing into—or being forced out of—her Kingdom, but Evalyn knew without a doubt that it was within sight. It took every ounce of the strength she had left to hold in her emotions as they crossed it. A breeze flicked her loose hair, and the Alpha gave a light chuckle—the only sound anyone made. Evalyn wanted to laugh and dance as much as sink to the ground and cry.

But she didn't. Simply stormed closer to the city, never faltering her southwest gaze.

The next day, they remained quick and light-stepped. Koathe was in sight.

It was an indistinguishable speck in the distance, but in sight. It'd take the entire day to reach the capital gates.

Despite the King and his desires, his army and plans, their relief had stayed well into the darkness of night that no longer seemed as black.

Chapter Twenty Three

Three months. Evalyn had been gone for three months, and the Queen and Kalan, weeks.

The gates of Koathe were taller than the Princess remembered.

"Open the gates!" a deep, pleading voice cried out. "*Open the gates!*"

Walfien Pax.

The four stepped faster. *They were home, they were home, they were home.*

She struggled to stifle her sob as they stumbled onto the Main Road, hundreds of Fae observing their return from a distance. Evalyn wanted to do so many things—run to Walfien, apologize to her Kingdom, explain her absence—but she sensed the stillness behind her and whirled on Kalan, collapsed to the ground. He attempted to push himself up, but it was useless. When beings swarmed around Evalyn—healers and sentinels and anyone who could help—she began panicking.

Too many people, and they were too close—

Time was in slow motion. Walfien's eyes were full of shock and solace as he neared them. The Princess couldn't comprehend his questions; only saw Tania being slipped off of Recks' back, unmoving. Walfien's mouth opened, but Evalyn couldn't hear; she was unable to decipher anything as a pulse grew in her hands, head, body. She couldn't remove her gaze from her mother—nurses surrounded the Queen, their hands quick and skilled, pressing against her skin.

Stripes of glowing gold shot across her body, visibly racing through her veins. When the Queen was transported away by guards, Evalyn reached out a hand.

Her body began giving out.

She stumbled in a circle, gaze fixating on Kalan. Capital nurses poured over him, examining his chest with unfazed faces. Nimble fingers traced his scars; flurries of purple mist rose from within him and sucked into the healer's palms. Kalan's eyes closed.

Walfien gripped the Princess' elbow, but her lips parted and shut, no words escaping. Before she could regain a grasp on reality, Evalyn dropped to the ground, the beating in her head turning to an aching pound. Hands reached for her, but she jerked away—they couldn't touch her. Help her mother, help Kalan, but don't touch her, don't touch her—

The Princess' only reaction to the pain was to scream. To cry out at the searing within her back. She shook in the street, tunic shredding as she frantically clawed at the stabbing in her spine—

Gods, what was it? Her magic again? Or Death with a warning?

Her howl must've echoed across the Kingdom. *Please make it stop, make it stop*—the girl's face was splotched with tears, and hands gripped her own as her cries became silent whimpers from the agony. *Gods help her, the pain...* Something—there was *something* in her, coming from inside. It sliced between her shoulder blades, pushing and stretching her skin—

She didn't feel her body slump to the ground.

Chapter Twenty Four

Evalyn didn't budge upon waking. She was on her stomach, half-curled into a ball under the thin sheets of a cot, when she grew wary of the presences beside her.

"We know about Primascul and his own—*including the fact* that they were never passed onto any Fae after."

Kinz.

Mags responded, "It'd make sense, sister. That Oberon is a descendant, so she's part of the bloodline. It's the only explanation—"

"This isn't something that remains millennia later. Explanations mean nothing. She is a miracle."

Astonishment and joy swelled in Evalyn. Kinz was here.

The Princess blinked her eyes, observing them from her sideways angle. The witches weren't identical—Kinz was a blunt mountain, with her fire-red braids and thick-cloaked attire, whereas Mags was the deep sea, with cleansing hands and translucent-jeweled accessories. But even if Mags hadn't already declared it, their familial tie would've been undoubtable. Both were wise and healing and unconditionally welcoming.

"Evalyn!" the women both exclaimed at the Faerie's movement. Evalyn attempted a smile, cut short by a throbbing headache as she sat up. She placed her head in her hands from the dizziness.

Then she felt them; reached behind to a smoothness. Softness. And sensed it in her fingers *and* her back. In *them*; the new part of her.

Wings.

They were a deep bronze along the entire length, flecked with gold-dust. Made of feathers, yet... not. The wings were solid, but a haze around the edges turned them to translucent shadows. Or rays of light. The Princess peered over the other shoulder, comprehending their size—tucked together, they were already wider than her body and rose above her head. Fully spread... she couldn't imagine. Evalyn's head spun as she looked at Kinz and Mags. She gripped the cot edge as her body swayed. "How... are they what you were discussing?"

Mags sucked in a breath. "We don't yet understand their existence, dear. There could be many factors leading to them—we haven't pinpointed a reason."

"Nevertheless, they're gorgeous, and an utter sensation to our lands." Kinz smiled. "Once your body becomes familiar with the weight, we can figure out how to work them. In due time, of course." The woman reached for the Princess' hand. "I promised we'd see each other again."

Evalyn squeezed the matron's fingers. "When did you arrive? How long ago did we return?"

"A few days. I arrived last night." Her eyes twinkled.

Evalyn reached for her wings, gulping as she realized what Kinz had meant. After who knew how long... she could potentially fly. The Princess shifted to the edge of the cot—using substantially more effort than she recalled ever needing. The wings were lighter than expected, but the weight was vast and strange. She released a breath.

She'd eventually have to do it. Might as well get it done.

Closing her eyes, the Faerie searched for the muscle to command the movement. Sucking in a sharp breath, she willed her wings to shift.

Kinz and Mags gripped her shoulders and hands as Evalyn cried out, nearly plunging to the floor. Gods... she'd have to learn how to do everything over again. Walking, standing—fighting. She'd become her strongest in Braena, but had lost that power during captivity and travel. Evalyn would be in the training room before sunrise until after it set, no matter her mother's approval. She had to strengthen every newfound skill and learn to wield her abilities to maximum use.

The Princess straightened, standing with minimal aid from the witches. Evalyn was no less broken, but she was unique, she supposed. And as much as she didn't want to be... a weapon in this War.

Evalyn was brought to her bedroom following her visit with Kinz and Mags the previous day. After slipping in and out of sleep for hours, she allowed the rest control, although with subsequent punishment—nightmare after nightmare woke her from the slumber. The exhaustion of traveling had temporarily stopped them, but they were back.

And horrible in return.

Six months ago, Evalyn couldn't have fathomed her current life: Princess of a Kingdom endangered by her father, a ruthless King empowered by fear and evil.

The terrors forced her to face Oberon, sickening her no matter that he wasn't actually beside her, taunting her, mercilessly torturing those she loved: Kalan, her mother, then Walfien, Kinz, Mags, her maids. She was surrounded by them all, dead—the Princess was in a room of corpses, the murdered citizens of her Kingdom, gone, lost, because of her selfishness.

It was her fault.

Her fault.

Her fault.

A pair of strong and stable hands shook her shoulders, but she was sobbing, gasping ragged breaths, scared to believe the visions were over.

"It's okay. Evalyn, it's okay."

She released her grip on the bed sheets, teeth chattering and body shaking. Walfien Pax mirrored her—on his knees, hands outstretched, eyes wide, dark hair disheveled from sleep. "It's okay," he repeated. "You're here. You're safe."

Walfien had supported her for so long. Through so much. And then they were separated, alone in the Kingdoms, and she'd come back as they'd first met—a frightened girl, kept awake by terrors and broken by what she'd gone through.

But he was unchanged—he was a shining light guiding her from internal darkness.

She was crying again as she gripped him. His returning touch under her wings was light yet affirming. Their breathing intermingled before syncing; the tension in her chest drained away. He said, "I'm here for you through the rough just as much as the easy. Even if there aren't as many of those anymore."

She pulled away. "I Saw your arrival. I rode from midmorning to reach Koathe in time and entered the capital moments before you reached the northern gate. Seeing all of you return... it was like a weight lifted off my chest."

Evalyn's lips curled, although her vision blurred with more tears. "I'm sorry, Walfien. I'm sorry for everything you had to go through in our absence. How did you fare?"

He sat back and shook his head, half a smile on his lips. When she didn't soften her stare, his facade dropped. Walfien released a long breath, his words soft. "I was Hand of the Queen whilst you and your mother were gone—only that. Unseeing, unfeeling; I lost the ability to function, for a while. Mags withheld me from turning wholly bitter." He truly smiled now, although the feature comprised exhaustion, sorrow, ache. "I missed you so much, Evalyn."

"I missed you too," she whispered. His blue and green eyes sparkled in the calm morning light as he observed her wings and face. "What?" she breathed.

"They're astounding."

She bit her lip, touching her wings—she still couldn't believe they were real. "I don't know what to do with them. Where to begin."

"We'll figure it out. We always do. Like any new ability, you have to practice and get used to it—them."

Evalyn sighed; his presence was soothing. "Will you stay?"

His face lit up. "I wouldn't leave if I had to."

She simpered. "We can attempt the basic skills. May I?"

She moved to the edge of the bed; her open fingers were clasped by a warm embrace as Walfien found her side. With a heave, she slipped off the bed, willing her legs to hold. Although the pressure of her wings tugged her down, she didn't immediately crash to the floor. The Princess shuffled her feet, maintaining a solid stance as more weight released across her body. She wasn't surprised by the soreness along her spine, but with days' rest, was unprepared to take her first step.

Evalyn stumbled forward, hands scrambling for a hold—Walfien threw his arms under her own as she fell, legs giving out.

"Slow and steady," he chuckled.

She winced.

But by evening, Evalyn managed to stand on her own and take slow, careful steps to and from her balcony.

Her chamber door clicked open. Reclining on her bed, Evalyn straightened as Walfien entered with a tray of steaming food—and a beaming Kalan. The Princess shoved herself forward, exhaustion and soreness replaced with overwhelming glee. The Alpha was in front of her within a second.

"How are you?" he questioned, voice low. Their gazes locked, and she knew he meant more than physically. How comfortable was she? How far was he allowed to go?

Evalyn glanced at Walfien. Something in his face asked what Kalan could possibly mean when she'd been lively all day—Evalyn smiled to ward off his curiosity. She didn't want either of them bearing her burdens. Yet... the Princess needed to move on. Push away the memories holding her back for the prosperity of Faylinn, if not herself.

She answered, "Better."

Within a moment, he wrapped arms around her shoulders and settled his lips onto her forehead. A considerate, caring restart of intimacy.

Eyes closed, she hummed, "Do you like the new addition?"

"They're beautiful."

Evalyn opened her eyes. His expression was of complete adoration. "And how are you? Healed?"

"Only scars remain. I didn't want them wiped by magic."

She understood; had demanded the same upon waking in the infirmary. Internal healing had been unarguable with the nurses, but the surface scars already formed had been easier untouched, anyway. Like Kalan's, they were reminders of what Braena would get back. "What about Recks?"

"You'll have to see yourself," Kalan said. "Later," he added as she opened her mouth to question. "Have you seen Tania?"

The Princess halted, appalled. How had her first concern not been to see her mother?

"You didn't have the strength until now. She'll understand," Walfien piped from the doorway.

Kalan reached out a hand, but she batted it away. "I can do this." As practiced with Walfien, her focus shifted not on the work it took to move, but on placing one foot in front of the other. A simple, effortless task. Her mind even strayed to Walfien's watching eyes as she neared him. The Hand nodded in assurance when she grasped the door handle. It took the Princess' remaining will to cross the hallway and reach her mother's bedside. Walfien and Kalan remained outside; a warmth left her at the closed door.

The Queen's skin was a sickly green, eyes dark and sunken. Her hair hung in tired curls atop her shoulders, and the bedsheets were so flat, tucked tight against the Faerie's body, the bed almost appeared empty. She was frail—had thinned dramatically in the days they'd been apart.

It was so unbearably true: her mother was dying.

Tania's eyes opened. She sluggishly dragged herself to sit, the tiniest of smiles on her lips when she noticed Evalyn's wings. "My Lost Princess, home at last."

The bright, warm colors of her room now seemed like Death's manner of humor. A mockery of the life Tania was barely clinging to. "How bad is it?" Evalyn whispered, staunching her tears, fearful that even a word too loud would ruin their time remaining.

"I've commenced preparation for the coronation." The Queen's voice broke, but no tears fell from her eyes.

Evalyn squeezed her quivering lips. She would match her mother's strength. "I wish we never had to."

"Don't worry—I'm ready. As for you, never doubt the future laid ahead. You will outshine all who've come before you, just as Faylinn believes. As I believe."

"I'll make you proud," Evalyn promised. "I'll make you proud, mother." Tania's hand brushed Evalyn's cheek in response. It was stiff and cold.

Sunlight melted the chill in Evalyn's skin as Kalan guided her to the Mediocris Woods. A week ago, they'd trudged the opposite way, destined to save themselves.

Everything had changed since.

The truth of Tania's sickness had been revealed: the Queen was soon to pass, and the Princess would rise. Talk of coronation had begun, but kept far from Evalyn at her behest. Her mother wasn't gone yet. For now, she'd give a speech to explain the months of her absence; another of Evalyn's requests. Her Kingdom deserved to know the course of their future due to what she'd done.

Kalan squeezed her hand. "What's on your mind?"

"It's just... nerves. I'm meeting your father, after all—"

"You aren't worried about meeting Recks. This is more than that." He stopped, facing her. "You don't have to hide from me. You're allowed to feel upset and scared and wronged. Oberon took everything from you—"

"From us. We went through that together."

"And we came out stronger. But for so long, I wasn't there for you."

"That's nothing to fault you for." She brushed his cheek with a hand. "Let's go."

They continued into the trees, steps light. Nights ago, the Princess had discovered a new form of magic when she'd willed her wings away—instantaneously returning to her normal Fae body, free from the work and strain—and insufficient sleep due to their size. Nevertheless, she'd continued training with her wings. They were a symbol, if nothing else—of her bloodline, and how she'd be better than her father.

The buzzing forest welcomed the Princess. They arrived at the edge of the Moon Clan camp, where the pack circled around a gentle morning fire. The air was finally cooling; days shortening. Autumn was en route.

They reached Kye and Jan on a cabin porch. "Princess Evalyn," they crooned in unison, bowing at the waist.

She smiled. "I'm pleased that you're both well."

"We're happy to see you home," Janson piped, eyes crinkling in a beam.

Kye said to Kalan, "Felicity didn't ask me today why you left. What made her stop?"

"We had a long talk after my healing. Along with my mother." Kalan sighed. "As Alpha, there are things I have to do that no one can understand. Make sacrifices that seem incomprehensible or take chances that feel unwinnable."

Kye nodded. "We know. Just... don't leave us like that again." A request, brother to brother. The Alpha dipped his chin in firm agreement.

A shadow at Evalyn's shoulder sent the Faerie into action, spinning to shield the wolves with her arms spread wide, sending a flurry of pine needles whipping in a wind—but it was Recks.

Human Recks.

His appearance as a wolf matched that of his human form, but the male was unlike the Alpha. Aside from the air of authority, Kalan had none of his father's attributes. Recks stood higher, with a brawny, tan-skinned body and dark beard concealing the bottom half of his face. Graying, brunette hair glimmered in the morning sunrays.

"I understand we've already been acquainted. However, allow me to properly introduce myself: Recks Delta, Your Highness. I'm at your service and will." He inclined at the waist into a low, respectful bow.

The Alpha, now scowling, led Recks and Evalyn to a nearby cabin, past a group of onlooking pack members who were just as curious to discover what entailed the new male's arrival. This wolf had likely undergone greater adventures and explored more of Liatue than all wolfkind.

Inside, the three seated themselves at a round table. Recks' voice was gruff as he said, "You deserve to know why I'm here." His son nodded for his explanation. Recks sighed as if preparing for his own speech. "Two decades ago, I left you and your mother. It's clear Oberon's words were truthful—but they were what *he* thought to be true. I didn't think I was fit to raise you, but I *wanted* to. I desperately tried to convince myself that I could give you a life far from mine, but my guilt overpowered that. No matter what I did, you'd be in the spotlight of my deeds, forced into a life you couldn't possibly want. It was for you that I ran. As cowardly as it was, I thought I was making the right choice.

"But I heard about what happened to your pack—to Paiton, and where that put you. As soon as I heard your name and Diana's, I knew I had to come back. No matter if you knew of me or not... I had to know *you*. Even if you eternally despised me for what I did." The man stared blankly. "It was the worst decision of my existence, to leave you and your mother behind."

The Alpha seemed to wholly ignore the legend's intent. "It was the best thing that ever happened to me. Without you, I've become the leader and Alpha I was meant to be." Kalan stood, hands scratching the table. He'd wanted rectification from his father, not an apology. He continued although Evalyn gripped his arm, silently begging him to sit. "And you're right. I would've lived in your shadow, and hated who I would've had to become to please the scathing eyes of your supporters. You would have ruined what I've spent my whole life building. Did you think aiding our escape from Braena would grant you free entry into my life?"

"That's enough, Kalan," Evalyn hissed. His face snapped to her own, softening immediately.

Recks seemed to expect as much. Golden eyes strayed to the table between them, fingers tracing the age-worn scores in the wood.

Evalyn said, "Times are different, Kalan. We need to direct our anger in opposite directions from each other." The woman slowly looked at Recks. "But you..." It was the legend's turn to receive the Princess' sweltering stare. "You cannot waltz into this Kingdom and expect a wholly welcoming approach. Regaining the trust from pack elders—and a relationship with your son—will take time. Until then, we shall collaborate as ruling figures. With influence across Liatue, you can significantly steady our side."

The man scrunched his eyebrows. "What do you propose, Highness?"

"I'm tasking you with scheduling a continental tour to gather forces. Whatever wolves you can rally, Faylinn will have them. I'm sure you made a friend or two in the years of your absence—perhaps there is a debt to call in. You have two days to acquaint yourself with the Moon Clan. After my speech, the countdown to your mission begins." Because in two days, she'd stand before the citizens of Faylinn, her friends and family, to explain what had occurred in Braena, and what would happen to their Kingdom because of it. Even with

King Oberon's plans on public display, it would only be a matter of time—and effort—before he gathered allies and grew his army. Faylinn had to move first.

Recks' vision danced between them.

Kalan said, "If you want to come back into my life... you're going to help us win this War."

The Princess paced at her bedroom door, stomach twisting as she recited the words she'd memorized. There were hours until her speech—she'd forced herself to have *some* idea about what to say. The Faerie couldn't stand before her Kingdom wordlessly. Having to do the same for his clan, Kalan had left her room either ten minutes or two hours ago; she'd lost track.

Even with her planning, she was a flurry of emotions, so when the knob turned and her door swung wide, Evalyn gasped in both joy and shock as Beverly, Ida, and Vixie hurtled for their Princess. With a chorus of laughter, the Faeries sank to the floor in a huddle.

"I missed you all greatly," Evalyn chortled.

Beverly gripped Evalyn's hands with a grin. Her plump cheeks were a deep pink. "When we heard you were back—" She looked at Ida and Vixie happily— "oh, we were astounded! Lord Pax graciously ensured we'd remain in service to you, and we weren't even temporarily relocated to another Lady! Of course, we helped around the castle—we couldn't leave the work to everyone else, that wouldn't be kind nor a good use of our time, but he granted us a two-week leave to visit our families and we weren't due to come back for another three days, but then your return spread—"

"I'm sure Evalyn understands," Vixie giggled. "We were told of your disappearance, Princess, although it was obvious that you were gone after a day—then your absence was followed by Queen Tania and the Alpha. The full account has been a secret among few, but we're simply pleased for your return—our carriages just arrived this morning."

"You weren't told?" Evalyn's voice quieted. The handmaids shook their heads, beams faltering. Her closest friends had no idea where she'd been taken. Knew nothing about the holding of Faylinn's leaders.

"Don't worry, Evalyn," peeped Ida from under thick, dark lashes. "Whatever you need to say will be announced in a few hours. You don't have to speak of what you endured unless you're ready and willing." The Princess reached out to the Fae's small hands. Beverly and Vixie held onto each other as if they were to let go, they'd wake from a dream; Ida watched with adoration and understanding—despite their lack of knowledge on the past three months. The Princess would never be able to repay them for their unfailing devotion.

No one would fit in more perfectly than Luca. She'd tell the girls about her once the truth was uncovered—because even if the entire Kingdom spited the Princess for her actions, these Faeries would never leave her side.

It broke her heart more than the alternative of being alone.

Vixie tugged her arm. "Let's get you in the bath; we've much to do. Three months' absence calls for a thoroughly dramatic entrance."

The Princess was grateful for every miniscule act as they readied her. They didn't stumble at the foul scars on her shoulder and arm, nor question her hesitancy to reveal them. The girl savored every moment of the manicuring, brushing, and washing, and when the Faeries were done, singing through the process, Evalyn embraced them before being whisked out of her quarters and ushered into the Great Hall.

Despite the length of her absence, her speech wouldn't be held in the capital. Those aware of the reality of her disappearance wouldn't allow her outside castle grounds—except when the Alpha personally escorted her to and from the Mediocris Woods—until they were prepared to take the risk. According to Walfien, they weren't. She couldn't yet bear the thought of leaving again anyways, even for a day-trip to the most sealed and secure city in the Kingdom.

Princess Evalyn strode through the center of the Great Hall, taking her place at the Royal throne as Faeries filed in. The Great Hall filled to the brim with nobles and castle guests, but staff of The Palace and common folk from Koathe and nearby villages carried on their attempts to enter when the guards began shutting the entry. Shouts rose into a loud wave of complaint—the foyer remained overflowing with Fae wishing to hear.

"Leave them open," her voice boomed. Every being in the Hall shifted toward the Princess. "Leave them open for those who want to hear." The immediate swing of the re-opening doorway echoed.

When all movement halted, countless silent gazes were her cue to begin.

Where were you?

Explain what you've done.

How broken are you?

The Princess ignored everything she memorized.

"Over three months ago, I was kidnapped and smuggled to the Kingdom of Braena." Gasps trickled through the room. "I was forced to do things that hurt me, but made me stronger in the end. It's with desperate desire that I ask you to attempt to understand why I made several of the choices I did. It was for each and every one of you, and your family and friends and those you have never met and never will, that I tried my best to save Faylinn." Evalyn paused; forced her emotions down. No matter how recalling it made her feel, they had the right to know. "Over the course of my captivity in Braena, Oberon informed me of the plans for his Kingdom. He is building a monstrous army of creatures called Sanguin, which he intends to set upon us. He is willing to gain power over the Kingdom of Ausor and use them, if necessary, to destroy and dominate Liatue. And he wants me at his side whilst doing it, to convince all of our peoples that his desires are best."

She willed her wings to arise from the magic within. All eyes turned to circles as whispered astonishment sparked between neighbors and strangers. It was the first time she'd publicly shown them; there'd been rumors about her wings since their appearance in Koathe, but no mass confirmation until now. The crowd seemed to lean ever closer. "You may wonder why I'm alive, then. Why I'm in The Palace with such crucial information about Oberon Romen's schemes, and speaking about it as plainly as describing the sky." She sucked in a deep breath. "I am his daughter."

Now her audience tripped backward. Hissed rumor and chiding comments began immediately, but was impounded by the overwhelming silence of the Faeries' curiosity.

She continued. "Being so, Oberon wouldn't kill me, but gave me two choices: join him and rule by his side, leaving those I love to bow at our feet, or return home and share what I learned to win this War. You see, he believes we have no savior. That Faylinn is doomed, and no matter my attempts, we will lose. But I believe we will have victory. So I escaped to fight for you." She pointed at a man before her, who gulped, startled at her acknowledgement. "And you." The Princess continued, a young girl coming into view. "And you." Her hand moved to the back of the room. "And every Faerie in this Kingdom. I will protect and defend *everyday* to defeat the creature that is the King, because I know we have a chance. He's taken too much from too many!" she shouted. The crowd's voices shifted from hushed support to blatant cries of rejoice. Across the hall, acceding clapping rang. "Oberon has ruined and torn us apart and broken our souls over and over and over... but we must not be deterred from this battle. Whether I push through or die trying, I will fight. *I will fight.* For us. *For Faylinn.*" Evalyn lifted her chin. She wouldn't look away. Oberon could take, destroy, obliterate—

But she had something he didn't.

True fire in her veins. Determination that couldn't be stifled. Her father lived for himself and his rule, but she had something truly worth dying for: them.

Her last words were a cry to the Gods. "*Will you?*"

The Princess was pulled from the chaos; from the shouts and hurrahs by hundreds of Fae that had miraculously found hope in her mess of words. She was outside her living quarters within a moment, but the cries of the citizens remained deafening. Evalyn hadn't intended for the explanation to turn into a rallying speech, but... it was where she'd been led. They knew enough of what she'd gone through, and Evalyn couldn't have left the chamber without talk of War. There was no use denying it. Oberon would come, and they had to be prepared.

Despite the dire need for preparation, she entered her chamber and slumped onto her bed.

Chapter Twenty Five

It made sense why her mother was ready to let go.

Tania had spent years—decades—taking charge of what Faylinn and its people would say and do, what they would *be*. A role certain to be fatally grueling. After her commitment and contribution to Faylinn, it was past time to give up the life of power and pass it on.

Evalyn had tried to prepare for Tania's last goodbye, when the light faded from her eyes and she found a place of peace and light. It was a perfect day: they'd encountered the Autumnal Equinox, marking the change in season whilst the Kingdom rejoiced over the return of harvests and prosperity.

But a personal warning from Death himself couldn't have readied the Princess.

When her pale-faced handmaids met the end of the hallway she walked down, they didn't have to say what was happening. Tears already coated Evalyn's cheeks when she whipped into the room. Tania's Keepers and the maids and nurses remained at the door. Healing would no longer provide comfort nor aid.

Evalyn stumbled to the bedside. Her mother was still beautiful, despite her cool gray skin and the deep purple under her eyes. She gripped Tania's hand, frail and bony. The Queen angled her face towards her daughter, voice a raspy murmur. "I'm sorry we didn't have more time." Despite her thinning breaths and slowing heartbeat, despite the fact that everything would change in simple seconds, Tania's eyes were clear while they looked over the Princess, crouched as close to the Queen as she could get.

Evalyn squeezed a hand, laying her forehead over their intertwined fingers. Hot tears splattered on their skin.

The pounding in her ears was overwhelming, yet the Princess choked out, "Thank you for bringing me back to this life. So I was able to better your own, if nothing else." No matter that the Queen was leaving it, no matter that Oberon was destroying it day by day, no matter that one of the few reasons Evalyn had pushed through so long was because of the woman in front of her.

Tania's blink declared her agreement. The Princess watched her mother, anticipating, hoping for a final, dying scrap of wisdom, or a last memory to add to the strength and experience Evalyn only possessed because of the Queen.

But Tania smiled and took a breath. Closed her eyes. Exhaled.

Her chest rose no more.

A sob escaped Evalyn's lips. She squeezed Tania's hand, and the Faeries at the door knelt in honor and remembrance; the Gods had taken the Queen into their embrace. But all that swirled through Evalyn's mind was the knowledge that her mother would never wake up. Heat and cold rushed through the Princess' body as she slumped against the bedside. Emotions surged through her; grief from the loss, uncertainty of her next steps, relief that her mother was no longer hurting. But above the rest, she felt boiling anger.

Enragement.

A wave of power rushed to her fingertips.

The Princess didn't contain it. The cries of the distant females became unheard, and the quaking of the room, *the castle*, was not felt by her body.

After everything her wretched father had done, she couldn't blame him for this: her mother's end. Despite what he'd caused Evalyn... there was nothing and no one she could fault but the forces of nature in their duty. It was that truth which sent something formerly slumbering within her to awaken; to open its eyes and blink in the first of its sight.

A power without end stirred from the pit of her soul.

Evalyn didn't move from Tania's body—the Queen's chilling, lifeless body. Walfien Pax braced himself between the huddle of females at the door as Evalyn sent a rolling wave of power—a thick and tangible black shadow exuding from her fingertips—through the durable stone building. Or what had once been thought to be unwavering. The magical swaying of the castle said otherwise.

Self-shielded, the Hand shoved through the panting servants in the doorway before diving towards the Princess. A mass surge of this... *darkness*, this raw force surely passed down from Oberon, and she knew everyone would be in worse states than the pains her burst had put them through. But she couldn't withhold the magic—it had a will of its own.

Walfien pried Evalyn's hands from Tania. Through the murky shadow, she found him white faced, glassy-eyed, and scowling as she attempted to pull from his hold, but he didn't let go—the Hand knew he had to get her out and calmed down. Quickly. What a greater release of the darkness could do was unknown.

"Evalyn, please." He pulled on her arm. She didn't budge.

"*No*."

"You can't stay here like this." Another tug, and she wrenched from his grasp, curling her knees to her chest with a sob. Canvases fell from the walls and stone dust crumbled from the ceiling.

The Princess rocked back and forth, shielding her face with her hands. She couldn't think straight beyond acknowledging the aching sorrow in her chest. Her wings flared out—stretching nearly across the full depth of the room. A gust of wind sent Walfien to the ground, but he was on his feet in an instant—throwing Evalyn over his shoulder before she could object.

He was at the doorway when she noticed their retreat.

"No, no—take me back!" Her shout echoed down the hallway, and Walfien scrambled faster to her room as she began pushing on his body, howling, "*Take me back! Take me back!*" But they were in her quarters within a second, on her bed, the Princess' eyes wide and gaping. He restrained her wrists at her sides against the pillows, their bodies an inch apart, tears endlessly dripping down pink cheeks. She struggled harder—

"She's gone, Evalyn! *She's gone!*" Walfien blurted.

Evalyn stilled. Silenced.

Along with the rocking castle and groaning sentinels and sniffling females in the hallway. The shadow mass billowing through the castle drifted back into her bedroom, into her fingers; the magic returned to the girl's veins.

Unending saltwater flowed down Evalyn's skin. The color in her wings faded; the hazy light they contained shrunk and folded in on itself, as if being sucked into a realm of dark lament. In a blink, the wings were gone. Walfien released his hold, but Evalyn didn't move.

The Hand crouched in the corner of her room; watching carefully and distantly.

Waiting for words or calm or acknowledgement.

But when the sun escaped their vision, the room was enveloped in a blackness deeper than the Princess' grief.

Chapter Twenty Six

Blonde hair stuck to the Princess' forehead with sweat. She clenched her hands and faced Walfien, an impeccable, mute focus tying them together. Evalyn shoved down the fatigue circling in her veins—she'd begged to be taught this.

Control and power.

To maintain self-will when another's magic tried to overtake her.

To barricade her mind from attacking forces like the King.

Walfien had met her at the training room without protest. The last she'd tested her physical limits, pushed herself so hard, had been in Braena. With Asodu, whose ways were made for soldiers preparing for battle. His unforgiving teaching declared breaks meant insufferable consequences, that understanding your limit was weakness—there were no ends to a Fae's strength. Anyone could keep going. To him, breaking point was a sheer matter of will.

But now was no time to dwell on the past. For the past week, she'd used vigorous training sessions to divert the crushing thoughts of just that, and what its events entailed for her future. Easy enough, considering the multitude of skills demanding upkeeping. Evalyn had come to possess the creation of every element—fire, water and ice, wind, and land—and her mother's empathy. But the Princess hadn't been able to reproduce the dark magic that'd emerged after her mother's passing. She'd have to wait until it showed itself to practice and study it.

As for the current power test... her mind settled into a place of stillness. Walfien lightly curled his hand into a fist, contorting his magic into a version of the power Oberon held. Albeit different, it was all they had to practice against. The Hand's invisible yet tangible strikes of magic demanded specific responses from her senses and nerves; it was a physical version of Oberon's power, who's true attacks would be equivalent attempts to control her, but using his mental command. Defeating Walfien came when she could maintain her self control enough to overthrow her reactionary dodges and counterattacks. Withholding the desire to defend herself translated into restraining unhelpful instincts in battle—and instead forming a barrier around her mind to shield herself from Oberon.

Walfien shot his hand out, slowly closing his grip. Standing, limbs taut, Evalyn ignored the hit at her hips and the tightening sensation on her arms. But the repeated magical slices at the base of her neck became more ticklish and annoying by the second and before she could stop herself, her fingers swiped the air. She growled at her response, eyes opening.

The Hand stepped back. "Your defenses are weak, Evalyn. I can't sense your thoughts, but I can feel your struggle. Brick by brick, you have to build the power to block your mind. Otherwise Oberon will be able to do whatever he wants if he gets through."

The Princess heaved a breath. "Just go again." Keeping to anywhere except her bedroom, making sure everyday that she was busy from dawn to dusk with hearing civil cases, council meetings, or studying The Door and Vynus, Evalyn had fallen into a bustling routine. Training had become both a nightly and morning ritual, filling the gaps between fitful sleep and a new day of work.

Although it was appallingly tiring, she had to follow the gripping routine. Admitting that she wanted a break meant recognizing her exhaustion, and the girl had made herself busy with Royal obligations to specifically divert her attention from all feelings beyond preoccupation. Once Evalyn acknowledged her weariness, she'd have to acknowledge the despair and hurt, and she wasn't ready for the beginning it would lead to. To move on from the aching loss of her mother, the only true parent the Gods had given her. The only one that mattered. Moving on meant accepting that she was alone.

Nonetheless, in a few short days, Evalyn would have no choice. The end of the week marked the memorial speech for Tania; a consolation for the Kingdom-wide tragedy the night before Evalyn's coronation.

But for now, the Princess could blot out her sorrow with exertion. Her and Walfien's repeated fight offered the same result, this time with both of them stumbling to the sides of the mat from the gale of wind she abruptly formed.

Evalyn sucked in a breath. "You're holding back."

"I'm already hurting you," he said.

"I can handle the sting."

The Hand rolled his neck without retort. Three strikes impacted her at once, then a flurry of back-to-back magic punches that amplified the pressure in her chest. Evalyn suppressed the urge to sink to her knees, and her face scrunched in concentration, lips drawn. She was holding out longer. A coil of his power swirled her head, tugging her hair and scratching her face and shoulders—but dissolved after a couple seconds.

"Why did you stop?" she complained. "My defense was solid and stable."

Walfien flung his arms to the sides of the room, and they both crashed to the ground.

"What..." Evalyn gulped air, "was that for?"

"That's what it would feel like with Oberon—sudden and powerful. That portion of my power was more than I've given you this entire session," Walfien returned breathlessly, "and a minute amount compared to your father. And you weren't prepared because you're trying to impossibly master a great feat in one sitting. This progress feels like nothing, but you have to go slow or you'll hit burnout."

"But I can do more," she pleaded as the Hand picked her up from the ground. Walfien didn't release his grip on her forearms.

"I think we're done for today."

"No. I have to keep going. If I want to have any chance against my father, I can't stop until I'm stronger—"

"You *are* strong," he countered. "You're more powerful in your magic than most Guard soldiers, and equally as active." She pulled away sharply, eyebrows furrowing. The Hand closed his eyes before asking, "Your training hasn't been about building skills this week, has it?"

She wasn't going to talk about her mother. The Faerie swallowed. "Can we go one last time?"

"You've done enough."

"Please."

"I'm sorry."

"*Please*, Walfien. Training and fighting is *all I have left*. To prepare Faylinn for victory in this War. If I can't do this, what hope do I have when true battle comes?"

"What do you not understand? *It doesn't matter!*" he declared, shaking his head. "If you aren't mentally sound, you will fail in any war that comes. Wild emotions lead to recklessness and anger that overwhelm any common sense you possess—*that* is how you slip up and die. Right now, your unchecked grief is lethal."

"But I—"

"You're going to rest. Especially with Tania's memorial and your coronation at the week's end. Acknowledge yourself, Evalyn."

"I can't. You know why—I can see it in your eyes, you *know* what this despair feels like—"

"No training until after your coronation," Walfien commanded, although his tone was apologetic.

"You can't tell me what to do."

His chin dropped to his chest, yet he said, "I don't want to see you in this room until I can trust you're going to care for yourself outside of it. Tania wouldn't desire your suffering because of her."

She stumbled backwards. There was an overarching kindness in his demand, some tucked-away part of her knew, but... "Fine. Get out of my sight until then."

Evalyn had loathed Walfien in those moments.

Engrossing herself in mindless activity of training meant she didn't have to deal with her pain yet. The Faerie had despised Walfien—her *friend*—for taking that choice away.

He'd even had the audacity to order the sentries to deny her access to the training room when she attempted to sneak a half hour session the same evening.

She detested Walfien more in the following days, when he took charge of almost all her duties, leaving her with insurmountable spare time during which she wandered the gardens in pained silence or vented her annoyance to her handmaids or studied whatever she could find of The Door and Vynus. The afternoon following his demand, Walfien had apologized—or it's what he'd tried to do before Evalyn slammed her bedroom door in his face in petty rage.

The Princess had done much thinking since—had been *forced* to, thanks to him.

She crouched at the head of a row of yellow flowers, brushing her fingers along the sunlit petals and inhaling the aroma of pollen and soil. With the twist of her wrist, a puddle of water pooled at the base of the bushes before gently seeping into the ground. The tending was unnecessary, as castle servants nurtured every species in the gardens year round, but the activity eased the knots in her chest.

"Befriending the carnations?"

Kalan leaned against the wall of the Great Tower, head skimming the bottom lip of a long, half round window sill.

"Sometimes I think they're better companions than ourselves," Evalyn said. "Their only concern, to be. A peaceful existence." She stood. "And they're yarrows, not carnations."

The Alpha strode onto the grounds with a smile. Evalyn followed him to her usual hiding spot, the secluded pouch of grass nestled within the lines of hibiscus shrubs. He plopped onto the dirt, patting the space beside him. "How long have you been out here for?"

Evalyn sat, bringing her knees to her chest with palms wrapped around her legs. "An hour. Maybe two. I wasn't keeping track."

"Everyone will arrive in a few more," Kalan said. "This very spot will be filled." With many more Fae willing to travel to The Palace for their fallen Queen than the Great Hall could hold, Tania's service would be held in both the gardens. It felt Evalyn had just explained her absence yesterday, and now she was to recollect her portion of Tania's life to Faylinn. The Alpha intertwined their fingers. "It'll be good. To say goodbye."

Evalyn leaned a cheek onto her knees, watching the Alpha. Birds tweeted in the hawthorn tree before them. "How's Recks?"

A deep inhale. "Actually... great. You can see his clear effort in council meetings; he adds a stopover in his route almost daily and is constantly cleaning up his plan. He isn't leaving until it's perfected, apparently."

"We did give him an order to obtain as many allies as possible."

Kalan chuckled. "Beyond that, he truly is trying to get to know me. Everyday at sunset he asks to sit around the main fire and talk. He tells me of his travels and I reveal my life. He's entirely soft spoken and more gentle than you'd expect of a legendary wolf... but I am used to Jan and Kye's chaos. It isn't saying much that I'm surprised."

"That's wonderful," she murmured. Although she could never again sit with and learn about her mother. Never again could the Queen bestow her knowledge or grace onto others. She straightened.

"You don't have to hold it in." Kalan swept back Evalyn's hair, holding her face in his hands until she met his gaze. "I did the same when my father was killed," he added. "Kept everything inside and never thought it was too much—until I exploded. And realized I had to give myself the time to grieve, and continue on with my life because that's what he would want."

"I know."

Kalan tilted his head. "Your mother would want you to do the same."

"I know."

"Do you want to talk about it?"

"Ask me after her service." She had a feeling it'd be easier after tonight.

He smiled. "Okay."

When the sun hugged the western horizon, the Faeries flooding the gardens began lifting their whoops and exclamation. All were dressed in multitudes of colors, as was standard; Fae memorials were held to remember and celebrate the life of those passed, and glorify the beauty of the afterlife they had entered. The plant-swathed hilltop was vibrant and shining.

Voices of Guard leaders, Conclave Lords, prestigious nobles, and chosen common-folk rebounded over the grounds from their elevated stage at the castle's edge as they reflected on the Queen Mother's dreams and accomplishments. Tania's Keepers—who remained at the Palace with their only remaining duty to live full lives as Court members—watched on tearfully but brightly, erupting into praise after Serene sang a melody she had written for Tania in their youth. Only because of Walfien and Kalan's encouragement was Evalyn able to study and retain the stories claimed by everyone.

When it was her time to speak, her stomach flipped and legs trembled as she marched onto the platform. This time she'd actually brought the parchment containing her outlined speech to ensure she noted all of her desired thoughts, if not out of fear of forgetting everything and drawing a blank. This memorial was not the time to turn speechless—nor invoke a spontaneous call to arms for War. Her speech was short, despite the fact. Simple and to the point, summarizing what Walfien had covered more extravagantly in his speech just before her. The Princess' thin, emerald gown brushed against her legs as a breeze cooled her sweating frame. A long inhale eased her nerves.

"There isn't a word that could approach defining who Tania Impur was to me," Evalyn said. "My mother was a fierce fighter, who desired the best for Faylinn. But she desired the best for me, too. Through the journey of resettling into my Fae life, she was ready for every question and concern. Tania consistently reminded me of her unwavering trust and belief, and I am a stronger woman today because of the strength she possessed in my darkest moments. I will not fail in accomplishing my mother's dreams, and I will make her proud."

Shoulder to shoulder before the Princess, the people of Faylinn tilted their chins up to the darkening sky. Tears leaked from some eyes; others stood motionless with closed lids; even more beamed in the face of the above.

Evalyn had never spoken any of the Faerie adages. She'd received the one of fun and fortune on her nameday, but hadn't vocalized any of the universal sayings that brought together folk of every stature and regard. It seemed fitting that her first was to commemorate Tania.

"The bereaved find relief!" she declared.

"As they will!" returned the crowd, a spirited thrum that reverberated across the entire Palace grounds.

It was true. Evalyn could heal. She could grow, and move on, and do what her mother had wanted her to. She could find peace in achievement, starting with clearing Liatue of its evil and woe.

As Faylinn exalted Tania's afterlife existence, the empty pit in Evalyn's chest stopped expanding.

Chapter Twenty Seven

By the morning of her coronation, the pit had started to fill.

The unforgettable esteem that Faylinn held Tania in proved that although her mother was gone in form, she lived on in spirit. Evalyn still ached to think that she couldn't hug her mother, but her fading sadness was proof that Tania remained walking alongside her.

A knock sounded at the door, snapping the Princess' out of her awakening daze. Granting her permission for entry, Walfien stepped through the threshold. His eyes darted around the room, from her position in a new canopy bed to the woven rug and fresh set of slow-burning candles. Her quarters had been refurbished, along with the Queen's chamber—the royal residence that Evalyn would soon take up for the length of her official rule.

Walfien wasn't in his guard uniform, instead clad in a tunic and trousers, his hair rumpled. He'd woken recently as well. When he brought his stare to Evalyn, their words came out together.

"I'm sorry I didn't see you were trying to help."

"It was wrong of me to stick you in here."

They chortled, but quieted after the confessions. Walfien rubbed the back of his neck. Evalyn left her bed, morning light shining through her windows and a cooling breeze sweeping into her room as she walked onto the balcony. Walfien approached her side, inches from the edge of the wings she'd summoned. They'd become a presence she longed for.

"Thank you," she exclaimed, voice airy from sleep. Walfien turned. "If it wasn't for you, I'd still be stuck in my grief and doubt." The Princess sighed. "At first I hated it—I couldn't absorb myself in the things that wrenched me from reality. But you were right: that was my problem. I didn't want to accept that my mother was gone, or that it was okay to continue without her. You helped me do that." She counted the minutes as a shaded breeze ruffled her feathers. "Braena did... many things to me. To all of us. Everything has changed. But I didn't endure what happened on my own."

His blue and green irises traced the tips of her wings. "Despite the atrocity, I'm sure it helped that Kalan and your mother were with you through it. Recks too, if you want to count him—"

"My *point*, Walfien, is that I wouldn't be here without you, either." Walfien stilled; shook his head. She laughed, "Your humility is infuriating. Accept my gratitude."

"I've failed to protect you from every horror."

"You're the reason I was able to protect myself."

He nodded slowly, the corners of his lips rising.

"Thank you, again. I'm sorry for losing my temper."

Walfien reclined his arms on the balcony railing. "You're always thanking me although I do so little."

"I think that means I have numerous favors to return." Evalyn lifted her chin.

"What kind of favors?"

"Anything. Do you desire my suite when I move to my mother's? What's your favorite breakfast course? I can request it to be freshly prepared everyday! Or should you want a personal steed, I'll order the finest stallion Flordem can breed. Oh, you could get a foal to be raised in The Palace, he would be so precious—"

"I get your meaning," he laughed, eyeing her gently. "What if I want other things?"

"Then you shall receive them, Lord Pax."

Walfien fully faced her. "Can I call in one now?" A wind lifted the locks of hair grazing his forehead. His slow heartbeat divulged calm intent, yet something about his expression struck Evalyn, and her response came out as a whisper.

"Yes."

A flutter in her stomach betrayed the thoughts she attempted to push away. The ones that wished he would step closer, that made her forget all sense. She'd never felt drawn to Walfien like this—or maybe she'd never let herself realize it. Maybe she'd stubbornly overlooked his comfort and kindness and care as thoughtless and obligatory duties.

She knew it was true when he placed his lips on hers.

Her heart stopped for a second, then beat out of her chest. She should pull away. It was wrong of her—what would Kalan think? What would she tell him—

Yet the Princess didn't stop the kiss. The pace of her pounding heart said not all in the world had gone to chaos. Selfishly, this felt... right.

Walfien's hands draped down her jawline, onto her neck. The kiss was smooth and warm as his lips brushed against hers. Then he pulled away; they opened their eyes, taking unified breaths. Evalyn staggered away. Heat rose to her cheeks, already flushed with the wild emotions coursing through her, and her hand involuntarily moved to her mouth, the ghost of Walfien's own remaining. She could still feel the soft touch of his lips.

Guilt was an awfully faint afterthought, Gods save her.

The Hand looked as confounded as Evalyn felt. He opened his mouth as if to explain—but was gone from the room in seconds.

Evalyn didn't move from the spot for a long while.

"What's with the pacing?"

The Princess halted her steps in the castle gardens. She faced Kye Kallister, his freckles dark under the sun. She cleared her throat, brows furrowing. "I—well... it's nothing, really—"

"That's not much of an answer," he said. "Actually, it wasn't an answer in the slightest." Brown eyes observed her, then his voice lowered as he leaned towards the Princess. "Why, may I ask, are you distressed on your coronation day?"

"It's not about the coronation," Evalyn spluttered. Kye raised his brows. "I can't tell you. I didn't expect anyone to find me here like this—"

"Not my fault, Princess. Kalan is on castle grounds for the coronation and I was simply heading through for a patrol debrief. Didn't think I'd catch the Princess on the scenic route."

She winced. She would *not* tell one of Kalan's closest friends what had happened that morning. What had put her in a dilemma.

"I haven't seen you at camp in a while," Kye said.

He hadn't? She could swear she'd gone just the other day—no, he was right. The Princess hadn't visited in weeks. Evalyn bit her lip. "You aren't making me feel better, Kye."

A smile. "Sorry. That's Jan's specialty." He tilted his head. "Do you, maybe... want to talk about it? Honestly, the abundance of emotions radiating from you is unnerving, and I don't think you want to feel this way tonight."

No way. *No way* would she tell. But he was right *again*—she couldn't keep this in. She wouldn't be able to focus for the coronation or the subsequent ball, both events requiring complete concentration so she didn't mess up within the first *day* of her reign—"Walfien and I kissed," she exploded. The words tumbled out like a roaring waterfall. "A few hours ago. It's never happened before—truthfully, I didn't think he thought of me as anything more than a friend or ruling partner, but there were so many withheld feelings in the kiss and I didn't stop it, which made me realize I liked it and that I've liked Walfien for a while but hadn't let myself accept it because I love Kalan—and I do, I love Kalan with all I have—" she fumbled for a breath—"yet I can't get Walfien or the kiss out of my head. But I can't tell Kalan because he's *everything* to me and it would hurt him—after the heartache he's suffered, it'd hurt him even more and I can't do that to him—"

Evalyn slammed a hand over her mouth.

Kye gulped, stare wide. He began, words slow, "That's... quite something—"

"You can't say a word." The Princess pounced towards him, gripping the hands that the male raised in surrender. "Please don't tell Kalan," she begged.

"I'll do it eventually. I will. But you can't share a word that I just said, Kye, *please—"*

"I won't," he inserted with a long breath. "I won't tell anyone, Princess. On the Spirits. Trade in that distress for some ale tonight, won't you?"

Chapter Twenty Eight

Kalan let out a shocked puff of air as Evalyn exited her quarters.

She knew what she looked like: no longer the girl she'd once been, but a woman destined for the Crown.

Ready to rule.

Her dress was a rich emerald, with lace along the waistline and hems. The hues of her wings complimented the gown, draping down her back in a mystic veil. Her blonde locks, loosely curled with the top half braided at the back, highlighted the skin that had regained color. Her maids matched her heels and the jewels on her dress with the Crown that'd soon be placed upon her head.

She blushed at Kalan's wordless compliment, smile broad. His suit was cream, with hints of emerald that flawlessly matched her dress. He was more handsome than ever. "Evening, Alpha," she responded, linking her arm through his. Without a mother or father—or any she wanted present—Evalyn had been able to choose her partner for the aisle walk to the throne. As Alpha of Faylinn's only ally, the declaration was obvious. The title was important for an imprint on the crowd, but she also wanted Kalan there, at her side. They hadn't yet discussed their future—a future together—but she loved him, and it was enough.

She forced thoughts of Walfien away.

A fraction of noble Fae and Sages were allowed into the ceremonial throne room; the rest of the Kingdom would view her when she was Queen, greeting them during the celebration in the ballroom. When they reached the doors to the throne room, Evalyn could sense chatting voices through the door. A slab of wood was all that withheld her from her destined future.

"Are you ready?" Kalan asked.

She gave a deep inhale. Nodded. For the first time in her life, she was. She was ready for what awaited her. No matter that War was brewing, that ruling would inevitably be the most difficult time of her life, that she'd eventually have to face her father... she'd persevere.

A harmony of strings sounded as the doors opened.

The rest of her life began.

Hundreds of eyes turned as the sounds of conversation died instantly. Evalyn reminded herself to place one foot in front of the other. Her wings were a steadying presence at her shoulders, and the touch of Kalan kept her nerves at bay. As they approached the front of the room, past rows of standing strangers, most of whom Evalyn would surely know in a week's time, she saw Walfien. He was at the top of the steps to which she neared, watching Kalan at her side. It was a feat to pretend as if nothing had happened, like they were okay and she wasn't overthinking every second they'd spent together, every word they'd shared, all the feelings that had aroused with his departure this morning.

She squeezed Kalan's arm, returning to the task at hand. When they reached their destination, the Alpha slid from her grip and stepped to the side, feet away from the throne she'd occupy in a moment. The Princess met the first step.

The High Minister stood before her in a jeweled, green cloak over black clothing. At Evalyn's look, he gave a pleasant smile and gazed at the crowd. The last whispers silenced. His thick, old voice echoed in the chamber. "Ladies and Gentlemen, Wolf and Fae, I am the High Minister. We gather here today to formally recognize our Royal leader under the blessings of the Gods: Your Highness, Evalyn Impur." The ensuing clapping cut off abruptly at his raised hand. "Before we begin, the Princess has requested to merge two ceremonies in one. Without previous time to receive her signarum, there is no better moment to pronounce her loyalty than now." He gestured to the back of the room, where two Sages strode forth. "Princess Evalyn, where would you desire the forever-mark of Faylinn?"

She'd made her decision days ago—before the kiss. But maybe the Gods had intended her choice to mean even more to Walfien than the Fae had meant—since she was choosing his spot. The Princess pulled down the long sleeve of her dress, revealing the delicate skin of her upper arm. The Sages shifted to her side and lifted their hands; she sucked in a breath as magical ink transferred onto her body. The burning was sudden, but bearable. When they finished the process, the emblem of her Kingdom eternally marked on her skin, a wave of soothing cool flowed from their fingertips before they retreated to the corners of the chamber.

"If you will, Your Highness." The Minister gestured to the object at her feet.

She dropped to her knees and flipped open the renowned book of Faylinn, full of the beginnings of Fae and the Kingdom. The mark of Faylinn was etched into the cover, their symbol of safety and comfort. The tips of her wings touched the ground, their wideness blocking the view of the nobles behind.

"Do you, Evalyn Impur, Daughter of the Queen Mother Tania Impur, Princess of Faylinn and Heir to the Throne and Royal Crown, promise that your words in this ceremony will remain true until your dying breath?"

"I do." Her voice was soft compared to his.

"Let us begin," The Minister announced. He spoke the ancient-script questions without needing to read them from the page. "Will you uphold the beneficial workings of the past leaders of the Kingdom of Faylinn?"

"I will."

"Will you share the purpose of our race as the Gods intended it?"

"I will."

It went on. Question after question of what she'd do as the head of countless others.

Evalyn found herself focused on everything else: the afternoon sun nearing dusk, falling over the back of The Palace; the waiting folk mingling on the castle grounds, whose buzzing energy seemed grand enough to grasp.

Walfien.

He hadn't taken his eyes from Evalyn since the moment she entered the hall. She couldn't help but look. His features transformed to astonishment, as if he hadn't expected her acknowledgement and didn't know what to do with it. The Princess cleared her throat. This was her time; Faylinn's time; her people's time. Later, she'd deal with the matter, deal with the emotions pooled in her stomach.

"And will you swear to follow through with your duties as Ruler, even if your life shall be at stake?"

"I will," Evalyn promised.

The Minister dipped his head to the crowd, and Evalyn rose as he recited the final words of the ceremony. "By the competence of my class and the order of our fallen Queen Mother, it is my duty and utmost honor to announce you as Her Majesty, Queen Evalyn Impur of Faylinn."

Praise and elation and honor erupted from the crowd.

Evalyn lost her breath, reality pausing as she took in the life she'd adopted. She climbed the final steps and stepped closer to her fate. She knelt before the High Minister a last time as a Citadel pupil strode up the steps, pillow in hand. Atop it sat the Royal Crown, which the High Minister lifted and placed on her head.

The weight of it magically suspended atop her hair. She couldn't stop her lips from rising as she approached the jeweled throne. Perched upon it.

The Faeries before her continued their deafening clapping, whooping, rejoicing.

Evalyn simpered. *I will make you proud.*

Music already played inside the Great Hall, along with the whir of hundreds of chatting voices. The corners of the Queen's lips lifted as the ballroom entrance opened.

With a fleeting glance at Kalan, they sauntered forth as the Libcerus' instrumental melody grew in her ears. Although Evalyn had previously stepped to the dance with countless males, the Royal occasion meant the dance could be executed with one of her desire.

As she remembered, the music started slow; an acoustic beat to set the tempo. Her and Kalan's feet moved in turn, their steps perfectly synced. Evalyn tucked nearer to the Alpha; it was the closest they'd been in months. She'd learned how to push away the unsettling panic such proximity gave her—yet although Evalyn welcomed his comforting presence, she was dismayed by the assessing stares from around the hall.

Many Faeries, including her own Court members, dissented from the popular acceptance of her leadership. She was too young and too inexperienced, and had wrought irreversible destruction onto her own Kingdom because of both.

Yet... she could momentarily set aside rules and etiquette. She was Queen. This was her ball, and she wouldn't let it be ruined by the pressure of impressing imperious nobles.

Besides, half the crowd wasn't watching, already tipsy. The citizenry took their drinking seriously.

The music quickened at the Libcerus' pounding chorus. "Time for a show," Kalan declared. She grinned back, words dying in her throat as Kalan flung her into a spin. Laughter dripped from their lips as they circled the floor; the Royal Crown stayed atop her head by some ancient magic she'd never understand.

Her cheeks ached from smiling by the song's close. Kalan spun her one last time, dipping her on the concluding beat; the weight at her back declared her wings had involuntarily spread wide.

The guests began clapping as if it had indeed been a show.

Evalyn rose and closed her wings. A swift, lively tune echoed through the chamber and other Faeries took up the floor. Dresses flared and feet stomped until a layer of sweat coated any visible skin. The music was a uniting melody, linking passionate dancers and drunk Lords and all other guests in a state of joy for hours. Evalyn barely took breaks, swinging through the arms of common-men and Lords and sharing dances with Ladies and their children.

The Moon Clan's arrival brought a wave of celebration that dragged even more guests onto the dancing floor. Evalyn had never seen so many nobles jovial, for once not attacking another's honor as they did in meetings and trials. Felicity Lupien and her friends instantly found Evalyn, lingering in her presence before Diana swept them away and capered with the Queen herself.

Numerous males took their turn in dances, questioning not only her well-being but her readiness for rule. She answered them all honestly—although purposefully vague—and thanked them for their kindness. Their intentions were far from genuine politeness; they were suitors, practically begging for a piece of her power and wealth, even more intrigued and ravenous for attention from Evalyn now that she was Queen.

After a couple dozen, she slipped away from the dancing to find Kalan and a drink. His look was somber enough as she approached to summon gnawing anxiety. "What is it?"

"I'm afraid my efforts to fascinate you are inadequate," he said.

She rolled her eyes. "It's only polite to entertain their efforts—especially since we aren't married."

Kalan scrunched his face. "Then do you suppose right now is a supremely appropriate time for my proposal?"

The events of her morning blurred with the woman's melting insides, but she dropped her chin in understanding. "You're *jealous*, Kalan Lupien!"

"I am not."

"Yes, you are!"

The Alpha stared across the room, head turned excessively far away from her eyes as he countered, "Never would I be so irresolute of our mutual affection to envy the splendor gained by other men from being near your ethereal presence."

"You're jealous, and a fool." The male was unresponsive. "Kalan, I don't intend to accept any of their hands. But I have to please the ogling eyes of my constant observers, otherwise they'd chase me around like thirsty hound pups. If I amuse them, they won't be able to say I wholly ignored them."

Kalan still said nothing, but when his rigid posture slackened and a goofy, unbothered smile grew on his face, a laugh bubbled out from Evalyn's throat.

Once the moon peaked in the sky and began its descent—when even the wolves found seats to breathe—Evalyn staggered away from the dancing and found Kalan at the head of the Great Hall, mingling with a pair of Lords beside the Queen's table, where her high-backed chair sat so far unused.

Evalyn neared the table for a much needed breath, but her eye caught the woman, at pace with the male linked to her arm, and knew her rest was to wait. In likewise realization, Kalan stepped to her side, just as pleasant of an expression on his face.

The unrecognized Faeries halted a comfortable space in front of Evalyn and Kalan. If the woman's elegant gown crafted from her Kingdom colors of dusty rose and silver, with majestic hoops and beads decorating the layered silk, wasn't a sign of her homeland, then her dark, velvet skin—naturally shades deeper than those of any other Fae in Liatue—was the teller. The duo looked only years older than Evalyn, but their grace and ease revealed that they'd been raised to wield whatever authority they possessed.

The male stepped forward, a hand gesturing to the woman. His trimmed hair matched the thick expanse of mocha flowing over her shoulders. "Your Majesty, allow me to introduce Queen Veda Kroghe of the Kingdom of Ausor." His wide smile, showing two rows of straight, pearly teeth, wasn't one of swagger, but evident pride of the declaration.

Queen Veda's eyes glinted playfully. "It's a pleasure to be in your company, Queen Evalyn." The words were gentle and unhurried; her voice was honey.

"Please, call me Evalyn."

The Queen of Ausor chuckled. "It seems the Gods have given us one mind. I prefer Veda, as well. I've always thought such formality between us leaders was wasteful." Evalyn beamed, unable to restrain studying the similarities between Veda and her companion. Identical hazel eyes, with a piercing gold swirling through brown and green; not an inch of height difference; their speech one and the same. Veda tilted her head, cherry lips in a knowing smile. "This is my twin brother, Kiran."

Kiran's beam was unfaltering. Evalyn parted her lips but he said, "You're wondering why my sister is the crowned leader of Ausor, and not me?" Evalyn confirmed her inquiry. The Ausorian leader had previously—recently—been a King. "In our Kingdom, we have no restrictions, no traditions of sole male or female leadership. The mothers and fathers of Ausor's Royalty teach their children the ways and life of jurisdiction. When the time comes, our household decides, as one, who we believe is most fit for leadership. For a millennium, this has brought contentment and prosperity to our people. They trust the judgment of our forefathers, and therefore trust in us who are elected."

It was a wonderful, unique system—one of faith between Ausor's people and their governance.

Veda added, "Kiran is my closest friend—the other half of myself. As my Emissary, he can show others what I desire and convey the needs for our

Kingdom before anything else." Kiran gingerly linked arms with the Queen, and his gaze wandered around the room.

"It sounds remarkable," Evalyn responded, reminded of the presence at her own side. She wrapped a hand around his forearm, linking their fingers. "This is Kalan Lupien, Alpha of the Moon Clan."

Queen Veda's eyebrows rose. "A charming one. Wolves are said to be fiercely loyal and brave."

Evalyn gripped the Alpha's arm tighter, sensing his growing beam. "Oh, he'll be boasting about that compliment for weeks now!" The Ausorian Queen chuckled, but Evalyn added, "Thank you for coming, Veda. It means more than you know. I apologize for not being in attendance to your own celebrations—I'm just getting into the rhythm of leading."

"I've heard about your situation and past. I understand," Veda returned. "However, I'd say our debts are matched and canceled. I was unable to be present for many things until recently." A pause. "Your absence was not by mistake. No one, save my household, was in attendance to my coronation. There were no celebrations." Kiran's vision darted to his sister, the flicker of a glance enough communication. "Our father, the King, was assassinated several months ago. Royal responsibilities overcame us quickly, and I was selected and coronated before I could begin to mourn. Despite my childhood, I hadn't thought I'd be chosen—I'd always thought Kiran would be King. I wasn't entirely prepared." Her gaze faltered to the ground. She was silent only for a second before lifting her chin with a soft smile—as if she'd remembered to remain calm and unbothered. Evalyn understood too well. Veda smoothed out her dress with a free hand and cleared her throat, but the lingering pain in her eyes said enough.

"We aren't alone in the hardship of holding the fragile future of our people in our hands," Evalyn exclaimed. She couldn't decide whether she meant it more to Veda or herself. "We can get through it together."

The distraught in the Queen's eyes slowly faded until entrancing, golden shimmer remained. They turned to the ballroom, and Veda said, "This set-up is breathtaking. My nieces would never want to leave." Her laugh was flawless.

Kiran smiled. "Arabel would ask for her quarters to be decorated exactly like it."

"Your children?" Evalyn marveled.

He nodded. "Arabel is seven, and Guinn, three."

"And both more beautiful than any child I've ever laid eyes on," Queen Veda remarked. "But I'm certainly biased."

Kalan noted, "Perhaps Evalyn can one day meet them. She adores children."

The twin's eyes poured into the Queen. "Yes," she stated slowly, "I do." She then grasped Kalan's motive. "After my youth in the human lands, and now knowing the life that many may not have... I'll fight for them if it means my end. They are who we must heal this world for."

Veda's stare turned somber. "War truly is upon us, then. I'd thought it mere hearsay among my people, but... you have confirmed it as truth."

Evalyn dipped her chin. The Faeries of Ausor exchanged a long, complex look. Perhaps it was the similarities she held with Veda—the mutual surprise by their rise to power, their love of adolescents, their painful losses—but Evalyn couldn't refrain from blurting, "We need Ausor. We *need* you—but you need Faylinn, too. Neither of our Kingdoms stand a chance against the King of Braena if we don't unite. Veda... I have to ask you to fight with us. Forget the meetings, the formal contracts, the schedules and travels—the King could strike at any moment, and I can no longer trust we have the advantage of time. I understand how much I'm asking—"

"If it comes to battle, honor compels me to fight for my kin. No questions asked, no conditions required," Veda interjected. She shook her head gently. "You remind me of my father—strong-willed and fierce and blunt. He'd have done anything for Ausor." Her eyes glimmered. "He was a fighter. So I'll fight for you, Evalyn, and I'll fight for my people. I don't need a speech to convince me you're worth it."

Evalyn couldn't breathe. Without any context of what stood against them, with no knowledge of the odds stacked tall in favor of their enemy... the Queen of Ausor had said yes.

"Thank—thank you," Evalyn stuttered out. "I don't—I don't know what—"

"Nothing more must be said. Vengeance will be taken for our father, as well," Veda voiced. "I have many reasons to believe the King was associated with his death."

"Queen Evalyn, we came knowing you had already proven yourself," Kiran explained. "We're aware of what you've gone through—and I'm inclined to believe it worse than our tragedy. Do not think we traveled here solely to establish monetary relationships with Faylinn."

"How can I repay you?"

Veda smiled. "Get us through this War, my fellow Queen. Then perhaps we'll consider asking any more of you." Evalyn nodded, still struggling to comprehend what was happening. "I wish to stay longer, but there's much to do—including preparing for battle. My Kingdom sends their utmost congratulations to you, Evalyn. I have a feeling we're going to grow into fast friends."

Evalyn nodded. "You must come again, eventually, when it can be just the two of us."

"Of course," Veda responded. With an exchanged beam, the Faeries turned away and were gone in an instant.

Evalyn faced Kalan, who stared at the spot the Faeries had stood. "What just happened?" she murmured. He gradually lifted his eyes.

"I know what they were."

"The first Royals we've met that didn't want to overtake Faylinn?"

"They weren't just twins," he voiced, disregarding her joke. "They were *jumeas*. Linked through their souls—a connection so rare it's said to happen once in a millennium, if not less."

"How do you know? And what does that mean—what can they do?"

"Their eyes," he stated. "The swirling gold? It was magic—fire, and something else outside common knowledge. An unrelenting power that nothing, even other magic, can stop. Walfien told me about them when we were children. A Fae can hone in the strength of their jumeas in a single, desperate time of need; they can use their magic only once, for it's so powerful that they immediately reach burnout in the process. There are whispers of another pair of jumeas—long, long ago, before Liatue was inhabited; before these Kingdoms were a thought."

"So having them on our side..."

"Having them on our side is a greater gift than we could wish for if things go wrong," Kalan finished. They both were shocked from everything they'd learned. Eventually, Kalan's focus centered on Evalyn, and he pulled her close.

She sighed. "No more talk of War. Not today."

"I know." He tugged her into a tender embrace and her thoughts returned to the ballroom and party at hand. This was all they needed to think about.

Servants floated around the guests seated at wooden, oval tables that encircled the dancing floor, handling trays of glasses filled with a familiar, fizzing liquid. As one swept past the Queen and Alpha, Kalan reached for a pair of drinks. Evalyn swirled the cup's contents.

"It's called campabor," Kalan stated.

She lowered her glass. "I had some during my Bonum Vitae."

"Daring."

"Why?"

The Alpha chuckled. "Well, you're obviously aware of its effects, but more than a sip, if not under proper, watching eyes... can lead to mornings of confusion and regret. In more than bedrooms. The magic used in its formulation does strange things to your thinking."

She smirked and lifted the drink into the air, tapping the side with silverware from the table. The ballroom quieted.

"Good evening to all—or morning, I suppose," Evalyn declared. Glasses clinked and laughter chimed. "Thanks be to the Gods for your health, support, and spirit. I've made a promise to my mother, and with your help, I aim to fulfill that oath. Let us remain united as a Kingdom, and closer as one people. As family." The guests raised their glasses. "To Faylinn," she toasted.

"*To Faylinn!*" repeated the crowd, shouting with hurrahs and grins. Some glasses were sipped at, others wholly set aside. Kalan met her stare, and she downed the entire glass.

"Was it pointless to assume you'd remain sober?"

"Abstinence is but a state of mind," Evalyn crooned, emptying Kalan's drink as well. He rolled his eyes—any attempt at stopping her would be useless.

Not that she'd need more. Her vision blurred, body already rocking; she recognized the warmth streaming through her veins. She was embraced in lightness, pleasure, exuberance. A chortle rose from her core, and she leaned onto the table.

"What's so funny?"

She faced Kalan at his question, laughter slipping through her teeth. His eyes twinkled. "The dancing folk are flowers in the wind," Evalyn returned breathily. Curls fell over her shoulder as she hunched forward with a giggle. The music pounding in the chamber, the Faeries swirling around each other, the exquisite grooming and outfits—everything was ludicrous. Why had she ever been worried about ruling? This would be *fun*—

The Faerie stumbled into Kalan's arms, who gazed upon her, amused, earning yet another laugh from the Queen. Evalyn rose to Kalan's ear. "I want a kiss."

A snort. "Shall I fetch one of the Lords?"

"No, I want a kiss from *you*. Here." She puckered her lips.

"You're half out of your wits." But he placed one between her brows.

"What a bore," she tutted.

The Alpha sighed, smiling, and wrapped his arms around her.

An hour later, Evalyn and Kalan were slumped, as gracefully as they could be, in a pair of elegant chairs beside a window. They'd danced through several more songs before retreating to the private, dim corner of the ballroom, despite the celebration continuing behind them. Evalyn's head pounded as the campabor struggled to wear off, and she leaned on Kalan's shoulder in observation of the starlight-draped land through the glass.

The Queen sensed motion behind them—and rose to see Walfien.

"We need to talk," he declared. She nodded. The campabor's final effects involuntarily dissipated.

"We won't be long," she told Kalan. Eyes drooping, he grinned in return.

Miraculously, the pair left the ballroom unnoticed. They ambled through the corridors in silence; the early morning shadows only built their tension. Every step tightened Evalyn's chest until she couldn't breathe. When the Queen slowed to a stop, Walfien did too.

"I haven't seen you all night," she remarked quietly. Walfien nodded, but didn't give an explanation—not that she'd asked for one. "Why did you do it? And why did you leave?" she questioned. He just stared. "Do you expect me to understand when you tell me nothing, Walfien? I might as well be talking to a wall, Gods spare me—"

"You didn't stop it." His calmness was aggravating.

"What?"

"You stand and demand answers, but you didn't stop the kiss."

It was her turn to stare.

He nodded, as if her lack of response was answer enough, but she shook her head and backed away, wings brushing the wall behind her. He sighed. "I'm sorry, Evalyn. I know... I should've asked to kiss you. And I shouldn't have left. It's hard to put into words—"

"It can't happen again. If Kalan finds out—"

"You haven't told him?"

Evalyn gulped. "You haven't either. He's your best friend."

"You love him *very* differently," he argued. It was unfairly true. "His reaction may be much less harsh if you were the one to tell him it was a mistake."

"A mistake? You initiated it, and that's—that's what you want to call it?"

"You say that as if you don't agree."

She flushed, unable to respond. What would she say, anyway? That he was right, but she couldn't admit it? That he was nearing the truth she'd stupidly spilled to Kye, but telling Walfien might ruin the little joy she had tried so hard to keep intact with Kalan because it'd hurt the Alpha beyond measure?

"I can tell you felt what I did," Walfien murmured. Evalyn cursed herself for letting her emotions show. "You just don't want to say so."

"I—I just..."

"You aren't going to tell him, are you?"

"No," she breathed, feeling sick. Even though the girl had wanted to this morning, had told Kye as much... she didn't plan to—not anymore. Seeing Kalan so happy tonight... she couldn't bring him that torment. Walfien's eyes widened, as if she'd said she was going to confess what he'd done to her—what this entire situation was doing to her. Making the Queen realize there was more between the two than either of them had ever let on.

Because of that kiss... nothing would be the same. With them *and* with Kalan.

Yet she didn't hate Walfien for it. Their intimacy had been... natural.

She couldn't accept that. Not with War brewing, not with the King's threat of an army, not with the duties she'd accepted under oath half a day ago.

The Queen straightened. "After everything him and I went through together, don't you think he deserves to at least know about our feelings?"

"Like I said: I should've done things differently. But I care about you, Evalyn. I hope that much is clear. It's *your* choice to acknowledge whether you feel the same, or pretend it never happened. Not Kalan's."

"What about Ahstra?" The words were out of her mouth before she could stop them.

He froze. "What *about* Ahstra?"

"She... she left you, and Oberon—"

"I know what he did. I know who she was." His voice was now full of fire.

"Then I understand even less. What about my father's note?"

Walfien's eyes traced her face twice before he answered. "Since the day his messengers dropped her at the gate, I believed I would be alone for the rest of my life. I was an ineligible bachelor for the foreseeable future; no one dared to touch the cursed commoner, no matter his rank or wealth." His throat bobbed. "But then I let you in—and you didn't shun me. You saw me for what I'm trying to be. And yesterday, in the seconds you kissed me back... I felt hope for the first time in five years. But I will never let love get so near me just to tear me to pieces again. I'll only pursue this if you let me."

Her jaw fidgeted for a response. He added, "I know we've barely had time to discuss what happened, so it's hard to understand—"

"What, this? *Us*?" she blurted. "I know. I've been struggling to do it since this morning, but your absence made it significantly harder. And I—I can't begin to imagine the state that Ahstra left you in, but now you want me to decide... what? If I'm in love with you? After one kiss?"

"No. Just if you're going to be honest with yourself." Walfien stared. "You should get back to your ball." He gave a deep sigh, and began to back down the hallway. He paused at the end of the corridor. "I wish you the utmost happiness, Evalyn. No matter what happens."

For some reason, as he rounded the corner, she didn't feel happy at all.

Chapter Twenty Nine

"*These children deserve better!*" Evalyn roared, reclining further into her throne in the Great Hall, glaring at the three unfazed southern-Flordem Lords standing before her. "You mean to tell me that because a *miniscule fraction* of folks in each of your districts are unable to scrounge up the remnants of what little coin they earn, *every* Faerie cannot grant their children schooling?"

A bony, angular male leaned forward, his hand raised—Lord Taphe. It was the only name she could recall from the introduction ten minutes earlier. His mouth was a line. "Your Majesty, if they didn't want their descendants to live as ignorant as themselves, they'd be able to provide the necessary cost we request."

"Remind me again how much that is?"

"The funding averages to around one hundred and seventy-two emerald coins per household, annually."

The Queen pinched the bridge of her nose. For over a week, the hearings of lesser Lords had gotten on her last nerve. "You'll personally make up for the absence of funds. I don't care if lessons are taught in a shop's storefront, they will happen for all children in your districts." The company tensed, eyes widening at the demand and darting to the sentries scattered across the walls. Lord Taphe opened his mouth, but Evalyn lifted her hand. "Find the money, space, and personnel without trickery against innocent civilians to obtain any of them. In three days, if I do not receive confirmation that the necessary resources have been acquired... it would not pain me in the slightest to strip you of your land and titles for disobeying my request to meet this *simple* demand."

"But, Your Majesty," the middle Lord began, near choking on his words, "that's not what standard policy dictates—"

"I don't care. This is about making the world a better place for those who can't do it themselves." The silence of the room was deafening. She shrugged. "Make it happen."

Two hours later, the case was still fresh in her mind as she marched from the Great Hall with a grumbling stomach. The proceedings always started out calm and collected—but by the end, the Fae's mind never failed to pound out of her head.

According to Walfien—from a fleeting, strained conversation—she'd eventually preside over only the most important hearings. Which would, soon, be solely focused on War. Walfien had taken on the Queen's meetings with the High Minister, so, currently, it was critical she knew of the ongoing, daily complications present in both her Court and villages amongst the main cities. Town infrastructure issues and neighbor quarrels, although easily resolved, consumed her waking hours. But in due time, the woman wouldn't have to deal with pointless arguments between arrogant Lords over their daughters' engagements with the same, wretched noble; the job of settling such matters would fall to any free Courtier. Her selection was vast; the woman hadn't grasped the true size of the Queen's Court until she'd gained command of them.

The Faerie had taken it upon herself to use the early stages of her reign to make herself clear: Faylinn's goals would not be the same. This was a fresh start for the entire Kingdom to realize that everyone was equal—that injustice would not escape her attention.

When Evalyn entered the foyer, she paused. "You were listening outside? Again?"

Walfien straightened at the courtyard entrance. "Despite being able to attend those meetings, I prefer watching from a distance as the Lords fumble over the demands from a Queen less than half their age. Free entertainment." She detected his itch to smile. But the woman hadn't given him more than a curt nod in greeting, even when they saw each other well more than thrice a day.

Evalyn rolled her eyes, clasped her hands before her, and continued walking. Walfien fell into step with her and declared, "Technically, you can't strip those Flordem Lords of their titles unless they've committed a crime—which doesn't *exactly* mean disobeying orders. Murder, theft, yes... but—"

"I know how it works. But the conversation is over and that's all that matters. Although my headache hasn't lessened in the slightest," she complained, rubbing her head. She neared the dining hall, where she'd consumed meals since her coronation. Eating with her people, as a part of her people, was another way to publicize her intentions. Walfien snapped his chin toward her—

"Don't start," she groaned. "I'm fine."

"I won't apologize for worrying. You *are* Tania's daughter, which means you could be susceptible to the disease that took her."

"I'm also *Oberon's* daughter, and we both know he won't let me die until he gets what he wants." She gave a fleeting, sarcastic grin.

Walfien's presence remained close as she sat in the now familiar seat in the center of the head table. He was making her insane. Past the guilt and anger and irritation that ran through her—the same emotions as every time she saw the Hand—deep down, Evalyn couldn't deny that he'd sparked something irreversible.

But they hadn't brought up the kiss again. Who knew if they ever would.

She certainly hadn't told Kalan anything. And as if her mere thought summoned him, the Alpha appeared in the seat next to her, across from Walfien. She placed down her fork with a glance at the Hand—who lifted his chin, meeting her stare. He hadn't spoken a word, either.

Evalyn looked away first. Kalan intertwined their hands. Walfien began eating. "How did the hearing session go?" Kalan inquired.

"Like the others—I give my orders and hope the Lords are wise enough to follow them." She grumbled, "Why is it so inconvenient to help those below them? So many have enough wealth to provide for multiple times their own families' needs."

Walfien commented, "They were raised, as they raise their own children, believing that it doesn't matter if they have more than enough to satisfy their day-to-day lives; to them, the money and titles they have is just that—their own, and no one else's. Asking them to give some of it up—even an amount that wouldn't make a dent in what they possess—is taken as an insult."

Kalan nodded. "That's how the clan used to be. When my father was here, we were more of a population than a family. Everyone acted for themselves. They didn't live in the harmony we do now."

"If only they could see how well the Moon Clan prospers," she retorted. Kalan squeezed her hand, vision wandering down the table. Evalyn's eyes shifted to Walfien, who watched their hands, and she restrained from pulling her fingers out of Kalan's grasp.

The Alpha sat up, smirking as always, oblivious to their silent battle. "Have you heard the rumors of me being your consort? Apparently you have a hidden lover stowed away in the dungeons, intent on taking my place." He threw his head back with a chuckle. "Perhaps we *should* marry soon just to stop the gossip."

Yes, she'd heard it all. Everyone asked when the union would be; marriage meant Kalan would become the Queen's consort, a position as powerful as Evalyn herself considering his title as Alpha. His lighthearted fun made her stomach twist—and she wanted to flip the table for feeling so upset by it.

Kalan laughed and kissed the back of her hand. "I'm teasing." Evalyn lifted her lips, the most she could manage. "Are you busy tonight?" he questioned.

She exclaimed swiftly, "Yes. Additional meetings... and such." She gulped, throat simmering with the fierce backlash of Viitor. "I know I'll be tired by this evening." She was utterly horrid for denying him when he'd come all the way to the castle for her company. She'd lost count of how many times she'd pushed away his offers over the past week, but at least his requests had been mere letters.

"Of course. Soon, or I'll start thinking you don't want to see me." He winked before striding off.

Her stare fell to the table. Walfien monitored her.

Nothing had been the same since their argument during her ball—even her and Kalan's relationship was changed. Every moment with the Alpha wasn't like before, but she couldn't bring herself to tell him of her tension because it would lead to why—and boil down to the incident overtaking her every thought.

These feelings. The kiss. Her betrayal.

"I'm ready to talk when you are," the Hand said. "It's eating you up inside but you keep pushing me away."

Silence. Walfien downed a goblet of water. She finished eating. More silence.

"*Stop looking at me like that,*" she hissed. A group of Ladies at the table behind Walfien glanced their way, but returned to their conversation swiftly.

Walfien's voice was unfailingly level. "Tell me you don't feel happy with leaving our feelings unspoken and I will. I'll never look at you again in any way, if that's what you want. But I gave you my answer. You've returned me nothing."

"I don't feel like talking to you." When he nodded, standing, the Queen scowled. "Where are you going?"

"To those meetings you lied about having tonight."

The Lords accomplished her demand within an hour of the three-day deadline. It took every ounce of effort to contain her rage at the pure defiance in their waiting. Nevertheless, her order had been followed, and she, unfortunately for her head, withheld punishment.

It'd prove irritating to sort out replacements, anyway.

She went to the training room straight after the updating consultation and spent two hours practicing combat with a spare sentry. To her relief, her secret training was no more. The Guard had even invited her to some of their pre-dawn unit-training sessions. Milid was a fierce instructor, but Evalyn kept up with the sentinels. No one had shown a lick of surprise.

Luckily, the exhaustion sometimes granted her nights free of the terrors that hadn't faded. But on the mornings where she woke screaming and clinging to her sheets, lighting every candle in her room with the slightest lift of a finger, her scarred shoulder and mangled arm often throbbing in remembrance of their cause, the Queen took slow breaths, folded one leg over the other, and poured the emotions into her magic practice.

She'd stopped crying.

Evalyn resorted to strolling the castle's upper hallways when the sun caressed the horizon. It was the second day in over a fortnight she had a free evening. Although she would rather have roamed the gardens, the Faerie couldn't bring herself to a situation in which she might cross paths with Kalan. She'd denied an offer of his company once more.

Evalyn prayed about the day she'd have to tell him everything, because it would come—

But not yet. There was too much work to do.

What little peace she'd obtained from the sunset disappeared as she turned towards the grand staircase. Lord Pavan Ziffoy and his son, Jaino, began striding promptly for her, and before she could take another step they were at her front, blocking the intended escape to her quarters.

"Queen Evalyn! Just the person we were looking for!" Pavan exclaimed. Jaino bowed kindly; when she lifted her brows, the Lord plastered a fake smile and bowed as well, as if the act of respect had simply slipped his wild thoughts.

She hummed, "I would be *most* honored to assist you, Lord Ziffoy. What are your concerns?"

Jaino's youth-splotched face burned red. He stared at the floor as if it was the most intriguing ground he'd stepped foot on. His father answered, "My son and I traveled all this way from Mearley to procure a moment of amity between the two of you. You see, his interests at present are specified to horse-riding, reading, swimming, and bladesmithing. I'm sure there's common ground somewhere to begin forming your relationship."

Evalyn restrained a sigh. His statement was half-true; there was a small council meeting tonight requiring the presence of the Conclave, and the week-long Sanator celebrations began tomorrow at dawn. Jaino had certainly not been a priority for their travels. But she said, "I'll speak to Jaino alone for a moment."

The Lord sauntered down the hallway triumphantly. As soon as he was out of earshot, the Queen faced the boy—he was nearly as tall as her.

"Would you like to marry me, Jaino?"

His dark brown eyes lifted. His voice was faint, but low; a sign of spurring growth. "No, your Majesty."

She smiled. "Would you like to marry someone else?"

"Yes, your Majesty."

"As I thought. May I ask who?"

"There—there's a girl from home." He shifted on his toes.

"Is she a fair bride?"

His face lit up. "Much more than. She's the most *wonderful* girl I've ever met—no offense."

"I didn't take any. What's your favorite thing to do at home?"

His answer was immediate. "Swim with my cousins in the United Lake."

"Even now, while it's freezing?"

"Sometimes," he exclaimed, standing taller. "Mother gets worried about us blueing, but we don't go after the first snow. Father screams and shouts about our adventures, even when Spring arrives. He says it's an abomination to my lordly obligations."

Evalyn rolled her shoulders as Pavan returned to his son's side. "Should I fetch him in an hour?" the Lord inquired.

A grin rose on the Queen's lips. She watched the boy as she said, "After allowing him to participate in all of Sanator's festivities, Jaino will return home. You won't need to bring him back to the Palace unless he desires so." A chuckle escaped Jaino's otherwise innocent expression. "And under my authority... he shall be allowed to swim in the United Lake whenever he pleases. I'll require regular letters from him detailing his fun, and if I hear about any prohibition, there will be ramifications. How does that sound, Jaino?"

The boy nodded vigorously. Pavan breathed heavily, motionless and silent.

Evalyn smiled brightly. "I'll see you tonight, my Lord."

That evening, the council meeting was swift and humorous; every look at Pavan's angry stare nearly brought her to laughter, much to the confusion of every other member. The Lord took every opportunity to spout ire on her propositions in return; it wasn't until Kinz and Mags, in unison, snapped direct jibes at Pavan that he shut up.

Straight after the session, the Queen closed her bedroom door. A fresh, clean scent filled her nostrils as she faced her three maids, who curtsied in unison. Evalyn returned a smile and slipped out of heels that Ida returned to her closet. "I'll take care of myself for the night. The three of you, relax."

"Oh, we don't need it," Beverly retorted half-heartedly. But with an unwavering stare from Evalyn, they swiftly exited the room, giggling about something a baker-boy had shouted in the kitchens at dinner.

Evalyn traded her day gown for a training uniform, braiding her hair over a shoulder, gaze catching on the stacks of parchment atop her desk. She'd been transferred into the Queen's Quarters—her mother's room—a week earlier. It was when she'd discovered the notes—as if waiting to be scoured. With the slightest of glances, she'd instantly known what they concerned.

And subsequently put off looking at the vital information they possibly contained. The trouble with Walfien was distraction enough from her duties.

Evalyn made for the practice quarters.

It was for more than stress-relief to push herself to harder limits everyday; to grow stronger, faster. She needed impervious defensive and offensive technique. Wing strengthening came after; although extending and contracting them was now painless, building muscle was as crucial.

One day, the Queen hoped to fly.

War called for it.

When her vigor was depleted, she practiced her elemental powers, then called in Micka Roshium. The Second in Command of the Guard was one of few undoubtedly trustworthy sentries and a willing subject to practice her newfound mental power on. At her wish, Micka started to weep, then began laughing so forcefully he dropped to the ground in a shaking ball. She severed the link to his mind, and in the same second he was standing, shaking off the emotional shift.

The Queen had scant ideas about how to utilize the empathy, but honing the power was better than leaving it weak and ineffective, should it be the only magic available—or necessary—to use at any point.

During breaks—despite it being a time for both of their minds to rest—Micka shared everything he could recall: the beauty of his fond but unidentified lover, as well as his attempts to sway her to have his hand; pestering and schemes with other guards during his shifts around The Palace; or his family, from a small village district in Dusston and their memories together before he'd come into service as a sentry. Evalyn had become inclined to share details from her own past, and began to care for him. He was like a brother—the sibling she'd never had.

Although exhausted and hungry, Evalyn was refreshed as she opened her chamber door, the wooden creak a calming reminder of the warm bed awaiting her. After filling her tub in the bathing chambers, she returned to the chamber for her sleepwear when her door snapped shut.

Someone had just been in here.

The Faerie swept for the door, placing an ear to the wood—not even the candle fixtures hissed from the corridor. Only when she shifted back to her quarters did she notice the neatly folded letter at the end of her bed. She didn't need to see the seal before ripping the wax apart, unfurling the parchment as fast as her fingers could handle.

The color drained from Evalyn's face, but she wasn't surprised by the sender. Although it'd been weeks, the woman unfailingly knew his work. A sense from their shared blood, likely.

> *My daughter, I hope your journey found you well and the re-acclimation to the Faylinn elements met you joyfully. That is as far as my grace extends. As I've heard, your mother recently died—and you became the Crowned Ruler. It's a shame I wasn't invited to the coronation.*

Evalyn's throat dried as she tried to maintain her composure.

> *Alas, I digress. Let me make our state clear: there will never be peace between our Kingdoms. I gave you chance and chance again to prove your loyalty to me—to diminish this thought*

of War—but it seems you haven't yet learned what happens when you refuse my mercy.

The Queen was going to faint. *Why* had she sent her maids away?

Since you're determined to have a fight—a fight I shall give. When Winter greets Liatue, we'll meet between the boundaries of our Kingdoms. At the home of another being—Crawlers, I believe they're called. You passed over the terrain on your escape from here; you'll find it again. Then and there, our clash will occur, unless you want your castle to become a bloodbath. Nevertheless, when you send your troops into battle, when they still die at the hands of my Sanguin and you're left alone... remember you brought this onto yourself.

The parchment burst into flames, ashes staining Evalyn's palm. She stared blankly at the opposing wall, all thoughts of nightly relaxation completely and forever abandoned.

War War War War War War—

It thumped in her head; pounding like her heart.

Evalyn staggered to the frame of her bed, sliding to the floor. She had to focus—*breathe*. No fear, no hesitation. Frost-burns webbed across the ground, inhibiting the fire that threatened to saturate all she could see. Sanator began tomorrow, and the Rising Sun ceremony—the commencement of the occasion—required her attentive participation. She could do it; pretend all was fine, if only for some hours.

But sleep wouldn't come tonight.

She had two months to prepare Faylinn for the fight of its life.

Chapter Thirty

Evalyn was already sitting at the vanity when her maids arrived. The Faeries rushed around excitedly as they readied Evalyn; after an entertaining debate over what color best suited her locks, they settled for a long-sleeved, auburn dress with a ruched bodice. A delicate golden tiara, formed like intertwined twigs, was placed atop her head, the sheen of metal a perfect complement to the flecks in the wings that poked over her shoulders. Evalyn faced the girls, in a neat line admiring their work.

After last night, the Queen couldn't wait any longer.

No hesitation.

She said, "I declare the three of you my Keepers."

Their eyes widened, and Beverly dropped the products in her hands to cover her mouth, but Evalyn continued, "Your new shared chambers shall be in the Princess' suite—closer than the traditional quadrant. I want you to attend all formal celebrations with me; small council meetings and throne room hearings are discretionary, but I encourage you to make friends within and outside of Court." Tears streamed down Beverly's face. Vixie looked close to crying as well, but a wide beam stretched across her lips, and Ida smiled broadly, her honey-tan face tingeing pink. "You'll be my eyes and ears in places where my own are insufficient. Any whisper of gossip, any threats or rumors—I want them brought to my attention. I'll put in the official paperwork after Sanator—but starting today, you'll receive proper pay and the benefits of any other Lady in Court, including a portion of coin being sent to your families." Ida gasped—it meant she could afford advanced healing for her father. The Queen beamed. "Most of all, *enjoy* it. You three are close friends—and some of my first, at that. You deserve it and more."

The women were wholly lost to emotion. Shrieks and laughter and sobbing pierced Evalyn's heart, and they were wildly uncontrolled with excitement for ten minutes.

After the maids regained their composures and ushered the Queen to the foyer, Evalyn took in a brightening sky: sunrise was within the hour. With a silent demand, the beaming trio returned to their chambers to prepare themselves.

Evalyn wouldn't allow them to miss out. Not now—never again.

Despite the time, the foyer was full of noble Faeries, sentries lining the walls, and bustling servants finishing the last touches on the castle before the real crowd arrived. Once a year, Fae across Faylinn traveled to The Palace to see the Rising Sun ceremony on the first day of Sanator, to witness the works of their Queen and thank the long-passed warrior-saviors of Dricormie and Beolah.

Evalyn waited at a side of the Grand Staircase. A pair of bright-eyed boys watched her wings trail behind her as she took in the decorations. The Palace staff had reigned in the essence of Autumn: maroon and golden leaved vines were strewn along every rail and magic-lit column; spice-and-cider scents coated every surface; warm, bronze candles huddled atop scattered benches with dried goods and cream-coated roots.

"Pondering whom in the crowd fits your likings?" said a voice at Evalyn's side.

The Queen took a slow inhale, forcing a grin as she faced the source. "What a delightful idea, Lord Ziffoy." The Faerie watched Evalyn with feigned intrigue. His silver-red hair was slicked back, and the black cloak was nothing short of a show of wealth. "In fact, I think I've found the male of my dreams," she exclaimed with a hand over her heart.

Having spotted him upon arriving, it took only a second to turn to the guard stationed left of the entrance to the courtyard and beckon him to her side. A hidden gesture explained her meaning, and a beam rose to his face, his hand sliding along her back when he arrived at her side. The ribbons and patches were outnumbered by few—more astonishing when in such close range to their monarch. She leaned in to whisper the simplest of stories for him to go along with, making sure a faint bloom of color rose to her cheeks as she finished with a laugh—the sound a result of a joke made between lovers.

"Isn't he handsome, Lord Ziffoy?" She fluttered her lashes, placing a manicured hand on his chest, beside the Kingdom sigil.

The Lord looked near to twitching, yet he retorted smoothly, "I suppose I've missed the parting of you and the Alpha—yet I never paid much attention to the romantic squabbles of adolescents. Nevertheless... I would think it unwise, Your Majesty, to settle so easily. Especially for..." He trailed off as he looked the Faerie up and down, nose cringing.

"Second in Command of the Faylinn Guard is the title you're searching for," Micka Roshium responded. His voice was no less chipper than if they were discussing the fine meals soon to be served.

"I wouldn't expect you to understand, Lord Ziffoy. Happiness—love, even—seems something you lack comprehension of." Evalyn met the Lord's near-black, piercing eyes. He licked his lips, bristling as she further remarked, "I sleep well at night knowing I'm in some of the safest hands in Faylinn. I daresay Jaino's skills could compare." A part of her wished she didn't have to stoop so low as to degrade the Lord's poor son, but she couldn't deny the fun it was to mess with Pavan. A smug beam found her face, and she leaned ever closer to the sentry at her hip.

"Do you sleep so well?" the Lord questioned with a rising smirk. Evalyn's lips thinned. It was impossible for him to know about the terrors that plagued her sleep—"With the Braenian conflict and all," he added, head tilting to one side. "I, for one, find it troublesome that our enemy's forces could launch an unannounced assault at any moment. War is soon to come, is it not?" Her expression turned to stone. He certainly wouldn't be the first she told about the definite schedule. "Resting at night seems a trivial feat in the daunting face of combat."

Unblinking, she snapped, "I wholly reject Jaino's offer of marriage. Do not attempt to persuade my hand again. Your son deserves better than to suffer the repercussions of Royal existence."

The Lord chuckled as if she'd spoken the most clever jest. But when her features remained cold, he grasped her truth with a twitch. The male's lips twisted. "You can't be—"

"I believe the ceremony is about to start, Lord Ziffoy." Evalyn flicked her gaze to the doors, where the crowd began filing into the courtyard and through the castle gate.

"If you hurry, you might still find a good spot to watch your Queen," Micka added.

Pavan clenched his jaw. After a momental glare, he stalked off to pester a noble. Evalyn silently thanked the Gods that his involvement was over. She wished she'd conversed more with any of the other Lords of the Conclave, if only to uncover their opinions of Pavan Ziffoy and determine whether there was anything that could be done about his ferocity.

When the Lord of Mearley was well out of sight, the Queen pulled away. Micka's curly, lapis hair was a blinding contrast to their surroundings. "I apologize for the performance. I knew it'd get under his skin," Evalyn clarified.

"It's perfectly alright! This serves as another story to tell during my shift later tonight. I think we both needed a bit of distraction, amid the fun of it."

The Queen forgot the Faerie was as young as herself—and surrounded by even more pressure and stress where battle was concerned. He moved to return to his place by the entrance, but Evalyn gripped his wrist. "About our—*my* training... you're okay with it?" she inquired. "You agreed when I first asked, but if it's become a hassle—"

"Evalyn, that's a splendid part of my day. Not only because I get to rave about myself," he countered with a laugh, "but because it's an honor to serve you in doing so."

"You still can't show me your powers?" she pouted.

"I have a limited set of manipulations, all of which I use in my work. If I showed you my identities, I'd have to kill you." She rolled her eyes, simpering. "Our usual time this week?" he questioned. The Queen nodded, relieved to hear his reassurance. The Fae sauntered to his position at the foyer entrance with a grin.

It wasn't five minutes later—a time spent watching the lively group of high guests and nobility gossip and swoon over the circumstances of the day—that Beverly, Ida, and Vixie met Queen's side, and followed her through the courtyard and past the castle's inner gate. On the level expanse of land nestled between the internal and external stone barricades of the castle, already surrounded by thousands of Fae, was a wide platform set to hold the Queen. The Hand, her Ladies, and an excessive multitude of guards were to remain on shorter podiums on either side of Evalyn. Kalan and the Moon Clan had opted to remain in their camp for the first ceremony, a tradition special to the Fae kind.

When there were five minutes to dawn and the last straggling Fae became part of the endless sea of faces, the Queen stepped to the edge of the stand. She'd been instructed about her part of the ritual a week previous, but hoped the Gods forgave her if she messed it up.

A cool breeze blew hair out of her face and countered the heat emitting from her wings. The Queen inhaled deeply as a hush overwhelmed the crowd—yet didn't silence the exhilaration radiating from them. It was a different atmosphere than the one of apprehension and unease which had captivated The Palace the past week, when everyone's thoughts had been consumed by War—the War of Kin, it'd been unanimously named.

Evalyn smiled easily under the welcoming gazes of her people. "My fellow Fae, today we stand hand in hand with one another, united not only as a Kingdom but as beings of one creation. We celebrate the defeat of our enemy, Deilok, at the hands of two leaders who took it upon themselves to give Faeries another chance at life. Dricormie and Beolah will be remembered as long as Faylinn stands, and we revel this week at the fact that our Kingdom is doing that." The Queen smiled at the Ladies by her side. Even Walfien, who she hadn't seen in days, showed encouragement at her words. Despite the feelings they hadn't discussed, despite the encounters that had consisted solely of business and confusion and annoyance since the ball... his current stare was gentle, and full of pride and encouragement.

Whether it was her recent accruement of stress or the absence of the Alpha, Evalyn smiled back. From the beginning, he'd kept up with her chaos.

There was little over a minute until the sun peeked over the horizon. By some unspoken communication, the Faerie crowd, as one, lowered to the grassy field over their knees. Evalyn readied for the ritual—a show of her power and a commemoration to the Fae couple who'd risked themselves for the fate of those they loved.

She, too, was willing to put her life on hold if it meant destroying Oberon for the betterment of Liatue.

In unison to the Queen's uplifted palms, the hands of five thousand Faeries reached to the sky; sparks of amber and teal and marigold formed at every fingertip, lighting the dwindling darkness. A magic-made sunrise in itself. Evalyn created a ball of flame; a living creature which, with the fluttering of her fingers, formed into a flaring mass that shaped around her wings—a coating of magic, of liquid fire, that became an additional layer around the feathers.

She breathed slowly, feeling the power in her bones—waiting to decipher what it desired to be seen as.

An itch, then... there. The magic was securely wrapped like branches around her limbs.

Evalyn lifted her arms and angled them to her front. She clenched her hands into fists, and a gust of misty wind flowed from the far east. The current carried nature's imprint: pine needles and dried leaves and fallen wildflowers, all rising over the outer gate of the castle and floating neatly above the gathered Fae. The airstream shaped the plant-life into woven garlands and placed them on whatever head was closest. Gasps sounded from throughout the crowd and the Queen smiled greater. Before the first ray of light peeked over the distance, she pulled the sparkling colors from the Faeries' hands and willed them into a writhing ball of magic, her hands outstretched toward it.

"Rise," she exclaimed, beginning the ceremonial phrase as dawn transpired. "Rise as the light does, in recognition of those who bestowed the gift of another morning onto us. Rise with the day, and do not forget the sacrifices of those behind us. *Rise,*" Evalyn shouted as the heads of the Fae lifted, "*like the sun.*"

As the final portion of light crossed the horizon, the Queen exploded the ball of sparks, sending a wave of color onto the Faeries which stuck to their hair and faces and clothes. Together, they erupted into praise, into a chorus of one species—lifting a song that would forever be passed down to convey their hope and joy in the most desolate of times. The Queen watched in jubilation as music intermingled with their cries. Within moments, every body danced to the melody, the residue of the sparks shimmering under morning sunlight.

For a majority of the morning, Evalyn watched play after play concerning the battle in which Dricormie and Beolah had defeated Deilok. Although she couldn't help recall the beliefs of the Rogues—that Deilok had never truly been killed; that he'd arise to exact revenge—Evalyn thoroughly enjoyed the humorous reenactments by the young Fae. Each adolescent producer asked the Queen for her opinion, and each of her encouraging responses caused the children to jump ecstatically. After the spectacles, she dined the extravagant midday feast prepared by the humble and easily-moved servants of the castle, then observed still-youthful nobles play games and test their magic in comparison to another. Twice, they concluded with someone drenched in a tide of spiced ale.

It was during one of these games that Walfien appeared before Evalyn, hand outstretched. "Would you dance with me?" His mismatched eyes twinkled in the sun's setting rays.

She placed her hand in his without a single thought of refusal. The Hand swung them into motion right in their place; the grounds' music seemed to drown out all other background noise. She didn't say anything; didn't want to break the peaceful ambience wrapping around them. They simply danced and danced. When Faeries joined them to form a massive crowd of twirling and jumping bodies, they extracted themselves from the center, giddy with the exhilaration of each other's company.

"That was outstanding!" Evalyn exclaimed breathily.

"I used to be fun, believe it or not," Walfien beamed. "I figured I may as well enjoy one of the seven days the castle has paused most work. What do you say to drinks and returning for another song?"

Evalyn nodded. All reluctance she'd previously held toward him seemed to have disappeared; truly, she found herself suddenly dreading the absence of his company. The Queen wanted to celebrate the remaining festivities with him, and to not have to abandon him after they ended. She wanted this joy to persist into the face of War. To eternally accompany his soothing presence.

No matter her concerns after Sanator, she was grateful to be with him now. The woman clutched his arm as they turned. At the edges of the crowd stood a pair of individually swaying Fae, their arms swirling through the air as if they were swatting a pest, and their feet moving in a jig too confusing to have any pattern. Evalyn and Walfien met each other's eyes before exploding into laughter, essentially falling onto the refreshments stand, unable to catch their breath enough to give the bewildered server their order.

With as festive a mood as any Fae, Kalan suddenly found them there. Although outwardly in hysterics, Evalyn's mind sobered up at once in the face of the Alpha's unabating joy. "What mighty fun did I just miss?"

Walfien straightened steadily, face bright. "Nothing you can't see now." He pointed at the awkwardly dancing couple. Kalan chuckled, but Evalyn didn't find it funny anymore.

The Alpha twisted back towards her with a grin. "Do you want to go show them how it's done?" His face fell. "What's wrong?"

Evalyn had been frowning. She cleared her throat, lifting a smile. "Oh, it's nothing. Come on, we can dance." She gave a fleeting glance at Walfien; his face showed he knew what thoughts had captured her focus. But before she could say anything, Kalan had led her back into the horde.

The Alpha smiled, a hand around her waist as they bounced on their toes. He leaned his mouth to her ear. "After so long, I'm pleased to spend any amount of time with you—even if it has to be during this manifold of celebrations instead of your private company. I missed you."

His gesture, although kind, as it was meant—and expected behavior from the male she loved—sent a suffocating pang through her chest.

Because it established the truth Evalyn had been trying, albeit badly, to push away: the feelings between her and Walfien were growing. Slowly, but growing all the same. Without Kalan's presence the past couple of weeks holding her accountable to reveal the kiss, and thus, her feelings, there hadn't lately been any reason to deny Evalyn's attraction to Walfien. This evening, she'd let them manifest into tangible results.

And Gods, she *knew* the lack of walls between herself and Walfien while she remained in a public relationship with Kalan made her a devious crone, but... it was far past the time for her to be honest with herself, at least. She'd learned veering from the truth did nothing besides bring further hurt.

Yet although the festivities continued until the moon appeared, Kalan didn't leave her side once.

She found that she didn't have as much fun as she had with Walfien.

Eventually, she made it back to her quarters. Sheer olive curtains draped over the corner posts of Evalyn's bed, brushing the apex of her wing. She restrained from slumping onto the nest of plush cushions, despite the unabating exhaustion that lingered with every inhale. The balance required from her show of magic in the ceremony this morning meant a fatigue strong enough to yearn for the comfort of her bedsheets beyond all other needs.

But regardless of her tiredness and emotional confusion, Evalyn's current focus lay within the stack of parchment atop her desk. Without any males to steal her concentration, the Fae couldn't restrain from dragging her gaze to it, and after a minute of consideration, settled into the linen-backed chair and spread the sheets across the length of the table.

It took an hour to read through every note, every scribble; an hour to contemplate what her mother had left behind for her daughter to see.

Whether Tania had known about Evalyn's awareness of the matter—whether her mother had intentionally placed the information somewhere she'd find it—was impossible to figure out. But what Evalyn knew for certain... she gulped and skimmed over the documents a second time. The Queen leaned over the workspace, head in her hands.

Tania had transcribed the entire translation of the markings on The Door, save the final, ending phrase. The Vynus markings claimed that only one person could enter the room without repercussions; it would be the woman's luck that the specific person permitted was what Tania hadn't identified.

But all Evalyn had left to solve was its meaning... and she'd have a foothold over her father.

The Queen spent the rest of the evening studying and learning the old language, but to no avail. The markings were in no book, no document.

As if they didn't exist outside of their use on The Door.

She slammed the titles shut and went to bed.

The Queen underwent the same routine for the rest of Sanator: parties and feasts and plays and games from dawn into the evening, then studying and training at night until she couldn't keep her eyes open. The full schedule gave her a few hours of unbothered sleep on some nights—on others, she was incapable of resting, her mind crazed on thoughts of War preparations, The Door, Walfien and Kalan. The entire Court had taken a break for the seven days of celebration; Evalyn had no meetings or civil cases to deal with. Her duties consisted of showing at every meal and ensuring Lord Ziffoy wasn't too bothersome to her Keepers—whom the Queen introduced to most of her Court throughout the week.

When she woke the morning after Sanator—which had ended with nothing less than a full night of dancing and belting vigorous songs around a magic-made bonfire in the gardens—Evalyn wasn't shocked that her ankles and lungs were sore beyond measure. She was, however, astounded to find herself eager to return to a normal day of work—even without the campabor and steady hum of strings.

Evalyn stopped her Keepers' duties with the flick of a hand, gray-blue sparks sizzling at her fingertips. With Sanator over, she had a new idea of emphasizing her power.

The trio were nothing short of bewildered at first, but standing at her mirror half an hour later, their guileful smiles announced their attendance with her for the day. A few turns down the hallway brought the Queen to the first of many judges. Before he even laid eyes on her, the Ladies knew to continue on and wait for Evalyn in the Great Hall.

Walfien reached her side moments later, eyes wide and gaping down her body. She couldn't tell if he was cross or plainly taken aback as he muttered, "What are you *wearing*, Evalyn?"

She smirked. The Queen clad a wine-red gown, layered with a thin, flowing fabric that cinched at the waist; the double slits in her skirt rose to mid-thigh. Her bodice was a tight thing, cutting low in the front with loose sleeves that draped over her arms.

"What will best prove I'm not some inexperienced girl, but a woman to be taken seriously upon her Crowning. I'm ensuring those within my Court know who they're dealing with." She brushed a finger along the tail of her wing, tugging it close as a noblewoman might with her cloak.

The Queen decided Walfien was, in fact, cross with her as he scoffed, "You're proving you have a fresh body for any castle occupant to daydream about.

People will gossip and chide your name for this—they'll turn it into a scandal that will diminish your budding reputation." He shook his head. "Wasn't Sanator enough proof for you? That your people adore and respect you? Believe in your power?"

Evalyn's lips thinned. She'd seen such things. But there would always be those who despised her for her youth, for her way of assimilating into the Fae world. Half of the Court was in line with Pavan Ziffoy; this was for them as much as herself. She wasn't a child any longer. "You act like I've walked out naked."

"You act like you *haven't*." His voice grew stern. She hadn't expected this reaction from *him*. "I'm trying to help you."

"You're dictating who I am."

"I'm doing nothing to *dictate* you—"

"Well, you don't seem to care about my feelings—"

"You *know* I care!" Walfien exploded, hands grasping Evalyn's arms suddenly but gently. She instantly shrugged him off, but when she stumbled into the corridor wall, the visions—the memories—appeared.

She was back in Braena, in that too-dim corridor, Rouhs closing in with a cackling, wide-lipped grin, red irises gaping over her body. Then she was in the Sanguin-housing dungeons, the creatures inches from her face. In a split-second, she tripped back, and the Sanguin latched its claws onto her shoulder. The warmth of blood on her skin felt too real as Evalyn collapsed to the floor in a shout of pain.

She watched Pellima before a bellowing Kalan, the mistress' hands rising and falling with the scoring of the Alpha's chest, and the light in Kalan's eyes was gone. At the side, Tania was a second from Death's grip, smashing into the stone floor over and over again.

The Queen took a sharp inhale. Hot, fresh tears dripped down her chin.

The worst of them all began; what still haunted her little hours of sleep.

Rouhs was in front of her again, so close, his breath in her ear, "What fun I'll have with my toy." He brushed golden locks behind her ears, then there were countless iron blades in his grasp as he scored her hands and stomach and thighs, and the burn was everywhere, unending, encasing, and she was convinced the blazing was true. The Faerie screamed and twisted and sobbed, it was too real, too real, *too real*—

She was back in her Kingdom.

Both her and Walfien were crumpled on the floor, less than a foot from each other. Tracks of saltwater covered her cheeks. Evalyn leaned her head into the coolness of the corridor wall and stared at Walfien, whose face was paler than hers, full of sheer disbelief. He'd somehow seen the visions too, then, by some link in their magic—with his Sight and the mental powers she'd strengthened.

With a long sigh, Evalyn wiped her nose. Walfien was silent aside from his heavy breathing, the shock on his face unfading, and they remained frozen on the floor. "I—I'm sorry," Walfien stammered. Evalyn shook her head, but didn't know whether she was in dissent with his apology or the fact that he'd caused the horrors in her mind to be relived. Both, likely.

She was at fault for everyone's suffering, including her own.

"Those were... that was real, wasn't it?" His voice rasped.

Her gaze wandered around the corridor, to the gold detailing and sage green of the walls. She was home—not in Braena, not in the dungeon, not in the Shadow's corridors. The woman steadily lifted her sleeve, the pale, jagged lettering prominent against her sunned skin. *Broken*: carved into her flesh like an engraved tomb.

She returned to Walfien's unwavering look. "No one was supposed to know."

Only Luca and her trio knew of her wounds. Everyone else had been unaware that her sleep was consistently plagued by nightmares—she'd never let anyone enter her chambers beyond midnight to glimpse her attempt at rest—and the cooling weather had made it uncomplicated to hide the scars. She knew the public response would be a strange mixture of pity and fright and disgust.

So Evalyn didn't expect Walfien to reach for her hand; to allow such emotion in his eyes to show. And after the trauma that'd resurfaced—the feelings and haunting touches that had returned—she didn't expect to allow him to do so. Or to grip his hand in return, and feel profoundly relieved that the secrets that tormented her waking moments were no longer hers to hold alone.

Walfien pulled them to stand. "Why not?"

She didn't meet his eyes, and brought her hands to wrap around herself. "I've caused pain for my people. They already shunned how I was brought to power... and now, they don't like me as a young and inexperienced leader." The Fae hugged herself tighter. "Nobody wants a broken one."

The Hand lifted her chin. "You are nothing less than perfect. No matter what has been done to you. But if it's what you think... we'll just have to put the pieces back together."

The woman didn't have the heart to tell him she wasn't who he thought she was. Because she'd become anything—she'd *sacrifice* anything—if it meant saving her people. Including whatever trace of goodness he detected. Evalyn's lip wobbled and she nodded, her cheek resting in his palm. He stroked a thumb across her skin. All felt right with him knowing the truth.

All felt right with *him*.

She pulled away.

Walfien dropped his hand but didn't put distance between them. Evalyn didn't know if she wanted him to. Their eyes stayed on each other, and she gulped, "I... I want things to be better. For everyone. And what's going on between us... it's—"

"New," he provided.

The Queen nodded. "Can we just... can we wait until this War is over to figure it out? For the sake of our Kingdom?" Walfien inclined his chin, finally stepping back. Evalyn followed suit—but before they could part, she exclaimed, "Please keep it."

"Keep what?"

"Your hope," she said.

Evalyn didn't think he moved until long after she'd gone.

The Queen spent more hours than necessary in meetings with the Court.

But the use of her time was all she could do to help with preparations that were crucial for her Kingdom to have a chance at ending this War in their favor. Upon the first meeting, she'd ensured every individual knew how vital it was that immediate action be taken. Festivities were over—they had to muster all the funds, weapons, travel and housing supplies, and troops Faylinn could possibly contain. Despite her father's claims, despite the two months he'd given them to prepare, Evalyn wasn't sure the King would withhold an attack until the declared date of battle just to keep his word.

Within hours of the order, Commander Praesi had successfully increased protection at the border: numerous squads had been sent to various points along the Faylinn boundary. Additional divisions were released for active village guarding and scouting—not for outright fighting, as the Kingdom needed every Faerie available in the case the King truly desired a major battle—but to report suspicious activity that could possibly relate to Braenish activity.

Keeping up with training and ensuring she consumed three meals a day was a grand feat; it took the Queen's utmost restraint not to allow her growing magic to burst at every beck and call.

The days were moving far too fast.

Suddenly there was a single month left. When Evalyn awoke the morning of the halfway mark, her actions were a result of training as much as a final, dire attempt to decompress.

The Queen wore a skin-tight, full-body training uniform, her wings half outstretched and trailing at her back. She glided leisurely across the keep floor—something she hadn't experienced in months. Something she wasn't supposed to be doing at all, considering she had a consultation with Lord Relfou of the Conclave concerning the importation of several thousand standing soldiers in two hours. Apparently the citizens residing in the mountainous, southwestern region of Faylinn were taught combative skills from a young age.

Still, Evalyn forced herself to breathe, and take what felt like her last free moment to do something for herself before she ran out of time entirely.

The Faerie entered the Great Tower. The pair of servants she passed didn't balk at her travels, nor did the sentry changing shifts that strolled down the stairs with a respectful dip of his chin. It'd become odd not to be rushing around the castle with strict arrivals and discussing valuable information with various nobles.

Evalyn reached the topmost level of the tower—a circular-floored space, with elegant archways carved on four sides of the stone walls. It was the highest position in any structure in Faylinn. The woman wandered to the archway that opened to the courtyard of The Palace, a view that stretched to the Mediocris Woods, hands resting on the stone edges. She leaned forward, and a forceful breeze swept curled locks across her face.

Perfect.

Evalyn stepped onto the ledge, wings flaring in anticipation. She'd been practicing small heights over the weeks, and something told her she was finally ready to attempt a true test.

To fly.

She sensed an uneasy presence behind her halt at the top of the stairs. Walfien's eyes were broad, his face still. He'd Seen what she was about to do.

The Hand's lips parted in dissent—but Evalyn stepped back, let herself sway, and plunged off the ledge. She caught a peek of Walfien's windblown hair at the edge of the tower before she tucked her wings tight against her body and flipped around, facing the rapidly approaching ground, where a group of noblewomen and handful of servants watched their Queen risk everything.

Not that she was going to die.

No, she'd attempted her strength because Walfien had shown. The Hand would save her if she needed it. But she hadn't begun screaming to indicate she'd failed her experiment and required saving.

She wouldn't begin now.

When Evalyn heard the cream-and-burgundy-clothed Lady cry out, and when even the busiest of servants paused at her dropping figure, the Queen of Faylinn expanded her wings to their full length. As she caught the wind, it took her a moment to grasp her distance to the hilltop.

An arm's reach had separated her from Death.

The realization galvanized her bones.

She began pounding her wings as a rush of laughter escaped her lips—she was *flying*.

The Queen veered right, into a south-bound wind that swept her towards an edge of the Mediocris Woods, but she gave a mighty beat and swerved back for The Palace, circling around it once, twice. Although it required an intense focus and determination—and she knew the faint ache in the muscles in her back would be far greater the next morning—there was an ease to the flying she couldn't quite grasp. Not that she needed to; the motions felt natural, as if she'd known what to do her entire life.

A grand beam broke through her lips. Despite her father and his War... this goodness lingered.

The Fae rode a current to the Aternalis Creek, where she loosened her arms to skim spark-tipped fingers across the water, leaving trails of luster in their wake. Pixies streamed around her, keeping up with her wingbeats and veering in patterns under and over the Queen. When the woman raised her chin to soar higher, her wings faltered ever so slightly—she dipped several inches into the rushing river, dunking both legs in bitter water and sending the pixies into rambunctious laughter. A sudden, sharp intake of breath had her steadying and hovering for several moments before she took off for the castle.

Wind whipped at her hair as she landed on the ledge of the Great Tower. The pixies trampled over one another as their spindly green limbs pushed and shoved to enter the chamber first.

Walfien leaned against the stone wall, arms crossed and head bowed. Evalyn dropped onto the tower floor, apologetic for the fright she'd given him, but smiled at the rush in her veins. She tucked strands of blonde behind her ears as the Hand pushed off the wall and neared her.

"Don't tell me that was the first time you tried that."

The edges of her wings rested at her shoulders. She stepped to the side, slouching against the stone, her half-dried pants leaking river water onto the floor. "I won't." The pixies' snickering turned to hissing when Walfien shot them a look.

He shook his head, dark wisps of uncut hair falling over his forehead. "You're outrageous, in case you didn't know."

"I mean to be. It's a favored tactic of keeping men like you on their toes."

A laugh sputtered out of Walfien. "I suppose you'll be keeping future methods to yourself, my Queen?"

"Most certainly, my Lord Hand. But if you'll excuse me, I do have an appointment with our dearly adored Lord Relfou." She passed him, his eyes tracking her every move, as well as the pixies that floated above her head and zoomed around the trail of her wings. The Queen halted at the top of the stairs, finding the male staring and open-mouthed at her casual manner. She beamed. "Happy nameday, Walfien."

Sunlight promptly became a necessity as its presence each day decreased. Constant snow drizzle—although lighter than it would soon be—was of no assistance to battle arrangements, as was the dropping temperature. Castle inhabitants meandering outside without purpose were rare and insane, and even the laziest, most privileged nobles found themselves contributing to preparations. Making space for incoming soldiers and surplus assistance became a hassle, especially as the majority of resources compiled onto The Palace's grounds.

With apparent weeks until battle, joy had dimmed to a faint flicker; laughter and Court gossip dwindled, and even Evalyn's trio quieted.

The Queen's days entailed back-to-back War counselings, and she resorted to practicing her magic late into the night when the rest of the castle endeavored for a few hours of sleep.

It was a little less than a week after her flight show when Evalyn gained half an hour to spare between meetings. When the final Courtier closed the chamber door behind him, she didn't delay in slumping onto the table—and was a breath away from rest when a creak at the threshold sent her flying into an upright stance, wiping down her gown and adjusting her plaited hair.

However, her gaze met Kalan and Recks Delta, and she returned to the slab of wood before her. An upbeat Kalan seated himself on her left, announcing, "My favorite woman. Let's settle this!" Evalyn leaned a cheek over her fist—she'd wholly forgotten about their planned interim catch-up.

Recks Delta paced in front of her table, gaze fluttering between his son and the Queen of Faylinn. Potentially wondering why he hadn't seen Evalyn accompany the Alpha since they'd formally met.

Before any unwanted emotions could arise in the woman, she straightened and declared, "My council has the expectation that your power and reputation will prove advantageous for Faylinn in the War of Kin."

The man seated himself in the chair opposite Kalan. "My route is nearly finalized. If I can get a sliver more time..."

"I understand your care for perfection, but we're in dire need of assistance," she retorted. "Our troops—even with those of our allies—are substantial, but not enough."

Kalan added, "Not for the army we predict the King has—the one he could be growing at this moment."

"You will leave tomorrow at sunrise to gather whatever forces possible," the Queen commanded. Recks opened his mouth, but she said, "I understand you have arranged a precise journey, but I don't know how long you have. We'll respond to only the most certain confirmation that the King is readying for battle, but until then... you have your mission."

The Alpha folded his hands over the table. "You've shown a valiant effort to galvanize the Moon Clan. I know you can do the same for those who have no one."

The wolf-legend dipped his chin. "I'll do my best." He made for the exit.

"Recks Delta," Evalyn remarked. The man's golden-brown eyes held her firm gaze. "Thank you."

With a smile, the wolf departed.

Kalan slouched, rubbing his eyes. "Every turn I make in The Palace is occupied by a pair of Lords boasting about their share of investment in this fight. Recks and I encountered three alone on our way up the grand staircase."

The corners of Evalyn's lips perked. "The Conclave has supplied the vast majority of resources. They're simply desperate to have their egos groomed. Although... it *is* a beneficial way of growing our supplies." She picked at her nails. "Perhaps I should hold a contest to see who can provide the most. What entertainment that would be."

Kalan chuckled. Evalyn found herself reaching for his hand. Yearning overwhelmed all other thoughts in her mind. They'd both been so hounded with duties and personal meetings and ensuring the safety of everyone else they loved that they'd barely seen each other after Sanator.

Not that it was Kalan's fault. On the contrary, the Queen had become panicked. By not being at his side for so long, she'd set aside the honorable—the *right*—thing to do and tell him about the kiss. But the idea of revealing all the feelings that went with it to Kalan was beyond frightening, and she'd dodged every possible encounter with him because of it.

It was a brutal instinct to plaster a pleasant look on her face; to forcibly replace her surely pungent scent of iniquity with calm focus as she asked, "How are you?"

He scrunched his brows. "Good. Better than I should be, considering the circumstances."

"You're happy?"

"Of course I'm happy, Evalyn." He gripped her hand. "With you, always."

She inhaled his scent of fresh pine, closing her eyes momentarily.

"Are you?"

Evalyn peered into golden eyes. "You make me happy." It was true. They'd endured so much, and she'd received boundless comfort and support from him.

But the guilt from everything she'd kept inside brought bile to her throat. She stood, knocking down the seat behind her. Kalan rose too, but she exclaimed—despite the choking burn in her mouth at the falsehood, "Bad lunch. I—I need air."

So much for picking up the broken pieces and building herself into a Queen deserving of her people when the woman didn't have the decency to be honest with the male she loved.

"Don't exhaust yourself. I'll get it," he said. In a moment he'd cracked a window and returned to her side, fixing her chair. "There's a meeting with the clan elders, otherwise I'd stay longer. Plan another extravagant sunset dinner, maybe." He kissed the top of her head. "No matter what happens with this War, I love you."

Before she could respond, he'd exited the room. As she lowered into her seat, the armrests cracked and splintered from freezing over. She was shaking.

Chapter Thirty One

Evalyn's head spun.

Her Keepers clothed her in a piece they'd designed; a gown crafted of fabric capturing midnight, which wrapped across her waist. A billowing cloak of the same shade clasped around her neck and pooled to the floor at her feet. The dizziness didn't subside.

The Faerie's chin tilted as she observed herself in the mirror. Blonde waves spilled over her shoulders, and her eyes strayed to the parchment in her palm.

The reason she was preparing for the first Royal criminal trial of her reign.

Despite the fact that they had no inclination as to what the case was about—who it was for—the Queen's trio was silent as they cleaned her nails, swept product onto her lips, and placed the Royal Crown atop her head.

Within minutes, she headed for the Great Hall, Keepers in tow. Kalan and Walfien would meet her there—additional markers of the authority she wielded. Nearing the entrance, her blank expression formed into an intentional smirk. No one but herself, a select pair of sentries, and the Faerie who'd delivered the slip of parchment in her grip knew anything of the prosecution. It didn't stop the whispers that echoed through the corridors, nor did it halt rumors of the trial already spreading across the castle.

The Great Hall was absent of noise when Evalyn strode through the doors and made for her throne atop the dais. The group of nobles that had gathered to witness the morning's events swiftly split into two groups on either side of the sentry-lined chamber. The Queen summoned her wings through the slits in her outfit a moment before she sat down, the sunray-feathered limbs unfurling at her sides. Walfien and Kalan were erect at the edges of her throne, embodiments of impassive confidence, and Beverly, Ida, and Vixie took up spots in the front row of the left group, the obedient and implicit attendants their roles demanded.

It was when the doors opened once more that the spectators realized only three members of the Conclave were present beside Evalyn's trio, and one of the Queen Mother's trusted Keepers were missing.

Serene, Nickie, and the Mim twins clutched each other with horrified gasps as Hali Maytora was dragged into the Great Hall, red-eyed and slovenly. Lord Pavan Ziffoy was hauled to Hali's side, both shoved to their knees. The nobles' faces stained with bewilderment, and all rotated to Evalyn in wordless query as to why such distinguished individuals were in chains with three guards at each of their backs.

She smiled and raised the neatly folded parchment. "This was delivered to me last night. Filip, would you be so kind as to come forth?"

The young servant stopped at the base of the dais with lowered eyes and sloped shoulders. With so many piercing gazes and listening ears, Evalyn restrained from softening her tone. "Stand straight and look at me."

The wispy haired boy revealed bright green eyes. "Apologies, Majesty."

She dipped her chin. "Filip came to possess this letter after glimpsing the recipient address when cleaning the chambers of Lord Ziffoy, and wisely brought it to my attention before it was too late."

Murmurs escaped from the crowd, and the leader of Mearley jerked against his binds.

"Do you have something to say, Lord Ziffoy?"

"You don't know what you've gotten yourself into, girl," he hissed, russet hair draping over his brows.

"I'm sure it's no worse than the pit you've dug yourself. Now it's time to read my favorite contents within your letter."

Pavan's face paled.

The Queen made a show of unfolding the parchment. "Let's see... ah. Here." She cleared her throat. "*I wish to have a place in your Court, my King. There is none with grander power, and Braena deserves nothing less than a staff worthy of serving you.*" Gasps echoed across the hall. "*My techniques to reach the most exclusive of Faylinn's Court have been successful. The woman is more than willing to share necessary information. I will do anything I must to satisfy you.*" The Queen paused. Her sight drifted to the Lady crouched on the floor. Hali began sobbing, the restraints on her wrists taut as she pulled from the guards. Tendrils of frozen mist expanded from her body, slithering across the floor.

Pavan's face scrunched into a scowl. "That... this is some—some ploy against me, to rid of my presence in this Court, and I will have *none of it!*"

He did have a way with words.

"Your inclement to defend only yourself—and not the Lady whose reputation you have ruined—doesn't aid you in the slightest." Evalyn turned. "What do you have to say for yourself, Hali?"

The Faerie didn't even meet the Queen's eyes before breaking down. Evalyn withheld the urge to roll her eyes. It would have been feasible that Hali had been pressured into sharing knowledge with the Lord—but her own handmaidens had revealed the Keeper's natural and willing tendency to visit Pavan during every stay he took at The Palace, hours at a time, no servants allowed inside his reserved quarters. And her two attacks: *only we will remain.*

Not anymore. Not after her and Pavan's nasty misconduct had been discovered.

"Hali Maytora, you are hereby stripped of your title as a Lady of the Court and Keeper of the Queen Mother. You will return to your home village within the week with whatever belongings you can carry, and are indefinitely banned from The Palace. Should you dare return, you shall be persecuted on sight."

The sentinels behind Hali marched forth to grab her—but the Faerie began screaming, loud and echoing. "*I'm pregnant! I'm pregnant!*" she screeched, the blood draining from her face as she crawled toward the Queen. "*Please, please, Majesty,*" the Keeper sobbed, "*I'm with his child. Please.*"

"Then you should be grateful for your future circumstances. After all, adulterous duplicity is a pinnacle offense."

"*No!* You slithering, senseless Queen—don't think this changes *anything*! You'll see! Only we will remain! *We will last through the end*, and you'll regret—"

It wasn't a second after the guards had whisked the thrashing Faerie from the chamber that Pavan opened his mouth to argue, but the Queen raised her hand, silencing him. "I suppose I should also mention the scheme concerning your bargain with the King in which you promised your son, Jaino, would be wed to me—linking your name to Royalty—in return for..." With a chortle, she recited the phrase she'd memorized. "*Being bestowed the title of Right Hand, Your Grace.*"

Someone in the crowd swore.

Indeed, Evalyn had read the contents of the letter and had the Lord instantly imprisoned before getting his chambers searched—where they found many interesting documents occupying an iron-locked drawer. There were certain to be more in his home city, but she'd found all she desired.

"I'm sure several of you remain dubious without proof of the evidence that has condemned Lord Ziffoy." The Queen clapped her hands twice. "That's why I've taken it upon myself to do you a favor." The doors swung open for a pair of sentinels hauling a crate full of inked parchment and scrolls, who placed it at Filip's side. When Evalyn held out a hand, the servant transferred a light stack of documents into it, which the Queen sifted through. "Letters, bargains, coded messages; all of which date back as far as months prior to my arrival to Faylinn—and address the King of Braena in Lord Ziffoy's handwriting, which has been identified by several Fae familiar with it."

Evalyn had never seen someone's face turn such a rich shade of scarlet so swiftly, nor had she ever seen a Faerie so easily overpower two trained sentries as Pavan did, yanking on the chains binding his wrists so abruptly that the guards lost their holds and stumbled to their knees. The crowd's startled voices filled the air.

As the guards regained their composure and pounced for the restraints, the Lord began shouting between thick breaths, "This is madness! *Madness*! This—this is—"

"A lie?" the Queen offered. The hall muted. "Lord Ziffoy, according to these documents, you have apportioned confidential information about Faylinn's monarchs, armies, and security and defenses, to our enemy. You aided Braenish soldiers to capture me and my mother, as well as orchestrated prior castle attacks, and engaged in unlawful relations with another Court member to secure your lineage in the Royal bloodline." The files in her hand fluttered to the floor. "Your defense?"

He snarled, "This wasn't a trial to begin with. Your decision was made the moment you obtained that letter. This is a display—a way to see if I'd confess under force."

"And you put on an *astounding* performance," she hummed. Her vision bounced between the nobles' glares of loathing and sentries' entertained stares. How many had despised the Lord and never had anything to say for it? How many had attempted and failed to do as she was—disposing of the Faerie entirely?

She guessed quite a few, for when she stood from her throne and made way to the floor announcing: "Pavan of House Ziffoy, Lord of Mearley and member of Faylinn's Conclave, you are sentenced to execution under my Royal authority for the crime of treason," not a single being objected to the penalty.

The Lord's body went rigid. The remaining sneer on his face faded.

Evalyn merely stroked the velvet-soft edge of her wing. "Would you like documentation of your last words?"

The sentinels that had reclaimed the Fae's shackles tugged as Pavan proceeded forward a step, features transfiguring into a maniacal grin as he hissed quietly enough that only she heard, "When you awake each night, quaking and weeping from the terrors of being vanquished—of being a pawn in a game you know not of—remember I will be blithely watching from the other side. Even after death... *only we will remain.*"

Evalyn set her features into a cool, unmoving state.

The male flew away, landing on his rear. He bent backwards, neck tugging down under the force, his cry of pain quickly becoming a pleading sob as his body configured into a terrible form. Only when he silenced did the Faerie jerk forward, in such agony that his arms couldn't catch his upper body as it slammed into the floor. He awkwardly lifted his head, soulless eyes meeting Evalyn's.

"Should I do it again, *my Lord*?"

The chamber filled with gasps and whispers. They were surprised and—not disbelieving, but... admiring. Astonished.

Evalyn had controlled her magic without physical instruction.

Successfully performing any tendril of power solely with her mind was a feat so rare that only a handful of Fae had been able to do it in a millennium—thus, her Kingdom was aware of her advantage. She could be bound, or blind, or lost—but unless her magic was smothered by iron... the Queen of Faylinn had a limitless, defending power.

But Evalyn ignored the reactions of the nobles, ignored the wondrous surprise she felt radiating from the two males at her back, and kept her eyes on the traitor at her feet.

Pavan, breathless and twitching, glared back.

A smirk formed on Evalyn's lips as she crossed her hands at her hips. Slowly tilted her head.

The Faerie was swept to his knees, arms spreading wide from his body. Stretching. Straining, as the Great Hall doors parted again and a masked, hooded Fae emerged. A sharpened longsword swung at the executioner's side as he silently neared the Queen. She raised a beckoning hand; he raised it over Pavan, whose body she forced to lower.

Yet the Queen waited.

Inciting a horror and helplessness in the Lord that she understood all too greatly because of him.

When the male took a long, shuddering breath, she permitted the sword's descent.

Evalyn didn't move—didn't blink as the crunch of metal through bone rang across the room; as his body tumbled forward, halting inches from her feet, and crimson spilled onto the floor from where the sword impaled his figure.

The Queen stepped over the pooling blood, discarded each appalled noble, and marched out of the chamber without another sound.

Chapter Thirty Two

"The Lords think there's nothing they can do to help themselves," Evalyn said, running fingers through her curls. "Is my assistance *imperative* to accomplish any sort of matter?" Her eyes bulged, and she scoffed at Walfien, who was slumped in the high-backed chair behind his desk whilst she sprawled across the sofa. "I don't understand how you've dealt with them for so long."

The Hand dragged fingers down his face—down the dark scruff along his cheeks and chin that had grown over the past few days. "You get used to it."

Evalyn grumbled.

Walfien cleared his throat and folded his arms over the desktop. "Lord Gilian has made some encouraging efforts to transport his inventory of longbows for the archers."

She laid her head over the armrest, vision flipping. "The unrefined sack of a man from... what was it?"

"Windrew. It's a miniscule town between the southern peak of the Timoke Mountains and Mediocris Woods."

She rolled her eyes. "I assume he desires speedy compensation beforehand."

"He can be denied it."

Her ears perked. "*And* be promised that should he not supply our troops with higher chances of survival, his lands may go unprotected from any..." She nibbled at her lip as she rose to sit. "Unwanted guests."

Walfien shook his head with the hint of a smile. "You have an eye for schemery."

"One of us has to. Besides," she added, "if, by now, the Lords of my Kingdom don't believe I'll follow through with my promises, I'll simply rid of more liabilities." No one doubted her after Pavan Ziffoy's execution last week. The Hand dipped his head in agreement, although he shielded a grin. Evalyn scrunched her forehead. "I'm serious."

"I know."

"Yet you're amused?"

"Your mother was just as feisty about carelessness; I noticed the similarity."

A huddle of footsteps sounded outside the doorway. They both straightened instantly—only a guard shift.

Walfien sighed. "We're scrambling for space with the inpouring of troops. Commander Praesi declared the groups today should be the last from Lubbum, but some soldiers have already relocated to Pheelo until we leave for battle."

"That's supplementary protection for the clan, if nothing else. What of Koathe for the divisions from Flordem? They're scheduled for arrival in two days' time. Surely that's long enough to send them to the capital without complaint?"

"There will be protests to any changes we make," he answered, "but it's a viable alternative. I'll meet with the Commander this afternoon. Perhaps we should send our excess in The Palace there too."

"If all goes our way, we'll be marching north anyways. Gathering well rested and sufficiently supplied soldiers can only help," Evalyn offered. Walfien absently nodded his head, likely formulating the best course of action for a smooth week.

She paced towards the bookshelves. They were always doing that: ensuring everyone was safe; paranoid that her father would attack at any given moment despite his claims and lack of movement; speeding through every meeting and meal and public appearance merely to get them over and done with. The Queen was simply going through the motions, feeling nothing except exhaustion and strain and a yearning for War to *start* just so it could finally end—

"Breathe." A soothing and deep purr of comfort.

The Queen returned to reality, her hands grasping the shelf above her head. She'd summoned her wings, instinctively enveloping herself in warm shadows. With a slow, deep inhale, she dropped her right wing to view Walfien inclined against the wall, a foot away. Mismatched irises searched her face.

When Evalyn lowered her hands, sending her wings away with half a thought, he said, "I understand."

She leaned into his embrace. Another inhale made his scent clear: leather, parchment, a hint of cardamom. She'd never understood it before, but suddenly it was everywhere: within the chamber, lingering on her plum gown, clinging to his hair.

Their arms settled around each other, and Evalyn lifted her chin. In his eyes, she saw her own weariness. The burdens and tension.

"I'm right here with you."

She pouted her lips. "I'm sorry we're in this mess."

The corners of his eyes crinkled. "Aren't you always?"

"Don't make me send Oberon's army your way first."

"I know better than to doubt you won't."

A chuckle rose to her lips, but a creak sounded behind her and Walfien's expression swiftly transformed into something she rarely glimpsed from his unshakeable soul—fear. She turned uneasily.

Kalan stood at the door, a bundle of sky-blue geraniums clutched in his hand, fingers blooming pale from his tightening grip. "I was looking for you before your next meeting, Evalyn."

Walfien cleared his throat. Evalyn immediately pulled away, fluffing her gown. "You found me."

"I can see you're a little preoccupied."

Evalyn glanced at Walfien but stepped towards the sofa. "I'm not. Would you like to join me for lunch?"

The wolf's face was stone. "I'd like to be told what I walked into. Were you just starting? Or finishing up before anyone could see?"

Evalyn responded, "That wasn't what you think it was," when Walfien said, "These times aren't easy, Kalan."

A muscle feathered in the Alpha's jaw as he shifted to Walfien. "You're trying to stay on neutral ground, *brother*."

"You'd protect your family. I'm trying to protect her."

"That is *not* the same thing," Kalan snarled. "You couldn't protect your parents, and you sure couldn't save Ahstra! What makes you think you can keep her safe?"

Evalyn noted the astonishment on the Hand's face. She said, "Let's talk about this—"

"So you can toss the story around like this is some *game?*"

"I've never done that, Kalan."

"I don't believe you."

Walfien interjected, "She is your *Queen* and you'll listen to her—"

"You don't get to do that to me!" the Alpha bellowed.

"We can when you won't let us explain ourselves!" Evalyn shouted.

"Now you're teaming against me." The side of Kalan's mouth was upturned, but he wasn't amused in the slightest. "I assumed you'd been distant because of War. And I hadn't pondered how you coped with the struggles—the *same ones* I feel—but I didn't expect... this." Evalyn restrained from looking at Walfien now. "What I saw wasn't a pair of close friends. Do yourself a favor and save your breath trying to convince me otherwise."

The Queen clutched at the fabric of her dress, stunned. Why hadn't she told him of the kiss—of her feelings—when she'd had the chance? When it wouldn't have created such a dramatic scene and she could've moved on feeling a little less of a sick liar?

So much for her truth-honed blood.

The Alpha's mouth thinned. "*Days* ago, we were good." He shook his head at the ceiling. "You said you were *happy*. And this... with *him*—" He took a shuddering breath.

"Kalan," Walfien attempted.

"I can't do this." The wolf's face crumpled. "Not before this War."

"Kalan, please." The Queen stepped around the sofa. "We have to discuss this. We need to talk—"

"*You don't have a say in what I need anymore,*" he choked out. "*Neither of you.*" Shimmering eyes met Evalyn's. "How long? How long has something been going on?" Bile rose in her throat when she attempted to part her lips. "Have you gone so far as to—"

"*Never*," Evalyn blustered swiftly, "Gods, never more than—"

A terrible silence.

"But you've been this close before. Okay. I get it. While I claimed my *unfaltering* love for you, after so much heartbreak—which we shared together—you were just as personal with my best friend. I suppose it proves my naivety." Color leached from Evalyn's cheeks. Gods, she truly was as vile as the Faeries she'd rid from The Palace. The Alpha shifted his gaze past her. "And *you*—" Kalan's voice thickened. Walfien was silent. "I've trusted you my whole life. And after our share of troubles, I found *her*—" he pointed at Evalyn, voice cracking—"and she made it all go away. You knew that. *You knew*. But you didn't have the decency to push her away, even out of respect for me? Perhaps Ahstra got what she wanted. To end everything rather than be with you."

Kalan *knew* that wasn't what had happened—but the Alpha whipped in Evalyn's direction. "These were for you. They match your eyes." In a swift motion, the flowers scattered across the floor in distressed fragments. Something in her did the same. "Go ahead; you can finish. Don't pretend now that you care about boundaries. You obviously never did."

He turned on his heel and exited the office.

Evalyn didn't realize she'd reached out for him until her wrist began aching. She rotated towards Walfien, their states of shock mirrored. She sputtered, "I'm going after him. He was just... angry, and I need to explain—"

"He wasn't. That was... beyond. And to come back from that... we'll have to spend our lifetimes righting this."

Evalyn growled, dragging hands through her hair, down her face. This was her fault. Kalan hadn't allowed her to explain, but she deserved this. The guilt and sorrow and ire. Her wings returned, resolute and reliable at the sides of her fingertips. She'd debated telling Kalan and had consciously decided not to. Decided to hurt him, instead.

This was her punishment.

Pine needles crackled under her feet, and frigid winds seared her eyes. Evalyn slowed as she approached the edge of the Moon Clan's camp, silently pacing around the clearing as she searched for him. She had to make things right. Or try to.

The Queen found him marching towards a cabin, where Bre, Janson, and Kye lounged outside on stumps around a long-burning fire. Her body froze at the rear corner of a neighboring cabin.

"Canceled your business with the Commander?" Kye surmised over the flames at Kalan's approaching figure.

"No."

"Then why are you here?"

"I don't need your snark right now," Kalan barked.

Kye lifted his hands. "I didn't know you were in such an uptight mood—"

Janson spluttered, "What Kye *means* to say is that you can tell us why you're upset." He combed through coal-black hair, muttering, "*Spirits, Kye,* you'll get us all yelled at one day..."

Kalan watched the fire. "I found Evalyn... having a moment. With Walfien." The Queen's stomach dropped at the sorrow in his voice.

Jan sucked in a breath. "Oh."

"It's been going on for a while," the Alpha huffed. "I don't know the details, but they must've thought I was stupid, because they almost tried to pretend like I'd imagined them wrapped around one another."

"*Oh,*" Janson repeated.

Evalyn flinched when Kalan hurled a rock into the fire, sending sparks dancing in the sky. "I have been waiting *weeks* for Evalyn to look at me like she did him. I know the King did some cruel things to her in Braena, so I made sure she knew I was here if she needed any comfort... but I have seen *Commander Praesi* more times than my own partner in the last month and I concluded it to be an issue with our schedules. Now I doubt her's was ever as full as she made it out to be. With real conferences, anyways. No one would dare think twice if the Queen's free time was filled with her Hand's company—especially stupid, gullible Kalan Lupien."

"Don't say that," Bre protested.

"That's not your fault," Jan stressed. "She's forever earned my respect, but Evalyn has to be every level of foolish to cheat you."

Kalan shook his head, eyes closed against the cracking fire. "What say you, Kye?"

The Queen sucked in a breath. Kye was a man of his word; he hadn't told. The male cleared his throat. "I'm nonplussed. You know I don't do well with stuff like this."

"Normally, you'd be raging more than anyone and begging for a name to beat up."

Kye inched closer to Bre. "Sorry, Kalan. Not in the mood to fight, I guess."

"Stand up," Kalan demanded. "I can feel your trepidation. *Stand up.*" The wolf did, matching the Alpha's gaze. "Look me in the eyes and tell me that outside War, this is the most surprising news you've received in three months."

"I can't."

Jan's eyes widened.

"I already knew," Kye worsened. Kalan marched forth, but the male threw his hands up as Jan stepped between them. "Look, I didn't think it was a big deal. Truly, I thought Evalyn would have told you before the night was over, but I didn't see her again—how was I supposed to know if she did? I assumed her swift confession left you relatively unbothered, so I never said anything. And... I kind of swore to her that I wouldn't tell."

"You promised you wouldn't tell *what?*"

Kye shook his head, but Kalan growled his demand and the wolf mumbled begrudgingly, "That, before her coronation... Walfien kissed her. And she didn't stop it. She realized they had feelings for each other but didn't want to hurt you."

"Walfien Pax did *what?*" Bre snapped.

Kalan shoved Janson, sending his fist flying for Kye's face as soon as he was in range. Kye crashed to the ground, swearing and clutching his jaw. The Alpha stepped back, huffing.

"You know, I think this is worse," Kalan puffed. "That you knew instead of Janson. He's usually the one to think about other people's feelings—not Kye Kallister, master brawler and expert in the art of pushing rebellion to the limit without summoning punishment." Kye gritted his teeth as he stood. "I could've understood if Jan was concerned about both my and Evalyn's feelings... but *you—*" Kalan prodded a finger into the male's chest—"are supposed to be the one that comes to me immediately with information like that."

"I'm sorry."

Kalan lifted his chin. "I'm done with apologies."

Evalyn pressed against the cabin, hiding from sight as Kalan shifted to his wolf and stormed off into the forest. When the evening shadows overwhelmed his figure, she crumpled to the ground.

It was hours later when a servant knocked on the Queen's door and handed her a letter. She hadn't slept, but assumed all others in the Palace were—who had such dire need to send a message while the sun remained slumbering? It took a moment to light the candles upon her desk before she could observe the contents; she'd become acquainted with the dark to wallow in what had gone so wrong so quickly.

But when the stamp came into view, she was *certain* she'd fallen into a nightmare. She nearly shredded the parchment in an effort to open it quick enough.

Evalyn read it through three times. With a wobbly breath, she sprinted to find Walfien.

Millo Ten, Overseer of the Rogues, had written one line.

They're coming.

Chapter Thirty Three

The marching would begin at dawn.

After alerting her council—and in turn, the entire castle—of the letter's contents, Evalyn returned to her quarters and only opened the doors for her Keepers.

They weren't easy to convince to stay behind. They protested like children, begging to go with the Queen for every number of outrageous reasons—and Evalyn *did* want them with her—but as Queen, as their *friend*, she couldn't dare hope they'd remain safe if they left the walls of the castle. With that firm declaration, the trio had fallen into tears and dared to plead for Evalyn to stay.

She gave a miserable laugh. They knew she couldn't.

When Evalyn exited her chambers, she continued not to the foyer, but to the Great Tower, rounding the steps up and up and up to an entrance she'd never neared.

She pushed against the castle Steeple's tall, wooden doors—which, by some magic, remained silent in spite of their age.

She stopped in her tracks when a familiar face made way in her direction, towards the exit of the multi-leveled chamber. Walfien halted before Evalyn, who leaned against the door, holding it open to reveal the stout hallway at her back. She wasn't surprised to see him; on the contrary, it was a relief that they'd both spared an ounce of their time to ask for a miracle in the War, but the Hand had never spoken about his spiritual beliefs, let alone be seen in any form of worship or prayer to the Gods. Evalyn hadn't either—hadn't been any amount of a proper believer. She'd never sacrificed time to thank the Gods—just beg for help. It was a wonder why the woman bothered to do so now.

Walfien scanned her. They hadn't again acknowledged anything about Kalan—and seeing as she was moments from entering holy ground, it was likely better not to. Her current concern was a prayer before they traveled. So Evalyn gave a faint smile, and the Hand continued with the dip of his chin.

The tall doors closed behind her, the hour of morning leaving the mute, candle-lit Steeple to herself. Warmth emitted from the nooks in the stone walls; cream candles were packed into the countless shelves embedded within the curving, windowless walls of the tower, and smothered the floorspace save a thin, direct pathway to the wallside opposite of the doors. Against the blank wall resided a statue—a figureless silhouette that represented both Omforteu and Deeam in a way that only an abstract fragment of art could manage. Evalyn felt the comfort it'd been intended to create as she neared it. The slight drag of her wings echoed.

When there was less than a foot between her and the shrine, she dropped to her knees, instinctively placing her hands on the floor, keeping her eyes lowered. Not out of fright or obligation, but respect. The Queen had long since accepted her Creation, and had yet to find any reason to doubt it.

She took a shuddering breath.

"We're to depart on this journey within the hour—we'll head north to meet my father's forces." Her voice sounded horribly vulnerable in the vastness of the tower. Evalyn closed her eyes, head lowering. "Please provide me with guidance. The travels won't be smooth, and I know however we greet battle, the end of this War won't be what anyone expects." Candle-heat spread across her wings. It'd be the last time she was warm for a while. "Still, I... I can't comprehend why my Kingdom cares for me. My growing power is meaningless in comparison to who I am, yet so many are willing to die for me—*to die.* To lose their lives so I can live mine." Her lips trembled. "I want to be worthy of their praise. I want to fight. To save my people. Prove that I'm more than the broken child my father formulated."

Desperation tore through her, and the candles around her sailed into the walls. The flames winked out, sending her into darkness. She gave heaving breaths, squeezing her fists and flaring her wings as her vision adjusted.

"I know this War is punishment for what I've caused in Liatue. For what my people have to go through." Her words turned deep and guttural. "But however the course of this battle shall go... I ask one thing." She leaned back and peered into the face of the statue. "Make my father regret it."

The trudging troops were specks of dust. Evalyn soared far above in calm, Winter air. Horse-drawn wagons hauled loads of foodstuffs, weaponry, and camp gear—everything they would need to survive for a couple weeks, if necessary. The entirety of the Queen's civil Court had remained at The Palace with the exception of Kinz and Mags, who hadn't spared Evalyn a word before they'd settled onto their mounts. Few carriages dotted the line of travel, transporting martial Lords and the Guard's upper leaders who could afford not to walk alongside the platoons.

It'd been an unexpected surprise when anonymous complaints had arisen from her Court pertaining to her decision to march with her troops into battle—but Evalyn didn't particularly care for their opinions. No matter where their disapproval stemmed, she wouldn't let the citizens of Faylinn fight alone.

This was *her* father, which meant it was her battle.

Her War. Nothing would stop Evalyn from putting an end to this horror.

She'd sent messages to every noble in reprimand.

The Queen chose to fly for the first day not only to partake in any additional training she could, but for this: to take in all she was risking—using—in this War. The lives, supplies, and connections in her Kingdom. Her insides twisted as she observed the mass below; the leather and steel scented breeze did nothing to soothe her, so she rose higher, until a blanket of clouds lay beneath her and the moist wind shifted to icy, fresh air.

The sun, bright and warm, was a finger's width above the clouds.

It would be a long day.

She dipped back below the clouds, making three circles around the route of Fae. The effort to find accommodations for the extra soldiers had proved pointless—they'd been commanded to convene with the main army during their travels to Faylinn's northern border. Queen Veda's army would join them just before, and Evalyn was sure they'd encounter the Rogues soon after.

The Moon Clan trotted at the front of the procession. Every single wolf in the pack had assailed the Alpha upon hearing Braena had begun their march for battle and demanded to fight. Kalan was at the very head, guiding them to Oberon; to the Faerie who'd taken and ruined so much for the wolf. Although she hadn't yet conversed with him, to explain *everything*—because he had nothing but rightful contempt for her—Evalyn was proud of him.

The great Alpha who had helped and saved so many. Saved her.

By the third day of travel, Evalyn opted for horseback rather than exacerbate her flying fatigue. At least they'd rested at a local village last night, where Evalyn and other Court staffers had been forced to take up rooms in the inn to receive half-decent rest.

The two days of flying had left a sharp ache in the Queen's shoulders, although something told her the growing pain in her groin was no better a result. Still, the hours had provided decent training. Despite the necessity of saving her energy and building her magic reserve, she'd also practiced her abilities above the clouds, forming fire-arrows and barriers of parchment-thin ice.

Her stamina had grown strong; a mighty reservoir in comparison to the shallow pool of her adolescent body. Perhaps her present strength could've warded off the toxins that incapacitated her fifteen-year-old self.

Or sensed the betrayal of her parents beforehand and found this life a little earlier.

She pondered how different things may have been. The people she might've met; who she would've become. If it would've been different than this life, full of War and brokenness and sorrow.

Something told her no.

That, no matter what, her fate would've led here. To this fight and all it accompanied.

"How are you holding up?" Walfien asked, steering their mounts away from the trudging parade.

After two days on horseback, the Queen was strongly considering returning to the air until they reached the border. At least her rear would receive some alleviation. She fidgeted in her saddle. "Not as bad as I thought I'd be. A little tender and sleep-deprived, but... I'm managing. I'm sure I'll say otherwise when we meet my father's forces."

She gazed at the grassy field before them, covered in half-frozen dew. The landscape was captivatingly vibrant, with multi-colored wildflowers dotting the scenery as if in revolt against the sheer season. Evalyn twirled a finger as they passed a patch, and two blush, lacy flowers floated into her open palm. She smiled at it, untouched and unbridled by the turmoil of the vile creatures of Liatue.

A cool wind kissed her nape, sending shivers down her spine—she wished summoning her wings didn't frighten her mare. The only time she'd tried, the horse had bucked the Queen off and nearly stomped on her feathers.

"What are you thinking about?" Walfien inquired.

She peered into the pale sky. "I was once convinced I'd never see this land again. But I'm willfully giving it up now to keep this Kingdom safe."

Walfien's gaze was observant. And... private.

"Stop, Walfien. Someone will see."

He turned. "I'm sorry."

She sighed. "A thought for a thought. Your turn."

"You still care for him."

"Of course. I can't forget everything we went through." The dozens of wolves were near-imperceptible marks in the landscape ahead. "He sacrificed so much."

Hush overcame them.

After some minutes, the Hand voiced, "It tears me apart—what happened. How it happened. I never wanted to hurt him. Especially like that. But... what's done is done, and we have to accept that when he moves on... he won't come back. Not like we knew him."

Evalyn stroked her mare, furrowing her brows as she understood, and profound anguish subsequently overwhelmed her. The sound of chatting troops and trotting stallions echoed around her head. Finally, she murmured, "They brought the children."

"They did."

"Kalan allowed them to fight."

"If they asked to fight... he wouldn't have told them they were unfit in any way. And he knows too well they all have something to fight for."

"Willing or not, it makes it no easier to see children marching onto a battlefield." The Queen lifted her shoulders. "But they're strong. If they endured the attack that claimed half of their pack... they're warriors in their own right."

"There are adolescents among our own troops. A handful haven't reached their Bonum Vitae—others may never. Most aren't as young, but... Guard leaders had to set aside the fact that they're still growing youth. Because their choice is to either watch those they hold dear sacrifice their lives, or do it alongside them. Who are we to demand which way they must suffer?"

Evalyn hated that thought. Her vision set on nothing. "We should return."

Walfien closed his eyes, sighing, "I'll gather an update from Commander Praesi." With a parting nod, he trotted into the mass of Fae.

The wretched truth was that most young Fae would die on the field. Many grown ones, too. But the stakes of this War had been made clear to all volunteer troops; she wouldn't ruin the chance of revenge for those who'd given up everything to take it.

Yet there *was* one final way she could help Faylinn. One more ally she could convince, who could aid the adolescent Fae who'd joined the battalion with desperate hopes of victory but were unable to bring any true defense.

Come nightfall, Evalyn leaned against a foot-high crate, unbothered by the pacing and wandering Fae before her. Petite fires had arisen throughout the village-wide resting area, glowing in the faces of passersbyers. She shifted to the darkened plains at her back. From her scouting at sunset, the area matched the one described in her research. The woman gingerly stepped towards the abyss; all that remained was a small hike. Twenty feet from the edge of the camp-grounds, she tugged a hooded cloak around herself, checking only once to ensure no one spotted her.

Then sprinted into the wilderness.

Ten minutes later, she spotted the cluster of vine-covered boulders sheltered by a mesmerizing, gnarled sapling.

The Sacred Tree.

Its ancient limbs expanded to the length of a thunderstorm cloud; the broad, round-lobed leaves were thick and healthy. The magic sheltering them from Fae-induced harm had also kept the tree from natural deterioration over the centuries.

An orb of flame appeared in her palm, and the bark creaked, seeming to yearn for the raw power. The Faerie extended threads of fire from the ball in her hand; berry-red strands wove living flame around the trunk, illuminating a leave-strewn ground. A simple thought permitted the magic to emit light yet withhold its destructive heat.

When she dropped her cloak and revealed her wings, a chorus of gasps sounded above. The Queen of Faylinn lifted her head to thousands of awestruck pixies. Glittering specks of eyes blinked among olive-skinned bodies, human only in form. Needle-thin arms and legs stretched long, and translucent, golden wings sprouted at their backs. They were the only living beings she knew to be immortal. Primitive, yet elegantly magnificent creatures.

She dropped to a knee, lowering her chin in respect and gratitude, and they leaned ever closer, a shrill wave of sound sending chills down her back. Their greeting and demand.

Hello, Newborn Queen. What assistance do you require?

They knew she'd come for one reason.

And with a display of her powers, the show of her wings... the presence of the daughter of King Oberon Romen and Queen Tania Impur meant a significant deal.

Evalyn had read about the ways of the pixies and their method of trading and bargaining; what they required in return and the restrictions they applied to deals.

"Assist Faylinn in the War of Kin." She asked not that they serve her cause, because they bowed to no one; there were no leaders, no governance among them, yet the pixies understood how to cooperate in eternal peace. She only asked for their physical help in battle—no more, no less. "Should my enemy be vanquished, I will immediately enforce your ability to roam the whole of Liatue for as long as I live. I leave a second favor to you."

It was an offer they couldn't resist. She'd researched and uncovered ancient findings of the injustice towards their kind, the ways in which many had shielded their lands so as to block the pixies' exploration. And an additional favor of their choosing—it was risky, as the favor could be as broad or specific as it declared, but the method was the only known way to assuredly gain pixie agreement.

After several minutes amidst untranslatable whisperings, a band of the creatures descended to the group of rocks at the Queen's side. When a single, finger-tall one stepped forward and reached out, she laid her hand at its feet. The pain at the pad of her finger—where the pixie placed feather-light hands—was a pinprick, followed by a delicate tingle that traveled up her arm. Even through her tunic, she glimpsed the lucent circle that followed the path of a vein to her heart.

It meant her bargain was accepted—and secured with the pixies' peculiar magic that ensured she would keep her word.

The snap of Evalyn's fingers plunged them into black night.

Chapter Thirty Four

The soldiers were chaos outside of Evalyn's cottage. They were to reach the boundary tomorrow evening, but the swift-stepped, final addition of Faylinn troops had united with the main army a day earlier than planned. As the last evening of objective-less respite that they could wager to spare along the trek, all were celebrating the overnight stop-over at the final Faylinn village they'd pass. Fire-songs echoed across the grounds, along with stumbling groups of friends disoriented from ale and exhaustion.

Although going off little sleep due to the prior night's adrenaline from the pixies' alliance, the Queen hadn't relaxed during the four hours she'd been waiting in the single-room cottage hollowed out for her needs. She mindlessly paced at the door frame. On the edge of the bed, Walfien was absorbed in his own thoughts since his return from a fleeting encounter with the newly-joined captains. She didn't have to ask what was in his goblet.

Resting around a conference table, Mags crossed her fingers along the wooden top. "There must exist some last way to bargain with the King."

The Queen paused her stride, shaking her head. "It'll never work." The witches had been trying to convince her for half an hour to make peace with Oberon and call off the whole War.

Kinz raised her brows. "This is but a hasty response in the midst of his fervent power grab. We've seen battles like this over the years, dear. Neither side truly desires the wretched aftermath."

"You don't know my father, Kinz."

Mags sighed. "Evalyn, there are ways of appearing—"

"*Not him.* This is not a facade. He cares for *nothing* beyond his supremacy."

"He cares for you," Kinz said.

Evalyn's eyes flew wide. She thought of all the torture and treachery she'd experienced in The Shadow Coumpound, all her father had done to bring her *home*. "You're a fool to believe so."

The elder woman snapped back, "*You* are a fool to think care always depicts tenderness and mercy. Don't dare to presume I've overlooked his cruelty. But you yourself said there was one thing he wanted more than this War."

Evalyn shook her head. "It's too late, in any case."

The witches shared an indiscernible look.

A rustle sounded outside, and the Hand was at Evalyn's side before her head had snapped up. The witches' whispers halted.

Commander Praesi strolled in, fingers perpetually set atop her longsword. The handle of a mace peeked from behind light-streaked, coal-tinted hair, which lay closely trimmed to her head. Her dark-eyed gaze respectfully acknowledged Kinz and Mags before matching Evalyn's stare. The scars flecking her face blended with endless freckles, stark against the woman's bronze complexion. She lowered her chin, partially bowing at the waist. "Your Majesty. Lord Pax. We're minutes from sundown; I daresay our meeting should proceed."

"A messenger delivered a note shortly after we arrived," Walfien responded. "Veda insisted she'd be present by dusk. It's a matter of moments, Commander—"

"The Queen of Ausor is here! She's—" Micka plowed inside, eyes widening as he discerned the Fae before him. "Oh, you're already..." He slowed his steps, disheveled blue hair falling over his forehead. "Waiting. Cool." A smile found his lips, as it always seemed to do, and he bowed swiftly, clearing his throat. "Their units reached the east border of camp two minutes ago, which means she should be—"

"I hope I find you in good health, Alpha," voiced a sweet tone outside the open door.

"Likewise, Your Grace," came the return. Walfien and Evalyn shared a wary look.

Queen Veda seemed to glide through the door, clad in a silver and rose battle-uniform, followed by Kalan, Kiran Kroghe, and an additional Fae—a large male with a sideways smirk, whose chest was decorated with the Ausorian emblem of three overlapping hearts.

Micka audibly gulped, whispering although everyone could hear, "She is the second most angelic Fae to grace my sight."

Kiran raised his brows, likely wondering who the first could be, but Veda veered directly for her fellow Queen, gripped the woman in a friendly embrace, and pulled away without looking at the others. "You are well, Evalyn?"

"Well enough. If looks are any indication, I'm inclined to believe the same of you," she chuckled. The Faerie nodded in agreement, shifting to observe Evalyn's companions as the Faylinn Queen introduced them. "You've met Kalan, Alpha of the Moon Clan; this is Milid Praesi, Commander of the Faylinn Guard; Micka Roshium, Second in Command; Walfien Pax, my Hand; and my dearest friends, Mags and Kinz Alatar, florvi witches in service to and inhabitants of my Kingdom."

Veda beamed, pacing to her brother's side. "My brother, Kiran, is Emissary to Ausor," she said to the others, "and this is the Commander of Ausor's forces, Javin Kallias." Javin dipped his chin. "Now that we're acquainted," she added with sparkling eyes, "I would ask for a moment. Surely our Commanders would appreciate familiarizing themselves?"

Before Evalyn turned her way, Milid was already leading Javin and Micka outside, in discussion about their unit numbers.

The rest of the delegation discussed soldiers, travels, and life within both of the southern Kingdoms for over an hour.

"It's a relief to hear of your desire to aid us in this War," Walfien said, after Veda proclaimed for the fourth time her Kingdom's pride in serving Faylinn in battle.

"Liatue deserves to be rid of the disease that is the King. Any further power means more destruction, and we've seen the aftermath of that. So we're determined," Veda proclaimed, "to fight. And we *want* to fight—for Faylinn, but for our father as well. For Ausor. Do not doubt our willingness to be here."

Evalyn nodded, her hand sliding to cover the other woman's. "That tenacity is something we greatly need." Her eyes briefly flicked to Kalan—who's returning stare made her soul tremble. She'd restrained from looking at him since he'd arrived, worried that he would ignore her forever and the woman would never get the chance to state her piece. Within a heartbeat, she'd returned to Ausor's rulers, saying, "It's getting late. We should retire to bed; travels will continue before dawn."

Everyone stood. The Queens gripped each other tightly, and Veda whispered into Evalyn's ear. "Maybe when this is all over, your artists can design my future children's rooms. I may not yet be married, but I know I want a warm floral theme with accents of a charming gold—the color of your hair." She chuckled, adding, "Keep it from Kiran, though, or he'll use the idea for his own little ones." They pulled away with matching desolate smiles—as lighthearted as the comment was, there would be no decorating soon. Both were too aware that War would end, as it had started, in tragedy and death.

The jumeas exited the cottage; Mags and Kinz followed with wishes of full sleep. The Alpha stepped around the table, but Evalyn faced him.

"Will you stay for a moment?" she asked.

The Alpha's glowing, golden eyes were captivating. Despite how she'd hurt him, something held Kalan at the table. He never took his gaze off the Queen, even as she flicked a wrist to the Hand, who gave a mulling stare before departing to his own room.

Leaving them alone, at long last.

It seemed years since they'd last spoken.

Evalyn met the side of her bed, voice light. Cautious. "I saw the clan earlier. They seem to contain the highest spirit in all of camp. Any spirit left, actually." Her gaze twinkled.

"What is it that you want to say, Evalyn?"

She closed her eyes. Steadied her breathing. "I want to apologize."

"You don't. You're sorry for none of it."

"*I am.* I still care for you, Kalan—"

"*And I am still in love with you,*" he retorted. "I know you know that." The crackling of fire and muffled chatting sounded from outside. It wasn't until she looked at him that he said, "I will always love you, Evalyn. *Always.*" He shook his chin. "But I need the space—the *time*—to breathe. To process. To figure out what I'm supposed to do next."

"Kalan, we just—we don't have that kind of time. I want to talk this out now, to answer your questions and—"

"There's nothing I have to ask. Not about us, and certainly not concerning Walfien." The Alpha made to leave, but the softest of touches grazed his elbow. He faced her.

Evalyn parted her lips.

"Go to bed," he said. Before she could say her own three words that would hurt him more than help. "There are *lamentable* times ahead, Evalyn. Get your rest, and focus on this War." Her hands fell to her sides and she stepped back, heart empty and overflowing at once.

Kalan returned to his pack.

The longer they marched—the closer they came to meeting Oberon's forces and commencing battle—the more the soldiers' states eroded. By the time they reached the edge of the Silent Slopes, the mood of the procession was dwindling on mental burnouts.

Queen Evalyn lingered at Veda Kroghe's side when she wasn't airborne. The northern winds had become something of a hindrance to her flying, yet the woman was determined to strengthen her skills in all circumstances.

Battle would make no exceptions for her when it arrived.

Despite their unsettling future, a light smile surfaced on Evalyn's face as she reclined around a fire, extending her legs in front of her and wings behind. A group of soldiers rested around the other side, shimmering bottles of campabor in their hands that they ensured the Queen hadn't been stolen.

"Y-Your Majesties," slurred a dark-eyed male. "Have—have some!" he hiccuped, tossing the bottle across the flames. Evalyn halted the open drink mid-air, lifting her brows at the encouraging roars that followed the Fae's request.

Veda, at her side, met the woman's stare. Perhaps stupidly, they emptied the bottle.

Alas, this was War. Consequences were few and far between for such imprudence.

Evalyn's vision cleared and muscles eased. Veda leaned into her with a giggle, and on the Ausorian's other side, Kiran snickered. The Faylinn Queen's companions were nowhere to be seen, likely being significantly more productive instead of cavorting around a bonfire with half a dozen Guard soldiers—but Evalyn didn't particularly care.

When the campabor effects drifted away and the joking soldiers calmed, she asked the soldiers about their stories.

A deep and croaking voice echoed across the blaze. "M'mate passed sixteen years ago. Three months later, our girl passed. She'd just had her second nameday. Both got a sickness too quick to fend off. Couldn't afford a healer." The beginning of wrinkles lined the male's face, along with a deep brown beard. He clasped large, muscular hands. "I thought there was nothing left to fight for. Been in forestry since I was a boy, so it didn't come as a shock when m'village urged me to join the Guard. They said I could fight for m'girls." A pause. "I've been part of it for fifteen years now. Sometimes I think the Gods intended for 'em to pass so I could find this."

The woman at his side lifted her cup. Her voice was considerably lighter, but contained years of knowledge. Of seeing and doing things that couldn't be put into words. "I came from nothing. Lived on the edge of the Screaming Cliffs with my Pa until I had my Bonum Vitae—and discovered all that remained of my mother was my magic. After a month, I could unfailingly pin a critter to a tree with rocks and stone. My Pa gathered the little we had and dragged us to the capital, set on finding me a job if it was the last thing he did. I showed my skills to anyone who cared to watch." A nostalgic smile rose to her lips. "Apparently a capital sentry saw what I could do and reported to The Palace. Commander Praesi found me the next day. My Pa had never been happier in his life to hear a Sentinel Recruiting."

For hours they lingered there, gathering more and more troops to share their tales. Even Veda revealed a glimpse of life in Ausor—how the most desolate and shoddy of Fae were reborn in the Ausorian army. Young and old, legendary guards and fresh-recruits, every soldier came from something unique.

It made the Queen loathe War infinitely more than she already did.

The glow of the moon, centered in the midnight sky, illuminated the Faeries' faces alongside the rolling flames as the last one finished his piece. The final drops of campabor had long since been consumed, and the crowd of troops silently leaned into one another around the fire that'd grown three times over since dusk.

The ancient flame-song began with a boy, melancholic and sacred and meaningful. The swaying limbs of the trees above stilled to hear; the fire halted its crackles and pops; the wind slowed to a listening breeze.

Say, the Gods sent Him down
baring truth in a broad-lipped beam
that time shall, here and now,
be put to use fair and wisely.

The other soldiers joined in harmony, as if the words were a bedtime tale eternally resting in their memories.

Heartened by honor,
awaiting riches to own,
We claim Him our pressure
to forever roam
'til We reach home;
to forever roam
even when We can't go on;
to forever roam
or face His grim throne.

Chapter Thirty Five

Evalyn woke to the rustle of her tent, flying forward before Walfien had reached her side. Growling, hair frizzed and eyes piercing, she asked what in the *world* had him waking her an hour after she'd fallen asleep, but the Hand simply conveyed Recks had returned.

They were outside her tent within a minute. The massive bonfires surrounding camp were meant to ward off irritated Crawlers, but their inherent purpose did naught against the frigid wind blowing every which way.

"Where?" she questioned, voice barely rising over the gales.

Walfien gave a sleep-deprived simper. "Waiting."

The Hand led her through camp, towards the northwestern patrol, through rows of sizzling embers and tents housing passed-out soldiers. She pulled her cloak tight, too sleepy to care to summon her wings.

The Queen spotted the male before he did her. Recks turned from a sentinel with a pleased smile, inclining at the waist. "I'm sorry to wake you, Your Majesty."

Evalyn shook her head. "You gathered no one?"

His eyes widened. "On the contrary..." The wolf-legend shifted to the open grounds of blackness at their side.

When Evalyn rotated on her heel, hundreds of glowing, lupine orbs stared back, extending as far as her vision allowed.

"You... how many?"

"Over seventy-five. Among numerous self-dwellers and omegas, members from the Ice-Rider Clan, Ambers Pack, and Starlight Clan have declared themselves in service to you, Evalyn." Ancient, autonomous groups of wolves whose rivalries and grudges typically set them on opposing sides of battle. It was for reasons like the War of Kin that most packs roamed the uncharted territory of Liatue and disregarded the Faerie Kingdoms and their squabbles.

So why they were here, fighting with the Moon Clan, Evalyn had no guess. Only gratitude.

Recks lifted his chin. "They were all I managed to round up before I heard about the outset of your travels. We hoped to meet your troops before it was too late."

Evalyn exhaled a breath. "Thank the Gods. Without you... without this..." She swallowed. "Your effort will be forever remembered, Recks Delta." She was appalled at the amount of support he had gathered, at the additional warriors that had miraculously pledged themselves to Faylinn's cause.

But any speck of placidity the Queen felt had sorely abandoned her once they made landfall upon the southern edge of a vast, circular pocket of land within the Silent Slopes. Nestled at a makeshift conference table in the Commander's tent, Evalyn wrapped her wings around her shoulders in an effort to draw out the cold that had seeped into her bones. Milid, Walfien, Micka, and Kalan resided closest to her sides; Commander Javin Killians and Queen Veda down the table; and the three Faylinn Generals, Kip, Rooke, and Darion, each overseeing their respective units—the archers, magic-wielding foot-soldiers, and cavalry—lounged across from Evalyn at the opposite end of the table. They were well-trained soldiers, experienced from minor land-disputes and neighbor quarrels, with reputable titles from decades passed. Still, the Queen could sense their miniscule disdain.

She'd prove she was greater than her past. Greater than the actions she'd taken—and the things that had been done to her.

"We have patrols covering every inch of dirt bordering camp," General Rooke proclaimed. "We arrived at sundown with nothing in the distance—no faraway sounds, no change in wildlife... yet the hair on my neck stood up. And not because of the Crawlers. We're keeping multiple eyes on every side of our base as a precaution."

Evalyn straightened. "I scoured the entire battle-space from above when we stopped. There's no trace of Braena, but this is where my father deemed battle to be. I daresay it's a relief we have temporary rest."

"Not when we can be ambushed at any given moment," Darion noted.

The Queen nodded slowly, shifting her head to Milid. "Our first plan of action?"

"Luckily, each of our units are scattered across the encampment," the Commander began, "with the cavalry predominantly on our outskirts. In a weaker raid, our riders can mount immediately and are trained at defending the inner regions of camp. In the case of a full-fledged siege, however..." She tilted her head. "There would, undoubtedly, be great casualties. The magnitude of our defensive efficacy purely depends on the size of King Oberon's army and the methods he utilizes."

Micka piped in, "As for the approach to a mutually-timed battle... the odds are difficult to construe, especially without the numbers of the King's force. It's difficult to formulate a plan of action with half the factors." The Faerie retrieved a thick sheet of mapped parchment, spreading it across the table. "But we can easily outline the optimal routes of our forces with consideration to the landscape. I had this drawn based on the ground-scouters and aerial reports." A brief nod to the Queen. "We have the advantage of being stationed at this hill's peak, for monitoring surprise attacks and the offensive of our own troops. The northern slope of our base has a steeper drop, which proves a rougher decline for our troops, but if Braena presumes to claim the opposing hill, it lends an extra level of defense for our base."

Walfien leaned forward. "What of the troops' starting positions?"

"I hadn't planned on running them by anyone before we knew our other factors, but..." Micka shrugged his shoulders, "we can't trust there will be another chance for debate. Oberon's forces could arrive at any moment."

"Ideas will suffice, Micka," Commander Praesi declared.

"Yes, right." The Second cleared his throat. "Our archers could be stationed along this southern edge of the field." He brushed his fingers against the map.

Commander Javin inclined over an elbow. "A wise choice. That's an additional line of defense for our base camp, beyond reasonable placement."

General Kip nodded. "The basin is barren of trees, and along that woodline, the bowmen would be shielded yet maintain sufficient visibility to volley fire. There's nothing I dislike for my unit."

"Indeed, we can put the treeline to good use." Micka pointed to the east and west outskirts of the pocket of land. "We can place our cavalry along these regions, where they can charge directly for the King's flanks. The strongest of our infantries can reside in front of the archers under the cover of the trees. This leaves the wolf packs to line along our side of the basin—our first method of attack on all sides of the battlefront. Maybe they won't expect a non-magic offset."

The majority dipped their chins, more or less impressed with Micka's layout, and turned to Evalyn, but the woman's focus sat on Kalan. "You're okay with this?"

He merely responded, "We prepared ourselves for every scenario."

The Queen stared, but a tremor in her wings sent her upright, the chair at her rear shifting backwards. Her eyes widened as Walfien stood with her, a question on his lips already forming—

"What of my troops?"

Evalyn exhaled at the voice—what it insinuated. She spun to greet Overseer Ten at the entrance of the tent, who somehow appeared years younger than when they'd first met. With her background, the time spent preparing for her own enemy... perhaps Millo flourished amidst the conflict. Her deep chestnut hair was slicked into two plaits that balled into a knot at the base of her head.

The Queen tilted her chin. "I doubted I'd see you any less than hours before battle, Millo."

The woman's eyes glinted. "As did I, Majesty."

Evalyn's hand instinctively gestured outward. "Millo Ten, Overseer of the Rogues. The last of our allies." No protests or gasps at the sudden declaration. The better half of them were military experts, after all. Very little surprised those that had endured the indescribable.

Micka responded, "Where would you like them, Overseer?"

Millo smirked. "Wherever your Queen stations them."

"Place them alongside the infantry, strongest magic-wielders up front." Evalyn inhaled. "If there are no objections..." Silence echoed. Mags and Kinz' take caught her mind. What if she *was* preparing to sacrifice countless lives for no reason? What if she could've saved them all without means of warfare and death?

No—her father made the choice to start this fight. Now, there was no route but to kill him; to take back their freedom. Evalyn lifted her chin. "With whatever adjustments necessary, Commanders, make it happen."

Chapter Thirty Six

There were growls at sunrise. Then the shouting began.

But not Crawlers—their clacking had stopped the day prior.

The King's host had arrived.

"I flew over," Evalyn panted at the Commander's table. "The base is endless. I didn't go too far, but... I couldn't find the rear. Or my father."

Commander Praesi's eyes peered from under lowered brows. "Our scouts said as much. I think we safely assume forty thousand for King Oberon's forces."

"And hope we're overcounting," crooned Millo Ten.

Walfien's head slowly lifted. "We have twenty-five thousand at *best*."

"Then... we properly section our soldiers," Commander Javin declared. "We release our troops—use our strength—in waves. Let them think we have just as endless an amount of resources and supplication."

"We remain at a vast disadvantage!" Evalyn stressed. "It doesn't matter how many troops he thinks we have—the Sanguin are *ruthless*. I've seen them." She pulled down the tunic over her shoulder, displaying four thick scars. "I've *felt* them. Do not underestimate their power, or we'll wind up in the clutches of Oberon with fates worse than death. We stick with our plan. Use your heads, but don't back down."

Commander Praesi dipped her chin. "To your lines, then. Battle has begun."

Only the crackling of morning fires and rustling of nurses and servants could be heard along the edges of the battlefield.

The King's forces stood tall and unmoving atop the opposing hill.

The wolves leisurely prowled between the Faeries, step by step making their way to the forefront of the army lines.

From her spot at the front line of the infantry, Evalyn watched the Alpha. Wind unsettled his fur; he looked along the line of his own kind, stood shoulder-to-shoulder and stretched along the curve of their half of the basin. Felicity and Diana marked Kalan's sides, paws digging into the dirt and nostrils flaring.

As a heavy wind caressed Faylinn's forces, wolves and Fae alike gagged. King Oberon's forces smelled like death.

But the breathing of the soldiers around Evalyn paused not for the stench—for Kalan, who placed a foot forward, followed by a growling bark. The signal for the offensive charge. For the wolf clans to attack, and the subsequent Faerie march.

Chaotic mumbles at her side stole Evalyn's focus; she whipped towards Walfien as he stumbled around—his heart pounded frantically and he groaned in pain, clutching his head—

"What is it?" she exclaimed, gripping his uniform to stabilize him. "What do you See?"

The wolves began their assault. Five dozen swarmed down, followed by their second lines, howling and snarling at the chance to defeat their prey. It could be a song to other ears.

The Hand doubled over, but Evalyn kept a firm hold on his arms—

"It's a trap," he choked out, face white. "He's trapped them, Evalyn, the wolves—"

The first wolves met the bottom of the slope, and Kalan began trotting, Recks Delta at his front. It was too late to stop any of them. Their concentration was too tunneled, their awareness too slim of a thread to notice her shout if she tried. So Evalyn threw her magic over the front of the pack lines. A shield against whatever was coming, for whatever Walfien had Seen.

The forces of Braena didn't move an inch. As if they knew what was coming. Evalyn held her breath. Held her shield.

When the wolves reached the center of the field, the first explosion sounded.

The impact shook the hills. The soldiers at the Queen's back tumbled down with shouts, and Evalyn slammed into soil, the magnitude of the force crumbling her shield instantly. The land shook as flames grew, capturing dozens of wolves—but they weren't howling any longer. Those were yelps and cries reverberating across the field.

Three more explosions followed.

Fire. Shards. Destruction.

Her ears rang, but the Queen yelled out, reaching for any sign of life with her mind—

Nothing. There was *nothing*. She was standing in a split-second, mindlessly racing for the field—until she wasn't. The Queen could move no further, couldn't step forward—

She slammed her hands into a shimmering barrier. Her father had created his own shield around the pit, to block them from saving the wolves. She banged again. "No, no, no, they—they're dying—*they're dying!*" Fear and anger rippled through her as she shoved her shoulder into the wall of magic. "*Let me through! Let me through!*"

Her shouts echoed. Around her, every soldier halted, appalled and understanding.

Evalyn pounded at the barrier, flinging out magic that simply rebounded, screaming in the hopes that some ounce of her power would hinder a fraction of it, enough for her to break through and save *one of them*—

She didn't feel the hands at her sides, the hushing and warmth of Walfien from behind her. Evalyn didn't halt her shouting, didn't ease her attempts to shatter the shield with her magic, even as she was pried from her spot. When the Faerie was on her back, wrists pinned to the dirt at her sides with Walfien's face inches from her own, she stilled.

"Stop, Evalyn!" he begged. "You have to stop. This is what he wants—to frighten and hinder us so shockingly that we give up without retort. What we're *going* to do is get up and fight for them." Walfien loosened his grip. "We get up and fight."

She gave a sob, but staunched the threat of tears as she returned to the barrier, eyes straining against the wreckage of ground and body. Not even halfway down their slope was a rising, groaning Kalan, and Recks Delta, feet away, lunging low to the ground.

Alive. *Alive.* But they were the only ones who would stay so. Whether by their Spirits' mercy or the strength of the Delta bloodline, they'd missed the fatal impacts.

All in front of the pair, wolves burned—blown apart, unmoving, lifeless.

They were already too late, even if the males wanted to save the survivors. Most were gone the moment the explosions had gone off.

Kalan stepped forward, seemingly careless of precautions... until she saw the culprit of his recklessness. His family, right there, together. Waiting. Diana and Felicity's paws overlapped; crimson leaked from Janson's disfigured leg; Kye slumped between him and Bre, wailing for his already gone mate.

Kalan plodded forth, and the males lifted their heads. After a moment of wordless communication between the three, Kye's snout dropped atop Bre's and Janson slumped to the ground.

Kalan seemed to fold into himself, but his shadow fell over his sister. The Alpha shook his head at something, and Diana's head shifted towards her children before falling abruptly. Felicity released a last breath. The Alpha remained mute and motionless.

Recks watched the Faylinn soldiers near the shield and stretch around the sides of the field, reforming the lines—ready to take down what had already defeated them.

Evalyn's tears blurred her vision until the basin was a dark, flaming blur of nothing.

A deep, rumbling growl arose from Kalan's throat, a sound so distressed yet vengeful that it further rallied the Faerie soldiers.

But—*hours.*

The wall stayed for hours. Forcing them to watch the suffering, and look upon what had been done within the second battle had begun.

While the last of the wolves met the Spirits, Kalan never wavered. Never moved.

When the barrier dropped, Braena's forces surged down the hillside.

Evalyn didn't stop. Although her lungs were on fire and legs felt as if they'd collapse if she took another step, she didn't stop.

Ice shield, then arrows of flame in sync with the real ones soaring overhead. A tornado of frozen rock and ice crystals. Sparked lashes at the enemy's back. Flaming spears and spiked wood found home in the sides of Braenish soldiers. Any form of magic she could imagine configured with half a thought and sunk into the nearest soldier. She didn't care to see their faces. Strike, move; strike, move. Onto the next one. They'd never halt for her, so she wouldn't dare stop for them.

Evalyn didn't glimpse Oberon all day—didn't see a single creature of the army he'd built. Only pure, living Fae, clad with the mark of their respective side.

There were ten minutes to dusk when it finally slunk down the hill, out from the darkness of the forest.

A Sanguin.

All battle paused as it strode onto the field. Its wrinkled, gray skin could only be seen on its head, the rest of its body covered in a long tunic of black fabric, with a plate of thick chainmail guarding its chest and shoulders. The creature was living shadow.

It tilted its chin as it stopped, peering onto the field with depthless eyes. Horrified, Evalyn couldn't help but note the Fae-likeness of it. The way it perched on its feet, wholly erect and alert, as if with a mind of its own. The Sanguin didn't falter when Faylinn soldiers attacked. It simply lifted its hands, revealing clawed limbs of bone.

Try me.

Ten Faeries slumped dead to the ground before they could manage a single mark.

When it turned back to its base, the Braenish forces wordlessly followed suit.

Evalyn paused outside of Kalan's tent, sweat streaming down her chin onto a blood-stained uniform. Battle had rendered her brain fuzzy; she'd come here as soon as she'd withdrawn from the field. Although the male was done and wordless, she wanted to attempt to erect this suffering, if even a portion could be so.

The woman thought the tent was empty when she entered. But the soft patting of liquid meeting the ground caused her hearing to hone in, and she noticed the near-silent breathing under the dripping. Evalyn turned toward the corner.

There Kalan sat on a stool, sweat and soil slicked through his hair, blood dripping from every clothing-edge and limb. The sounding drizzle stemmed from his fingertips. The male's blank stare declared him—at least outwardly—unfazed by the battlefield and his actions on it. Good, considering they needed relentless and unforgiving soldiers on the frontlines.

But she knew it was only because he was wholly consumed by grief and despair. "Alpha," she said, hoping the formality would force him into a communicating state.

"Don't call me that," he spat. His eyes flickered up to her face. "Don't ever call me that again."

"I'm sorry." There was no point in asking how he was, nor how battle was faring for him. All she could think to do was apologize. Offer whatever comfort came to mind. "There was nothing anyone could do."

Kalan rose, pacing across the tent. He shook his chin rapidly, back and forth, sucking in and blowing out deep breaths, wrapping his hands around the back of his head. "I've ignored it since. Pushed it aside to stay alive and keep from collapsing completely." His voice thickened; he faced away from Evalyn as he continued. "But when we came back, all I saw was him." Recks. "*Just him.* He is all I will ever be able to see again."

"It will never be your fault," she tried.

Kalan sunk claws into his cot's side table. It landed in splintered pieces across the tent. "*That doesn't bring them back!*" he roared, his face transfiguring between his wolf features and human shape.

Evalyn gulped. He paced faster, and the frantic beating of his heart was a constant vibration within her hearing. His sobbing echoed, and he plummeted to his knees. "*What did I do to deserve this?*"

"*Nothing*," Evalyn instantly retorted. "You don't deserve any of it. This is *my* punishment." She knelt to his side. "What can I do?"

He froze. Red-rimmed golden eyes pierced Evalyn's as he said, "Kill me."

Her heart exploded. She was so taken aback that he had time to hurl her to the floor, his hands tight around her neck and squeezing until she could do nothing but fling shards of ice crystals into his face. He cried out but maintained his grip, and Evalyn contorted her body under him. She had to focus *not* to kill him with her magic, especially as every instinct hollered to destroy her attacker as she'd done all day. She rammed her knee into his groin; Kalan's partial release gave her enough leeway to suck in a breath and send her entire body into flames, causing him to jump away and giving her time to soar to the opposite edge of the tent.

"*Please*," he gasped, voice breaking. He was on his knees. "I will give *anything* to be dead in their place."

Evalyn was crying now, too. "Your death isn't the answer, Kalan." She stepped forward. "Allow their absence to fuel you. Don't let it rip you apart. You know they would want you to keep going." The pain encasing his form was horribly recognizable—the same torment filled her bones. They were both so utterly broken, but they couldn't heal each other anymore.

"Even Oberon's death couldn't balance the scale," Kalan said. Because righting the loss of his family wasn't the only thing holding him back. Evalyn found his side again, unafraid despite his attack. The woman intertwined their dirty and bloody hands. Down Kalan's cheeks, tears spilled. She knew what he was going to say. What else needed to happen. "I have to let you go," he whispered. His hands were shaking.

Evalyn closed her eyes. "Okay," she said.

"I love you."

"I love you, too."

Kalan gave a shuddering exhale. "Goodbye."

Chapter Thirty Seven

At dawn, a thick blanket of snow covered the battlefield, intertwining with scarlet splotches that turned it a deep pink. Death's canvas. By mid-morning, the bodies littering the field ruined any essence of artful creation, as did the constant, pained cries of injured soldiers and grunts of Fae struggling to survive against their opponent. The breaths of the troops were white-puffed clouds as they marched to hold the lines. Sparks and wisps of magic whistled, a light show at the surface.

Walfien pounced, magic from one hand, shortsword in another. He grunted as a soldier charged into him, but the Fae didn't stand a chance. The Hand whirled, slicing with a forceful, raging cry.

At another corner of Evalyn's vision, Micka fought—a boy no more. Not as he hurled a mace fifteen feet away into the side of a soldier with less than a huff. No sooner than he retrieved his weapon was he already striking another. Stationed somewhere was Commander Praesi—she'd be pleased by her Second's offensive skill. The woman had taught him well.

Walfien swiped at an outstretched arm, but before the metal found skin, a figure barrelled into the Braenish Faerie. Kalan's force brought demise as he collided with the slick, brown slosh of the ground. The wolf growled, sprinting away as a line of cavalry cut through the area. Every which way, gusts of magic flared out beside the chaos of combat; the clanking of metal became a constant beat. Evalyn sucked in frozen air and rose from the ground, pulling her sword from a Faerie's chest.

Her eyes met the male feet away, slicing into a Faylinn troop.

Her scarred forearm seared.

Rouhs laughed at the woman he stabbed.

Blistering fire swooped onto the male's head, and Evalyn plowed into his rear, skidding across blood and bodies before jamming a shortsword into his side. Rouhs cried out and flipped, swiping up with a fist—but his wrist froze in the air, eyes dancing between it and her. She smiled. His arm twisted, bone snapping. The Queen plunged her magic into his chest. The male sputtered, crimson dribbling down his cheek, then sagged onto the battleground.

When Evalyn stood, she raised a dagger in Walfien's direction, who stepped aside as she whipped her arm. The blade met a sprinting foe.

They swept back into battle.

They'd been fighting for three days, with barely a breath to take between nightfall and sunrise before they were back facing the endlessly charging lines of Oberon's Fae host. He'd recalled his side each dusk—likely drawing out the battle. Making Faylinn suffer by letting them believe they could get away with slivers of rest before the fighting continued at sunrise. They hadn't laid overnight siege to the Braenish camp; although Faylinn was making more of a dent than what was being made in them, a direct assault on their forces would undoubtedly end with the obliteration of Faylinn's forces. Evalyn knew this wasn't Braena's true army.

She didn't have to wait long for it to show.

The King unleashed more Sanguin that afternoon.

Evalyn watched them swarm down the hill, into the pocket of land that quickly turned into a chasm too steep to climb out of. Shouts turned to screams and cries as the Sanguin shredded and bit into their victims—injecting their venom as they killed them.

She had to find Oberon before it was too late. *She had to end this.*

So many of the Sanguin crawled on all fours, hissing and yowling, bodies mangled and skin taut. Their claws sunk into the iced-over, blood-soaked ground as they tackled the closest lines of Fae.

Evalyn was more petrified by the others.

The ones that mirrored that first Sanguin, standing tall and walking calmly onto the field, confident they wouldn't be defeated. She didn't realize she was trembling until one turned in her direction.

It never looked away from the Queen.

Although soldiers from every direction acknowledged its intent and shifted to defend her, the creature's black stare was unfaltering whilst it killed those standing in its way, slinking ever nearer.

It didn't spare her a thought before pouncing.

She went down with a hoarse cry, her voice deep and raw as its claws tightened and pinched the skin of her arms. Evalyn wriggled and contorted underneath, its heavy weight halting the flow of air into her neck. The pressure in her head grew until it was a steady ache; the stinging of her arms turned numb. But she pushed and fought and flung out her magic—which disintegrated into nothing upon contact with the armor. Where it grazed her skin, sizzling blisters remained.

She'd memorized that pain—iron. It couldn't hurt the Sanguin, since they were already dead, but it was the best defense against living Fae. The Sanguin clambered over her, every inch of the breastplate searing her skin. She bit her tongue—withheld the roar of pain.

The creature swiped at her face. She dodged, sending another string of magic out, shoving down her panic—it'd do her no good. A past version of herself may have let it overwhelm instinct, but not anymore. She searched and searched for an entrance to kill it; the heaviest armor shielded its heart.

There.

A space under its arm, wide enough for her magic to fling past the iron's natural repellent qualities and sift through the clothing like dust, through skin and muscle, directly into its limp heart where Oberon housed his control over the monsters. The organ froze and sweltered, then blasted apart.

The Sanguin collapsed to the side.

Evalyn's head slumped onto dirt.

"We're down to twenty thousand, with several hundred injured," Commander Praesi voiced.

Queen Evalyn groaned. All heads turned her way.

"You need to rest," Walfien grumbled. "You were closer to dying than any of us today."

It was true. After her predicament with the Sanguin, she'd passed out—and been more than lucky that several had seen the fight and instantly called for backup to retrieve her unconscious body from the field. She stared Walfien down, words airy. "Did anyone else manage to kill a Sanguin?" No one at the table answered. She stood, grimacing at her stiff, bandaged arms, but glared at the hand Walfien provided. "I did. I barely managed to take it down before I was too weak to go on, but I did."

General Rooke threw his hands into the air, bursting aloud, "We can't *defeat* them. These are truly powerful beasts, invincible monsters—"

"All monsters die." She eyed him and his shaky breaths. The leaders around the table shifted at her tone. "They *are* killable. The Sanguin may be strong and ruthless, General, but they're not invincible. I used my magic to slip past the armor; there's no additional protection underneath. It wasn't difficult to send ice into its chest and destroy it from the inside out." She placed a hand on the table; the motion sent sharpness into her bandaged, bruised arms. "A blow to the heart is all it takes. That's how they die. The hard part is not getting killed while you do it."

"Some are stronger than others," Commander Javin stated. "I watched one of the creatures strain to take down five soldiers, while another wiped out a unit of two dozen without blinking."

The Queen dipped her chin. "It depends on their age. The older they are—the longer they've been turned—the stronger. They stand; walk. Pretend not to be animals." Evalyn loosed a breath, turning to Micka. "All soldiers are to be informed of the trick with the armor, unless they can find an easier way around the iron." He nodded and made for the exit, but she added, "Tell them to be *smart*. You get reckless... you get killed."

The Queen flopped onto the edge of her cot, arms too sore to do anything but dangle at her sides. "Sit down," she demanded. There were hours until dawn.

Walfien slouched at her side. She peered at him.

He was already watching her. "How're you doing?"

"I haven't slept in four days," the woman returned, leaning back. The tight, bruising plaits atop her head were of no help to relax. "Kalan hasn't turned back to his human form since the first night."

"He'll come back on his own terms."

She already knew. She'd told Walfien about the incident with the Alpha, and the Hand had agreed with all that she'd guessed: Kalan would use battle to cope, and never be the same once it was over. Because whether it was a curse or blessing, something told her this War wouldn't bring Kalan into Death's embrace.

Evalyn yawned as Walfien stood and crossed her path, pouring them both goblets of lukewarm water. She wrinkled her nose as she met his side at the benchtable.

"What?" he huffed, handing her a cup.

"Gods, you stink!" she exclaimed. He raised his brows. "I'm serious, it's horrendous!" It was half-truth, really—although their smell was surely unfathomable, everything melded together at this point. Clean air was a far-away dream. But she fake-gagged, bending over solely for dramatic effect.

Evalyn's water spilled onto the floor, splashing on their uniforms, and she instinctively jumped, tripping over her own feet and colliding into the Hand. They fell to the floor with a thump, groaning yet laughing. Before she knew it, she was stuck under his hold, both of them breathless.

On the sides of her head, Walfien's hands lifted himself from the floor—but he slipped on her spilled water, and his face halted a hair's width from her own. They both huffed through their noses with mirroring smiles. She knew they needed this—to distract themselves from distressing over the battle; over their odds of winning. She was desperate to learn whether there was still some part of her that could laugh or smile or think happy thoughts without fear of losing them.

Because War was already changing her. When she was on the field... there was no line between where surviving ended and killing began.

Their persistent silence conveyed the feelings they couldn't find words to describe. Evalyn rose onto her elbows; he lifted with her. Everything ached and spun, but Walfien was steadying. He was constant.

Slowly, he leaned in, and their noses skimmed. Lightning sparked in her veins.

The Queen pushed at his chest. "You still stink."

Chapter Thirty Eight

Crimson and black blood began seeping together on the fourth day of battle.

On the fifth, the field was a portrait of slick, dark mud swamped by the dead they'd been forced to stop collecting each night.

Queen Evalyn heaved a breath, and although she'd adapted to the stench of rotting corpses and dead Sanguin, her nostrils burned. Her head pounded from magically attacking the Sanguin—her father had sent a larger wave this time. Triple his previous ones.

She rubbed her aching neck, the blood on her fingers tracing down her skin to her uniform. A reminder of what she was there for and who was at the cause of this War. Evalyn wiped at the splatters along her forehead and moved on.

Although she was so, so tired. Although Breana sent more men no matter how many troops Faylinn took down. Although her Kingdom was losing more resources than they could resupply and more willpower than the Gods could ever give them.

She kept going. Pushing. Searching for her father.

Flames slipped past metal, and solid rock formed at the core of the creature's heart. Two Fae went down with swords slicing their sides. A trickle of water crystallized around the next Sanguin heart. Another Faerie—ice shield and crystal arrows in his chest. Wind slipped past chainmail and breastplates, ending Oberon's monsters in half a second.

Push.

The sun was close to its peak. Halfway through the day.

A figure appeared before her, blocking out what little light Evalyn recognized. She lifted her head, pushing aside the instinct to succumb to the elements and instead shoved up her sleeves as she recognized the Faerie's face. When Asodu swung at her head, she ducked, following up with a strike to his face, enough of a surprise to throw him off balance. But he shook his chin and spat at her feet.

Evalyn chuckled—but he caught her moment of breath and surged towards the woman, sending her face-first into mud and blood slop. Stars danced in her vision, and she waited breathlessly for the next attack, what surely would be the killing strike—

It never came. When she regained her composure and flipped around, wiping away the slosh on her face, the male was enveloped in a swarm of pixies. Olive and gold threads of magic wrapped around him, faster than her eyes could perceive, tightening and sucking his limbs against his body until the Faerie was bursting out of the magical case.

He imploded into dust and fabric and crimson flakes.

The Queen shuddered when the pixies turned to her. But they dipped their heads and shot towards a Sanguin, forming a whirlwind of magic around the creature. A moment later, it was obliterated.

Her gratitude dissolved as a whistling scream sounded across the field. Walfien appeared at Evalyn's shoulder, breathing heavily. "We have to get out of here. Whatever I just Saw..." He shook his head. "It was phenomenal. Terrifying."

Evalyn's stomach dropped as they moved, attempting to sound retreat to every Faylinn soldier they could reach—and through the havoc, watched a Braenish soldier stab Kiran Kroghe through the chest. Veda crumpled towards her brother—not before taking the Fae down with her. But when she met Kiran's side, she gasped and spluttered as if a part of her own heart had stopped beating too.

It very well might have.

Tears slipped down Evalyn's cheeks. The Hand gripped her arm and pulled back. She knew why when Veda whipped in her direction, bloodied and distraught. *Go*, the Ausorian Queen mouthed. A blessing and a parting.

Veda's eyes began to glow, a burning light against the black warzone.

Walfien hauled Evalyn back to the base camp. "Retreat!" he shouted. "Retreat!" The seconds ticked by, and his tone became urgent. "*Fall back!*" Soldiers swarmed around them—they'd heard the voice of the Hand. Something was upon them.

They reached the edge of camp a second before it happened.

Evalyn spun to see gold intertwine itself around Veda, heat and light take shape.

But she was also sorrow and revenge.

Veda's cries grew until they were one with the wind. When her power reached its peak, forming a hemisphere of woven, golden magic expanding between the two bases, everything within was consumed in rose-colored flames. The Faeries in the Queen's line collided with the ground at the force. Evalyn's vision vanished against the brightness, but she blinked away the pain in the back of her head. The field returned into view when Veda's magic winked out.

Every being in its path plunged to the ground. Five thousand Braenish troops taken out with one stroke.

Walfien paused his panting. Faylinn's remaining army exhaled breaths of relief and embraced one another. Evalyn slouched, her hands covering her mouth. Finally, a true moment of rest and relief.

Until figures began standing. Until the dead weren't as forever-gone as they should be.

Every burned corpse rose with unprecedented ease. Unliving, yet alive once more. Anyone who had been pricked with Sanguin venom—they'd been instantaneously Changed and commanded to Rise.

Evalyn's entire body ached as she stood, clutching Walfien's side. Faylinn's base began praying to the Gods. Soldiers cursed and broke into tears. They were outnumbered nearly three to one, and they would have to kill their friends, allies, family. Would have to see them die once more—now at their own hands.

"I'll make it quick. I promise," murmured a woman at Evalyn's side. Then she wiped her nose, glanced at the Queen, and charged.

Every soldier followed. They were desolate and stunned, but they were determined. Make it easy for their loved ones. End them for their own comfort.

Evalyn pushed off Walfien and stumbled onto the field. The Ausorian would've done it without a second thought for Evalyn. She had to do the same. Even though Veda's sacrifice had been for nothing. She *pushed*. After two minutes and the slaughter of three soldiers, Evalyn found the Queen facing her as if Veda knew what she'd come to do. On the ground, an untouched Kiran was burn-free and gone.

Veda's eyes were already depthless—the confirmation Evalyn needed that she was exactly where she was meant to be. When the reincarnated Queen attacked, Evalyn let her. The slash in her forearm was barely deep enough to draw blood, but she knew if she let her guard down, Veda wouldn't hesitate to rip her throat from her body. Still, Evalyn waited, saltwater staining the sides of her face, releasing enough magic to restrain Veda's full strength. Because she deserved to see the Queen like this. To suffer, knowing it was her fault the woman had met this end.

Veda snarled, and black liquid spilled from the corner of her mouth. The twist of Evalyn's fingers sent magic straight through a tear in the Ausorian Queen's uniform. The quickest—kindest—way was to solidify her heart and crumble it to dust.

She didn't have a moment to weep as Veda fell. Sanguin poured onto the battlefield, a ceaselessly growing shadow. On they fought.

Yet despite the Rising, Braena's fresh host retreated after less than an hour. Evalyn didn't trust it was to give Faylinn a few hours of reprieve. In fact, the Queen felt like her father used the time to strengthen his own forces—not that the Sanguin needed any amount of relief. They couldn't tire; their killing instincts were constant. Whatever Oberon's plan was, Evalyn wouldn't fall for it.

But perhaps she already had.

From numbers alone, Faylinn was doomed. Even with every able troop on the field—many without helpful magic and fewer with weapons or proper rest—it was physically infeasible to hold out long enough to kill Oberon's entire army.

However, maybe... they didn't need to. Back in battle the next morning, Evalyn halted mid-air, sucking in deep breaths as she watched the carnage unfolding underneath her. It suddenly seemed so obvious: Oberon was the source and control of the Sanguin. She'd once asked him about it; whether killing him killed his host. Perhaps it was true. Perhaps, if the Sanguin's guider and creator died, they would too.

She prayed that despite all of Oberon's strength, there existed this weakness. No matter what, Evalyn would try, even if she went down with him. Even if the plan proved futile, Liatue remained better off without Oberon's presence, and they'd deal with the Sanguin another way.

But this *would* work. It had to.

The Queen scoped out the warzone, eyes darting between every face and body, from the treelines to the center of the field-pit. The Winter sun was harsh against her wings; worse for her vision against the snow that had fallen through the night, creating blinding flashes of white where fighting remained minimal.

Evalyn spotted him, watching the battle from the treeline of his base's edge—no guards; plain and visible as if he'd been there all along.

She knew he hadn't.

It was midday now. Circling above her father's legion, she observed the King move his station into a wood-canopied pavilion, surrounded by a huddle of sentinels and Sanguin.

Diving through the pocket of warfare, past singing metal and roaring Fae, the Queen neared her target. Two flicks of her arm sent the first guard down. At his collapse, the others' concentration erupted, and Evalyn soared by, a medley of burning flames and impaling stakes of wood bringing them all to the ground. The Sanguin were leashed and bare-skinned—young, too, if their crouched stances were of any indication.

Before she could start her second attack, an arrow whizzed past her face and hooked into the tip of her wing. She cried out, dropping several feet, but batted her wings harder to keep from plummeting to the field. The arrow slipped out; blood matted her shimmering feathers. Evalyn restrained from landing and groaned against the searing flare. She veered for the Sanguin, dodging sizzling sparks from the Fae below, and bolted under the tree limbs along her father's camp. Luring the ground-snow into a camouflaging current, she shot ice into the chests of each Sanguin, who had no chance to escape with their waists chained to the surrounding trees.

They sank to the floor with screeching cries. What effective guard dogs.

She didn't let her better judgment take hold before landing in front of the King.

Chapter Thirty Nine

Flames rose around them, licking the blazing forest overhead and scorching the apex of Evalyn wings as blackness consumed the sky. A river of crimson pooled at Evalyn's feet from the fallen guard beside her.

She froze with dread. Before the King stood Kinz and Mags, speaking to Oberon from half a pace away, unfazed by the proximity to their enemy. The florvis didn't so much as blink at the girl's presence at their side; Mags continued snarling at her father: "They have just as large a stake in this fight. They'll come for you for this hindrance and seek retribution."

"I have plans for that, too," the King hummed, his gaze stroking Evalyn. He stood in front of a set of makeshift seats, one hand resting on the edge of his sheathed sword. His jeweled cloak, so blood-red it was almost black, hung heavily from his shoulders, unmoving in the wind.

Evalyn's lungs seemed to collapse as she faced the elder sisters. "Why would you come here? I told you bargaining wouldn't work."

They met her gaze, eyes clear. Kinz tilted her chin. "There's been enough bloodshed. We came to the source to plead our case."

Glaring at Oberon as if he was as much of a child to her as Evalyn was, Mags snapped, "But it seems he's stubbornly occupied and unwavering from his ways." In another life, Evalyn may have hissed that she'd told them so.

The King gave a throaty chuckle. "Ah—this War wouldn't be possible without my daughter's dissent. Had she agreed to my simple desires, there would be only *necessary* death—unlike the innocent lives being taken every moment on this ground. Nonetheless, this War has become vital."

Kinz hissed, "She's but a *child*, with years ahead of her! How *dare* you entail her time with such horror."

"It is only temporarily full of such, witless witches." He met Evalyn's gaze with a wicked smile. "It stands that I have bigger plans for her future."

Mags cursed his name, stepping a pace forward, her wrinkled hands twisting whilst she uttered a string of sounds. Oberon flinched, and three splotches of blood began oozing from under the King's dark tunic, turning the cloth a deeper black in the places where it spread. Seething, his hands fisted—but Kinz voiced her own spell and swirled her fingers along the dirt, where an earth-split formed at her touch, jolting the Queen into a crouch while the ground shook under their feet. As far as Evalyn could see through the smoking, flaming trees, a gaping ravine formed, separating Oberon from the females. The witches stood slowly, clutching one another.

The King tutted his tongue. "Clearly, you've outgrown the limitless magic of your youth, ladies." He lifted a finger, and Mags and Kinz began gasping, clutching at their necks as they rose into the air.

"No!" Evalyn lunged forward with a scream—but that invisible hand of the King's gripped her, followed by shadows and darkness that wiped her vision of everything except the frail, captured women before her. She knew Oberon wouldn't have given into begging. There was only one path to finish this. Evalyn growled, struggling against the hold, fighting for the women that had fought for her, that even in their pain, looked upon her with care and adoration.

"I gave you more chances than you deserve, darling, yet you continue to oppose me," Oberon said. His voice echoed in every part of her head. "I suppose you're craving to see the consequential waste that your disagreement has prompted. Do you enjoy your own suffering so dearly? Or, better yet: did you come here under the pretense that you could enact my defeat?"

"I *will* kill you, even if it's the last thing I do!" she shouted, squirming and pushing.

The overwhelming calmness of his words raked gouges in her chest. "Go ahead, then. Try. Save yourself; save them, too."

Mags and Kinz froze in their positions, a few paces in front of Evalyn.

Her left hand rose, forced by the King, and she strained to deflect his control like she'd practiced with Walfien. Down, she pulled herself, not letting in his command. *Down, down* against his *up*—but it wasn't good enough. Her mental shield disintegrated upon formation, over and over, and her own magic was being contorted by her father. Still she tried—tried again and again to counter his power, but she wasn't ready. She hadn't practiced enough.

She wasn't good enough.

The King laughed. He knew. And she'd played right into his scheme.

Her frost-flames rushed the witches. She attempted to extinguish her power, to wholly rid of the magic, but their figures turned ashen, and the pair's bodies crumbled into a dust that was whipped away with the flaring fire-wind around them.

Evalyn staunched the tears before they came. Forced away any trace of pain before it could overtake her.

And the Queen fought. With all her might, she shoved and twisted and *pushed* as the King's power squeezed in on her. With a cry, the first of her magic slipped through. A sliver of starlight in the face of his darkness. With another shout, more wisps rose. Evalyn shoved again, harder, harder, *harder* at the shadow ropes tightening around her body. There. A hiss of Oberon's power as it confronted her light. Another, and her arm was free. She could feel her legs.

Evalyn's magic tore apart her restraints. She fell to the ground as the darkness dissipated and her vision returned.

No fear.

No hesitation.

The King was immobile as she lifted onto her hands and knees. He remained still when she pounced across the ravine, putting all of her might into a punch across his cheek, sending his head twisting to one side. She stepped away with a heaving breath as he turned his head back. A smear of blood rose at the base of his nose.

The King lifted a finger to the spot. "*Ow.*"

Evalyn braced as he flicked a hand, sending the woman flying over the earth-pit and impacting the edge of the battlefield, the world upside down from her place against the steep hillslope. Her wings itched and ached, crushed against the dirt beneath her, but the Queen shook her head, golden hair obscuring her vision, and with a heave, rolled onto her stomach. Then attacked again. Back and forth, they struck with their magic, blocking and firing, the power of the assaults growing with each shot, until an ounce of darkness marked her chest. She gasped for air, slipping on the edge of the ravine.

Her hands grasped a flimsy tree root, fingers squeezing whilst she helplessly dangled over the endless black pit. The King's feet stopped an inch before her face. The Queen halted, holding her breath.

And let go.

Tumbling into the depths, she glimpsed the sneering face of her father observing her end.

But the Faerie flew up, wings pounding as she shot for the sky, rising and rising until the atmosphere pressed in on her.

The calmest of breezes kissed her face, and Evalyn stopped beating her wings. Allowed the downward force to plunge her towards the ground. Wings tucked tight, she plummeted faster, the battlefield racing at her with unimaginable speed.

Shadows swirled around her hands, electric and expanding. The King's darkness—*her* darkness—returned once more for rightful victory. It spewed out from itself, a mass of black at her fingertips formed from rage and misery and desperation.

When she was ten feet from the King, he smiled.

She flung out every particle of her magic as her wings expanded, holding the Faerie up whilst she blasted Oberon into the face of the land. The Fae pounded her wings, begging them to keep her suspended over the earth-pit as her darkness continued pouring out. Flames sparked in his place, and she launched a storm of stone and soil against him, the gushing, sparking shadows neverending. More, more, more, she let it flow out and obliterate the King and his cruelty and his threats and all the terrors he'd created and all the pain he'd wrought.

She couldn't feel a burn—didn't sense the itch that told her burnout was near—but the Queen ended her assault.

Not even ash remained where Oberon had stood.

The destruction on the field halted in a unified motion as every Sanguin collapsed. Dead—and for good, this time. The Braenish army laid down their weapons and dropped to their knees, silent and aware that begging was aimless. Not when they were as good as dead, too. The remaining troops of Faylinn backed away, swiftly and wisely, gathering any wounded they could.

Evalyn lowered to solid ground. Willed away her wings and peered onto the battlefield.

"You did it," she whispered to all that had gone. All who had given themselves up.

You did it.

Chapter Forty

For hours, they strode through the field of bodies as the Generals and their captains marked the casualties and compiled resources for return travels. Evalyn tried to mark every fallen face from Faylinn. Many she didn't recognize, but some, she did.

"Where do you think we go?" she asked. "When we die."

At her hip, Walfien shifted his vision to the sky. "Ancient writings never revealed what the Gods plan for us. An afterlife, but nothing specific. I've always imagined somewhere of our own making—somewhere lack of our faults and aversion, full of everything we desire."

"What about those who don't deserve such a haven?"

He shrugged. "Anywhere but."

Evalyn wiped her hands as she stood; tugged her cloak tight and watched the slow-paced soldiers answering their duty calls. No one danced for the Winter Solstice. Not when they had so many bodies to bury.

Her heart dropped as a strand of deep blonde hair blew in the wind—but it was a Braenish uniform that clothed the body. Still, she whipped toward Walfien. "Where's Kalan?"

Color drained from his face. "I... haven't seen him in two days."

Their leisurely pacing turned into maddened scrambling as they tore through piles of bodies, shouting and shaking any indiscernible figures.

When Walfien sank to his knees, Evalyn knew to go to him. He stared upon the body with terrible pain.

Kalan was human, clothed in a Faylinn Guard uniform. He'd taken his final stand not just for the Moon Clan, but as one of his Kingdom. She crouched down, hands shaking. "No, no, not you, Kalan, *not you*—you were supposed to make it." Her voice broke. *"You were supposed to live for the rest of them."* The Faerie gave a sobbing gasp—but the bare wrist she gripped was warm. She flattened an ear to his chest, where a light, patterned beat sounded.

"*He's alive*," Evalyn whispered. She rocked his body. "Kalan, wake up."

Walfien shook him too, calling his name, anything to make the Alpha rise—but the Queen glimpsed black liquid at his neck. Right atop the vein, oozing over his back and onto the muddied ground.

At some point, he'd been bitten; injected with the Sanguin venom—but her father was dead.

A Rising was impossible; he couldn't be roused by Oberon's magic when such a power was forever gone.

"He's not going to wake up," she realized.

Chapter Forty One

Evalyn's honey-gold gown flowed around her ankles. She summoned her wings as the meeting hall door swung open, showing an oval table surrounded by ten Fae. Her Keepers stood against the far wall; two sentinels resided at the threshold. As she glided in, features revealing naught, everyone faced the woman—waiting for the first word.

Evalyn's gaze landed on her seat. Instead of taking its place, the Faerie shifted to the windows with the beginning of a smile. "I took a walk in the gardens today. The armerias are starting to bloom, and the trees are full once more. The fragrances were calming, especially with the breeze." She half-turned, stroking the edge of a wing and looking up and down the table. Watching the Faeries as they did her. Walfien Pax was right of her chair, and the four Lords of the Conclave sat across from one another. Luckily, the newly acquainted Jaino was less unnerved than in his first meeting. Micka Roshium and Millo Ten crossed one another—advisors to the Queen and paired Emissaries for Faylinn, granted their titles upon return from the War of Kin.

At the end of the table sat three faces Evalyn had never seen. Her voice remained sweet as she declared, "Any loss of such sights will not be at fault of conflict between our Kingdoms." Her eyes darted between the triad of Fae. The first male was clothed in a silver outfit that complimented his brown skin, with a dusty-rose emblem of three overlapping hearts stitched on both sleeves. Hazel eyes squinted gently from under curly, mocha hair. The other male posed close to the woman at his side. Their attires matched: elegant, maroon cloaks lined with shining jewels over a black uniform and gown. They were an ethereal pair of Faeries, unlike anyone Evalyn had ever seen, with carved cheeks and slick, onyx hair. At last, the Queen of Faylinn settled onto the edge of her chair, folding her hands atop the table. "Will it, Your Majesties?"

The male with the woman spoke first, his voice silk. "I'll presume that is not a threat, Queen Evalyn."

She liked him. "King Eden Dexter of Braena. You were Crowned three weeks ago, weren't you?" He stared with gray, piercing eyes. "I'm rather amused by your pretension. On the contrary... it was a test." The Queen smiled. "You passed."

His returning look was wary—but the Fae's chin lifted.

The other male asserted, "We must commence with promises of peace in order for this to work." This one was Hil Kroghe of Ausor. "My Kingdom has felt enough torment with the losses of my cousins, uncle, and citizenry. Surely you understand such pain, Majesty."

This one had potential. He wasn't as feisty as Eden, but there was dominance in his tone.

"I've come to understand a great many things, King Hil." Evalyn traced the wood under her fingertips. "As the monarchs of our Kingdoms, we're supposed to do what everyone behind us did. Maintain our rules and principles, keep our people happy. Smile, wave—show no sign of weakness." She leaned back. "You speak of peace as if you've seen it."

"I have seen what it's not."

"Those are very different things."

"Does anyone know what peace looks like?" King Eden placed a hand on the woman's thigh—his wife, Jade. A quiet, reserved, and loyal woman, obvious in her messages to Queen Evalyn from the recent two weeks.

Evalyn exhaled. "I called you here to discuss forming an alliance, as my letters projected. Should you agree to my terms... perhaps, one day, we'll be able to answer that question."

Slowly, Eden nodded. "Braena has never experienced peace. After all these years... I'd appreciate that for my Kingdom."

The Queen hadn't yet asked what it was like without her father overlooking the thoughts and actions of every citizen. She supposed she didn't need to; the new King's tone was explanatory enough.

Her gaze shifted to Hil. After a moment, he dropped his head. "I know I'm not Veda, nor will I ever be. She was a soul gifted to us by the Gods that comes once in a lifetime." He paused. "But I hope I can be half as notable as my cousin. I believe this alliance would do her justice. She never wanted the people of Ausor to be happy—she wanted the people of Liatue to be. State your terms."

Evalyn gestured to the table. "Those of my council have been allowed to formulate a single demand each."

The Conclave's conditions were relatively simple: improve inter-Kingdom emigration, increase communication between the three leaders, inform one another prior to any mass-effective actions, and establish shipping and trading routes. Easy and modest criteria, covering the majority of their concerns. Micka and Millo had similar demands. Walfien was slightly less industrial with his request.

"Wholly abolish the provision of marriage between Braena and Faylinn," he said.

King Eden tapped his wife's leg. "Done."

Evalyn had forgotten about the arrangement between the two Kingdoms that declared their leaders to be in continuous bondage. Her mother had ended her marriage with Oberon, but it'd still been written—and, in the chance Evalyn met Eden's bad side, could've been used against Faylinn to declare War by claiming a breakage of the previous alliance's terms. The Queen restrained from shaking her head, from questioning why—out of anything he could've demanded from the King of Braena—the Hand had gone down such a route. She met his eyes, but Walfien reclined in his chair without another word.

"What do *you* want, Evalyn?" Hil's voice was soft—there was Veda's selflessness. The Queen was warming up to his credulity.

Evalyn took a moment to think. The Kings had already made decent impressions on her with their seeking of peace and prosperity and... not having anything in common with the previously sinister motives of her father. "All I want is to not regret bargaining with either of you."

King Eden closed his eyes. "It'd prove awful to see another War in our time. We have less life than we ever believe."

Evalyn nodded. "I'll have our terms documented. We'll sign before you return to your homes. Enjoy your time in Faylinn." The Kings nodded, and after a moment, sound erupted in the room as the Lords of the Conclave swarmed Hil and Eden with every number of inquiries.

Walfien found Evalyn's side, his voice half a whisper. "That was a calm start, considering we formed an unprecedented alliance with Ausor and renewed one with the Kingdom that was just our enemy."

Evalyn tilted her chin. "There's something different about them." Across the room, Hil laughed at something Jaino said. The boy's face reddened, but he grinned. "I think we—"

"Oh, King Eden is *dashing*!" Vixiw exploded at the Queen's side, her fluffy curls of hair bouncing.

Beverly and Ida came around Walfien's side, the former rolling her eyes and latter stating, "He's married. That means he's taken for life." Ida would know, considering the blue-jeweled ring on her finger. The girl's admirer had made his move and proposed after the War, although Ida remained unwilling to reveal her secret lover. Soon, she claimed, but not yet.

"It doesn't mean he can't have a *mistress*," Vixie returned with a mischievous giggle.

Laughter bubbled in Evalyn. "You can't become the mistress of King Eden, Vixie, however attractive he is. The Kings are here to show they can be trusted, not swooned over."

The Lady tutted her tongue but dropped the topic. Within a moment she'd turned to Walfien, questioning about altered guard shifts because there'd been a *handsome* man at their hall for weeks on end and he'd disappeared. The Queen waited until King Eden closed his discussion with Lord Blaze and swept his wife from the chamber before going after him.

The hallway was light and quiet. She still wasn't used to the lack of tension and paranoia. Halfway down the corridor, Eden and Jade sauntered arm in arm.

"Eden," Evalyn exclaimed, striding forward until she was feet away. "Wait."

The King turned. "What can I do for my gracious host?"

"I have something to ask of you."

He raised his brows. "I presume it's unrelated to our prior meeting."

"Yes. Could you send for someone?"

"From Braena?"

"From the Shadow Compound itself."

Jade swayed her hips at the King's side. Eden glanced at her with a smile. "I like you, Evalyn. I appreciate you." His eyes darted to the ground. "I was elected by the other High Houses. I know what you think of them; I was there when you were in the castle, suffering through our meetings. Suffering through your father. I'm sorry I didn't help you—he was not a... *kind* being."

"No, he wasn't."

"I don't intend on following a similar path."

"What an immense consolation."

He huffed gently. "What is their name?"

"Luca Eaton. She works as a nobility handmaid."

King Eden nodded. There was a glint in his eyes—something the Queen couldn't place. But... it was good. The Faerie could feel it. "She'll be here before I depart."

"Is there any news?" Evalyn asked, reclining on the stool at her vanity and peering into her mirror. She began pulling at the pins in her hair, but the swift and gentle hands of Vixie immediately took up the task.

From across the room, Walfien leaned against the wall by her closet. "If there *was*, you'd know before me. But... no. He's unchanged."

The clinking from the dining chamber indicated Beverly and Ida had begun cleaning their dinner. Vixie removed the last pin before untwining the small plaits in Evalyn's hair.

It'd been two months since they returned from battle. Two months since the end of War. Two months since Kalan had been bitten and impacted by the venom that kept him alive yet lifeless. He resided in the castle, with no family to return to—other than Recks, who lodged in The Palace as a guest. Elyse and her healers attended the Alpha day and night, keeping him clean and fed and cared for with their magic.

But the Queen had taken it upon herself to figure out how to wake him up—because as long as Kalan was breathing, as long as his heart remained beating, she'd spend the rest of her life searching for a cure if it meant helping him. He was the one that deserved the joy that had at last returned to The Palace. The one that earned the thrills and festivity that had sprouted among the Fae servants and common-folk and Court following the culmination of the War of Kin. Evalyn had gone to at least a dozen gatherings and celebrations in the recent fortnight alone, witnessing the rejoicement and elation of her Kingdom after so much sorrow.

But Kalan hadn't been there to experience it, or see Spring's early hints, bringing fresh colors and new scents and weighty feelings that were almost foreign to the Queen—wonder and warmth and pleasure. It was such a stark contrast to what the Alpha had last endured, and he couldn't see or hear or feel any of it. He'd missed his twenty-third nameday.

"I want to check on him," she stated.

"You've visited him at least twice a day since you returned from the battle," Vixie voiced.

Walfien sighed. "Vixie's not wrong, Evalyn. He'll still be there when you wake tomorrow."

"But I owe it to him." Vixie paused at the woman's tone, and after a breath, patted Evalyn's head, declaring that Beverly and Ida could use help with the dishes. When the doors to the dining chamber swung closed, Walfien eyed the Queen. She stood, brushing through golden-blonde curls. "I know what you're going to say."

The Keepers swept through the bedroom chamber, the hallway door closing with a click as they ventured to the kitchens.

Walfien eyed her. "If you think I'm going to say what happened to Kalan isn't your fault, you'd be correct. And although *I* know no matter how many times those words come out of my mouth, you'll ignore them, I will repeat myself until you believe it." He pushed off the wall, meeting the Queen at the end of her bed. "You can't blame yourself forever."

Evalyn tugged on a knot, but quickly gave up and crossed her arms. "Look... my father created the Sanguin. It's their venom running through Kalan's veins—but *I'm* the one that got him on that battlefield. That War began because of *my* actions."

"He chose to be there, Evalyn. *He did.* Not you. And *that War* would never have happened without Oberon."

They stared at each other for a long while. Finally, she dropped her gaze and sat atop the bed frame.

Walfien asked, "Did you ask the librarians about the beasts? The ones your father used to begin the Sanguin line?"

"Oh, sure," she scoffed. "*Could you tell me the name of this creature—although I have no idea what it looks like, where it comes from, or any inkling of a clue as to what—*"

"I get your point," Walfien smirked, settling next to her.

Evalyn swung her legs. "I never told you... what it was like to kill my father. How easy it'd been. He barely fought back, near the end. As if he *wanted* to die." She hadn't spoken a single word about her end of the battle. What had occurred under the pavilion behind enemy lines.

"Maybe he did."

"And I'm supposed to believe that everyone that died because of him were... parts of what? A ruse to get me to kill him?"

Walfien looked sideways at her. "That's not what I meant. He was a monstrous King, and he knew what he was doing. But maybe you showed up, and... maybe, in his own twisted way, he realized he didn't want to fight anymore."

"That makes it seem like he had a shred of humanity left." She stopped swinging her legs. "And he didn't."

"I think you're not letting yourself feel relieved he's gone. He tortured Faylinn—tortured *you*—for so long, and it's hard to accept it's over. But if we start looking too much into his last actions, we may never come out of that spiral."

She bit her lip. "It's quiet without them. Mags and Kinz." Her voice lowered. "Sometimes I forget they're gone and go to their quarters and it isn't until I open the door to an empty chamber that I remember what happened. They were trying to bargain with Oberon, to make him stop. It was a suicide mission. But they knew that. They had to." She blinked away the burning in her eyes.

Walfien slid his hand over hers. "No matter why they did what they did... Mags and Kinz wouldn't have wanted us to be upset. They wouldn't have wanted the end of their lives to hinder the course of our own. They *would* have wanted us to keep going, do good, and make Liatue a better place in honor of what they sacrificed."

"You always know what to say."

He shook his head. "I never know what's going to come out of my mouth."

She faced Walfien fully, reaching up and brushing back the grown-out hair that had fallen over his eyes. "We met today. A year ago, I found you in the cabin."

"I think *I* found you behind the sofa, creeping on the conversation."

"A conversation about *myself*, as I recall. That means I had every right to creep."

Walfien's gaze drifted. "I didn't realize how long it's been. The months went by so fast and... everything changed so quickly." Blue and green eyes poured into her own. She grasped the hand Walfien slid down her cheek. His voice was a breath. "We haven't discussed this yet."

She gulped. "We can't. Not with Kalan as he is. He deserves to be awake for the result of that conversation. And we made it—*we did*. War is over and we made an agreement, but... not yet."

"Not yet," he repeated. "But..."

She smiled, pulling away as she stood. "Soon."

Walfien rose with her, his hand claiming the place above her hip, the other sweeping to the nape of her neck. The woman froze as he leaned forward, and she lifted her chin, lips parting—but he leaned back on his heels. "Soon," he whispered.

There were screams.

Screams and crying a week later as the Queen collided with the woman that had kept her afloat in the depths of the Shadow six months ago.

She couldn't understand how it'd been so long—couldn't fathom how time had slipped out from underneath them and Luca was *here* with Evalyn's promise unbroken. Their embracing grips were breathtaking as they fell into hysterics, not caring for the dozens of nobles around them, staring and judging the scene they'd made of their reunion.

Luca pulled away first, black hair styled in an elegant plait whipping around her shoulders. She held Evalyn's cheeks. "I didn't believe when King Eden sent for me. I didn't believe he knew my name or needed my assistance—but the letter said the Queen of Faylinn had asked for me, and" —she broke into sobs again—"I packed my things in ten minutes and was on a carriage by nightfall."

Evalyn clutched her wrists, laughing and crying at once. "There's so much I want to show you. How are you?"

"Proud of my greatest friend. Elated that she saved me. Grateful to be with her again."

Evalyn hugged her once more. "Welcome home, Luca." She stood back. "Get settled; I'll find you soon. I want you to meet my friends."

Luca nodded, lifting her maroon skirts and reaching for her things, but a servant was already there, escorting her to the Queen's quarters where she'd stay until they figured out a rooming situation. Luca turned back, jaw dropped, but ran after the servant with a chortle.

Evalyn glanced at the courtyard entrance. King Eden leaned against a pillar, alone and clothed in a significantly less extravagant outfit than when she'd last seen him at their meeting the week previous. As if sensing the Queen's gaze, he lifted his head.

In a few steps she was at his side. "Thank you for allowing her to stay."

"My people may wander wherever they desire. If Luca wants to stay here, she may do as she wishes."

"Truly?"

Eden looked out to the full, busy courtyard, and smiled. "We're free, Evalyn."

She smiled back. "Yes. Yes, we are."

Epilogue
Hand of the Queen

Walfien Pax folded his arms across his chest. He didn't like this. None of them liked this.

Evalyn had woken him half an hour ago, eyes so large he'd assumed there was an attack, but then she started speaking.

Rambling incomprehensible sounds were more like it, but he wouldn't tell her that.

The Hand leaned against the corridor wall opposite Ida, Vixie, Micka, Millo, and Luca, all surrounding The Door. Walfien had never cared to explore this section of The Palace; its entry had been forbidden for as long as he knew. But thirty minutes prior, the Queen had declared that she'd finally uncovered the meaning of the entry's markings.

Beverly had taken up the role of anxious caregiver, hoping to sway Evalyn from attempting to open The Door—because the Queen had a miraculous suspicion not only that she could open the door, but should be the sole one to do so. However, Walfien knew Evalyn had made up her mind and there would be no deterring her.

The Keeper stalked to Walfien's side with a defeated glower.

"You believe what's behind The Door is important... because King Oberon desired to know its contents?" Vixie questioned.

"Partially."

"And if it does open?" Luca asked. "What is our part in this?"

"You're to wait here in case anything happens. And I wanted witnesses." Evalyn shifted to The Door, where overgrown, red and violet vines masked the frame. "If I'm not back in a few minutes, do *not* come after me. Under any circumstances."

Millo nodded solemnly; Micka started, "This feels too risky, Evalyn—"

"That is an order as your Queen," the Faerie returned. "And a vehement request, as your friend, to trust me."

Walfien remained silent. He was just as uneasy, but he trusted her judgment. If the woman believed there was any chance of life-threatening danger, he'd know. If there was, they wouldn't have been drawn here in the first place.

Everyone took a unified inhale as Evalyn turned. She didn't look back before gripping the handle.

And disappearing—sucked to elsewhere. The immediate snap almost seemed like a result of the Western Continent witch portals he'd once read about. Her Keepers broke into gasps and speech at once, nearing the door although only a second had passed—

Walfien had barely taken a breath before a distant scream sounded.

Evalyn reappeared in their presence—quivering, tear-stained, hyperventilating. Everyone succumbed to utter quiet as the Queen dropped to the floor with a whimpering gasp. Then she gave a heaving breath, and stilled. Wiped her nose.

Her red-rimmed, blue eyes met his. "We aren't done."

Acknowledgements

Thank you God—my Lord, Father, Friend—for creating this story of life, that I have the chance to render my own imagination in your sight.

Maranda—thank you, a thousand times again. Your guidance and aid have been incomparable and vital. This book wouldn't be complete without your brilliant mind and humor, completely necessary (although sometimes harshly true) critiques, and never-ending love. I'm so grateful we get to journey together, sister.

Thank you, Mom and Dad, for raising me to push myself to the best of my ability, and thank you, Bub and B, for being such encouraging siblings. Each of you have taught me to follow my calling, chase my dreams, and embrace my creative passion. Thank you for your unceasing love. Thank you, Keith, for all your feedback and support, especially when I felt like giving up. I am so grateful.

Thank you, family, friends, peers, leaders, coworkers—all those I have met and crossed paths with, whether for a season or a lifetime, from middle school to college—you know who you are. Thank you for every breath of curiosity and intrigue about my creativity and storytelling. You have impacted me most greatly.

And thank you, reader. I hope you were able to glimpse the truth that I now know:

Broken people don't have to stay that way.

About the Author

Mallory Bautsch is an up-and-coming author of Young Adult Fantasy. She was born in southeast Texas, where she grew up reading books way past bedtime, enacting sword fights with sticks in the backyard, and imagining worlds of magic. Mallory currently attends Texas A&M University as a Marketing major, and loves taking long walks with her twin sister, making new friends, and serving at church. She adores her parents, siblings, and nephew, as well as her golden doodle.

CPSIA information can be obtained
at www.ICGtesting.com
Printed in the USA
BVHW041513120723
667134BV00014B/56